FIRESKY

First published 2021 by Solaris
an imprint of Rebellion Publishing Ltd,
Riverside House, Osney Mead,
Oxford, OX2 0ES, UK

www.solarisbooks.com

ISBN: 978 1 78108 908 8

10 9 8 7 6 5 4 3 2 1

A CIP catalogue record for this book is available
from the British Library.

Designed & typeset by Rebellion Publishing

Printed in Denmark

FIRESKY

Mark De Jager

SOLARIS

For the dreamers.

PROLOGUE

The Private Annals of Tiberius Talgoth, Archmage

MY FATHER DIED yesterday. He was a great scholar, and a warrior too. He had walked and fought beside the Battle Kings, wielding his power as they did their star-forged swords, felling creatures that would one day become legend and myth. It was his hand that wrote the first Codex of Power, and his teachings that set me upon the Path.

He was the greatest man I had known, and most likely will ever know, and yesterday I watched him die in his own filth, the hands that had once bent reality to his will crooked and twisted.

When the sun had set, I lit his pyre with the magic he had given me and watched his flesh turn to ash and ember. His vassals wept and the bards sang mournfully as the fire threw sparks high into the night, while the priests intoned their great rituals, assuring me with soft hands and voices that his soul had found its way to the gods.

They no doubt mistook my silence for mourning, but then they had sat with me and watched as time stole both his mind and the life from him. In his final moments of lucidity he begged for release, and I granted him it. And now my father was no more for Death had rendered every part of him meaningless.

Death.

It rules our lives, reaching into them with impunity. Even now I feel the subtle fingers of its murderous handmaiden, time, closing around my heart. When will they tighten and send all my dreams and achievements into the fire of oblivion?

CHAPTER 1

A FIERCE STORM was lashing the besieged city of Falkenburg as I made my way through the palace at the heart of it, and even now its bitter rain would be blowing in through the shattered windows of the church and lashing the bodies of Cardinal Polsson and his bodyguards. The Cardinal, a servant of the Worm Lord, had died in my fire, never knowing that his cruel tortures had helped me remember who and what I was. I had left his smouldering corpse where it fell and raced across the city to rescue Tatyana from the paladins that he had corrupted with his foul magic, and had finally shared my secret with her.

Tatyana stopped fiddling with the buckles of the armour she'd just stripped from the guard I'd killed on my way to rescue her and gawped at me.

'So you're telling me that you're a dragon?'

'Yes.' I stood as straight and tall as my currently human shaped body would allow me to.

'An actual, fire-breathing dragon?'

'It's more like spittle, but yes,' I said.

I was starting to think I had perhaps been too hasty in telling her the truth, but if I hadn't, I think I might have taken to standing on the roof and bellowing it at the city. Some secrets begged to be told, at least once. Since I had shared my secret, she'd done little save stand in one place, trying to fasten the same buckle while looking like she was expecting to wake up at any moment.

She shook her head again. 'No, no. It's not possible.'

I plucked the buckle from her grasp and threaded the strap through as I had seen her do with the others. 'I assure you that it is.'

She touched the bare skin of my arm, her hand as pale as bone against my ebon hide. 'You can't be him. The Dead Wind was just a legend, a song. A story that even my family had forgotten.'

I felt a prickly shiver of something run down my backbone as she said that long forgotten part of my name out loud. I was Stratus Firesky, the Dead Wind. The Destroyer. My memories had been fractured for too long, and reclaiming my name had woken a forgotten part of me. I felt the old fire kindle in my eyes and she gasped at the sight of it, dragging my attention back to the present.

I closed my eyes until I felt the tingle fade, then took a steadying breath. 'My answer is not going to change if you insist on asking the same question. Now, I must find Fronsac. That wizard knows—'

'Stratus, wait.' She grasped my arm as I turned away.

I paused, my teeth clenched to hold back a sharp retort. She didn't flinch from my gaze this time, but instead rubbed her hands together as if cold and shifted from foot to foot.

'Please. Is that... was that true? What you showed me?'

I could hear her heart racing without even trying, and even as I thought about it I tasted the sour edge of fear in her scent. Perhaps I had been wrong to offer her that glimpse of my old self, my true self, but as with most humans, if she didn't see something she wouldn't believe it. And sometimes not even then, it seemed.

'I would not lie to you,' I said. I lied. 'I am the Dead Wind.'

'But—' She gestured at me vaguely.

I bridled at the delay. Fronsac's scent wasn't getting any fresher, and the sooner I concluded my business with him the sooner I could be free of the city, and free away from roofs and walls and the rule of men.

'Enough of this. You are not making any sense.' She actually flinched as I stepped towards her, which I found hurtful given that I had just saved her life, and not for the first time. 'Why is the truth harder to believe than that I am some infernal creation?'

'I never believed that,' she said.

I heard her heartbeat skip at that, a murmur that I may not have sensed had I not known the sound and feel of it so well.

'You ask me not to lie, but then you do just that. That is not what friends do to each other, Tatyana Henkman.' I didn't put any power into saying her name, but I could feel the sorcery I had inadvertently embedded within her react to it nonetheless.

She opened her mouth to say something, but closed it and simply hugged her arms to her chest. The temptation to look into her mind was strong, but I resisted and simply folded my arms.

'Tell me, what more would you have me say or do that would convince you?'

She didn't say anything at first and simply stared at me as if seeing me for the first time.

'Your wings,' she blurted as I turned away. 'Where are your wings? And your tail?' She took a deep breath. 'I can understand demons, there are lots of stories about them. But a dragon? It's just not possible. I mean, how? I know it's magic and all that, but you're too small.'

A trio of servants who had stopped to stare at us quickly moved away as I looked in their direction, their excited whispers following them.

'My wings are inside me.' I held up a hand as she opened her mouth again. 'The enchantment that binds me to this shape very nearly killed me when I set it upon myself. I will not waste your time, nor mine, trying to explain it, other than to say that my flesh remembers them, like a seed carries the memory of the mighty oak it will one day become.'

'But why are you still a man?' She gestured to me as if I wasn't painfully aware of the body I was wearing.

I grimaced for that was a question I couldn't yet answer. 'It is not by choice. It is...'

Now she folded her arms. 'Complicated?'

'Yes,' I said, with no little relief. 'But now is not the time to try and explain it.'

Her brows creased in thought at this, and I took the moment to start walking again. I heard her start following again after a small pause. We walked in relative silence for some time, in so much that I could hear her muttering to herself but thankfully her questions seemed spent for now.

The traces of Fronsac's magic were easier to follow than his scent, letting me spend more thought in mentally rehearsing how I would announce myself to him until Tatyana spoke again, breaking into my thoughts.

'So how're you going to handle this? I mean, will Fronsac know?'

'Know what?'

She hurried forward until she was abreast with me. 'That you're a bloody dragon.'

'No. Why would he?'

'Well, he's the best wizard we have, isn't he?' She waved her hands at me. 'You're the one with the magic singing rainbows. How do you tell if someone's a wizard?'

I couldn't help but smile at her description of the

Songlines. I'd taken great care to explain how the currents of magic cradled the world but her attention span had clearly not been up to the task.

'I can usually smell it on them, like a burned spice, or sense the gathering of their power.' I slowed to save her from the undignified shuffle she was having to do to keep up with me. 'To divine who and what I truly am he would need to do far more than he has so far. I do not doubt that he senses that there is something inhuman about me, but for now I expect he believes it to be a distortion from my sorcery.'

'So are you going to tell him?'

The thought of a wizard, even a relatively friendly one like Fronsac knowing what I was sent an unpleasant shiver through me. The tortures that Navar Louw, my captor and the last wizard I had known, had visited upon me were not easily forgotten. His name was a curse to me now, and I felt my hands curling into fists at the mere thought of him. I had sworn to kill him, and thinking of the epically brutal ways in which I would do just that had become one of my favourite ways to fill the sadly rare moments I had to myself.

'Stratus?'

'What?' Startled back to awareness, I barked the word at her. 'Apologies. I do not have pleasant memories of wizards.'

The trail I had been following now led us along a passageway that ended in a small chamber with a wonderful pair of doors made almost entirely of coloured glass panels that together formed an attractive but somewhat bizarre picture of a man with a burning head sat upon a horse. I could see the shadows of at least half a dozen armed men milling around beyond the doors, and while they didn't seem particularly agitated, I knew it wouldn't take much to turn their primitive minds towards violence.

'Hold on, Stratus.' She pulled at my arm as I moved to open the doors. 'Slow down. Why have you brought us here?'

I glanced at the room and at the silhouettes of the men and shrugged. It all looked the same to me. 'Fronsac is somewhere close, just beyond those doors. I can smell him.'

'That passage leads up to Jean's private chambers. Those are his personal guards. They'll not let anyone past them without an invitation from him.'

'Not even you, the sworn sword of Prince Lucien?'

She snorted at that but didn't say anything. She was frowning, which was a good sign because it meant she was thinking about something. I had no issue with forcing my way into his chambers if I needed to, but it would undoubtedly be easier if I didn't need to burn my way into the Crown Prince's chambers. He was decidedly pricklier about such things than his brother Lucien.

'I'm going to try something,' she said, tugging at her borrowed armour. 'Don't do anything. Just follow what I do.'

'That would be doing something.'

'Gods, not now, Stratus.'

With that, she pulled the glass doors open and stepped through into the passage. She'd taken barely taken a step before her way was blocked.

'Hold please, milady,' said one of the men. 'Is Prince Jean expecting you?'

I stepped out into the passage and even though I was being peaceful, the guards reacted as if stung, recoiling away from me and laying their hands on their swords.

'Calm down, gentlemen,' Tatyana said with a smile, and for a few heartbeats it looked like it was going to work. What neither of us had considered was that somewhere in the maze of the palace behind us, the paladins who I had trapped in their dormitory while on my way to rescue Tatyana had eventually hacked their way through the door, and were now ringing every bell and sounding every horn they could lay their hands on.

The guards froze as the sonorous honk of the horns reached us. The one who'd spoken to Tatyana reacted first, stepping back from her and raising his hand.

'I'm afraid you need to leave. No one comes in or out until I know what is going on,' said the guard who had previously addressed her.

I leaned in close to Tatyana and covered her eyes with my hand. She gave a jolt at my touch, but I held her immobile against me and turned to the guard who had spoken.

'My apologies,' I said. 'It's neither personal nor permanent.'

He stared at me, his hand on his sword, and even I recognised the expression on his face as confusion. I closed my eyes and released the light spell I'd been holding. I hadn't added any heat to it, and so fully expected their sight to return, but there was no point in taking chances with my own vision. The pulse of magic light manifested above my head, and blazed like a small, silent sun for a brief moment before blinking away into nothingness. I released Tatyana and she pushed herself away from me.

'What did you do!' Her voice trailed away as the guards began shouting and clutching at their faces. 'God's beard, I told you not to do anything!'

'Your approach was being as useful as a goat's ear.'

'What?'

'It's an old expression. Come along,' I said, pushing my way through the reeling guards.

One of them clutched at my leg but I shook him off easily enough. Fronsac's scent strengthened once we were past the guards. Happily, he was quite close, and I gave Tatyana an encouraging smile as I knocked on the doors. The wizard opened them almost immediately, giving her no chance to protest.

'I thought I felt your sorcery,' he said. 'Stars, what is going on here?'

'Nothing serious,' I said. 'I found Tatyana.'

He watched the men in the passage for a few moments, then stepped aside. 'So you did. Come in, quickly now.'

JEAN'S CHAMBERS WERE far more spacious than Lucien's had been, and not only because of the lack of cluttered tables. The main room was set with a number of chairs, each of which looked comfortable enough to sleep in, all arranged around a single long table set with bowls of fruit and bread and several bottles of wine. The starchy smell of men was predominant, but there were also far more pleasant undertones of sweet resins and flowers, which made it tolerable.

Jean was sat in the largest of the chairs, watching us with a goblet held in his ink-stained fingers and a great number of papers upon his lap. A pale, muscular man I did not recognise stood behind him, his hands resting on the bone handles of the two swords that hung from his belt.

'Highness,' Tatyana said from behind me. Her finger dug into my back and I inclined my head in a shallow bow, if only to stop her from an angry outburst.

'Meneer Stratus,' the prince said, setting his goblet down and nodding to Tatyana. 'The mage was just talking about you.' He cocked his head towards the doors and the muffled sound of the bells. 'I would guess that a lot of people are talking about you at this moment, and I suspect not in such friendly tones.'

'My prince, may I just—' Fronsac began, but Jean raised

his hand and the wizard fell silent.

'No,' Jean said. 'I want him to tell me. To show me, as he did you.'

'My prince, in the mildest of terms, that is most irregular.'

'He has given you his word, has he not?'

I smiled as Fronsac glanced across at me. Prince Jean was proving to be far more interesting than my first impression of him had ever suggested. I had indeed given Fronsac my word that I would stand with them to destroy Navar Louw, the so called Worm Lord and my previous owner. It was a dangerous thing to offer a skilled wizard, but killing Navar was very much my first priority.

'I gave my word with sincerity and am bound by it,' I said to both of them. 'And I do not think our enemies will wait while I tell the story.'

'Time is something we all lack at this moment,' agreed the prince.

The man with the swords watched me closely as I pulled a chair across and sat in front of the prince, who was watching me even more intently. His scent was spiced with something like fear, his heartbeat rising, and I wondered whether he could sense the otherness in me as Fronsac had. I'd have been a fool to think that the wizard wasn't even now subtly scrutinising me for any clue as to what about me had changed, but I suspected that I would know the moment he discovered it.

I gave Jean an empty smile as I gathered my own thoughts. What secrets lurked in his head? If I knew them, would I regret giving my word to aid the descendants of the very men who had once set their armies against me and cost me my one love?

'What do I do?' asked Jean, pulling me back from my reverie as he laid the papers to one side.

'Just look into my eyes.'

'Can I blink?' I smiled at the same question that Tatyana had asked me, and fought the urge to suggest that something terrible would happen if he did.

'Of course.' I spread my legs slightly and rested my elbows on my knees so that my face was level with his, then woke my sorcery. I could feel Fronsac's magics swirling around us as he manipulated the sequence of wards he had set on Jean's mind. I could feel them shifting like the pieces of a puzzle box, but the sequence was too complicated and swift for me to follow. I waited until I felt the pressure fade, then looked into Jean's pale eyes.

There was some residual resistance from the wards, but these were easy enough to push past now. Jean shivered as our minds connected in a jumble of images and stray thoughts. That chaos lasted a brief moment before I exerted control and pulled him into my memories.

As I had with Fronsac, I let him see what I had seen, from my initial discovery of the enchanted corpses hidden beneath the sepulchre of St Tomas, then the battles Tatyana and I had fought against the dead in the dungeons, all the way to my confrontation with Cardinal Polsson, the corrupted leader of the Paladins that the city's defences were relying on. Again, as with Fronsac, I made sure to omit the truth of who and what I was.

I could feel the wonder and anger that the truth of Polsson's betrayal woke in Jean, and while he struggled to digest what I had shown him, I took the opportunity to peer into his mind as well, since it was doubtful that I would have another chance to do so again anytime soon. I would not have enough time to align my thoughts with his, so I had to settle for a more general approach, much as I had with Crow, the kind old tinker I had met on the road to Falkenburg. I would sift through these thoughts and memories later, when I had time alone.

I gently disengaged from his mind and let the connection fade before sitting back. Jean's knuckles were white as he clung to the sides of the chair and shook his head.

'That...' He reached for his goblet with a shaking hand and gulped at the remaining wine. 'That was unlike anything I have ever experienced.' He glanced up at Fronsac, who was standing close by. 'Is that what it is like to scry?'

'No, my prince,' answered Fronsac. 'Scrying is less intimate, and more like the vision of a bird passing overhead.'

The prince took another gulp of his wine, then sat back and stared at me. We sat like that for some time, with me steadily eating my way through the nearest bowl of fruit and him peering at me, his fingers steepled under his fleshy chin. Fronsac seemed content to simply stand there, but Tatyana marked the time by pacing the length of the room and sighing loudly on every turn. It was something of a relief when Jean eventually lowered his hands and cleared his throat.

'I want you to know that I appreciate everything you've done for us. I can't even begin to understand the full extent of the damage that Polsson has inflicted, but I know it would have been far worse without you.'

I was about to thank him when I felt Tatyana's heartbeat increase.

'That gratitude aside, you leave me in a difficult position. We are at war, Meneer Stratus, and the laws of this Kingdom are quite clear. The Law demands your death.'

Tatyana simply gasped, but I was on my feet, my chair sliding backwards and my hands curling into fists.

CHAPTER 2

'HIGHNESS, PLEASE, YOU cannot!' Tatyana's sword remained in its sheath as she dropped to a knee.

For my part, I fed power into my wind and fire construct so that it was ready to unleash with a thought. Fronsac must have sensed it because I felt his magics flicker to life as well, his now empowered wards making the air around him gleam like oil upon water.

If Jean was in anyway aware of how close he was to being immolated, he gave no sign of it. Instead, he simply waved his hand at his guard, who sheathed his vicious looking sword in the same swift movement he'd drawn it with.

'Sit down,' he said, his voice taking the hard edge that he had used in the war council. I didn't care for it, but I curled a finger of sorcery under my fallen chair and dragged it back towards me. Tatyana returned to the edge of her seat, her heart still beating like a drum and her scent clouded with anxiety. I glanced at Fronsac as his wards subsided; he was watching me as well, the green of his eyes glinting with gathered energy.

'Do you have any idea what you have done?' Jean snapped, pulling my attention away from the wizard. He didn't pause long enough for either of us to answer. 'You're a confessed necromancer. You killed the commander of my army, burned half of his camp and have now attacked the church on the eve of battle, slaying Drogah only knows how many of their holy knights, not to mention their spiritual leader. And from the bells, I am assuming you've done more damage since you came back here, yes?'

'They were torturing Tatyana. I will not stand for that.'

'I'll take that as a yes then. Do you have the remotest idea how it looks for me to have invited you into my confidence? Even now the guards outside are wondering why they haven't been ordered to drag you out in irons.'

'He disabled the guards,' Fronsac added helpfully.

'What does it matter?' I said. 'You know the truth of it.'

'*What does it matter?*' Jean's voice cracked out like a whip as he gripped the edge of the table. 'What does it matter? Are you a simpleton?'

I felt my lip curl into a sneer. Was this his gratitude for all I had done, for the blood I had shed?

'You ungrateful wretch.'

Jean started backwards as if slapped, and for a moment it was quiet enough for me to hear the soft buzz of the fruit flies that gathered over the bowls.

'You *dare* speak to me like that?' Despite the anger that flavoured his scent, Jean's voice was quiet, and as he spoke the guard behind him laid his hand on his sword again.

I looked up at the pale man. He was certainly fast, but I was confident that my thoughts were faster. 'If you draw that sword, I will burn the flesh from your very bones.'

'Your Highness,' Fronsac said, stepping forward between us. 'Stratus. Peace, I pray you.'

'I will *not* sit here and be spoken to like that,' snapped Jean. 'Not by anyone.'

'Of course not, Highness, and he will beg your forgiveness.' Fronsac glanced at me as he spoke. 'The night has been fraught, and full of strange magics, and I fear they have inflamed both pride and temper. I pray you, let us not add to the legion of enemies that we already face.'

'There is wisdom in Fronsac's words,' I said. 'I suggest you listen to him.'

Jean didn't respond other than to grind his teeth and stare at me in what I assumed he imagined was a threatening manner.

The wizard turned to me now. 'What my prince meant was that you have placed him in an awkward position, for while he values your service, when the high seneschal of the Order comes through that door not long from now, he has no proof of Cardinal Polsson's crimes.'

'The cardinal was an agent of the Worm Lord,' I replied.

'I understand that, as does my prince, but where is the proof?'

'I have shown you the proof you need.'

Fronsac shook his head. 'The Order would not recognise your magic as viable proof, so how, or what, would you show them? You have nothing they will accept.'

'What if you examine the bodies, and show them the worms?' offered Tatyana.

'Again, all of it the product of magic. Whatever else Polsson has done, he has ensured that wizards and the church will never stand side by side, so again, you cannot rely on magic to plead your case to them.'

I looked to Jean. 'You are the prince, the eldest son of the King, descended from the line of Kramm himself. Can you not command them?'

Jean threw his head back and laughed. *Laughed!* I felt the anger in me kindle anew but Tatyana spoke from behind me, distracting me before the embers could become a blaze.

'Who or what is Kramm?'

Fronsac answered for me, which was fortunate as in truth I had no real recollection of it aside from a murky memory of someone announcing the arrival of a visiting king by reciting all of his impressive sounding titles.

'Kramm was a pagan god of war, part of the pantheon of the Dawn Age. He was said to walk the world in the guise of a female avatar named Storm the Harbinger.'

'I like him already,' said Tatyana.

'That is most impressive, Fronsac,' I said, genuinely impressed.

He mimed taking a hat off. 'There's no point of being a wizard if you can't dazzle people with obscure knowledge.'

'Yes, we're all thrilled, Fronsac,' said Jean. 'But it changes nothing. As for commanding the paladins, I would gladly do it if it didn't violate at least six ancient laws and four very old and cleverly worded treaties. Which leaves me... *us*... where we started, with me bound to having you arrested and executed for high treason.'

'No one is executing us,' I growled. There was no sorcery in my words, but the voice I spoke to them with was older than this city, the timbre of it resonating with the deepest part of their brains, the part that reminded them to fear the dark.

Jean paled and sat back sharply, while his personal guard gripped his sword with suddenly clumsy hands, Behind me Tatyana's breath caught and even Fronsac took a step back, perhaps uncertain how to react to a non-magical threat.

'I... I have a proposal for you,' said Jean, his voice catching for a moment before its usual strength returned.

A thrill coursed through me as I studied their reactions. I had forgotten how *good* it felt to be feared, and perhaps it was because I hadn't felt that in so long that I decided to test Fronsac. I flexed my will against the touch of the wards he'd wrapped around me like gossamer curtains of light, and felt them solidify as I tried to brush them aside. They became the thinnest of blades now, cutting my energy into meaningless slivers and tightening around me like the great tree snakes of the far south, their ethereal edges a thought away from cutting me.

'Don't do it, my friend,' he said, but if anything his words only fed the anger waiting within me. He wasn't the first wizard to try and bind me, to trap me, and while I knew he did it without malice, at that moment I wanted nothing more than to rip the heart from his narrow chest.

A cool hand fell on my arm, and the small spark of raw sorcery that flickered between us let me know it was Tatyana even before she touched me. I let out the breath I had been holding, and the surge of anger subsided with it.

'Forgive me,' I said, turning to Fronsac for a moment. 'My curiosity is a beastly thing.' I sat back and offered Jean a toothy smile. 'What is your proposal?'

'Your lack of respect does you no favours, wizard.'

I opened my mouth to tell him that I was a sorcerer, not a wizard, but caught myself before I said too much. Wizard was such a very human term, coined by a race that had merely heard an echo of the Great Song and, in its arrogance, assumed that giving it a name made them its master.

'I am not a wizard,' I said, unable to stop myself. I might have argued the term with him, but there was no point to it. I had a sense of his mind now, and while it was the lightest of impressions it was enough to know that it was not one easily changed. I helped myself to more fruit as I waited for him to finish staring at me.

He sat back as I bit an apple in half. 'I do not have time for semantics or your wounded pride. Now, I may not like you, but I am not so churlish as to deny the debt we owe you. So this is what will happen: you will be arrested when you leave this room, and taken away to await execution.'

At this Tatyana drew a sharp breath. For my part, I glanced at Fronsac, who gave a small shake of his head. I could feel his wards, but there was no sense of him gathering any other power to himself, which I found reassuring. I ate the rest of the apple and waited for Jean to finish.

'You will be taken to the traitor's cells in the guard tower. This will be a mistake of course, since a wizard will surely have no trouble opening the door. You will escape, to my public disappointment, and secretly meet with Fronsac, who will take you somewhere out of the way until we see how this mess is going to play out.'

'I don't like prisons.'

Jean slapped his hand against the table. 'I don't care! You will do this, or by the gods, I will hand you over to them with a bloody ribbon around your neck.'

'Highness,' said Tatyana, edging forward. 'Prince Jean, what about Lucien? He is too close to them.'

'I have not forgotten my own brother.' He looked to the window, and the pinking sky beyond. 'He has ridden out to join his army this very morning, accompanied by Baron Karsten and his lancers.'

'The fourth cohort are Polsson's men,' I said. Had my warnings been for nothing?

'I have raised Baron Karsten to the position of High Seneschal,' Jean said, as if that explained anything.

'Karsten is a good man,' Tatyana said. 'As High Seneschal he will be close to Lucien at all times.' She looked back to Jean. 'But he doesn't know the truth. I should be at his side. It's where I belong. Let us go after them. Please, Jean.'

'And do what exactly? You'll both be strung up before you get within fifty yards of him.'

'It's time,' said Fronsac, before either of us could reply. 'They're coming up the stairs now.'

I understood his meaning, and while I saw the logic of Jean's scheme, the thought of being chained and imprisoned once more made my throat tighten and my hands curl into fists. Submission sat as poorly with me as it ever had.

'Let us get this mummery over with,' I said, rising to my feet. As I moved, the pale man behind Jean drew his sword. As he did, I loosened the grip on the wind construct I had been holding in my mind, slamming the sword against his chest and hurling him against the wall with enough force to empty a nearby bookshelf. He left a smear of blood on the stone as he slid down it, the whites of his eyes showing as his dazed brain tried to understand what had just happened to him.

At the sound of his body hitting the wall Jean all but threw himself from the chair to land sprawling at Fronsac's feet, but by then it was over. The wizard was staring at me too, his hands half raised, and even though I didn't care to try touch his mind with his wards woken, I was fairly certain he was trying to understand why he didn't sense me doing anything.

The door was thrown open a heartbeat later as the guards reacted to the noise and came charging in, swords raised and challenges spilling from their lips. I raised my hands and stood up as Fronsac helped Jean to his feet.

'Get them out of here!' he bawled, his plump cheeks almost as red as the blood on the wall. 'You keep those chains on, do you hear me? On!'

I couldn't help but wince as they closed the manacles on my wrists, with my hands behind my back. That I could snap them with just the strength of my arms was scant comfort from the indignity of submission. They led us out into a scene of complete chaos. The guards I had blinded were being tended by what I assumed were healers, while more guards were trying to hold back three grey bearded men wearing the white and red smocks of the paladins. These three and their similarly dressed escorts redoubled the amount of shouting they were doing as they caught sight of us and, in a surge of anger, barged their way through the first line of guards.

'Demon!'

'Murderer!'

'Heresy, my lord!'

The guards who Jean had tasked with taking us to the cells were calling out for them to drop their weapons and stand back, but even I could see they weren't going to obey. The greybeard's escorts rushed forward and fell upon the guards with their fists and feet, beating them to the ground. Everyone but me was shouting. One of my guards kicked a paladin hard enough in the eggs to drop him, which made me burst out laughing. As I did, the nearest of the greybeards shouted 'Bastard!' and leaped towards me, a dagger in his hand.

I flinched backwards, knocking Tatyana to the ground, and narrowly avoided his lunge. He was close, and in a moment of inspiration I rammed my head down into his face as one of his men had once done to me. I mistimed it though, and instead of striking with my forehead I ended up mashing my face against his. It saved him from a staved in head but I did take a bite out of his cheek instead, which really set him to howling. I spat the bloody wad at him as he staggered away clutching at his face.

'Enough!'

The word roared through the passage, the force of it

ripping several paintings from the walls, and making everyone within it stagger to an abrupt halt, fists raised and mouths open. I smelled Fronsac's magic as the roar faded to a ringing whine in my ears.

I helped Tatyana to her feet as best as I could with my hands behind me.

'That is quite enough,' Fronsac's voice was hard and laced with power as he strode into the passage. 'You men. Take the Prince's prisoners to the cells.' He jabbed his staff at the paladins. 'And you, gentlemen, will present your petitions to His Highness in the manner agreed. Church or not, if you so much as lay a hand on the King's men again you will be deemed a traitor to the Kingdom and dealt with under the old laws.'

I had expected them to protest, but the fire had apparently gone from their bellies. They were hauling their wounded to their feet when a sharp shove from the guardsmen set Tatyana and I walking again.

CHAPTER 3

THE MAZE-LIKE HALLWAYS of the palace still made little sense to me, but we hadn't walked too far from Jean's quarters before we came to a short stair that led up into a square tower. According to Fronsac this was where condemned noblemen were taken to await their execution. There were only four cells, all of which were dry and had beds, wooden floors with thick rugs and even glass windows. They left the chains on when they pushed me into a cell and Tatyana in the one alongside mine. The doors had small windows in them but were heavy things of ancient wood, bound in thick iron with strong locks that turned noisily as they shut us in.

Fronsac chose three of the uninjured guards to remain by the doors to the towers while the others returned to wherever they were supposed to go. He then sent these three to fetch food and drink while he ostensibly guarded us, a clever ploy on his part.

'That was well played, although I doubt that Falco appreciates it at this moment,' he said, pacing in front of our doors.

'Falco?'

'Jean's bodyguard. You all but scrambled his brain with that little trick.'

I had meant to kill him, and I expect that Fronsac misread my surprise that he was still alive as some sort of concern.

'Don't worry, he'll be fine in a day or so.'

'What a relief.' I sent a flash of sorcery into the manacles, popping the lock open so that I could shake my hands free. 'So, when do we leave?'

He shook his head. 'You don't. Not yet.'

'I agreed to this on the understanding that we would leave.'

'And you will leave, but not yet.'

'Why not?'

'We need to let some of the dust settle on this. We have won some time with our little display, but the Order will not be shaken off that easily, siege or not.'

I stepped up to the door and pressed my face to the little window. 'I saved this miserable city, and now I am to sit in this prison simply so that your prince is not embarrassed?'

'Lucien is out there, Fronsac,' called Tatyana from her cell. 'Every moment that we waste brings him closer to the worms. We have to get out of here.'

'I know. And I understand, really, I do.' He stepped close to the door as well and met my gaze frankly. 'My friend, do you think I want this? Do you not think I would prefer you at my side, hurling destruction down on the scum gathering outside our walls?' He paused for a steadying breath. 'I ask only that you trust me, just for a day, perhaps two. You will be safe here. And fed. Take it as a chance to rest and gather your strength, because I have no doubt that you will be needing it sooner than you realise.'

He had lowered his wards as he spoke and now met my gaze once more. Not one to waste an opportunity, I fed some power into mine and accepted his invitation. He was a skilled wizard, and I had no doubt that he could influence what I gleaned from his thoughts, but even so I would have sensed some doubt or hesitation if he was hiding anything. He kept his deep thoughts hidden, but I could sense his deep curiosity about me, some fear too, but nothing I associated with either malice nor falsehood. He believed what he was saying, which either made him a very good liar an honest fool.

I blinked the thoughts away and broke the connection. 'Fine, I will wait. But the morning after next, I am opening this door and leaving this city whether your Prince wants it or not.'

He nodded. 'The morning after next.' He tilted his staff and the torches set into the sconces all flared to life, dispelling the shadows. 'I'll tell the guards to remain outside, in the main passage. Until then.'

He touched his fingers to the edge of his cowl, then turned on his heel and left, shutting the main door behind him.

'Some reward, eh?' said Tatyana after a few moments.

'It feels more of a punishment than a reward.'

'I know that. So what are you going to do now?'

'Sleep.'

'And then what?'

'I hope to eat. Lamb, preferably.'

'Really? We're locked in a damned dungeon and that's your plan?'

I closed my eyes, set my hand against the wall and sent a few strands of sorcery running along the cold stone until I felt the wood and metal of her door, then sent them burrowing into the keyhole. The lock was a masterful piece of engineering, and it took me a fair amount of probing to find and move the correct part. I heard it spring open with my ears even as I felt it through the sorcery.

'What the Hel!' A few moments later I heard her shuffle out of the cell and come stand before mine.

'The doors are not keeping me here, only my promise to Fronsac,' I said, peering at her through the window.

'Let me in.'

I shivered at her words as she unknowingly echoed the voice of my draconic self. 'Are you going to hit me again?'

She laughed. 'No. I've just grown used to having you around.'

I pulled the sorcery back to me and opened my door too.

'Nice place,' she said, stepping inside.

'It's my favourite dungeon so far.'

'Did you just make an actual joke?'

'No.'

'No, I suppose not.'

She folded her arms and stared at me until I started wondering if there was some social convention that I had misinterpreted. I remained as I was as she slowly walked around me, her hand trailing across my borrowed tunic.

'A dragon,' she said when she finally stood before me again.

I fought the urge to sigh. 'That is still correct.'

Her eyes suddenly widened, and I turned, expected some assassin behind me, but the cell was empty.

'Sorry,' she said, a hand pressed to her breast. 'I just remembered what you said when you healed me. You used your blood.' She looked quite pale as she said it. 'Dragon blood.'

'It flows in your veins too now,' I said. The memory wasn't a pleasant one, seeing as I'd been impaled on a number of wooden beams and had to rip myself free to reach her before the wound to her heart killed her. I hadn't regretted it yet, and the realisation actually improved my mood. She gasped as I grabbed her hand and the sorcery within her drew some of my energy into her, sharpening her senses and filling her with a surge of strength.

'Tatyana Henkman,' I said, enjoying the sensation of the fire kindling in my eyes once more. 'The only other being in this world with the blood of dragons.'

She looked up at me, the green of her eyes glowing like sunlit emeralds. She didn't resist as I drew her into my mind and folded her into my memories.

THE NIGHT AIR was cool across my scales as I sank through the clouds, ribbons of vapour clinging to my wingtips. Below me the great plains were a dark mass broken only by rivers that gleamed like silver in the moonlight. I woke my vision and the heat from the migrating herds lit the dark earth in a moving patchwork of colour, red where the great bison roamed, gold to the west where the oryx grazed and the yellows of the striped horses to both the south and north. Between them were dozens of families of the small, dun buck that served as the ears and eyes for all of them, their small heat traces giving them the look of wandering fireflies.

I silently circled the herds. Their senses were attuned to the threat of the great cats that crept ever closer on the fringes of the herds, rather than what waited in the sky above them. I could fall upon them now and fill my jaws before the first warning call, but there was no sport in that.

I dipped my wings into a dive, my speed increasing until I could feel the strain of holding my wings level pull at my shoulders. I was mere moments from the edge of the first herd before I gave voice to my hunting call, the sound of it lighting a blind panic among the herds. As one, the plains exploded into movement, the colours brightening as their blood surged and the blind instinct to flee overwhelmed their senses. I skimmed over the nearest herd, low enough that I felt the males' antlers brush my thighs, the wind of my passing bowling over the weak and infirm.

With another roar I tilted my wings and powered my way upwards once more, exulting in the feel of the great muscles that spanned my chest and back working in perfect unison as I gained enough height to wheel on my wingtip and plunge down amongst them once more. It was time for the killing to begin.

I CLOSED MY eyes and pulled my mind from Tatyana's, then caught her as she fell against me.

'What was that?' she exclaimed in rush.

'A memory of a better time.'

'I could feel it. I felt it.' A smile crooked my lips as she closed her eyes and stretched out her arms, tilting them to the left. 'The wind, everything.'

'They were good years.'

'It was so fast. You were so fast.'

'Only in the hunt. I always preferred to fly above the clouds.' The smile found its way onto my face again. 'I could soar for days with nothing but cool air between me and the sun.'

'Can you show me?'

I considered it, and was surprised to find that I was not actually opposed to the idea. Quite the opposite. My own memories had been hidden from me for too long, and while there was a danger in dwelling in them too often, surely I deserved such a small indulgence. I bade her sit facing me, her on the bed and me on the floor. I could feel her excitement radiating from the connection between us, and it was hard not to feel flattered. I took her small, delicate hands in mine and looked into her eyes. I had many memories of flying, so it was no difficult matter to drag her consciousness into such strong memories, particularly when I enjoyed revisiting them too.

The shadows were lengthening when I finally closed the memory and released her hands, and I found myself feeling both strangely refreshed and tired at the same time. I had almost grown used to the body I was wearing, but after sinking so deeply into my older memories I could feel the unnatural shape of my flesh chafing against my soul.

'Is something wrong?' she asked, watching me from the edge of the bed with a furrowed brow.

'I should not have indulged myself so deeply,' I said. 'Some memories are dangerous to linger on.'

'Well, I have no regrets, if that's any consolation.' She sat back and crossed her legs under her in a way that made me wince, even though the knees of this body bent the same way as hers. 'But I know what you mean. I'm the same with anything from my childhood. Even after so many years, merely thinking of my father sets my teeth on edge.'

'I didn't like him either, if that's any consolation.'

'Sorry?'

'That's not necessary. It wasn't your fault.'

'No. I mean, what do you mean you didn't like him either?'

'Your father was the one who found me. After his father's father had abandoned the circus and left me to die.' I sat back as the memories of the overgrown barn I had spent so many decades in welled up, my mind conjuring the earthy scents of decaying wood and spreading moss that had been all I could smell for nigh on a hundred years. 'Another fifty years or so and the floor of my cage would have been soft enough to break, and then I would have been free. But instead your father found me, and I was still struggling to awaken from my long sleep to be able to do anything about it on that first day. He walked right into the cage and sat closer than you are now.' I forced the memories away. 'If I'd known what he was thinking I might have tried harder to get to him.'

'Why?' She edged forward. 'What did he do?'

'He sold me to Navar Louw.'

She recoiled as if I had struck her and pushed herself backwards until her back met the wall, then covered her face with her hands.

I shifted so that I could lean against the wall too, rolling the memory around in my mind once more like I would a pebble in my hand. *Navar Louw.* Even bereft of my sorcery and with my senses dulled by disuse and generations of old enchantments, I had sensed the corruption within him on our first meeting, but had then thought it merely a facet of his humanity and exposure to magic. As ever, hindsight chided for me for missing the obvious, but Navar was a master of deceit. For years he had sat in the centre of a vast web, ostensibly teaching the wizards who would take to the fields to fight the very army he was leading, all the while corrupting and subverting their will to his own. And even then he had pursued a greater prize: me. Forgotten and lost for two generations, left to die in an old barn because some old fool decided that owning a circus was too demeaning a profession for his illustrious family.

I glanced across as the bed creaked and saw that Tatyana had pushed herself back into a sitting position.

'You knew,' she said.

It was too obvious to be a question so I didn't bother answering her.

'Dad sold you. To *him*. Do you think he knew? He couldn't have. No one did. But he knew about you.'

'Eventually, yes. That was the first time I saw him. The last was the next day, when Navar's men came with their wagons and oxen to haul me away.'

'How did you survive?'

'That's a tale for another day I think.' I drew a deep breath and tasted the air. 'The food's almost here.'

She grunted and hauled herself to her feet. 'I suppose I'd better go back to my cell.'

She paused at the door. 'Stratus?'

'Yes?'

'Thank you. For, you know.' She tapped her head.

'I enjoyed it,' I said. It was true, after all. 'If only to have put an end to your questions.'

'Think again,' she said with a smile, then closed the door behind her.

CHAPTER 4

THE FOOD ARRIVED soon after she left. I sat quietly at the back of the cell while they carried it in, ignoring the posturing and the empty threats that went along with it. After a bit more shouting and the slamming of doors they left us alone and I unlocked both cells again, more for the principle of it than anything else, then set about eating. There wasn't much, barely enough for a man, but it was far tastier than what I was expecting. Tatyana seemed content to eat on her own and I was happy to do the same and then stretch myself out on the soft bed, which creaked and moaned but held my weight.

I woke to the sound of men arguing in the passage outside my cell, something about the doors having not been locked. I wiped the grit from my eyes and glanced at the narrow window; the gloom suggested that it was the middle of the night, but that felt wrong. I stood and fumbled at the clasp on the window, and after a bit of twisting and pulling it came away from the frame and the window swung open with a clatter, followed by a gust of cool air. Looking to the east, I could see slivers of sunlight amidst the clouds like embers within an ash covered fire. I drew a deep breath of the air, sifting out the usual odours of the city until I was left with a slightly bitter, metallic taste I had last experienced in the catacombs beneath the city. Tainted magic.

The argument in the passage resolved itself while I was watching the clouds, but I paid no heed to the men as they barged into the cell and replaced the food tray with another. They left quickly, but not before locking, unlocking and testing the door several times. I opened both doors again as soon as they were gone, and soon after Tatyana joined me with her tray of food.

'I'll trade you, eggs for oats.'

'Deal,' I said, happily handing over the bowl.

'You don't know what you're missing. This is the good stuff, made with butter and honey.'

'It's a matter of principle. And I like eggs.'

We ate in companionable silence until another gust of wind slapped the window open again, the frame clacking against the stone.

'You got yours open, I see.' She padded over to it and peered out. 'That's a big storm brewing.'

'It's not a storm,' I said between mouthfuls of egg.

'What do you mean?'

I swallowed the last bite and moved to join her. I drew a veil of sorcery across my vision and looked out across the city again. The clouds were heavy and dark, as if pregnant with rain, save on the fringes where the sunlight had forced its way through. There the vapours were a sickly green.

'These clouds have been drawn together by men, not nature,' I said. I closed my eyes. 'The pressure is all wrong too.'

'The pressure?'

'Air has a weight and form to it. You don't really feel it here, but to fly, you must learn to read the signs. Hot draws cold, as cold draws hot. It is how the winds and weather form.'

'Huh.'

'Yet I hardly feel any of that. This,' I pointed to the green tinged sky, 'is something entirely unnatural.'

'They can do that?'

'They can raise the dead, so there is little I count as impossible these days. The power involved would be considerable though.'

'Could you do it?'

I considered that. 'Yes, perhaps. But not on such a scale, nor for such a long time. Not alone.'

She closed the window, then sighed loudly as she picked up the clasp. ''Did you have to break it?'

'Poor craftsmanship.'

'I'm sure. Are you thinking what I'm thinking?'

I reached for her head but she flinched and swatted my hand away.

'Not like that!' She flinched as the window blew open again. 'What I meant is, do you think this means he's come with them? The Worm Lord.'

'Ah.'

I knew he was out there somewhere, but I hadn't really thought about him being so close. It was clearly a display meant to set fear running through the city, but was it more than that? Would frightening the population be worth such a cost? I had used fear as a weapon when I had owned the skies, but that had simply been a symptom of my size and ferocity.

'Do you hear that?' Tatyana asked, breaking me from my thoughts. 'Sounds like a lot of people.'

I turned my head and listened. Men were generally very noisy, especially when more than a few gathered together, but the sound of voices echoing from the streets outside did sound more enthusiastic than usual.

'What are they shouting?'

I paid more attention to the loudest of the chants. 'Having. No. *Hang him*,' I said.

'Oh shit. You're right.'

'What do you think it means?'

She stared at me until I repeated the question then said, 'You. It means you.'

'Me?'

She didn't reply at first and simply stared out the window.

'Do you want me to lift you up?'

'What? No. It sounds like they're moving along Eagle Road, probably down to the main gaol near the guardhouse. They probably think you're in there.'

'It's been a long time since I had a mob chasing me.'

'I bet the weasel is behind this.'

'Who?'

'Marshal Wilsenach. Weasel, get it? He is, was, Polsson's man. He's good, but I wonder if he's bitten off more than he can chew with this.'

I shrugged and went to sit down. Whatever would happen, would happen. I had one more day to gather myself before I left this city and sought my own path once more.

'What are you doing?'

'At the moment, I'm sitting down. After that, I want to explore the clouds.'

'We can't just ignore this.'

I looked up at her. 'I don't see why not.'

'That's a mob, Stratus. A scared mob with someone to blame their fears on.' She stepped closer. 'Have you ever seen a mob when it gets going?'

'Yes.' I sighed and looked up at her. 'They'll turn and flee as soon as things turn against them.'

In my experience, that had involved setting a few of them alight, especially the men. It was curious thing, but while a screaming woman could excite a mob into new savagery, when men started screaming it had entirely the opposite reaction.

'Then you've seen a different sort of mob than I have. Once the riot starts, they'll swarm.' She was pacing now, and punching one hand into another. 'Jean doesn't dare use force against them, not now.'

I leaned back against the comforting solidity of the wall and closed my eyes. Tatyana was still pacing and arguing the scenario with herself, but I closed my ears to her and turned my attention inward. The last few days had been hard on me, and while the Songlines had healed the rift in my mind, my body was another matter. *My body*. I flexed the muscles of my arms. This was not truly my body. It was my flesh, certainly, but it was as far removed from what it had been as leather boots were to the cow they had come from. I could feel my sorcery rising as I started to draw together the form of the enchantment that bound me to this body.

I was jerked back to the present by a kick to my leg. I lurched forward with a growl that sent Tatyana dancing backwards.

'What?' I snarled.

'Sorry,' she said, a tinge of fear mixing into her scent. 'I thought you were sleeping.'

I scowled against the sudden throb of pain that had woken above my right eye and was steadily working its way through my head, the price for having lost control of the sorcery I had begun to summon. A few drops of blood fell from my nose as I forced myself to swallow the anger that had risen within me.

'You're bleeding.'

'That's what happens when an idiot wrenches you from your sorcerous works.'

'Oh shit. I'm sorry, I just—'

'Just leave me alone,' I said, my voice thickened by the anger that accompanied the pain. 'Go.'

She stepped out of the door, but then hesitated. 'Maybe next time you decide to wander off halfway through a conversation to fiddle with your magic you'll have the goddamned courtesy to warn me.'

She shut the door firmly behind her before I could tell her what I thought about her so called conversation. Rather than the usual sense of confinement I felt in a closed room, the isolation actually felt quite comforting. My thoughts refused to settle though, so instead of directing them inward I began to form my own scrying construct, redirecting the energies, the exercise serving to sooth the ache before it could settle in and cloud my mind. It was quite satisfying when it held together and I carefully fed more power into it.

I splayed my hands against the floor to ground myself as my vision blurred and transferred to the construct's point of view. I looked down at myself and watched as I shook my head, the separation of seeing it a moment after feeling it quite disorienting. I turned away from my body and sent my vision flying out of the window. It was easier to control once I was outside of the walls, allowing me to simply focus on what I was seeing. It felt like I was flying again, and I spent some time swooping back and forth under the pretence of perfecting my control of the spell-work.

Once I was satisfied that I could control my movement and sight, I rose and looked down on where the mob had gathered outside the guardhouse. It was a good size crowd, some several hundred strong. Some of them were armed, but the rest were simply shaking their fists at the guards staring down at them from the walls. I didn't bother trying to identify the agitators as I could only see them, and without smell or sound I knew there was little chance of me recognising their all too human faces again.

I turned away and swept up and along the city walls, passing over the soldiers who were staring out into the gloomy fields beyond. There were far more of them as I approached the south and east, as well as several of the great siege-bows they had once been so fond of shooting at me. The streets below were empty now save for the occasional barricade where smaller groups of soldiers loitered, their mouths flapping in conversations I neither heard nor cared about.

I rose over the walls and looked out towards the Penullin camp that squatted in the shadow of the darkest clouds. That was where the answers would be. Was Navar there? Even without realising it, my vision had crossed the city walls and begun following the muddy ribbon of road that led to their camp. I fed a little more power into the construct, sharpening the clarity of what I was seeing and driving back the unnatural gloom bleeding from the clouds.

I could see the Penullin tents more clearly now, rank upon rank of them, all surrounded by small, busy figures. Amidst this forest of tents was a cluster of far larger constructions, each at least twice the height of a man and large enough to swallow several wagons. I sped towards these, eager to find my enemies, and in my haste I missed the shimmer of the wards their wizards had set about the camp waking. They flashed to life before me, the dense, angular runes of their construction giving them the appearance of snowflakes that had just come from a smith's forge. It took bare moments for me to recognise what they were, but by then it was too late.

They exploded into razor thin shards of red light that

flashed towards me at the speed of thought, shredding the framework of my construct and sending a discordant shockwave along the sorcerous line connecting me to it.

It was like being hit on the head with a hammer that had somehow bypassed my skull. My vision was still tied to the scrying construct, the now malformed structure of which was spewing raw energy into the air as it spun out of control, amplifying the disorientation that I was swiftly drowning in. The second shockwave hit even as some part of me registered that I had rolled across the floor back in the palace, the impact sending my limbs into spasms. I couldn't unbind my sight from the construct, and it felt like my eyes were twisting loose in their sockets. I might have screamed, but the third shockwave hit and what thoughts I had managed to muster splintered and vanished like sparks blown from a fire.

CHAPTER 5

WHEN I WOKE again, it wasn't a gradual realisation. One minute there was nothing, and the next I was there on my back, astonished that I could feel my hearts beating again and wondering why I couldn't open my eyes. My mouth was as dry as a desert afternoon and my tongue seemed too large and glued to my teeth, and I fell into a fit of coughing that made my chest ache before it eventually passed. I took several steadying breaths, then reached for my face. I felt cloth under my fingers, but before I could pull it off a hand touched mine.

'Not yet, Meneer,' said an unknown voice. I sniffed the air as I lowered my arms. It was a male, young, and imprinted with a familiar bouquet of spices and burned air. A wizard, or if not, at least a fledgling of Fronsac's. 'You are safe, but you must rest. We were not expecting you to wake for another week at least.'

'Where am I?' I asked, my voice barely a croak. I drew in another nose of air. Aside from the fledgling's scent, the room smelled largely of ash, hot metal and oil, almost like a blacksmith's forge, but nowhere near as overwhelming or hot.

'You are in Magus Fronsac's rooms. Can you lift your head?'

I did so and felt another cushion being pushed under it.

'Something to drink,' he said, and I felt a cup pressed to my lips. 'Slowly now.'

I opened my mouth and accepted the drink greedily, not bothering to taste it. I could almost feel my gums drawing it all in and swelling to grip my teeth more tightly again, so much so that I hardly had to swallow any.

'More.'

'Soon. I must return to my work, but I will let the Master know that you are awake.'

'Something woke me,' I whispered. I had felt it when I woke, but it had gone by the time I had begun to wonder about my eyes. 'A sharp pain, like a knife pulled from my flesh.'

'You are unharmed, Meneer, save for your eyes. But my Master will speak to you of this himself.'

I wanted to press him for more answers, but sleep claimed me once more and I didn't hear or feel anything else until Fronsac woke me sometime later.

'Welcome back,' he said as I turned my head towards the sound of his voice.

'What happened?'

'You did. You caused quite a stir.'

'You reek of magic,' I said, and it was true. He was, of course, an accomplished and powerful wizard in his own right and so always carried the stains of his craft with him, but what I could sense was sharper and stronger, and undercut with the bittersweet tang of physical exhaustion.

'Believe it or not, the war has not stopped simply because you decided to have a nap,' he said.

'How disappointing.' I said. 'I decided to have a look around the Penullin camp, but as I pressed closer, a rune materialised in the air before me and then exploded into slivers. The next I knew, your apprentice was soothing me.'

He grunted, and I could feel him drumming his fingers against the edge of the bed. 'What colour was it? What did it look like?'

'As red as fanned embers.' I pictured it in my mind. 'There were two large lines of runes, crossing each other, and several smaller ones off the lengths of these. Like frost spreading on glass, or a snowflake.'

'Are you sure?'

'It is quite an indelible memory.'

I felt his fingers drum against the bed once more. 'The ward you stumbled into is called *Kahr-meshu*. Very powerful, and very hard to divine or counter.' He rested his hand on my chest, right above my primary heart. 'You should be dead, my friend, and not simply blinded.'

'Blinded?' I reached for the wrappings on my head again but he slapped my hand away.

'Calm down. We do not know if it's permanent or not. God's beard, man, do you not understand? That ward should have flayed your mind, not just put you on your back for a week.'

'I can heal myself,' I said, reluctantly lowering my arms.

'I'm sure you can. But there is something you need to do for me first.'

As he spoke, the smell of lightning charged air that hung about him began to strengthen. He was gathering his magic, and I felt the same powerful wards I had encountered the first time I had met him flare to life.

'What are you doing?' I reached for my sorcery, but rather than the familiar harmony of the Songlines I felt a dull, empty ache in my head and a ghost of the stabbing pain in my chest.

'One of the things that makes Khar-meshu so deadly and hard to counter is the seed of necromantic energy it is imbued with,' he said, his calm tone betraying none of the strain that he surely must have felt. 'It's a greedy sort of energy that always strikes first. It disrupts your protective wards and prevents further spell-casting, thus allowing the full force of the core spell to strike its target. A bit like someone pulling your armour away before stabbing you.'

I couldn't feel my sorcery, but my arms were free and with his hand still on my chest, I knew he was close enough for me to strike or grab him. Wards or not, he wouldn't be doing anything very wizardly with my hand around his neck. I shifted my hips as I spoke.

'Fascinating. Now tell me, what are you doing?'

'Answering a troubling question.'

As he spoke the last word I felt his magic coalesce and pulse through his hand, into my chest. The tone of it was familiar, but when I tried to press in on it the dull ache in my head redoubled and I felt it slip away from me completely. I could hear him whispering as he directed the magic.

I twisted, swinging my right arm up to grab him. It felt heavy, as if a dozen men were hanging from it, but I welcomed the opportunity to push everything else away and focus on just one goal. I felt the grip of his magic slipping, and just as I opened my hand for the final lunge, the bed splintered beneath me, my weight and the unnatural pressures finally overcoming it.

My hand closed on clothing, rather than his neck, but that would do. If I could pull him towards my mouth my teeth would do more than my hands ever could.

I hadn't noticed that the whispering had stopped until he lifted his hand from my chest. 'You're not human.'

I held onto the clothing I had in my fist and forced my predator's teeth back into my jawbone before answering. 'I am not.'

I heard him take a deep breath and exhale slowly. I had

feared this moment, or worried about it anyway. He was the one person in Jean's court I had reason to fear, but also the one person I had originally come to the city to see, and the irony of being blindfolded at this point wasn't lost on me. I waited while he dealt with whatever thoughts were unfolding in his mind, ready to pull him over if he tried to cast something more troublesome than a divination spell.

'You're not a demon, nor anything crafted by necromancy.'

'Both true.' I let go of his robes and pushed myself away from the wreckage of the bed. I heard him step closer and the rustle of his clothes as he crouched opposite me. I flinched when he touched the bandage, but didn't offer any resistance as he worked at the knot.

'Would you tell me if I asked?'

'That depends on why you want to know.' I kept very still as he began to unwind the cloth.

'I think you know why.'

'Pretend that I don't.'

He sighed. 'We don't have time for these games. Despite everything, I actually like you, so please don't force me into issuing threats and warnings.' He paused. 'Is your name even Stratus?'

He was right, of course. I had already trusted him enough to give him my word, and I was curious to see how he would react.

'I have many names,' I said. 'First among them is Stratus Firesky. In the Dawn Age men knew me as the Dead Wind, and when Henkman vanquished me I was named the Destroyer, and the Doom of Krandin.'

He gasped, and I felt his hands drop away a moment before I heard the clatter of him sitting back on the broken bed. His heartbeat had surged, and I could feel pulses of magic flashing in and out of reality as his control slipped.

I smiled as I reached up and took over the unwrapping of the bandages.

'Now you know my name,' I said. 'And you're about to tell me that it's impossible.'

'Both true,' he said, his voice a shadow of its usual strength.

The bandage finally fell away, and I gently touched my eyes. They were puffy and painful to the touch, but they were still there.

'You shouldn't try to open them yet,' he said, but without much certainty.

I ignored him and slowly forced them open, and at last the black became shot with a rich red that began to fade into the familiar orange of lamplight. I tried once more to kindle my sorcery, and again felt the dull ache in my head resist the attempt, but its grip on my thoughts seemed weaker than it had before. I looked to where Fronsac sat, a dark and largely featureless blob against the light.

'How many fingers am I holding up?' he asked.

'Twelve.'

'Ha.' I could feel his magic drifting over me, the touch as light as a mountain mist.

'Cast as many divinations as you want, mage. I am telling you the truth, as I ever have.'

'You felt that?'

I probed at my sorcery again, and this time felt something different. A light touch, as if the ache was following my train of thought.

'Lift your spell,' I said, a lick of anger colouring my words. 'Now.'

'Will you—'

'Are you doubting my word now, as well as name? If I wished you ill I would have crushed you with my bare hands.'

'I was going to ask if you will permit me to lay my hands on you again.'

'Fine.'

He came forward and put a hand on my head, and even with my blurred vision I could see the bracelets on his wrist glittering with summoned power. He spoke a word and shifted his fingers in a quick pattern that my unfocused eyes couldn't follow, sending a brief flash of pain through my head. It was gone even as I flinched, and in its place I felt a surge of raw energy as my sorcery came to life once more, like a river finally breaking through a dam.

I sighed in relief and wasted no time in channelling it into a healing pattern and set it to work on my eyes as soon as I was able.

'Your rate of recovery is astounding.'

'How did you do that? How did you prevent me from summoning the power?'

'I didn't. I just slowed the rate that the Khar-meshu's taint faded.'

He was slowly coming into focus, and my vision had improved enough that I could see him fiddling with another bracelet.

'Damnation. I have to go,' he said. 'Duty calls. Please, stay here. We need to talk I have so many questions!' He rose quickly but then paused by the door. 'Is there anything you need?'

'Food,' I said. 'And where is Tatyana?'

'I will send for some and explain when I return,' he said, and my hearing was acute enough that I heard the false note in his tone.

However, he was also true to his word and soon enough food arrived, little more than bread and salted meat, but it was most welcome. By the time I finished the loaf the swelling around my eyes had subsided and my vision was almost back to normal. The room I was in was clearly a workshop of sorts, and almost as cluttered as Fronsac's own chambers. The only area that was relatively clear was the space where his apprentice was now back working in, having stared at me all the while that I was eating.

I found some clean clothes that would fit me, and retrieved my medallion from where it lay on a table alongside a parchment where someone had started copying the runes that covered its surfaces. I pocketed the medallion and with nothing else to do, watched the apprentice at work. He was hunched over a small but thick pot over an equally small but very intense magical fire, and chanting in a singsong voice as he emptied tiny spoons of powder into the molten metal within the pot. When he was satisfied, he took great care in pouring the glowing contents of the pot into what looked like a big brick, then sat back, sweating profusely and his chant slowing as it reached its conclusion.

Ever polite, I waited until his chant was finished and he'd bathed his face before asking him what he was doing. In reply, he pried the lid from a nearby box and handed me a delicate looking metal token. It was a thinner version of the eye-inside-a-triangle sort that I had seen the soldiers wearing. I sent a small push of sorcery into it and stared in amazement as the metal pulsed with a green light.

'Fascinating,' I said. 'I barely touched it with some unshaped energy. Why did it turn green like that?'

'Once treated, the metal reacts to magic. It's more sensitive and easier to enchant.'

'Fascinating,' I said again. I turned the token over in my fingers, sending another trickle of energy into it, and this time watching as it spread. It was a brittle metal, and I could have snapped it with ease but when the sorcery touched it, the metal seemed to swell, like a dry cloth soaking in water. When I stopped feeding it the energies, the strength and glow slowly evaporated again.

'How do you stop the magic from dissipating? Is there more alchemy?'

'No,' he said, gesturing to his work table. 'This is all the alchemy there is. I'm in charge of all of it, see?'

'A great responsibility.'

He nodded. 'It is. The spells are cast by Balar's team, and he seals them.'

'Seals them how?'

'Um. I'm not sure.' He gestured to the table. 'I'm an alchemist more than a wizard.'

'An alchemist.' I looked around the room again, this time paying more attention to the jars and pots that cluttered the shelves. 'Tell me, friend, do you have any stink-rock or glow-stone?'

'Any what?'

'Stink-rock. Dull and brown on the outside, but the inside looks like a nice cheese and smells like something that died a week ago.'

He rubbed his chin as he considered this, smearing the soot there into tapering streaks. 'It could be brimstone. We have a bit of that, but mind you, it's expensive stuff. Carted in all the way from Gadri. I've never heard of glow stone though.'

'It's a yellow-grey stone, often pockmarked or showing lots of layers when split. If you abrade it, it sometimes starts to glow.'

'I can't say I recognise it. But I have some unlabelled samples over there, in those two chests. You're welcome to look.'

'Thank you.'

I could feel him watching me, but he soon got bored of that and went back to work while I sifted through the chests, seeking the minerals my body was calling for.

CHAPTER 6

'IT WAS HER decision. You should know by now that it is hard to say no to her.'

I took another sip of the wine that Fronsac had poured but didn't taste it. As it transpired, the blast from the wards had left me unconscious for five whole days; it was nothing compared to the entire months and seasons that I would have slept through once, but as he'd said, neither the world nor the war had stopped simply because I had.

While I had lain there insensate, the rest of the Penullin general Novstan's army had caught up with the vanguard and begun establishing their camps, and by now the encirclement of the city was all but complete. That much had been expected, unlike the news that Lucien and his contingent of paladins had not arrived at their meeting with Baron Karsten, who had instead found himself being ambushed by Penullin cavalry and had escaped with less than half of his men.

Once that news had reached Tatyana's ears she had pressed Jean for permission to leave. I believed Fronsac when he said he'd tried all he could to persuade her to wait, but with me expected to either die or not wake for weeks she would not be dissuaded.

I lowered my now empty glass aside. 'I understand. I

think I would have been more surprised had she stayed.'

'Me too. I'm not sure if she takes her vows seriously or if she's simply too stubborn to change her mind.'

'I think it is both,' I said, making him laugh. I watched him for a moment, then set my glass down. 'Ask.'

'Ask what?'

'The questions hiding behind your teeth. You've barely tasted your wine, and if you spin that ring one more time I'm fairly certain your finger will come off.'

He laughed and ran his fingers through his hair. As blind as I was to the secret language of human expression, his anxiety was plain to see.

'I have so many,' he said, leaning forward, his curiosity suddenly strong enough that I could taste it in the aura of magic he radiated. 'I would ask them all if we had time, but since dawn is racing towards us, just answer me this: why are you here?'

I refilled my glass and went to the window. We were in his private chambers, having made our way along seldom used passageways in the palaces, a cloak and hood hiding me from casual observers. I preferred it here; his wards kept the strange pressures of the dark magics gathering outside the city at bay, and the windows were large, unbarred and open. They looked out across the west of the city, the hill the palace sat upon giving a view of streets where only a few lamps held back the menace of the unnatural clouds overhead. Their uniform blackness was broken only by sporadic flashes of green light, as if some eldritch thing was moving through them.

'Navar Louw,' I said, leaning against the frame. 'Your Worm Lord. I chose this form to escape from him. It was a desperate measure, but it was the only option I could see.'

'Couldn't you have flown away?'

He couldn't see my grimace from where he sat. 'No. He

cut my wings soon after I came into his charge.' I swallowed against an unexpected tightening of my throat for I had tried to avoid thinking of those days. 'And not just slashes, but actually cut parts of them away.' I finished my wine and turned away from the unsettling green of the clouds. 'Tracking a flightless dragon is easier than tracking a man.'

'Could you not have healed them?'

'We have a shared enemy in time. I could have healed them, and one day I will, but to regrow flesh from new takes longer than healing a simple wound. And the skin of my wings needs to be strong; if I had forced it to grow it would have been as soft as that of a hatchling.'

'So why come here?'

'I was looking for you, as it happens.' I smiled at his widening eyes. 'I mean a scholar, not you specifically. There was a flaw in my transmogrification which left a fissure in my mind and a hole in my memories. I could not remember all of my own name, let alone my purpose.'

'Fascinating. So this is not a glamour? That is your own body, your own, draconic flesh?'

'It is.' I stood a little straighter as he looked me up and down, his awe almost palpable and quite intoxicating.

'You must have been desperate to attempt something that dangerous. Foolish, even.'

I waved his comment away. 'It was a small flaw in an otherwise grand work.'

He sipped at his wine, then leaned forward. 'Is he still hunting you?'

'I believe so. All his minions, Polsson included, had a description and instructions to capture me.'

'Intriguing. Will you walk with me? I have duties to attend to that will not wait for the dawn.'

'Where to? As you are so fond of reminding me, I am a fugitive, wanted for treason and murder.'

'Leave that to me. Come now.'

And so it was that for the second time that night I found myself following Fronsac along deserted passageways. These led to a small metal gate that opened as we approached and I found myself walking out into the city streets. He had given me a staff, although it had so little magical potential that it was little more than an ornate branch, but with my hooded cloak and the darkness that lay so thick across the city he assured me that I was a passable apprentice. He seemed content to walk without speaking, which suited me too.

I had not appreciated how protected the palace was until we left its confines. The clouds felt lower and far more menacing out in the open. The roads we followed were empty save for a few stray cats that hissed and wailed as we passed, and the only lights I saw were those glowing behind the shuttered windows of a tavern, the sound of the laughter within strangely jarring after the silence that blanketed the streets.

'Why are they so happy?' I asked.

'Wine has its own magic,' he replied, pausing to re-light a tall lamp with a touch of his staff.

The light seemed hesitant at first, but then slowly strengthened. I fed a little power into my sorcery and let it drift out around me like a moth's antennae. The dark magics practised by Navar's wizards left an unpleasant but distinctive echo, and as I walked I began to sense it around me, a faint but pervasive buzz at the edge of hearing that was hard to ignore once you became aware of it. The grating buzz began to fade as we approached one of the guard towers that studded the city walls though, and I tugged my hood up a little more as we reached the fringes of the light cast by the lamps set at its entrance. The two guards at the foot of the stairs were already watching us.

Fronsac slowed and turned to me. 'Whatever happens, do not let go of the staff.'

With that, he touched his to the top of mine and I felt a jolt as a latent spell swelled to life within it. Like the metal used for the tokens, the staff I bore was largely unfinished but an effective channel for his spell. I felt nothing more than a brief chill that quickly washed over me, but I could feel the magic he'd transferred to the staff vibrating within it. He seemed to be satisfied with whatever he had done and strode up to the door without any further hesitation; I followed and tried to mimic his confidence. The guards quickly stepped back and opened the door, although I saw that both were still watching us closely.

For all that I had destroyed more than a few such fortifications in my time, I had never been inside one like this before. It was smaller than I imagined, possibly due to the thickness of the walls, but the starchy reek of a score or more men living within its confines made it almost impossible for me to concentrate on anything else except not choking on the smell. I pressed the thick sleeve of the cloak to my face and breathed through the fabric and hurried after Fronsac who, having greeted the surly men loitering in the central chamber, was now climbing the stairs to the top.

I took several deep breaths as we emerged onto the roof, where most of the space was taken up by one of their siege bows, which looked far bigger and more complicated up close. I felt my lip curl into a sneer as I saw the spear-sized arrows stacked next to it.

'What was all that about?' Fronsac said, his voice pitched low enough that the four soldiers who he'd just greeted could not hear him. 'It looked like you were going to throw up.'

'The air in there is as thick as cheese.'

'Nonsense. It's a bit stuffy, but what did you expect?'

'Perhaps if you had told me where we were going and why I would have known what to expect.'

It was a small lie, but he didn't need to know that. Rather than reply, he turned to the guards. 'Gentlemen, would you mind going downstairs while we take care of this?'

They didn't hesitate, and after a quick chorus of 'Yes sir' they disappeared through the hatch, which Fronsac shut behind them.

'Over here,' he said, tapping his staff to a large square of pale stone that I hadn't noticed before. A single, large rune was carved into it, and it didn't take much focus for me to see the dark blue light that suffused it.

'What is it?'

'It's a ward stone. I had a dozen or so made some time ago, although I had hoped never to use them.' He sat on the edge of one of the boxes holding spare shafts for the siege bow. 'Do you recognise it?'

I closed my eyes and brushed a frond of sorcery across it until I felt it react. I sensed a slow strength behind it, arcs of blue light meeting each of my golden strands, and as I maintained the touch I felt that strength rising like the blood of something roused from a long sleep, the arcs thickening until they pushed mine back. I slowly withdrew my touch and felt it subside, but slower than it had risen, as if wary of a trick.

'It's a rune of protection.'

'And?'

'What do you mean, and?'

'It's inscribed on a defensive tower. Any fool could have guessed that.'

I swallowed my irritation. 'Its strength is anchored somewhere beneath the city, somewhere deep and strong. It feels slower to react, but I sense that it reacts to what is put against it.'

'Excellent, and correct. This is the shielding rune. Its name means "the fortress" in the old tongue.'

'Your old tongue and mine are two different things.'

'Well, now you know.' He looked up at the skies, then to the east where the fires of the Penullin camp glittered like fallen stars. 'I know you've felt it. The darkness that hangs over the city like a shroud.'

'As soon as we stepped out of the palace.'

'These men, these soldiers, they're all waiting for the arrival of an army and a forest of siege towers to mark the start of the battle.' He leaned on his staff. 'They have no idea that it's already begun.'

'And this is your battleground,' I said, tapping the stone with my foot.

'Part of it. I have a stone in each of the twelve towers, and I have as many of my apprentices as I can spare setting a similar enchantment in the tokens that Niels is producing, but they are all near to exhaustion.'

'As are you. You smell like an old man on the edge of infirmity.'

'Well, that's a bit harsh,' he said with a fleeting smile. 'But you're not entirely wrong. The idea of sleeping more than two hours a night is fast becoming little more than a distant memory.'

'Drawing on your power to sustain you will only work for a short period. There will be a heavy price to pay.'

'Do you think I don't know that?'

'You're still doing it, so yes.'

He snorted. 'Well, I don't have the luxury of a choice. I can protect the soldiers, but out there? The fear that the darkness brings is already festering and there's little I can do about it. This city is going to tear itself apart long before the catapults rain down.'

'Why did you bring me here, Fronsac?'

'I needed you to feel it.' He waved his hand at the sky. 'To understand what we are facing. I have spent my days buried in every book I can find, looking for something, anything that could help us. And now I find that a dragon has been sleeping in my chambers for a week.'

'The.'

'The what?'

'*The* dragon. I am the last of my kind.'

'Really?' He shook his head. 'The point is, *you* are my miracle. Our miracle, do you not see that? If half the stories about you are true then we have a chance, a real chance, to destroy the Worm and everything he stands for.' He sighed. 'To avenge my sons.'

'I still do not understand why you have brought me here. I have already given my word to help cast him down.'

'But that was you, as a man.' He stepped close and clapped a hand to my shoulder. 'We need you. We need *the* dragon. I have retrieved a copy of *Henkman's Chronicle* from what remains of the library, and if half of it is true then you are our greatest hope.'

I shook his hand off. 'I gave my word to oppose Navar Louw, not be the nursemaid to a city of paranoid savages who will turn on me before his body is even cold.'

He took a few steps back, then turned away and stared out towards the Penullin camp. For my part, I folded my arms, leaned against the wall and waited.

'I'm not asking you to be our nursemaid,' he said, still looking out into the dark. 'Nor our champion.'

'If not that, then what?'

When he turned around, his shoulders were hunched like an old man's as he leaned on his staff. 'Destroy Louw, but do it soon.' He leaned on his staff, the shadows giving his face the cast of a skull. 'We cannot stand against what is coming.'

'Even with such protection?'

He sat back down on the box of spears and rubbed his face with both hands. 'I'm fighting a forest fire with a leaking bucket. For every yard I gain, I lose another two, and the real heat is yet to come.' He took a small flask from a hidden pocket and drank from it, wincing as he lowered it. 'We're all going to die here. Or worse.'

He rested his head against the wall and looked up at me. 'You're the only one I've said that to. Even Jean still thinks we have a chance.' He closed his eyes. 'I'm so tired, Stratus.'

It was the truth. I could see it in the aura surrounding him and taste it in his scent. This was no gambit for my sympathy, but actual honesty.

'So why are you still fighting?'

'I am sworn to...'

'Why are you still fighting?' I asked again. He opened his eyes, and I let him see the glimmer of sorcery in mine. 'Do not lie to me.'

I felt his heartbeat increase as his hands clenched into fists, the more familiar tinge of anger filtering into his aura and scent. He pressed his fists to his forehead for several heartbeats, then relaxed again although, if anything, the anger surrounding him increased as he did so.

'My sons.' His voice was quiet, but there was steel in it. 'They died calling for me, and I couldn't help them. I couldn't stop him. I see and hear them every time I close my eyes.' He gritted his teeth and, as I watched, every trace of anger in his aura and scent vanished like the light of a snuffed candle, an impressive feat of self-control. 'I would happily break every oath I have ever taken if it gave me one chance to kill that bastard. I should feel shame at this, but I cannot find it within myself.'

'That's because there is no shame in vengeance, my

friend.' He took the hand I offered and I pulled him to his feet. 'Anger and hate have ever been stronger than justice and duty.'

He tugged his robes into a neater arrangement. 'You have a talent for making me say things I have never told anyone else.'

'Vengeance is a cause close to my heart. I will do what I can to help you achieve it, but to do so you must help me too.'

'Anything.'

'A dangerous offer to make one such as me, wizard.'

Before I could say anything, a stabbing pain lanced through my chest. I fell back against the wall, vainly clutching at my breastbone, but there was no wound to clutch at. I groaned as the pain pulsed through me again, twisting and pulling, as if someone was pulling a barbed arrow from my flesh. I slid down the wall, gasping for breath even as Fronsac reacted, his wards rippling outwards.

I felt my sorcery rising in response to their touch, and as it did I at last realised what I was feeling. Something was forcibly drawing power from me. No, not something, but someone. Tatyana was hurt, and grievously so if the healing construct was reacting in this way.

CHAPTER 7

'BE PATIENT.'

'Patience is for the undecided,' I snarled as I continued to pace the length of Fronsac's chamber. 'Why does everything take so long?'

One of the nameless apprentices who was helping the mage manipulate the crystal artefact he was hunched over looked across to me.

'Scrying for a single person is hard enough, and it's going to take longer if you keep disturbing us,' he said, his tone sharpening.

Fighting the urge to throw him from the window, I contented myself with a growl. Tatyana had been sorely wounded, and was out there somewhere. I could feel the enchantment I had embedded within her steadily drawing power from me to speed her healing, so she was at least alive. That and Fronsac's promise to tell me where she was were the only things that had stopped me from leaving to find her immediately. A promise he was having trouble keeping, from the look of things.

I cursed again. I could feel the walls and roof pressing in on me again, something not helped by the apprentices having insisted on closing the windows and shutters once dawn broke. I marched over to these even as I thought about it and threw them open with a defiant snarl. The air in the city had never been fresh or invigorating, but the flood of refugees who had fled before the encirclement of the city was completed meant fewer morning fires and less foulness in the streets, a small improvement.

I stepped onto the small balcony and leaned forward until my legs were pressed against the decorative railing, toppling a few pots of herbs and sending them to explode on the cobbles below. It was dawn, but the unnatural clouds meant that the only sign of it was a few muted glimmers of gold that managed to stab through the eastern fringe of the cloud.

I took several deep breaths, seeking the calm centre that would let me weave my sorcery without real thought, but it remained elusive. I looked out across the city instead, seeking a distraction from my thoughts, and as I did I became aware of the sound of dogs barking. There were always dogs barking somewhere, but never all at the same time, and never like this. The barks were becoming more frenzied, and many were swiftly descending into the kind of howling that they normally reserved for when I was close by. Across the breadth of the city I could see flocks of birds rising into the air – sparrows, pigeons and crows, all taking to the wing together in a swirling mass, cawing and tweeting as if their lives depended on it. On a nearby roof three cats stood hunched, hissing and screeching loud enough to be heard over the cacophony beyond the palace walls. I couldn't hear it from there, but I guessed that something similar was happening in the stables.

'It's happening.' I jolted at the sound of Fronsac's voice behind me and nearly tipped over the balcony. 'Look there, to the gatehouse.'

He pointed past my shoulder, towards the gatehouse that stood by one of the side gates. Set in the wall above it was a pale stone, and even without sorcery aiding my vision I could see the protective rune inscribed on it glowing ever more brightly with a blue light. I spread my sorcery out and felt the touch of magic almost immediately, its tone shrill compared to Fronsac's steady harmonies. It seemed to be coming from every direction at once, the pitch of it rising and falling in waves.

'What is it?' I asked. Down below us the guards had barred the gates and drawn their weapons as soon as the howling started, but they seemed calm enough, unlike the people I could see in the streets beyond. They couldn't hear the magic rising in pitch like I could, but the sound of the animals was more than enough to put the fear in them.

'That's just it,' Fronsac said quietly, working his own magic. 'This is the third such incident. It's not directed at anything, but this is the first time the animals have reacted.'

The strangeness of the magical attack had entirely displaced the frustration that had dogged my mind, and I strengthened the veil of sorcery across my vision just in time to see the green light within the clouds pull the dark mass together like the stitches of a surgeon closing flesh, strangling out the few remaining traces of sunlight and plunging the city into a gloom that made it seem as if it were dusk, rather than dawn.

For several breathless moments the green light vanished entirely and every beast and bird fell silent. On the roof, the cats were scraping their heads against the tiles, hard enough that I could see the dark streaks of blood that they left. The magic in the air rippled again, but before I could ask Fronsac if he had felt it, every bird and beast across the city dropped dead in a single stroke. I watched the bodies of the cats tumble off the roof, their backs and legs as stiff as if they had died hours before, their fall accompanied by a dull drumming as thousands of birds fell to the ground.

Human shouts and screams replaced those of the animals. Fronsac said something over his shoulder that I didn't hear and his apprentices all sped from the room, leaving the two of us to watch in fascinated horror as the next part of the Penullin attack unfolded. Thunder boomed across the city as the clouds rippled like scum floating on turbulent waters. I felt Fronsac's wards bloom with new strength as he fed more power into them, and for once the pressure of his magic didn't feel oppressive. Below us the guards were holding out their arms and we watched with them as tendrils of pale, corposant energy danced across the metal of their armour and weapons.

A thin bolt of lightning leapfrogged across the sky as if in celebration, silently scoring the writhing clouds with a thin green line that seemed to linger for several seconds longer than it should have. The sight of it sent a stab of dread through my gut, and the sense of unease that had been lodged there since I woke rose once more. I glanced at Fronsac, who seemed paler than he had before.

'Gods above,' he said in a quiet voice. 'Have you ever seen anything like this?'

'No.'

It was the truth. Whichever way I turned the blanket of cloud seemed darker and almost palpably malevolent. Beyond the palace walls and the reach of Fronsac's ward stones people were hastening to their homes, and I wondered if they felt the same nameless sense of dread pressing down on them. The clouds rippled again, as if vomiting the apocalyptically loud thunderclap that followed. It was loud enough that I felt it in my chest and the stone under my feet at the same time. Most of the glass windows I could see shattered in their frames, the sound of the shards crashing to the cobbles lost to the ringing in my ears. We had barely shaken our heads when the first of a dozen bolts of green-tinged lightning speared from the sky with a series of sharp cracks, striking a church tower near the city gates and transforming it into a cloud of flying debris within the blink of an eye.

I kept watching the clouds as the bolts flashed down to blast the city, the veil of sorcery across my vision showing me the flicker of gathering energies that presaged every destructive blast. As the final bolt struck, I saw the energies within the clouds dim, and drain away towards the south and east like waters from a cracked bowl, back towards the Penullin camp.

'It is over,' I said.

'I think so too,' said Fronsac, his voice sounding thin after the brutal cacophony. 'For now.'

With the energies binding them dispersing, the churning of the clouds began to still, and as I watched the first drops of rain began to fall, heavy and blood-warm, a trickle that soon became torrential. I held out my hand and the slashing rain filled it almost immediately. I tasted it hesitantly and spat it out a moment later. Fronsac tried it too, with the same result.

'Stagnant,' he said, slipping the small flask from his pocket once more. He sipped from it, then passed it to me. It smelled of mint, which was unexpected, as was the fiery aftertaste that made me cough and splutter. It faded quickly though, leaving a pleasant taste.

'What is that? I like it.'

'The locals call it firewater. Keep it, I have more.'

I nodded my thanks and slipped the flask into a pocket. 'What will happen next?'

'Well,' he said, turning away from the window and grabbing a nearby satchel. 'A page is on his way to summon me to a war council, where I'll have to argue with the church while my apprentices try to restore the wards and test if there's anything more to what just happened.' He paused in the act of shoving a leather-bound book into the satchel. 'They did this for several days at Aknak, until half the city was mad with terror and the water was poisoned. I don't expect anything different here.'

'What about Tatyana? And me?'

He stopped what he was doing. 'There is nothing you can do for now. You said yourself that she is alive and healing.' He paused as someone pounded on the door. 'Wait for my return. There's too much at risk for you to go blundering about out there.'

He took up his satchel and staff and opened the door, ignoring the gaily dressed page who had been doing the knocking. 'Don't do anything stupid. Trust me, please.'

With that, he pulled the door shut and was gone, leaving me alone in his chambers. I went to sit down, but then remembered how bad the chair had creaked the first time I'd sat on it, so settled myself into Fronsac's chair instead. His chamber looked a bit bigger from that perspective, but no less chaotic. I helped myself to the rest of the bottle of wine he had on the desk and examined the arrangement of crystals and runes they had been working on. I had a sense of what it was supposed to do, but the symbolism involved didn't feel right to me.

I pushed it away and rested my head on my arms. The strength of the wards in the palace had spared us the worst effects of the attack, but I could still feel traces of it when I extended my sorcery. It was a spectacular display of power, and clearly meant to intimidate, but in the end it was simply the product of a choir of wizards casting their spells in unison, amplifying the power. It may have been a mighty work, but it was still the work of humans. The element I could not reconcile was the necromantic energies they were working with. The inclusion of such negative energies should have made it all but impossible for them to cast something so complicated, yet clearly they had. I sat up and looked over at the countless books and bundles of parchments that littered the room and felt oddly reassured that, for all the knowledge and wisdom distilled through generations of wizards, they didn't know what was going on either.

So then why was I here, waiting for Fronsac?

I accepted that he had different skills to myself, but for all of that, here he was, trapped in a city and fighting a battle he knew he couldn't win. Waiting for his guidance was like asking someone who watched a lot of birds for advice on how to fly. I was the one that Navar had hunted and tortured. I was the one who had escaped his cruelty, and I was the one who had sworn to watch him die. It was not Fronsac who he had sent his assassins after.

I sat up as the thought hit me. The assassins. They had come for me, or for Lucien's guard. *Tatyana.* They knew before I did that I would seek her out. She was as much of a prize to them as I was, so if they had her, it made sense that they would take her to *him.* To Navar. Thus, if I found her, I would find him, or at least someone who knew where he was. I barely noticed my fists closing into fists, nor the growl that escaped my clenched teeth.

Navar Louw. It all came back to him. I felt a certainty that I'd been missing for some time coalesce within me. I would seek him out, I would find him, and I would kill him.

CHAPTER 8

I ATE ALL the leftover food I could find, then tightened my belt and made ready to leave. I was almost tempted to find another satchel, but caught myself before I could act on the impulse. When had I become so affected by human habits? I did not even have much idea of what I would put in it beside food, and that I could find for myself, as I ever had. I was still quietly chiding myself when I discovered that Fronsac had locked the door, and not just with the mechanical lock.

After all his talk of trust, that he would do such a thing to me came as an entirely unpleasant surprise. It shouldn't have, of course. He was a wizard and a man, two aspects that were as treacherous as the other. Smashing the door was one option, but I had little doubt that doing so would trigger some other defence as well.

'So be it,' I said, walking across the room and vaulting from the balcony. It was on the third level of the palace, so perhaps he thought it was too high for me to jump from, but in that he was mistaken. The guards didn't see me until I landed behind them, my legs soaking up the impact. I managed to whip myself in the face with the corner of my cloak but the guards seemed impressed nonetheless, so much so that one of them fell backwards.

'The demon!' shouted the one who was still standing, and I groaned as I remembered the Prince's declaration that I was a criminal or worse. Whatever illusion Fronsac had put upon me had clearly ended the moment I left his room.

'Easy now,' I said, but he was already lunging towards me with his spear, fear and haste making it a wild thrust that a blind child could have avoided. I grabbed the shaft and wrenched it from his hands, then slapped him across his helmet with it hard enough that his helm rang like a bell. The other one was getting to his feet, but froze in place when I tapped him on the breastplate with the tip of the spear.

'Tell Fronsac I am going to go find her.' I repeated it until he nodded. 'Now tend to your friend.'

I tossed the bar from the gate and slipped out into the city. Overhead, the clouds had begun drifting apart but still hung low and heavy, as if unsure what to do with the rancid water trapped within them. The rain that had fallen earlier had left foul-smelling puddles everywhere, not a few of which had the small, stiff bodies of dead birds poking from the surface. The attack had at least left the streets emptier than they should have been, and with the hood of my cloak raised I passed along them without incident, all the way to the city wall. Once I was as close to the outer wall as I could get without raising the alarm I stepped into the shadowy entrance of a boarded-up shop to watch the soldiers as they patrolled along the wall and the cleared ground before it.

From what I had seen and what Fronsac had told me, the Penullin camp was little less than a mile from the city. It was a sprawling, voracious thing that had consumed anything that could be eaten or made to be of use to the invaders for miles around. It was already larger than most of the surrounding villages and still growing as the various elements of their army caught up to the vanguard and established themselves.

One of those elements was the cabal of dark wizards serving General Novstan, a cabal that Fronsac said was led by Navar's very own apprentice, the same man who had killed his sons. Precisely the man who they would take Tatyana to. All I needed to do was get out of the city, cross the open ground where both sides were happy to put a few arrows in anything that moved, then slip through the Penullin defences and then infiltrate the camp of the wizards who had recently blinded and quite nearly killed me, fetch her, then repeat the process. I felt a grin stretch my face at the thought.

Darkness would be my greatest ally. Come nightfall, I would cross the wall and make my way to the camp. I could see in the dark almost as well as they could by day, so I was confident that their guard posts would be all but blind to me stalking through the darkness. I pulled the planks from the shop's door and slipped inside, momentarily gagging on the smell of rotten onions before I became inured to it. A cursory search revealed a few crusts of old bread, and after nibbling these, I sat with my back against the wall and began to slow my breathing. It would be a busy night no matter what happened, and I wanted to meditate and prepare my sorcery. Despite the dangers I was walking in to, I finally found the calm I sought and let my mind drift. Memories of Navar rose unbidden and I forced them away, unwilling to dwell on the years of torture I had suffered at his hand.

I was still fighting them off when I heard the hiss. Navar had done many things, but he had never hissed at me. I blinked the fragments of the dream away and looked around. It was sometime after dusk, and with the windows covered in planks the empty shop was almost perfectly dark. I woke my night vision and looked around again as the red tint washed the shadows away.

The hiss came again and as I turned I saw a swaybacked cat edging towards me, its head hanging low as if it were too heavy for its scrawny neck to support. I'd seen something like this before, and a single sniff confirmed my fear: necromancy. The cat stopped and hissed again, thickened blood dripping from its nose and mouth.

I stood and began to circle it, readying my sorcery as it turned to watch me, a pale luminescence flickering faintly within its eyes. It was definitely dead, so I felt no pity for it when I flicked out a thin whip of sorcery and decapitated it, the heat of the construct searing the stump with a puff of foul steam.

Its eyes continued to track me as I knelt down next to the head and used a combination of knife and sorcery to split the tiny skull. I fed a little more power into my vision as I examined its brain. It would have been far easier if they'd infected a human, but I had to work with what was given to me. It took a lot of patience, but eventually I found it: a pale, white hair curled within the base of the skull where the spine connected. I teased it out with a splinter of wood and watched it whip back and forth.

I burned it away with a thought and sat back. The clouds and subsequent display of thunder and lightning had been impressive, and while they had destroyed a few houses and a tower, that destruction had been an expensive diversion, not the attack. Neither Fronsac nor I had felt its intent because it had targeted low beasts like the cats and other vermin, and as such we had not perceived its threat. It seemed that Cardinal Polsson had not contented himself with feeding his worms to the Paladins, and had secretly recruited an army of creatures to spread disease, fear and chaos on his behalf. I made a mental note to ask Tatyana if the same thing had happened to the animals during the siege of Aknak, then cleaned my knife and kicked the corpse away.

The night had settled in, and it was time for me to become the hunter rather than the hunted.

CHAPTER 9

THE AREA NEAR the city walls was lit by many lanterns, but that same light that the soldiers took comfort in also made the shadows pooling beyond it that much darker by comparison, and I used this to my advantage, quickly slipping from pool to pool. There was no question of me using any of the gates set in the walls, not with so many men watching them, but then I had no intention of using them or climbing the wall.

When I made my way from the palace earlier that day I had come to the conclusion that I was heartily sick of the smell of this city, and even more so the sight of walls and roofs squeezing me from every direction. My gaze had drifted up to the looming mass of the city wall, tracing the outline of it against the night sky, and an idea had found its way into my thoughts and lodged there, the simplicity of it making me shake my head. I had been wearing this body so long that I had been viewing the problem that escaping the wall presented as a man, not a dragon. As a man, it was a towering edifice and an unsurmountable obstacle, but as a dragon, walls had ever been little more than something to fly *over*. And while my wings were lost to me, at least for now, I still had my sorcery.

Despite how the clouds hid the stars, my sense of direction

was intact, and my attempt at scrying had shown me more than enough of the Penullin camp for me to find my way to it, and perhaps more importantly, where amongst that sprawl of tents I would find the wizards who would be holding Tatyana.

'Who goes there?'

The shout came from my right and I started in surprise. I had been so fixated on my thoughts of what lay *beyond* the wall that I had forgotten I was still inside it. A patrol of at least a dozen soldiers was advancing on me, the men in front holding their lanterns high. I squinted against the sudden brightness, and the men suddenly faltered. I'd forgotten that I'd woken my night vision, and as my eyes adjusted they would have shone a brilliant red.

'It's the demon!'

Flashing my eyes had been a favourite trick of mine for as long as men had been afraid of the dark, and while they could now build cities as high as mountains and parade their gods about, that same base fear still lived within them.

'Farewell,' I said, and released the wind construct that I had been holding ready while I sought a good location to leave from. Whatever they may have said in reply was lost amidst the roar of the air as it threw me high into the air and sent them reeling back out into the street.

I kept my arms in close as I rose into the night sky, high enough that the rooftops looked like a game-board below me. I passed over the wall high enough that not a single sentry on the wall looked up, and as I reached the top of the arc I threw out my arms and spun about so that I could watch the horizon as I fell. A second, less urgent blast of wind slowed my descent, throwing a corona of mud into the air but otherwise letting me land gracefully enough that I barely had to flex my knees.

The wall was perhaps a bowshot and a half behind me, and by my reckoning I was right where I wanted to be. I would strike out towards the south, then curve around to enter the camp from the swamp on the east boundary. I didn't much care for swamps, but as I saw it, neither would men, and muddy waters would provide far more cover than a horse trampled grassy plain. I fed a little power into my night vision and began walking.

I was outside of the city again, my feet on earth rather than cold stone and no walls hemming me in, but any celebration of this small freedom was quashed by the lingering reek of the stagnant rainwater and a pervasive smell of decay that the breeze could not disperse. Here and there traces of horse scat provided a temporary relief with their earthier tones, and I stopped near a large scattering of it and squatted down to roll a few of the lumps in my fingers. There was a lot of it about, and from the scent and texture it seemed that horsemen were riding through here regularly. The freshest of them was less than a few hours old, a clear reminder that I did not want to be lingering here when it grew light enough for them to start riding again.

I wiped my hands and squelched on through the night. Between the soft ground and my weight, I was leaving a trail a blind man could follow but there was nothing I could do about that save hope for another good storm, natural or otherwise. As the distance between me and the camp narrowed I began to make out the scent and glimmer of the Penullin outposts. These were arranged in two staggered lines, allowing one to watch the other, and while that may have been effective, it relied on them being able to see me in the first place. I increased my pace and was very pleased with myself when I caught the first whiff of swamp-water. I kept moving parallel to the outposts as they curved away to the west, and by the time that the pre-dawn light was lightening the eastern sky I was ankle deep in soft mud. I pushed on, moving deeper into the swamps until I was confident that the men in the outposts would not see me once the sun rose. Despite the fermented odours that my every footstep stirred up, the scent of rotting flesh was still on the breeze and, as I pushed past a clump of stubborn grasses, I finally discovered why.

Some thirty feet ahead of me a stake had been sunk into an increasingly rare mound of solid ground, and mounted at the top of this was a severed human head. At first I thought little of it, except a small sense of satisfaction at having found the source of the smell. Hanging trophies of conquered enemies wasn't a human invention, and in my day I had done my fair share of it, both to boast of my prowess and intimidate others who may have thought to challenge me. From how pervasive the smell had been across the line of Penullin outposts I assumed that there were a number of such trophies displayed in their camp. I kept walking, but before I could take more than a few steps I heard a wet crack and, as I looked back at the head, its jaw opened wide and it began to scream.

I stared at it dumbly for several long heartbeats as the toneless shriek displaced the sound of insects and bubbling water. Shaking my head in disbelief, I swiftly crossed over to it and rammed one of my knives through the rune carved on its forehead, destroying the enchantment in a flash of green light that made my hand tingle and left smoke curling from its leaking eye sockets.

'Idiot,' I said to myself. I should have known there would be more to it than that. Who puts a trophy in a swamp where no one can see it? And more than that, I should have noticed how the flies that had been competing so vigorously to feast on my exposed skin had avoided the free meal offered by its decaying flesh. I worked my knife free and cleaned it on a patch of brittle grass. With whatever enchantment the necromancers had bound to it destroyed, the head was now rapidly catching up on the decomposition that had been denied to it. I moved across the clearing and took up a position where I could still see it, then settled down to wait in the shadow of some gnarled shrubs, curious to see if its warning scream drew any attention. It was barely mid-morning, so I had plenty of time to reach the camp before nightfall. The novelty of watching the face slowly slide off the skull quickly gave way to boredom though, and I was on the verge of standing and moving away when I noticed the bird.

It wasn't a particularly interesting bird, nor even a pretty one, but since I hadn't seen nor heard any of them since yesterday's deadly spell-work, it drew my attention. It landed on a nearby bulrush and simply sat there, looking oddly dishevelled. I teased out a wisp of sorcery and touched it to my vision, taking care to do it slowly enough that it wouldn't be felt.

The more I watched, the more un-birdlike the bird's behaviour looked. Small birds rarely sat still long enough to become prey, and when they moved or looked around, it was with swift, jerky movements. This one didn't so much as tilt its head, and as the sorcery veiled my vision I saw the aura of cold white light surrounding it. I strengthened the flow of sorcery and my focus on it, appalled and fascinated by what I saw in equal measure. This was something or someone masquerading as a bird, using the dead flesh like a puppet. But as men didn't know how to fly, so they must have been using the memories and instincts locked within its tiny brain, a process which would require great finesse and a masterfully controlled application, neither of which I'd seen in any wizard in a very long time, save perhaps Fronsac. And even then such an illusion of life would not last very long.

The answer, when it came, made me gasp loud enough to stir the bird into a new alertness. *The worms.* It had to be them. I sunk deeper into the shrub, the bird and the vermin crawling over me temporarily forgotten. It all came back to the worms.

The brain of every ghoul that Tatyana and I had encountered had been infested with them, either a cluster of small, writhing ones or a single, engorged monster the size of a man's thumb. I knew they were integral to the spread of the undead scourge, but time and pressing enemies had not given me much opportunity to understand how. The worms were saturated with the negative energies that the necromancers wielded, and always found their way into the brain. Polsson had said something about a bridge just before a spell set upon him by his master killed him. A spell meant to prevent him from talking about the secrets of the worms, and that meant what he said was important. A bridge between what though?

Annoyingly, while I had been thinking about all of this the bird had flown off. I slowly stood and brushed the insects from my clothes. They were all but swarming over me now, and I indulged myself in a small flash of sorcerous heat that killed everything on or within three feet of me. It set my cloak to smouldering in several places, but otherwise dried it out quite nicely too, which was an unexpected but welcome benefit.

Moving on through the swamp was a slow and tiring process. It was a treacherous, foul smelling place where everything was designed to sting, bite or drown you. Pools that looked shallow had bottoms of soft, sucking mud, and spotting the skeletal hand of an unluckier traveller had been the only thing that saved me from ending my journey in one of them. On top of all of these pitfalls I had to also take care to avoid several more of the rotting heads that were embedded wherever the ground was firm enough to hold the stakes lest they betray my position with their unearthly screaming. I only saw one Penullin patrol as I drew closer to the camp, and the noise they were making provided plenty of warning of their approach and I hunkered down amidst the weeds and grasses to let them pass unmolested.

My grasp of Penullin was still improving, but the tone of their conversation left me in little doubt that they were *griping*, something which Tatyana had once assured me was the universal language for soldiers. It had made no sense, and she had only laughed when I asked her to teach it to me, which I thought quite rude. Of the ten who passed by my hiding place, only one was paying any real attention to the surroundings. The others seemed to be content to continually swat at their sun-browned arms and red necks in a vain attempt to stop the denizens of this awful place devouring them.

I let them pass, then hurried to the point I had chosen to enter the camp from. The ground there was fairly rough, and so would provide plenty of good, deep shadows for me to pass amongst. I found a relatively dry spot, killed everything living in or near it, then pulled my hood up and tried to get some rest while I waited for the night.

CHAPTER 10

THE SWAMPS CAME to life as the night took hold, the drone of the biting flies and mosquitoes dimming as the frogs began to croak their own song and other small, sleeping things readied themselves to eat or be eaten. I too rose and shook off the mud that had dried on me, rolling my neck and shoulders until they moved soundlessly. It was a good and dark night with little moonlight penetrating the blanket of cloud. I spent some time preparing my sorcery and now carefully fed power into the constructs that would muffle the sound of my footsteps and blur the colours of my cloak. Thus prepared, I began making my way through the undergrowth that formed the border of the swamp, stopping regularly to listen and taste the air for unseen enemies, but there was no sign of any other sentries, either living or dead. I could feel their magic in the air, a growing but as yet undirected pressure that would soon become quite unpleasant.

After some time my feet finally found solid ground and I pulled myself up amidst the broken rocks. The ground here was even rougher up close, broken into tight ravines as if some ancient god had smashed it with a hammer. I climbed along these carefully, using the cracks and stumps of hardy shrubs to pull myself up. I had chosen the hardest of the paths, one that I hoped a defender would not think any sane attacker would attempt.

The sharp rocks and spiny bushes gave way to softer grass and I took some time to let my arms recover their strength, all the while watching as the sickly green light flickered to life within the clouds once more. I fed a lick of power into my night vision as I started moving forward again, wary of it being spotted but unwilling to risk breaking my leg in a rabbit hole or falling into a pit of stakes without it.

Passing the first line of sentries posed little challenge. Unlike those facing the city directly, these were standing and talking openly in pairs and threes, some with lanterns and some without. I stayed low as I crept past them, listening carefully for any change in their conversations, crawling on my belly like a snake when I needed to. The rough, broken ridge that marked the border of the swamp soon gave way to the undulating grassland that was more typical of Krandin's heartland. I squatted in the dark, taking in the view of the Penullin camp spread out before me. It was well lit, so much so that even without my night vision it would have been no great feat to navigate it safely. Many of the lamps shed a disappointingly steady white light, marking them as the work of the wizards.

The lands outside Falkenburg were crudely divided by the great road that lead to the Southland, and each of these halves was then subdivided by numerous hedges and low walls marking the boundaries of the various houses that dotted the landscape. The Penullin camp straddled the road, and those same hedges now served to split the sprawling mass of the army into different parts. Thanks largely to my attempt at scrying it wasn't too difficult to find the wizards' enormous tents once more. These were almost at the very edge of the camp, separated from the regular soldiers' tents by a shadowy band where no lamps or torches burned. There were two large tents within the wizard's encampment, surrounded by at least two dozen smaller versions, and as I watched I saw a glimmer of green light dance across the roof of one of the larger tents then flash upwards, like lightning in reverse.

From where I was my path would lead me down to the camp past two ransacked houses, the smaller of which had suffered damage from a brief but hot fire, perhaps the work of the wizards. I couldn't see any movement in or around this burnt house, which I thought would offer a very useful point to plot the final part of my invasion from.

The ground was still soft as I moved through the grasses, and I was perhaps halfway to the smoking house when I first heard the dogs. Animals hardly ever reacted well to my scent, but there was something about it that sent dogs into all manner of apoplexy. For once it seemed that luck was with me and the wind remained in my favour as I hurried into the deeper shadows that clung to the walls of the ruined house, the familiar smell of ash and embers providing a welcome break from those of mud and swamp fumes.

I kept close to the wall as I picked my way around the side of the house, the centre of which had been ruined by the fire, leaving its timbers poking out like ribs. Two sentries stood by what must have been the front entrance, talking quietly. I moved slowly across the yard, trusting to my sorcery to muffle my sound and shape, cursing silently when broken pottery and glass crunched under my feet, but neither sentry so much as looked in my direction. I crossed the final few yards quickly before my usual luck could reassert itself, and clambered through a broken window, taking care to avoid most of the detritus littering the floor.

Smashed furniture was scattered about, along with yet

more glass and pottery. I could smell blood too, and I followed the scent to the far end of the room where a body had fallen beneath the remnants of a table. It was that of a man, his neck ending in an angry red stump just above the collar of his shirt. His hands were cut deeply, suggesting that he hadn't died without a fight, but even so, judging by his small frame and wrinkled skin, the violence visited upon him seemed greatly out of proportion to whatever threat he may have posed. I left his headless body where it was and was about to move to the next room when I heard footsteps from the floor above me, followed by the sound of muffled voices.

I crossed to the staircase, which looked to be in good enough shape to hold my weight. The upper windows would offer a better view of my route, and any information I could squeeze out of a prisoner couldn't hurt, but at the same time, if they managed to raise the alarm it could complicate things enormously, especially if the dogs caught my scent. I kept low and moved like a lizard, spreading my weight so that the wood wouldn't creak as much and freezing in place whenever they stopped moving or talking.

When I was far enough that I could see over the top step it was clear that I needn't have bothered. There were only two men in the room, but both were at the window and had their backs to me, talking quietly in Penullin.

'It is beginning,' said one, pointing to something in the darkness beyond. 'Attend and eye look.'

'You are sure we're sweet distant?'

'Stop being an old nag. We are being good here.'

I hauled myself up and, keeping to a crouch, inched closer. I was perhaps half a dozen paces behind them when the sky outside began to glow, silhouetting them against the sickly green shade tinting the night beyond, and the wind suddenly rushed and swirled, sending the shutters clacking loudly and their scent into my nose. A human scent, but one saturated with burned spices. *Wizards.*

CHAPTER 11

SUCH WAS MY eagerness at the thought of taking a wizard prisoner that I didn't look at the table next to them. If I had, I would have seen the row of severed heads and the open book, and may even have realised what they had been doing up here.

But I didn't, and so yelped like a kicked dog when three of those same heads began shrieking. My foot slipped on the last step as they spun to face me. They were ready for battle, and I felt their magic surge. The defensive shield I had woven earlier flared into life with a snap, and I had a moment of triumph as it deflected the first wizard's spell and sent it skipping along the wall, tearing a glowing groove into the wood. That shield had only ever been meant as an emergency measure though, and before I could even think about renewing it, the second wizard thrust his staff at my chest as if it was a spear.

I felt the thump of his spell releasing even as the force of it hurled me backwards to smash through the railing. I had barely rolled to a stop when the other lashed me with whips of crackling, violet energy that paralysed my muscles and made it feel as if a giant was throttling me. Whatever power I had managed to summon slipped away like oil between my fingers as my skin blistered beneath the ever tightening coils of his spell.

I gasped for air and willed my hands upwards to try and break the grip around my throat, but they were distant, numb things that I could barely feel. I sucked in another whistling breath but it was too little to give me the strength I needed. I sagged back as the ring darkening the edge of my vision swelled and I fell into a dark, bottomless shaft.

THE JOURNEY TO Navar's university had been unlike any I'd suffered through before. Henkman and his louts had been coarse and stupid creatures, but they had lacked the cruelty that stained Navar's men. Food was scarce and foul enough to suggest that pigs had rejected it and stopped coming entirely after I threw it back at them for the second time.

Heavy curtains were thrown over my cage, blocking the sunlight I was craving, and the chains and rutted tracks we were following made sleep impossible. Had I known what lay ahead of me, I would have tried to appreciate the comparative luxury of that experience. My arrival at the university was greeted with no fanfare save for a gaggle of excited wizards who bowed and fell silent as Navar emerged from his carriage. Their weak bodies were ripe with a brutality that far outmatched the casual cruelty of the thugs that had brought me here, and I would grow to hate and fear them all in the years to follow.

With no little amount of shouting and cursing, the drovers guided my cage through the doorway of the glorified barn that would be my new prison. The floor dropped away into something of an amphitheatre, the centre point of which was a rectangle of sawdust marked out by polished menhirs, each taller than a man and spaced at regular intervals like the teeth of some buried leviathan. It took me

MARK DE JAGER

a few moments to work it out, but I realised it was my new cage. It was bigger than the one I had lived in for so long but this looked far more permanent and deprived of direct, natural light. I was still debating how I felt when the cage ground to a halt near the threshold of the menhirs.

'Warders to their positions!' Navar's voice boomed out, jolting me from my scrutiny of the stones. The group of mages had put their books away and were spreading out to encircle the cage, their rings, torcs and heavy bracelets gleaming with awakening magic against their pale skin.

My senses sharpened as fear wormed its way into my mind. Both pairs of my nostrils flared open, flooding my nose with dozens of overlaying scents, both old and fresh. Horse sweat. Man-sweat. Rock-dust. Melted gold. Wax. Blood, both man and animal, old and new. And pervading it all was the smell of gathering magic, that slightly flat smell of lightning-burned air. And it was getting stronger. The mages were gathering their powers, following the chant that Navar was repeating, his voice echoing as if he was speaking with two voices.

The sensory pits dotted along my lower jaw translated all of this into something akin to a strong current of water that was swirling around me like floodwaters against a solitary tree. I resisted the pressure of it for as long as I could out of sheer stubbornness, but it was in vain. The wards that Tiberius Talgoth had carved into the bars of his cunning trap all those years before stripped me of any real form of defence as greedily as they had from the first day of my captivity. I felt my will being torn away from me as their awful magic squirmed into my body and mind, a more intimate violation than anything they could have accomplished with sword or lance. They were stealing my body from me, and there was nothing I could do but watch as my limbs began to tremble and twitch with movements

99

that weren't mine as the spell drew to its conclusion.

With a crack, the magic crystallised and lanced deep into my head. The touch of it was cold and foul, like a sharp clawed hand groping around inside my skull, utterly ignorant of the revulsion and horror that it generated within me. The magic that they were forcing through my body felt like a parasite worming its way through my muscle and bone. I could only move my eyes, and then only with a force of will that sent yet more blood oozing from my nostrils.

I looked over to Navar with great effort and confirmed my suspicions. He was the focus, the centre of this vile web and by the star, he was enjoying it. That was the first day that I really felt the touch of his mind, and had I been in control of my body, I would have vomited. As much as I wanted to, I couldn't even scream when he began to move me out of the suddenly open cage. His control over my limbs was crude and clumsy, and completely reliant on the brute force that his coven was feeding him to achieve his goal. All of which meant precisely nothing at that moment since brute force was going to succeed.

I stopped fighting him. All he would do was channel more force, and he clearly didn't have the finesse or skill to be able to stop it from damaging me. I lurched from the cage like a marionette in the hands of a drunk, falling clumsily to the ground because he didn't know how to move something with four limbs. I landed awkwardly, almost breaking a wing. Rather than have me stand, he poured more force into my legs, using the powerful muscles in my thighs to simply drive me forward in an ungainly heap, grinding my face and wing into the floor twice more until I passed between two of the strangely carved menhirs.

With a last burst of power, he hurled me forward and ripped himself free of my mind. It was a heartbeat of pure, blinding agony that cut to the bone and beyond. It felt like he'd pulled half my brain out through my eye socket and left it there for dwarves to pound with burning hammers.

My vision flickered once, then mercifully faded to a nothingness that I would soon wish had been permanent.

I OPENED MY eyes, the surprise that I was still alive burning through the last of the memories that had sprung out of my still healing mind. I took a deeper breath and choked on the pain that radiated from my abused throat.

I was still in the same ruined house, and one of the wizards was busily tying a length of rope around my feet, binding them as my hands already were. He looked up in surprise when I pulled my legs up, but rather than move away, he reached for his staff – a terrible mistake on his part and an opportunity I wasn't going to pass up. I kicked out with both feet, bending his knees back on themselves with the sound of a dozen apples being bit into. He didn't start screaming until he had hit the ground.

I heard his companion moving behind me a moment before he tried to kick me in the side of the head. It was a glancing blow from a man clearly unused to physical confrontation and barely made me blink. The wizard tried a second time, but he had lost the element of surprise.

I turned into the kick as his foot came down and felt his boot scrape my cheek. All I needed was a short lunge to sink my teeth into his ankle, my draconic teeth making short work of his boots. He shrieked in that strange way that men do and tried to leap back, which only helped to tear the wound open a bit further. I released him, gagging on the bitter taste of his blood, and he fell backwards clutching at the wound.

I clenched my fists and lifted my elbows sideways from

my body, snapping the ropes. He lunged for his staff but I ripped it from his hands before he could point it at me. It had a nice heft to it, and didn't even break when I smashed it into the head of the blubbering wizard at my feet.

'We need to do the talking,' I said in his language, which made him stare at me in what I took to be astonishment. He tried to cast another spell as I untangled my legs from his dead friend, but I'd felt him readying his bracelet and simply grabbed his hand and squeezed. He wasn't a strong man, and I felt something snap even before I'd exerted any real pressure, eliciting a sharp cry from him. He fell silent as I smiled with far more teeth than he was expecting, shocking him into silence.

'Let we talk,' I said pulling him towards me.

CHAPTER 12

'REMEMBER OUR DEAL, wizard.'

He muttered something in reply without looking up.

The bite had left him with a nasty limp, but there was nothing either of us could do about that now, and I liked to think that he was far more concerned about what I'd promised to do to him if he so much as thought about betraying me. With him leading the way we had passed through the outer ring of the camp with little real challenge. We were almost at the inner line of sentries now, and I could see several of them watching us as we moved into the outer ring of light cast by their lanterns. The entire camp was bathed in the same milky green light that pulsed within the clouds above the wizard's encampment, and the slow flicker of it was playing havoc with my night vision. I tensed my arms to warm up the muscles, an act that made the bag of heads that I was carrying as part of my disguise sway back and forth.

'Who approaches?' called one of the sentries. He had one of those crossed bows in his hands, although it was still pointed at the dirt in front of his feet.

'Borel of the second cabal,' the wizard called back, 'and one other. The watch word is *eagle's claw*.'

I smiled at that. Men loved naming things after predators,

as if it would somehow demean them to choose something pleasant.

'Come on then, wizard.'

They seemed to lose interest in us after that, although I saw at least two of them make the so called 'sign of the angels', a primitive gesture meant to ward off evil, most likely a fragment of a forgotten spell or ritual. Those who weren't watching quickly retreated under makeshift shelters set up amidst the two wide, banked trenches that ran along the full length of the camp, apparently unwilling to bask in the eerie luminescence that swirled above them for longer than absolutely necessary. I found myself following Borel along muddy paths marked with lengths of thin rope from which scraps of coloured cloth were tied.

'What are these meant for?' I asked tugging at a shred of blue.

'Blue is for cavalry,' he said. 'Red for heavy foot, and yellow the bow-shooters.' He leaned on his staff and stared up at me, his face a pattern of shadows and green tinted curves. 'What you think to succeed win here? You will never leave here a living.'

His speech was quick, forcing me to concentrate more on what he was saying. I almost had a grip on the language though, even if the niceties of it hadn't taken hold yet. 'It is of your concern none.'

He laughed at that, which surprised me. I had expected him to have tried to escape by now, even if it would have been suicidal.

'Don't be a liar to me,' he said. 'You will never let me go.'

'You are mistaken,' I said, and the lie fell from my lips without hesitation. 'You see that?'

I pointed to the largest of the wizard's tents and as he looked in that direction, I shot my arm forward and closed my hand around his throat. The first squeeze stopped his scream before it could leave his mouth, and the second crushed the soft flesh of his throat, silencing him forever. I caught him before he could fall, then began to walk towards the camp again with him cradled in my arms, the bag of heads discarded in a nearby ditch.

The pathways were almost deserted, and the few men I could not avoid were apparently not concerned enough about me carrying a wizard in my arms. They simply hurried past as far from me as they could be while staying on the path, their heads down to avoid the dirty emerald light crawling across the sky. I tossed the dead wizard into one of the ditches carrying the waste away from the camp as I finally drew close to the dark moat that surrounded the wizards' camp.

The first thing I noticed was that the ground here was churned up, and taken with the smell of horse scat, it seemed that the cavalry were using it as a tent free route out of the camp. The second and more pressing issue was that the necromancers amongst the cabal were also using it as a mustering ground for their ghouls. These stood in rows all around the wizards' camp, ten ranks deep on the short sides and five on the long, and at a glance I estimated there to be at least a thousand of them, and quite possibly more. The smell was quite something, and went some way to explaining the amount of incense being burned among the closest rows of tents.

I moved forward cautiously, keeping the cavalry path between me and the nearest of the dead lest they react to my presence. They seemed oblivious though, and simply stood there with their slack faces turned towards the sky, the putrescent glow above was reflected in their pearl white eyes. I tossed a clod of dirt at the nearest of them, catching it squarely on the head, but aside from swaying it showed no sign of being aware of my attack, which encouraged me to edge a bit closer. If this was the extent of their defences, this rescue was going to be easier than I had dared to hope. An uncharitable part of me wished that someone would hurt Tatyana again so that I could get a better sense of where she was, but I held out hope that I would catch her scent sooner rather than later.

I continued to move closer, watching for any reactions from the dead, and I was almost within touching distance of the outer rank when the buzz and whine of the magic began rising to a crescendo, and I joined them in watching the sky as a column of green light abruptly shot from the largest tent and stabbed into the clouds. For several long moments it remained there, bright enough to cast its own shadows and appearing almost solid before it vanished just as suddenly, plunging the camp back into darkness that the guttering lamps and torches struggled to hold back.

The sky rumbled like a wounded beast as the magic rippled outwards through the clouds. Flashes of vivid yellow-green lightning burst from the clouds intermittently as the glow spread through the dark mass. There was a crude pattern to the flashes, one that made it obvious that whatever dreadful spell they had just launched was rolling towards the city.

I was still watching the arcs of lightning and trying to understand why some of them were in different colours when a cold, heavy body crashed into me, the unexpected impact knocking me over and into the mud. Teeth champed and scraped along my arm and cracked fingernails raked my face, narrowly missing my eyes.

I dug my feet in and thrust upwards, bucking the ghoul off me. I grabbed its flailing arm and bent it against my chest as it landed, snapping the elbow. I let go as the dead man lunged forward with his head, teeth clacking together while his feet churned the mud in his desperation to get at me. I thrust a hand at him, spearing my thumb into his eye. My other hand found his chin and I twisted his head until I felt his spine coming away from the base his skull. He collapsed and lay there twitching as his body remembered that it was dead.

I looked up and saw the rest of them looking down at me with their pale eyes, hands trembling at their sides as they turned their heads from side to side as if silently admonishing me. I shuffled back, the indignity of dragging myself across the mud and horseshit a small price to pay to avoid being dragged into a fight with an entire legion of the dead.

They didn't pursue me, although the front row were still clearly agitated, their heads bobbing and swaying and their hands grabbing at the air. I quickly got to my feet and moved away from the fallen ghoul. In the distance thunder boomed and rattled across Falkenburg's walls, the silhouette of the towers briefly visible against the emerald lightning lashing down beyond them.

In the wake of the spell's release, the grating pitch of magic emanating from the camp ebbed away to something that was almost bearable. I used the opportunity to reset my wards and use some energy to scrub away the lethargy their spellwork had imparted. I looked over the wall of dead men that surrounded their camp, and then smiled. A *wall* of dead men.

Men loved walls, but walls were only effective against things that had to go *through* them and the memory of my escape from the city was still fresh in my mind. I smiled in the dark as I edged back and began looking for a strip of ground that wasn't too soft and muddy. Something firm enough to run across.

* * *

I LANDED IN a spray of mud some twenty paces behind the last of the ghouls. It wasn't my most graceful landing, but with the memory of the wizard's deadly wards still fresh in my mind I had not dared to risk anything more than the bare minimum of power required to fuel my wind spell. I pushed myself onto my knees and kept low as I put some distance between me and the ghouls, heading towards the nearest cover, an untidy pile of large wooden boxes.

The mud within the wizard's camp smelt even fouler than the stagnant rainwater that had pooled in the swamps, but I had no time to worry about that. They were still awake, and this close to the tents where they did their spellwork I could feel the unwholesome radiation of their dark magic pressing against my skin like a thick, freezing mist, the killing sort that leaches your warmth away a breath at a time until you fall asleep and die without realising it.

I moved closer to the boxes, each of which was as long as I was tall and half as wide, and waited to see if anyone had noticed my arrival. There were a number of who I assumed were wizards standing near the larger tents, talking quietly in groups of four or five or staring towards the city as they puffed on pipes like Crow's, the sweeter smell of the weed a relief from the stench of the dead and rancid mud.

The outer perimeter of their camp was littered with similar caches of crates and barrels, but beyond this untidy barrier their tents were laid out in the same neat lines as the rest of the army's. From what I could surmise there were at least forty wizards less than a spear's throw from where I was hiding, and that was without counting however many were lurking in each of the larger tents. I shivered at the thought of it. I hadn't been amongst so many wizards since my darkest days of my captivity.

I looked to the east and cursed. My infiltration had

taken longer than expected and dawn was already lighting the sky. I did not care for the odds of going unnoticed amongst so many wizards in such a small area in daylight and so, working as quietly as I could, I moved some of the boxes apart until I had created something of a refuge in the centre of them. I was careful not to disturb the mess on top of the large sheet covering them so that it would look no different to a passer-by, a cunning touch that I was quite pleased with.

By the time the morning horns rang out across the Penullin camp I had crawled into the shadowy space I had created and was preparing myself for a very long and uncomfortable day.

The Private Annals of Tiberius Talgoth, Archmage

I FELL DOWN the stairs yesterday. I had set out for the kitchen, the need to eat having eventually penetrated the grief of my father's meaningless death. It was a small and stupid thing to trip as I did, but in my weakened state, my knees buckled and I fell down the stairs, all the way to the bottom.

It was a strange experience, for it was as if I was watching myself fall. I returned to my body as it crashed to a halt, and lay there gasping as an ever tightening feeling closed around my chest. I knew death was near, but could do nothing but pant like a dog as I sank into the darkness. My breath stopped as the last point of light vanished and I felt the ground beneath me part like a leviathan's jaws. I fell into its ice cold throat, and found breath enough to scream as hollow-eyed, screaming faces and grasping hands burst from its walls to bite and claw at me as I fell past them. I turned as I fell, and the scream died on my lips when I beheld what waited beneath me.

It was a vast, frozen lake of milky water, and its shores were a mass of splintered bone and discarded flesh. I saw countless deformed shapes throwing themselves against that icy barrier in a mindless need to return to the light. I was a breath away from its brittle surface, close enough that I saw my reflection upon it, when my fall abruptly slowed. I hung there for what felt like an age, watching as ribbons of vapour rose to entwine themselves around me like vines, but even as their icy touch gripped me I felt myself rising once more, speeding back towards the golden light of life.

I woke in my own bed with a tremendous gasp, nearly startling Neville, my elderly manservant, right into his own death. It was he who had brought me back from the brink of oblivion, massaging my heart and blowing breath into my lungs until they had recovered enough to remember what they were supposed to be doing. I embraced him heartily.

Like the slap that stops a woman's hysterics, that brush with death had finally ended the dreadful melancholy that had gripped me for so long, and I rose from my bed as soon as I was able, gripped by a new clarity in both mind and vision. I saw anew the dust that lay upon everything within the tower, and how so many of my servants laughed and took their ease. These I chased from my home with rod and flame with only what they were wearing upon their backs, which cheered those who had remained loyal and steadfast. With their spirits lifted it wasn't long before the tower felt like a home again. I began to eat once more too, and returned to my study for the first time since my father's death, eager to begin my new work.

Death had come for me, but it had not been some menacing Reaper cloaked in black. I had felt no presence nor malice of thought gathering to claw the soul from my body and drag me to immortal judgement. Death was not sentient; it was just another force, not unlike magic. And if I could bend one to my will, there was no law that I could not bend the other to it too.

In death I had found a new lease of life, and in the weeks

and months that followed my home became something of a mausoleum as the demands of my research grew even more strident. My knowledge already exceeded that of the local mortuary priests, who consider anything not already written in their lore books to be heresy! Their wilful ignorance is galling, and so I have set out on this path with only a few of my more promising apprentices who also understand that morals are subservient to knowledge. Despite my withdrawal from society, my reputation grew, which both made it easier to harvest subjects for study but also drew the ire of the church, and it came as no surprise when I was labelled a heretic. I closed my borders and ignored their edicts.

No students came to the tower for two full years after their proclamation, but in the midst of the third year I woke to find a dozen armoured knights hammering on my gates. I prepared for the worst before I opened the viewport, whereupon the tallest of these announced himself to be Aethbert, son of Edmund Henkman, a retainer who had served my father with great loyalty and affection. I granted him an audience, and was pleased by how gracious and well-spoken he was. Such was his charm and manner that soon I had invited all of his company in, and the kitchens were filled with a vigour the tower had not seen for some years.

We feasted long into the night, toasting my father's memory many times, and even though I find warriors coarse and blunt, I enjoyed their company. Come the dawn, Aethbert and I watched the sun rise from the roof while we toasted bread over a brazier. I had waited for him to come to the purpose of his visit, and he did so now and I sat amazed, both sun and bread forgotten, as he asked me to join his great quest to slay a dragon.

I laughed at first, and called him foolish for seeking

the help of a wizard of my skill to help him best some overgrown lizard. My laughter swiftly died when he told me how King Jorak Ironfist, the last of the Battle Kings, had led his great army against the same *wyrm*. Jorak had ridden with my father, and was not the last because of some trick of age, but because he was the deadliest of all of them. The dragon had found them, and in a single pass had burned the king and all of his champions into an unrecognisable mass of steel and blackened flesh. Aethbert and his warrior priests were en route to a great mustering, where they would lead a crusade to destroy the creature. This was a true dragon, the stuff of legend. Brutal, powerful and *immortal*. The thought of what I could learn about death from a creature who defied it was enough to make me feel faint with anticipation. I knew I would agree to join the crusade right then, but I did not dare give voice to my true purpose before him.

CHAPTER 13

IT WAS AS dank and uncomfortable in the hole as I had imagined it would be, and rather than try and sleep, with all the risks that brought, I chose to meditate instead. It was restful but easily dispelled, and didn't risk stirring up any sorcery that a passing wizard might sense. I'd had precious little time to myself recently, so the opportunity to just rest and think was a welcome one, mud notwithstanding. Making myself as comfortable as I could, I let my eyes close and began concentrating on my breathing, willing myself into an alert but hopefully still restful meditative state; if nothing else, the challenge of achieving it would be a distraction.

I'd expected to be sharing the space with all manner of insects and worms, but the only threads of life I could sense were those of the nearest wizards; everything else had either fled the area or died in the attempt. I shook the thought away and felt myself slowly relax, and as my breathing slowed, long suppressed memories seeped into my restive mind.

THE DAY WAS *more beautiful than autumn had any right to offer. The sun hung in the sky as if reluctant to move, warming the air even in the deepest parts of the valley one last time. The breeze was gentle and carried the sound of birdsong to where I lay on the sunning rock, languid and splayed out with no thought of dignity, only the need to expose as much of myself to the light before winter began to assert itself.*

I had been there for some time when I heard her above me, a moment before I saw her shadow race across the golden canopy of the forest below. I didn't hear her land though, I never did, for her grace was such that she could come down behind a herd of gazelle without so much as an ear being flicked amongst them.

Her tail squirmed in under my wing and dug into my ribs. I sighed and folded the wing back to give her space to stretch out next to me, her neck pressed against mine and her head tucked under my chin. Neither of us spoke; there was no need to, not on a day like that. We lay there until the sun eventually relinquished its hold on the sky and slowly sunk beyond the end of the valley, then watched the stars emerge as night settled across our world. In the morning I would leave for the southern coast for a final hunt to ensure our larder was stocked for the winter, as I had done every year for as long as I could remember. I didn't like being away from her for any length of time, but I liked being cold and starving even less.

Neither of us knew then that it would be our last day together.

'I SHOULD HAVE stayed.'

My own words ended the meditation. I sagged against the mud, uncaring of its slimy touch, and tried to remember the feel of her skin against mine. Her scales were finer than mine, and where the edges of mine were brushed with red, hers had been chased with gold. I bit back an unexpected sob and rubbed my face vigorously, if only to distract myself from thinking about the painful hollow that the memory had opened within my breast. *My beautiful Anakhara.*

She was why I was here, lying in the mud. Or rather, her death was. Her terrible, lonely death, that most awful event which had driven me mad with rage for so long, the embers of which still lived on within me. My mind, once so miserly with its hoard of memories, now offered too much. I forced the cruel images away with a cry, grinding my palms into eyes until all I could see were stray motes of light. More than eight hundred years had passed but the pain was still as fresh and unbearable as the first day. I lowered my hands and forced myself to concentrate on my breathing until the thickness in my throat and rekindled rage within my breast both subsided.

Once I was recovered, I peered out from under the covering, and the fall of shadows told me that most of the afternoon had passed. I could hear a constant rumble of sound from the surrounding camp, the combination of men and horses sounding almost indistinguishable from the camp where Prince Jean's soldiers had once taken me.

I wasn't interested in the army though. I splayed my hands against the mud and dug my fingers in as deep as I could before sending a few threads of sorcery out through them, each of these splitting, then splitting again until they fanned out in a web that would make a spider jealous. I closed my eyes and began sifting through the vibrations I could sense through them, filtering out those of the main camp and concentrating on the soft thump of human feet closer to me.

It was a fairly delicate construct and not something that could be rushed, and the sun had set by the time I collapsed it. The wizards were nowhere near as active as the army was by any measure, and that lack of activity had made my subterranean scrying all the harder by denying me distinct vibrations to focus on, but I knew far more about them now than I had when I arrived. I knew that at least half the wizards had not left their tents at all that day, which I assumed was due to the fatigue from their spellcasting the night before. I also knew that every other wizard spent most of their time clustered in or around the second of the big tents. Having so many wizards in one place sent my skin crawling and sent memories that I really did not want to revisit crowding my mind. *What were they doing in there?*

I'd sent a gentle probe towards the tent where they'd gathered, but the strength of the wards set around it was staggering. Spreading my web of sorcery to probe at it had also yielded one last nugget of knowledge: Tatyana was not here. If she had been, I was confident I would have felt *something*, but there was simply no echo from the sorcery within her. The connection hadn't called for any more healing energies either, so at least I knew that she hadn't been harmed again. I would have to find her trail anew, but that was something I could only do once I left the suffocating sphere of the dark magic surrounding the camp.

After making sure no one was close by, I edged out from my improvised shelter. The stars were still hidden by the poisoned clouds, but I could just about see the sunset, a blood red strip shot through with gold threads, and I found the sight of it uplifting. After another check to make sure I hadn't missed any roving sentries, staked heads or necromancers sneaking about, I made my way along the edge of the camp, moving from rubbish pile to rubbish pile. There wasn't much cover beyond the outer fringe of their camp, which posed a problem as there were far more guards about than the night before, both living and dead, as well as more lamps of the wizard-made variety, each burning with a steady silver light that left the area around them entirely devoid of any sort of shadow. I didn't think that snuffing them would be too difficult, but someone was more likely to spot their failure. At least there weren't any dogs here.

I wanted to know what they were doing in the large tent, and from where I was, the most promising route I could see would have me cross over an entirely exposed path, then pass through two lines of tents. That would, however, let me use a natural dip along the edge of the camp to come up behind the next array of tents which, by my reckoning, would then bring me to a point where I could see inside the large tent. I thought it a fine plan, and taking care to do it slowly enough that I could stop if I felt any wards reacting, I woke the construct to blur my shape once more. It took some time to coax to life, but maintaining it was not as taxing as I feared it would be given the magic saturating the area.

I rose from where I had been crouched and moved across the path, keeping my pace steady and the glow of my eyes hidden beneath the rim of my hood as best I could. The nearest guards were two living soldiers, and the temptation to freeze in place when one of them looked in my direction was almost irresistible, but I kept moving, trusting to my sorcery and the hope that moving at an entirely normal pace wouldn't elicit the same suspicions that running would.

I risked a glance in their direction as I passed behind the first tent and saw that they were now walking towards the path I had crossed. I crouched and picked my way between the tents until I was out of their line of sight taking care not to catch myself on any of the ropes crisscrossing the path.

I could hear the men within the tents as I passed, either snoring or talking quietly amongst themselves. Most of the latter was inconsequential, the sort of talk that I could have overheard from any gathering of men, but a mention of Navar gave me pause.

'Navar's changed.'

'War changes everybody. Why should he be any different?'

'Doesn't it worry you?' A pause. 'Wait, you haven't done it, have you?'

'So what if I did?'

'Gods. You promised we'd talk about it and decide together!'

'Oh come on, what is there to talk about? He's our master. I don't know why you insist—'

'Navar Louw was my master. *He's* the one who I looked up to, not this damned Worm Lord character. It's not right.'

'Keep your voice down.'

'Or what? I'd end up in a basement somewhere stitching crawlers together for the rest of my life?'

'At least.'

'You see? This is what I'm talking about. Anyone who questions anything he says is labelled a spy or agitator these days. Or worse.'

'Ach, you're overreacting. Just go to sleep, Herman. You're on the morning rotation.'

I had hoped for more tangible information but their whispered conversation spiralled off into stories and rumours of wizards who meant nothing to me. I stepped over the last of the ropes and hurried towards the dip I wanted to follow.

There were a handful of ghouls on the far side. They were unmoving, but the glint of light in their moon-white eyes meant they weren't dormant like the serried ranks behind them. I took extra care as I moved forward, my every sense attuned to the slightest noise or change in the scents carried by the breeze. I crossed to the lip of the ditch without incident and quickly lowered myself into the depression without really paying much attention. The ground was strangely cold and lumpy as it shifted beneath me, swallowing my legs and sending them plunging into cold liquid. A liquid burbling preceded a waft of foetid air as I struggled to find my footing amongst the sponginess. I fed some power into my vision and gasped out loud as the shadows receded and resolved themselves into a sea of dismembered human bodies. I reached for the edge, pushing a limp hand out of my face as the layers shifted, releasing another belch of gas from the congealed blood beneath.

The nearest of the ghoul sentries lurched into life at the sound of my scrabbling, its eyes flaring into new brightness as it stepped up to the very lip of the ditch.

I didn't know how deep the ditch was, but as far as I could see, it was entirely filled with human bodies, some dismembered and savaged, some whole, but each as pale and lifeless as marble. I couldn't find enough purchase to put myself in a position to silence the ghoul, so had to settle for lying very still, ignoring the putrid fluids soaking into my robes and the sensation of slowly sinking into the pit.

Eventually it stepped back, the light in its eyes dimming once more. I shook myself loose and moved to pull myself out, but the fluids and fats that had leaked out of the bodies had saturated the walls of the pit, making it a slippery nightmare that saw me sink deeper with every failed attempt. Worse than that though was that noise of my efforts to get out had brought the ghoul back. I lay as still as I could as it came closer, clinging to a limbless torso like a drowning man would to driftwood. I had intended to let it move away again, but the anger that simmered within me was rising now, provoked by the indignity of the grotesque spectacle I found myself part of.

My sorcery flexed as the anger burned away the caution I had held so dear, and manifested as a spear of burning energy that lanced upwards through the ghoul's head, the white heat of it turning half its brain into steam even before the tip burst out the top of the skull. It stood for a heartbeat more, temporarily held up by my sorcery alone, then fell in a heap as the spear dissipated.

A sense of calm settled on me as its body tumbled into the pit, enough so that I had the clarity of mind to extend the long, black talons that nestled within my forearms and drive them into the slippery walls. They punched through the slippery mud and anchored me while I crouched at the lip and extended a thin fan of sorcery ahead of me to warn me if the ward, or even any wizards, were reacting to my foolish attack. There was nothing; perhaps it had been too sudden for them to notice amidst the constant murmur of spellcasting that emanated from the second tent.

I held my talons in place as I considered my position. No part of me had escaped the foul soup that had drained into the depths of the trench, and as much as I wanted to scrape myself clean, I had to accept that it would take a day standing under a waterfall to cleanse this stench from my skin. I chewed my lip as I considered this and immediately regretted it. Spitting the taste from my mouth, I pulled the closest of the whole bodies to me. He was beardless but a fairly stout specimen, typical of a farmer or soldier. His neck was sound, and there were a number of bruises on his body and his knuckles were scraped, but I could find no wound to suggest how he had died. I rolled him back into the pit and examined two more bodies.

The first showed signs of having been gnawed on after death, and the second had several deep cuts that had been closed with rough stitches, but again after their death. Neither of these showed any killing wounds, which meant that magic had slain them. There were hundreds of bodies discarded here, and while I had no true understanding of how necromancy worked in practice, it was no great leap to imagine that so much death and the power being gathered here were related.

I needed to see what was in that tent.

CHAPTER 14

ONCE UPON A time I would sooner have died than crawl through a pit full of rotting carrion simply to avoid a fight, but those cruel years under Navar's fiery whip had taught me a great deal about what could and could not be tolerated.

I was already covered in blood and muck, and so reckoned I could hardly get any filthier. The stench and filth actually complemented the blurring effect of my sorcery, making me all but invisible to the few living guards I passed, although it didn't make the experience any less disgusting or undignified. I reckoned the ditch to be an old riverbed from the smooth rocks that occasionally jutted from the sides and the way it tapered away towards the swamps.

What was worrying me far more than the threat of so many wizards and rank fluids soaking my clothes was the chanting that was becoming audible as I approached the main tent. It was a strange, sibilant sound that rose and fell with a cadence that made me feel strangely off balance even though I was already all but flat on my belly. I gritted my teeth and pulled myself through another jumble of body parts, fighting the growing urge to join in with the chanting which had wormed its way into my thoughts.

Even my precious medallion couldn't protect me from this, and as I fought my way forward I felt the blurring construct I had been holding together begin to fragment, the focus needed to maintain it failing under the eroding effect of the chanting.

The words themselves were completely nonsensical to me, but that was no surprise. Only the intonation and intent mattered, not the language. They could be reciting a list of the Worm Lord's favourite meals but as long as they said it in the right way it would not make a mote of difference to the effect.

The pressure peaked as I passed the tent, every part of me aching as if I had just pulled myself up a mountain rather than through that slimy ditch. The riverbed widened here, thinning the depth of the bodies beneath me and soon after that the pile tapered away amidst a tangle of bodies that were still warm. I slid to the bottom of the pile and once I was a good twenty yards from the last body I slowly pulled myself to the lip of the bank. I was now behind the last of the smaller tents that ringed the large tent, which was more or less exactly where I wanted to be.

I fought to draw my sorcery to me again, and even as skilled as I was, it was a struggle to channel more than a trickle into myself. I hoarded what power I managed to call, then carefully sent a sliver of it out over the edge and towards the tent, probing for wards and unseen dangers. What I found was that the tents ringing the large one were full of prisoners taken by the Penullin army, which went some way to explaining the riverbed of bodies. From the number of dead, they must have been bringing more in from somewhere else on a regular basis.

I also began to sense that the ward I had sensed wasn't a ward at all, but something altogether different. I had encountered a good number of them in my time, ranging from the most basic sort to the complex, interlinked kind that had nearly killed me recently. For all the differences and dangers they presented, they had a common underlying structure that anchored it to the source of power that fed them. The cold, shifting sphere of energy that was pressing back at me now felt nothing like that, and yet it was definitely anchored to something within the tent, as a ward would be.

Drawn in by my curiosity, I pushed too far and suddenly felt that same formless cold latch on to my sorcery like a striking snake. It pulled with a terrible force, tearing it from my mind before I even knew it was gone and devouring it in an instant. I tumbled gracelessly down the bank and lay there stunned, unable to do anything more than try to breathe through the unspeakable pain of having my sorcery ripped from my mind. It was fortunate that I had drawn so little; had I been caught unawares with more power summoned the result would most likely have been far, far worse than a nasty headache and bout of nausea. It may not have been a physical attack, but it was nonetheless a brutal and violent act. Once the nausea passed I focused on the anger that always followed an injury, savouring how righteous it felt.

I pulled myself up and over the lip and rolled onto the grass, enjoying the feel of something other than cold flesh against mine, then quickly moved across to crouch behind one of the tents that I now knew to be holding prisoners.

I edged around the canvas and risked a glance towards the larger tent and the glow within. The light within was a soft shimmer, like moonlight reflecting off water, the brightness waxing and waning in time with the pitch of the chanting. I was immediately gripped with the idea that if I would only look into the centre of the light I would understand the pattern; it *wanted* me to look at it, just as the chant *wanted* me to mouth the words that formed it. What harm was there in it, after all? I would finally see what the others saw, and know the truth. I would be part of something greater than me.

I felt myself turn towards the glow, my hand reaching up to pull my hood off, but a sudden heat against my breast made me flinch. I felt the allure of the light and its glow fade, and the sight of it suddenly felt as unwelcome as an unexpected lump in a mouthful of wine. I shrank back behind the tent and fumbled St Tomas' medallion from the sodden pocket I carried it in. The blue stone in the centre flickered briefly as if acknowledging my gratitude, then dimmed and cooled. I patted it with no little affection and carefully put it away again. Its intervention had won me a brief reprieve from the insidious effect of the chant, giving me the momentary clarity of thought I needed to protect myself from it. I felt my anger stir anew and welcomed the sensation. It had sustained me through seven centuries of captivity and degradation, and it would see me through this too.

I inched forward again and looked towards the tent, concentrating on what was happening on the fringes of the light, rather than within it. It was like trying to watch fish at the bottom of a fast river, but after a fair amount of quiet cursing the figures finally swam into focus. The swaying figures were prisoners from the look of them, each linked to the other by a glittering chain fastened about their necks. Interspersed between them I could see the darker shapes of necromancers, their eyes glowing as they raised their staffs and crashed them to the ground, sending white sparks which flew to join the brighter glow in the centre.

I dragged my gaze away and looked around, suddenly conscious that the spectacle of the ritual had kept my attention for far longer than it should have. Aside from the wizards, who could protect themselves from the side effect of the spellcasting, the only figures moving around this close to the main tent were a number of undead guards, who I supposed were likewise immune to it. These ghouls weren't the more common sort who only reacted to things, but were armoured like men and roving under what appeared to be their own will, their eyes permanently ablaze with the cold light that signified a higher awareness. I would have preferred normal, living soldiers who were far easier to distract or kill. I had no real idea of what these ghouls were capable of. What could they actually see with the blank white orbs that served as their eyes?

I watched as a pair passed near to me, my legs braced to charge if they reacted to me, but whatever they saw, it seemed it did not extend to their peripheral vision, something that I would try to remember. I edged a bit further around the tent as the pair passed, then abruptly froze in place as I saw another of them in front of the very tent I was hiding behind. He was clad in stiff looking leather armour with metal discs sewn onto them, and held a heavy looking mace which I quite liked the look of.

As I inched closer to make sure he was alone, a woman within the tent suddenly screamed, and after little or no respite from the sibilant chanting and buzzing vibrations, her shriek was like a blade being jammed into my ear. I recoiled, and as I did my foot caught one of the ropes. I caught myself before I fell, but by then the guard's helmeted head had already swung towards me and the same mace that I had been admiring was suddenly lifting.

CHAPTER 15

'THEY'VE COME FOR us!' shouted another within the tent, prompting more screams and cries.

'We're next!'

'Drogah have mercy!'

I stepped away from the ropes as the guard advanced, the mace suddenly looking very menacing. He followed as I backed away. Once we were behind the tent and out of sight of the wizards I dug my feet into the ground and launched myself at him before he could finish lifting his weapon. My shoulder drove into his breastplate with my not inconsiderable weight firmly behind it, sending him crashing backwards.

I barely winced as my black talons slid out between my knuckles again. I'd only recently remembered I had them, and how to use them. They were originally meant for defending my territory, and were made to pierce the hides of other dragons, along with anything else stupid enough to challenge me. As I had grown in strength and size my challengers had become fewer and fewer and as such I'd used them so rarely in my later life that I could almost forgive myself for having forgotten that I'd had them.

The ghoul didn't know or care about any of that though. I grabbed its ankle and pulled it towards me even as my other hand punched it in the face, driving the length of the talon through its eye and out through the back of its skull.

But I had underestimated how resiliently these ghouls could move, and even as I wrenched the talon from the wreckage of its skull it lashed out with the mace, the angular spikes digging into my flesh and scraping the bone beneath. The impact knocked me sideways to the ground, tearing more flesh as it ripped free. It tried to sit up, but the gaping hole in its skull finally registered and it fell back, its limbs trembling uncontrollably. My injured arm didn't want to move, so I simply threw myself onto it, using my greater weight to stifle its flailing until I could slip my right talon under the edge of its helmet and push it up through its flapping tongue and deep into its foul brain. It shook once more, then abruptly deflated, vomiting foul smelling blood across me as I twisted the talon and pulled it out. I stood up as quickly as I could, wincing as the movement sent pain shooting up along my shoulder and neck.

For all of the violence, the fight had been brief and, apart from my grunting and the sounds of impact, conducted in relative silence. The groan that broke from my lips as I stood and tested my shoulder was perhaps the loudest noise of all. The numbness imparted by the force of the blow was rapidly fading, and blood was running free from the gashes it had torn open. The women in the tent had stopped shrieking, and it seemed that none of the wizards seemed to have taken the slightest notice of it, but then with so many already dead perhaps they didn't notice them anymore. I peered into the tent and found myself being stared at by several dozen pairs of eyes set into gaunt faces.

'Go!' I almost had to shout it to hear myself over the sound of the ritual, 'Run, save yourselves!'

The first of them hesitated until they were outside the tent, at which point they seemed to realise that this wasn't some cruel trick and sped off as fast as their spindly limbs could carry them. The rest didn't need much encouragement after that and dashed out as one, most of them pouring between the largest gaps in the tents. It was a false hope, for that gap would lead them back towards the guard posts, but with hysteria gripping them there was no point in me even trying to warn them. The mass exodus of course sent the wizards into a fit of shouting, and several of the runaways were felled by brightly flashing spells, adding to the chaos. It was all a boon for me for though, and I ducked inside the tent to examine my shoulder. As I reckoned it, no one would come to investigate an empty tent, at least not yet, and I needed my arm working if I was going to get out of there in one piece. I winced as I moved it. The blood was still flowing freely, cutting red tracks through the mud and filth that had coated me in the ditch. I dredged up a mote of power and carefully settled it across the wound, letting it settle across the rawness like fine cloth. It wasn't strong enough to mend it there and then, but it would staunch the worst of the bleeding and at least start the process. I could then finish it once I was away from the corruption that hung in the air.

'Startus?' croaked a voice from the back of the tent.

I edged forward as a half-naked figure moved out of the gloom, his skin creased and folded across muscles and bone like the roots of an old vine. He shuffled closer and stared up at me through eyebrows like wild hedgerows.

'Stratus,' I corrected him. 'Hello, Crow.'

The old tinker gave the same wheezing laugh that I remembered from our time on the road together. 'Are you rescuing me?'

'I only rescue princesses.'

He bared his remaining teeth at me and grabbed onto my arm as he embraced me, and even his feeble strength was enough to send a flare of pain racing up my arm and into my neck. He must have felt me stiffen because he pulled back and stared at the blood I'd transferred onto his shirt with surprise.

'You're bleeding.'

'Yes I am,' I said.

'Is it bad?'

'It isn't good.'

'What are you doing here?'

'There's no time for that.' I peered out the tent. 'We have to go.'

'Won't argue with that.' His voice trailed away as he looked into the large tent, his mouth hanging open.

I turned his head away and twisted his nose for good measure when he resisted, which made him curse and flail.

'Don't look at it,' I said as he rubbed his nose. 'What do you know of it?' I said, tilting my head towards the tent. 'What have you seen?'

'Not much. They take prisoners from the tents and replace those who keel over while they're singing.' He spat into the mud. 'Whoever goes in there doesn't come out alive.'

I grunted to hide my disappointment. I had hoped he would have noticed something I hadn't. The ritual was clearly a time-consuming one, which meant that its form and purpose would be difficult to divine until the very end, something I dare not remain here long enough to witness. What I needed was someone who knew what was coming. Someone with the kind of knowledge that could only come from being involved with this terrible project, and who could point me to wherever they had taken Tatyana. Someone like a wizard.

'Come with me,' I said, ducking out of the tent and pulling my hood up. The night hadn't yet surrendered to the dawn, so I hoped the combination of the murky light and morning's mist would let me pass as a wizard from a distance.

'Where are we going?'

'I've seen as much as I need to. We need to get out of the camp now, somewhere I can heal myself.' I paused as three of the wizards rushed by towards where several of the prisoners had overpowered one of their fellows and were beating him soundly with his own staff. None of them so much as looked in our direction. 'But first I'm going to catch myself a wizard.'

'Ah,' Crow wheezed in reply. 'Clever. Like a disguise.'

'Something like that.' I lowered myself into the ditch, cursing as a disjointed arm rolled under my foot and forced me to grab at the wall to steady myself. I looked over my shoulder and saw Crow standing on the edge, his arms limp at his sides, his hands trembling.

'Get down before they see you.'

'Gods above and saints below,' he breathed, the words barely audible. He dropped to his knees, but remained stubbornly on the edge.

'Get in.'

He didn't even look at me, and one of Tatyana's favourite curses spilled from my lips before I realised I was saying it. He looked up at the sound of it, just in time to see me grab his arm and pull him into the pile of bodies. Whatever torpor had gripped him at the sight of the piled corpses vanished as he landed amongst them and, as small as he was, it was a struggle for me to keep him silent. By the time his struggles subsided into tears the trickle of blood from my shoulder was a steady flow once more.

'Crow.' He ignored me and simply sat there, arms

hugging his narrow chest, his gaze fixed on a nearby head. '*Crow*.' I turned his head towards me as gently as I could. He blinked rapidly, but didn't say anything. 'They're dead. They don't care anymore.'

He hugged himself tighter and whimpered as something in the layers below us gave way in a loud blast of gas and he tipped sideways onto the waxy torso of a younger man. He squirmed away from it and closed his eyes.

'So many,' he said, and I sighed, relieved that he had not in fact lost his wits entirely. He turned to me. 'I have to get out of here. I can't do this, Drogah forgive me.'

'If you do, you'll be as dead as them.'

'This is Hel!' he hissed.

I resisted the urge to shake him. 'It's just a riverbed full of corpses.'

'They're people.'

'Dead people.'

'They were *people*, damn you. People.'

'And now they're dead people. They don't care about your sandal on their head.' He opened his mouth to say something, but I jabbed a finger against his forehead, fixing his attention on me. 'And if you cannot stomach crawling over them, then you can march up back to that tent and wait to be killed like a sheep.'

He pulled himself upright, the fogged look in his eyes was gone, replaced by the clarity of anger.

'You monster.' Now he jabbed a finger at me. 'What if it was your family laying here? Would you be so careless? So disrespectful?'

'I have no family.' I didn't let the memories that rose within my mind show on my face.

'Everyone has family,' Crow was saying. 'Avoiding a question isn't the same as answering it.'

I felt my own anger brighten inside my chest, the tips of

my draconic teeth pushing against the inside of my mouth. I forced them back with some effort.

'Dead is dead,' I said, fighting to keep my voice above a growl. 'Live and avenge them, or die here. The choice is yours.'

I turned away and began the awkward journey back along the riverbed, hugging my injured arm to my chest. After some time I heard the wet rasp of Crow's breathing behind me, interspersed with whispered entreaties to his god, who I imagined was paying them as little heed as I was. I slowed as I reached the point where I had first entered the riverbed. My shoulder was throbbing, and I spent more of my carefully hoarded energy to slow the bleeding once more, something that was a bit easier to do further away from the ritual. I was still crouched there, peering over the lip of the embankment when Crow caught up with me. He didn't say anything and simply sat there, breathing like a half-submerged bellows.

'I came from that way,' I said it more to myself than him, but he pushed himself up and looked over the edge with me. 'There are far less of them on that side, but forcing my way will still be like kicking a wasps' nest. Dawn isn't going to make it any easier.'

'So what's your plan, son?'

I peered at him, looking for any sign of a head wound, but there was too much blood and dirt caked on his face to tell for certain. 'I am not your son.'

'You don't say.'

'Say what?'

He shook his head and slid back down into the muck. 'So what happens next?'

'First things first.' I closed my eyes and sought out the touch of the Songlines. They were faint, distorted by the unnatural echoes of the wizards' ongoing spells, but they were there. As strange and disturbing as their magic was, it still needed the raw energy of the Songlines to exist. I sighed as I drew power to myself and quickly sent more of it into my healing pattern, numbing the deep ache radiating from my torn shoulder.

'You don't have a plan, do you?' Crow's voice jolted me. I'd all but forgotten he was there.

'We go through the camp and escape.'

'That's your plan?' He gave a brief chuckle. 'You do know there's a bloody great army just behind that little hill?'

'It was more of an idea than a plan,' I growled. I clapped a hand over his mouth as he drew breath to reply. 'Someone's coming.'

I sank back from the edge of the embankment and watched as two figures came walking along the bank. I took the first to be a soldier, and a living one too from his gait and the scarf wrapped around his face. The other was clearly a wizard, judging by his staff and robes, quite possibly even a necromancer if I was really lucky.

'We're fucked,' whispered Crow.

'Wait here,' I replied.

CHAPTER 16

'THIS IS STUPID.'

'If you're going to insist on complaining then at least find something new to say.'

'We're going to die.'

'Everyone dies.'

'Well, that's bloody encouraging, thank you.'

'Just keep walking, and try to look angry,' I said. Fighting the urge to shout at him to go faster was at least distracting me from the lingering pain of my wounds, not to mention that it would ruin the mummery that had thus far seen us successfully pass by two pairs of sentries.

'It's hard to look angry when I'm trying not to fill my boots with something beside my feet.'

'Keep walking. If the hounds find our scent all this will be for naught,' I reminded him.

The sun had risen shortly after I'd ambushed the wizard and his bodyguard. They'd stared at me with wide eyes as I sprang from the ditch with outstretched arms; neither had a chance to scream before I bowled them over. It had torn my shoulder open again, but that small hurt had been a small price for the element of surprise.

The soldier had tried to draw his sword, a mistake given that I was already upon him. He'd drawn less than half of it before my hand closed on his neck. There was no time for finesse and I'd simply tightened my fist until I no longer felt any resistance. I'd been more careful with the wizard given how tricky they could be, and had angled my arm to catch him in the throat as part of my tackle, trusting to the pain and inability to breathe to divert his attention from trying to use any of his rings or bracelets. He'd been a feisty one though, leaving me with little choice but to kill him. I'd been careful to leave his head undamaged, and quickly cut it off and stowed it in an improvised sack while Crow stripped the soldier's body.

As a result, I was now clad in the ill-fitting uniform of a Penullin soldier, and Crow in the robe and cape of the necromancer, the dark materials and poor light hiding the bloodstains. I was optimistic that the necromancer's brain would yield its secrets once I was somewhere safer where I could bend my will to the task. If Crow noticed the bleeding sack I carried he made no comment on it, which suited me. So disguised, we had picked out a route that offered the largest gap in the sentries and begun making our escape from the camp, keeping to the lowest paths where the morning mist was thickest.

I steered us back towards the outlying guard-posts nearest the swamp, and was feeling quite optimistic when a party of four soldiers came walking through the mist, the vapours having hidden them as well as they were hiding us. They barked a challenge at us, but Crow had replied fluently in their own tongue, his tone brusque and conveying a sense of insult. They stepped aside to let us pass, but they were watching us closely and I'd have wagered gold that they were going to put a spear in our backs as we passed.

Nonetheless, I considered it an impressive feat on Crow's part given how strong the scent of fear radiating from him was. We were close to the refuge the swamp offered now, but a glance over my shoulder confirmed that the guards were still watching us.

'Heya, wizard!' one of them called. 'A word with you.'

'What do I do?' Crow whispered.

'Don't move,' I said, closing my hands to aid my concentration.

The guard called again, and I heard the jingle of armour as they started walking towards us.

'What do I do?' he said again, louder this time.

I kept my attention on the swamps. 'Look mysterious.'

What I was attempting was a risk, but one I thought worth taking. My wind construct was a familiar tool that came readily to mind, and I worked as quickly as I could. Reworking the potency was a relatively simple task, but moving the point of origin was harder than I thought given that I couldn't see the ground I was aiming for.

Somewhere behind us a trumpet honked three times, then thrice more. It meant nothing to me, but the guards who had called to us now began moving with new vigour.

'Come here, you two!'

I could hear the thud of their feet now; it was time. I released the construct and felt it ripple into being, hopefully in the right place.

'Stand where you are!' The guards were close now, slowed by the steep slope and the wet grasses.

'Make up your mind,' I called back at them, while next to me Crow's fear was quickly curdling into terror. I grabbed his arm before he could bolt. 'Trust me,' I said, staring into the mist.

Even as doubts touched me I saw the heavy, milk white vapours of the low ground ripple and begin racing up the slope towards us in a thick, pearly wave. It first swallowed us, then the guards, and even as close as I was to Crow I could barely make out his outline. I held fast to his arm and woke my night-vision; it couldn't penetrate the silvery mist but it did show me the ground as a darker strip, letting me lead us safely down the pockmarked and uneven slope.

There was no time to argue or explain, so I simply threw Crow over my shoulder and began to race down the slope. I stumbled into one of the screaming heads just as we reached the first thickets of tall reeds and rushes. There was no time for subtlety so I simply pushed it over and let the water muffle its scream. I kept wading, trusting my innate sense of direction to keep me heading in the right direction, that being a straight line away from both the Penullin camp and Falkenburg. We passed beyond the mist too early for my liking, but then I had used my wind spell to push as much of it towards the camp as I could, all but emptying the basin the wetlands nestled in.

'I'm going to vomit' were Crow's first words since I'd picked him up, and I quickly set him down. We were in a pool that was only ankle deep, and thick with strings of slimy little eggs and rotten leaves.

'Never thought I'd be so glad to see a swamp,' said Crow, his hands on his knees as he stared at the far bank of the river we had just crossed, which in truth was little more than a wide, slow stream that oozed rather than flowed between the tussocks and sandbanks that stretched out towards the west. He waded a bit deeper in before squatting down and washing his face.

'So,' he said, 'what do we do now?

I considered the bloodied sack tied to my belt. The necromancer's brain wasn't getting any fresher, and dragging it through a swamp wasn't going to help either, but then neither was getting caught up in a fight I couldn't win.

'That way,' I said, pointing deeper into the marsh. 'Where the dogs cannot find our scent and we can stop for a while.'

'Did you do that? With the mists?'

'Yes.'

He scratched his beard. 'You don't look like a wizard. Not any sort I've ever seen.'

'I'm not a wizard.'

'Here now, you just said you were.'

'No, I did not. We should go.'

He grunted. 'Do you think they'll be chasing us?'

'The wizards might.'

'I was afraid you'd say that,' Crow muttered as he finished blasting air and water from each nostril. 'We'll have to go slowly. The mud can be treacherous.'

As we soon discovered, that was something of an understatement. I led the way on the simple logic that anything that could take my weight could take his. The glutinous mud was greedy, and almost immediately sucked the sandals from his feet. It wasn't satisfied with just his sandals though and with every plunge into its depths, another layer of it stuck to our feet and legs until it felt like there were chains wrapped around our ankles, forcing us to slow down now and then to scrape it off, which in places meant sinking up to our knees. Crow was not a young man, and however brief his captivity had been, it had taken its toll and we had barely entered the swamp proper before his strength gave out.

He barely protested when I hoisted him onto my back, something which I should have done sooner since he weighed less than my armour had, and it let me move at a much better pace, even if it came with the price of his breath on the back of my neck. The mists burned off sooner than I would have liked, and as the sun rose the heat brought out more of the stinging flies as well, forcing me to wrap torn strips of Crow's robes around my face in a tattered veil. My skin was thick enough that they didn't bother me overmuch, save that they all seemed intent on flying into my eyes, nose and mouth.

The afternoon came and went as I walked, and despite the flies' best efforts, I found myself enjoying the simplicity of engaging in a purely physical challenge. My attention was fixed on what I could see and feel, and while it was taxing, by the time that the day softened into dusk my mind was clearer than it had been for some time. And, even better than that, I was now finding firmer ground under my feet more often than not as it began to rise from the depression that had fostered the swamps. The last hours of walking felt the longest, as they always did, but when I set Crow gently upon the ground again it was on firm grass.

'It's a shame you had to stop, I was just nodding off,' he said as he rubbed his legs.

I fought the urge to ask what that meant. From what I remembered of our first meeting, trying to ask Crow questions was like telling the wind which way to blow. 'There's a stream beyond those bushes where the water is still sweet and good,' I said instead. 'We'll take our rest and carry on at first light.'

'Can you make a fire?' He pointed at me and flexed his fingers and I took his meaning.

'Yes. We should be safe enough to do so here. You gather some wood and I'll see if I can find something to eat.'

'Nothing too spicy though. I've a delicate stomach.'

'If you don't eat, you will die, and I will have carried you for nothing.'

He shook his head, then laughed wetly. 'You're a strange one, son. Strangest by a country mile for sure.'

I watched him as he wandered off, still shaking his head. I would never understand humans, nor why I was trying to in the first place. The sooner I was rid of this form and their infectious mannerisms the happier I would be. After a long drink from the stream I sat down and sent my sorcery rippling out from me, a gentle probe seeking anything edible. The water had helped still the gnawing in my belly but it was a temporary measure at best. I felt the light touch of the small creatures hiding and hunting around us and pulsed an urge to come to the drinking hole along those same strands of sorcery, then waited.

They came from all directions, startling Crow while he dug a shallow pit for the fire. After the horrors he had seen it was quite comical watching him scrabble back from rabbits and a young doe as if they were ravening beasts. I quickly snapped the necks of the ones I wanted, and dispersed the traces of sorcery fogging the minds of the others, creating a small stampede as they came to their senses and fled the predator looming over them. Crow's initial protest at this 'unnatural' form of hunting vanished as the reality of the impending meal took hold.

'There's not much dry wood around here,' he said, gesturing to the pitiful bundle of sticks next to the hole. I looked up as his voice trailed off. 'What in name of Hel are you doing to that poor squirrel?'

I looked at the red thing in my hands. Using my sorcery had made me think of Tatyana, and I'd started seeking any trace of the connection without realising it. 'Skinning it?'

'Skinning it doesn't mean that you squeeze everything out of its arse.'

'If you think you can do better, do it yourself.' I offered him the squirrel but he pushed it back at me.

'There isn't anything anyone can do with that.'

'You skin the rest then,' I said, tossing him my knife. 'I'll get the wood.'

'I reckon that's a better idea.'

I wasn't one to waste a bounty and quickly devoured the squirrel before heading down the lee of hill where the bushes were more plentiful and the ground drier. It also gave me the opportunity to do what I'd been putting off the whole afternoon.

I sat down on a jutting slab of rock and upended the sack hanging from my belt, catching the necromancer's head and weighing it in my hand for a moment. I needed to do it sooner rather than later, and then seemed as good a time as any. I prepared to crack it open with a rock but stopped just as I was about to bring it crashing down, my attention caught by my nails.

They were still as dark as my skin, but they now jutted from my fingers for almost the length of my knuckles, and tapered in a way that human nails could never be. I curled my fingers and experimented with willing them back to a more human size and shape, but unlike my teeth and the fighting talons hidden in my arms, , I felt no response at all. Their shift seemed to be a more permanent, physical sort. I stared at them a while longer.

Why was this happening, and when did it happen? I hadn't paid attention to anything as mundane as my nails for some time.

I peeled the skin back from the skull as I considered what it might mean before cracking the bone against the rock as if it were a boiled egg. My thoughts remained elsewhere, at least until the gut-wrenching taste of his brain brought me back to the present. I fought the urge to gag and chewed the mouthful slowly, exposing as much of my tongue to the limp matter as I could. Ghostly images soon began to flash across my vision, glimpses into a life lived behind walls and in dark rooms. I choked more of it down, chewing through it until images of war and slaughter replaced those of books and bitter disappointments. I took another large mouthful and closed my eyes.

CHAPTER 17

THE SOLDIERS ALL *work with a quiet efficiency now, one that entirely justified the severity of the reprimands we'd been forced to deliver earlier in the campaign. The common foot soldiers were coarse and brutal creatures, animals really, and we soon found that their respect could only be given through domination and fear. We had whipped them at first, but they learned to tolerate the lash, and then sneered at us when our arms no longer proved up to the task.*

It was my idea to reward them with the gift of the Bloodseed, rather than punishing them with the rod and lash, a moment of genius that had earned me praise from the Master himself, an honour made all the sweeter by the even greater jealousy it fostered in Ludvig. He was Bone Lord of this cabal, but we all knew he'd only been promoted because he'd been one of the Master's first apprentices at the University, rather than from merit or any ability to think for himself.

Now, instead of wasting hours strengthening and conditioning clumsy host bodies, we had subjects whose instincts and sinews had been soaked with violence for years. And more than that, seeing the change come over their peers cowed the rest of the unruly brutes better than any whipping ever had. There was even a small mutiny, but that never happened again after we blessed the entire company who had rebelled against our command. It was an expensive gesture, and the General protested to the Master himself, but in the end he accepted it, as we all knew he would always have to. Their army was nothing without us, and we all knew it.

Ludvig may still have been in charge, but everyone knew it was me who had completed the final ritual at Aknak. This was my show now, and once Falkenburg's node was cracked, I would have my own cabal.

I made my way into the ritual tent where the others were carefully cutting the turf away and flattening the area, preparing the ground for the laying of the circles, while several acolytes carefully repainted the containment sigils that had been damaged when the tent was repacked for its journey here. Satisfied that all was in order, I ordered the Lance to be brought forth. The cradle that would hold it while the souls were bound was not yet ready, but there was still much to do before we could begin charging its power. Ludvig of course raged at me for opening it without him, but he couldn't argue the fact that there was little time to spare if Falkenburg was to fall on schedule.

Standing before the Lance, it was easy to put our differences aside though. It was a breathtaking artefact, even if you ignored that it had been crafted by the goddess herself. It was eighteen feet long and as smooth as polished marble, and the silver filled runes incised into its length were sharp enough to slice the whorls from careless fingers. Its tapering length was marked with three thick bands of silver, each bearing further runes chased in red gold, their meanings known only to the Master. Even now, with the ritual to wake its power yet to be performed I could feel the potency within it buzzing pleasantly against my skin.

To call it a Lance was of course entirely demeaning to something of such power and grace, but it was easier to speak than the name the Master had given it, the same name that the prisoners would chant as they offered their souls to it. Akusangai. I felt the Bloodseed within me shift like a cat waking from a long sleep as the word pressed at my lips, desperate to be said out loud. Despite my gift and skill in the Art, I felt something like fear creep along my spine and hastily pressed my lips tighter together. To summon it so, without the proper protections in place was to invite madness.

I forced such thoughts from my mind and focused on the task at hand. The Master's instructions left no room for argument; the Lance had to be ready before he arrived. If we failed in that, it wouldn't matter that the ultimate responsibility had rested with Ludvig. We were his cabal, and would all be punished alongside him.

CHAPTER 18

My EYES OPENED as the last of the visions faded, and I managed a single deep breath before my stomach rebelled and emptied itself with rare violence. I stumbled to a pool of relatively clear water and rinsed my mouth and face, which was about the time that I saw Crow watching me. His hands were at his sides, shaking enough that I was surprised he hadn't managed to cut himself with the knife he was holding. He raised it to shoulder height as I walked towards him.

'What are you doing?' I asked, stopping a few feet out of his reach. I doubted that the bowstrings masquerading as muscles would allow him to drive the knife deep enough to hurt me, but didn't want to tempt him into trying anything stupid.

He swung the knife to the left, then back at me. 'What is this?'

I darted a glimpse to the left and spotted the necromancer's empty head. His eyes had popped out at some point, giving the sunken face an almost comical look of astonishment.

'I ate his brain,' I said, too tired to bother fabricating platitudes for another ungrateful human. 'And no, I neither wanted to nor enjoyed it.' I stepped closer. 'Now put that knife away before I sheathe it somewhere you would not appreciate.'

'You going to eat mine?'

I grimaced at the thought. 'Stars, no.'

He chewed his lip for a moment, then lowered the blade.

'It's how I see his memories,' I said, answering the question I was sure was on its way to his lips. 'Did you not wonder why I took his head?'

'I just thought it was, you know, some sort of ritual or something.'

'Hardly.' I grimaced at the thought of doing something like that often enough that it became a ritual event. It was a strange and savage world where decapitating another of your own kind caused such scant outrage, or where such a deed was so common that it had become a cultural norm. A world where humans held dominion would be a dark and terrible thing to behold.

'I just meant...' He stared up at me. 'Hel, I don't know what I meant. You ate his brains!'

'Brain. Singular.' I kicked the empty head into a rancid smelling pool. 'If I meant you harm I would not have rescued you.'

'You didn't though, did you?' I could hear his old heart galloping inside his chest and the creak of his joints as he sat down. 'You brought me out of there, but you didn't come to rescue me, did you?'

'No.'

'So why then?'

'That is a question I have been asking myself a lot of late.' I looked up at the stars and exhaled slowly until the annoyance simmering within me subsided. 'And yet I still haven't found an answer that rings true.'

'You say a lot but say nothing. Why did you save me?'

'You were kind to me when there was no reason to be.' I

smiled at the memory of him giving me a clean, new tunic. My first gift. His heart was still racing as he watched me, and if I hadn't known better I would have thought he was going to flee or attack me.

'Who are you?' He licked his lips, his tongue a flash of pink amongst the white bristles. 'What are you?'

'You don't want to know.'

'Tell me. I'm too old for mysteries. Is Stratus even your name?'

That made me smile, for I could only agree with the sentiment; I too was growing too old and tired for mysteries and lies.

'My name *is* Stratus Firesky, and it has been so since before this world's first dawn.' I felt my spine straighten and my chest swell as I announced myself, and I feel no shame in admitting that I let a touch of sorcery colour my words, carrying the memory of the awe and fear I had once been met with. 'I am the Dead Wind, the Destroyer, and the Doom of Krandin.'

His brows lifted. 'You're what?'

'The Dead Wind.'

'That's what I thought you said.' His eyebrows settled back to their usual position. 'Are you some kind of royalty?'

'In a manner of speaking, I suppose that I am.' King Stratus did have a pleasant sound to it.

'I don't get it.'

'I am Fireborn, the last true son of the stars.'

'What?'

I shook my head at the absurdity of having to explain myself to this tiny, shrivelled man. 'I am a dragon.' *The last dragon*, my mind whispered, ever willing to remind me of my sorrow.

'How do you mean?'

I thought he might have been jesting, but there was no laughter in his voice. 'I am a dragon in human form.'

'A *dragon?* The fire-breathing sort, like from the old stories?'

'Yes.'

He stared at me, then burst out laughing. 'More stories and lies. I said—'

His protest stuttered as I set my hand on top of his head. 'What—'

I tilted his head up until his eyes met mine and summoned the same memory of the hunt that I had shown Tatyana.

'See me now,' I said, and gently pulsed the memory into his mind, holding onto his arms as his knees buckled.

He cried out like a child and tried to bolt, but I had anticipated that and held him to me. For a moment I thought his heart would surely burst, but it held and I lowered him to the rock, where he lay gulping air as if I had just saved him from drowning.

'I'll be damned,' he said once the initial panic lost its grip on him. 'Gods above and saints below, you're serious.'

'Very.'

'It's not possible, it's just not.' Unexpectedly, he rose and took a step forward until his chest was pressed against my lower ribs, his gaze roving across my face.

'How? You look normal. I mean, you're a big lump and all but still, you know, normal.'

'There is an enchantment binding me to this form,' I said. 'Although I fear its hold upon me is weakening.' I lifted my hand and showed him my nails.

'Long nails are proof of nothing, surely.'

I sighed and smiled at him with a mouth full of my real teeth and the red of my eyes woken. He cried out to his gods once more and shrunk back and then, quite bizarrely, began crying.

'Do not be afraid,' I offered once I had retracted my teeth.

'I'm not,' he said. He took a shuffling step then lunged forward to embrace me.

At first I stood quietly, waiting for him to let go, but eventually patted him on the back as gently as I could when he showed no signs of releasing me, unsure what else to do. 'There, there.'

Eventually he released me and wiped the wet from his face. 'Sorry.'

'Apology accepted.'

'This is amazing.' He bared his remaining teeth in a smile I'd prefer not to see again.

'I'm sure it is, but dinner would be even more so.'

The thought of a hot, meaty meal was apparently enough to return to him to his senses and we made our way back to our impromptu camp with haste, where he instructed me how best to stack the wood for a long fire, rather than a hot one, before remembering who he was speaking to. After that he didn't say much, not until he had eaten his fill and I was idly cracking the longer bones for the marrow.

'You still haven't told me where you're from.'

'Why does it matter so much to you?' I said around a mouthful of fatty meat.

'Just curious is all. You never did answer me back there.' He gestured vaguely towards the east.

I considered the stars, then pointed to one that shone like a wolf's eye. 'My home was far to the north and east of here, under the light of the Wolf. Or at least I think it was. Is.'

'You can't remember?'

'It has been a long time, and my last memories of it were not fond ones.'

'How long?'

'Seven hundred years, give or take a few decades.'

His whistle stirred the longer whiskers on his lip as he leaned forward to stare at me, the glow of the coals smudging the lines that creased his face. Did human skulls shrink as they aged? His face must have been much larger at some point for him to have all that skin stretched out across it.

'And?' he asked.

'And what?'

'I said why are we still walking through this bloody bog rather than flying wherever it is we're going?'

'I didn't know that you could fly,' I said.

'Ha!' He clapped his hands and sat back, and for a moment I dared to hope that his questions had come to an end.

'But why? Come on, answer me. That can't be more of a secret than what you've already told me.' He scratched at his beard. 'Is it the glamour?'

'I always liked that word. *Glamour.* It sounds so much grander than enchantment, or spell binding. But yes, that is why. I am bound to this form, including my wings, and while I have my sorcery, I cannot yet unbind myself.'

'Why?'

'I will tell you in the morning.'

'Why not now?'

'Because,' I said, a growl slipping into my voice, 'I am tired, and hurt, and still hungry. I need to sleep, and you need to let me.'

'Easy, son, I was just asking a question. I don't often get to yammer to a bloody dragon.'

'Yammer in the morning.' I watched through lidded eyes as he laid back, idly picking his beard, and I had no need to read his mind to know that his questions would not wait until morning. I teased out a strand of sorcery and whispered his name as I pulsed it towards him, catching his gaze just long enough to weaken any resistance he might have offered. He was old and tired, and the compulsion took hold faster than I had hoped. Within three long breaths he was fast asleep.

CHAPTER 19

DESPITE WHAT I'D told Crow, sleep wasn't calling to me yet. I curled myself around the fire and examined my nails while I chewed a leftover hoof. From the top, the nail simply looked as if I had a penchant for filing my nails, but underneath was a different matter entirely. Unlike human nails, which are thin and flat, mine were nearly as thick as they were long, my fingertips having split in the centre to accommodate the growth. At this rate they would soon begin to curve downwards until they were as long and sharp as those of an eagle. I would need to visit a carpenter or blacksmith to trim them if I wanted to continue walking amongst men in peace.

'Why now?' I whispered, tapping one of them against a rock. I had transmogrified myself into a human form, but what I hadn't appreciated when I was doing it was how many layers of enchantments and old curses still hung upon my draconic body. Talgoth, the archmage who Aethbert Henkman had been in thrall to, had not wasted the opportunity to experiment on a beast as famous as me, and the cage he had trapped me in had itself been heavily enchanted, both to keep me constrained to less than half my normal size and to cut me off from the Songlines. Such a long exposure to his aggressive magics had influenced my own works, especially when taken with my inability to bolster my own enchantments, much less resist his. Any enchantment, whether physical or bound to an inanimate object, would deteriorate over time if it wasn't refreshed. Sometimes they would simply weaken and fade away, like a mountainside eroded by a river, but other times they would collapse on themselves and become an unpredictable, and potentially catastrophic mess.

I suspected the latter was happening to my enchantment as a result of the years of neglect and corrupted dregs of the spells cast by generations of mediocre wizards. I had been stripped of my sorcery for centuries, leaving me with no way to plumb the intention and lingering effects of the countless spells cast on me over the years.

I swallowed the last of the hoof and laid my head upon my arm, slowing my breathing until I felt my mind settle. Closing my eyes, I drew my sorcery to me and turned it inward, letting it filter through my veins and sinews, attuning it to the embedded remnants of my original enchantment. The core of it was still there, ghostly filaments wrapped around the shrunken fibres of my being, inconsequential by themselves but together forming the imprint and mould that this body had been poured into. To break those chains in the wrong place would cause the enchantment to fold in upon itself in an unpredictable manner, potentially releasing an uncontrolled, violent and undoubtedly fatal blast of raw energy inside my very flesh.

Time had faded the memory of how I had compiled the initial enchantment, and the countless spells from the curious and the cruel that I had weathered over the years had left their mark too, twisting parts of it, corrupting its purpose and the ways it interacted with my flesh to such an extent that I no longer knew where my work ended and theirs began.

The thought of stray magic touched something in me, and I fumbled the medallion from its hiding place inside my tattered clothing by touch alone, tracing my fingers across the tight engravings and smooth blue stone until I felt the gentle spark of the power contained within it kiss my fingertip as it woke. Before I had recovered my mind, the part of me I had called the Beast had taken its strength from the magic I had been exposed to, an ability that the medallion had certainly affected. I knew it was powerful, but precious little else about it. Could it draw some of the corruption left by the wizards' spell from me, like a poultice draws foulness from a septic wound? And if it could, how would that affect the rest of the enchantment, warped as it was? Was the medallion the cause of my steadily growing claws, or was it helping to stabilise the enchantment?

I set it down on my chest and looked up at the night sky, trying to recognise the constellations above from the fleeting glimpses the broken clouds offered. Something was happening to me, but I had yet to fathom why. Was it the result of the exposure to so much dark magic in the necromancer's camp, the insidious influence of the medallion or simply entropy? Or even all of them together?

I would have liked to find the time and a place of safety to discover the truth of it, but time was something I did not really have the luxury of. I'd let myself be drawn into Lucien's stupid little war and was now bound to it by virtue of having given my word to end Navar Louw, the source of the hate that burned inside me as steadily as the stars above. On top of all that I had also promised to help Tatyana find Lucien before the paladins corrupted him and, quite possibly, filled his head with worms.

The Master's instructions left no room for argument; the Lance had to be ready before he arrived.

The dead necromancer's memory rose in my mind, at first a reminder that time was not something I had, but then I realised that it was also a reminder that I now knew where Navar Louw was going to be. At some point soon he would be coming to Falkenburg, and since he apparently didn't care to lend his strength to the siege, I surmised that it would be to oversee whatever they intended to do once the city fell. Something that had to do with the Lance that the necromancers were working so hard to enchant. *The Lance*. I could see it in my mind, but the meanings of the runes were lost on me and not for the first time I felt a stab of envy at Fronsac's ability to read and understand them.

I sat up as an idea bloomed in my mind. Fronsac had shown a firm grip on rune-craft in the wards that covered his body and protected the palace. If anyone could decipher the writings upon the Lance, it would surely be him. Returning to the city now was not a viable option, so I would need him to come to me. When I had showed him my battles with the Cardinal I had let him into my mind as a demonstration of mutual trust, which wasn't something I did very often, but as a result of that connection I could still feel the impression of his mind and thoughts. And more than that, I could still recall the sound and feel of his magic.

I took all of these memories and impressions of him and carefully wove them together, infusing them with the sound of his name and his magic, slowly shaping it until I could hear and feel the essence of him within it. I held this essence in mind as I summoned a pulse of energy and carefully melded the two. Once I was satisfied that it would hold, I fed more power into it until it materialised between my hands as a ball of shimmering blue energy and the thought and sound of him had driven all other thoughts from my mind.

'Fronsac,' I said, my voice as close to his as I could manage. I released the energy and watched it arc towards the city like a comet. I couldn't imagine that he or his apprentices wouldn't be watching over the enemy camp, and such a brazen call would surely be impossible to miss.

'Fronsac,' I repeated, binding the sound of his magic into the spoken word. *'Fronsac.'*

With my sorcery woken and alert for any reply I felt the brush of another mind against mine. It wasn't him, but I heard an echo of his magic within the projection. An apprentice then, most likely using some device to scry. I'd hoped for Fronsac himself, since his apprentices may have been swayed by the lies Prince Jean had told to hide the purpose of our quest.

'Hurry,' I whispered as I drew a circle around myself. Unlike wizards, I didn't need props and tools, but I understood the basic symbolism of their craft. If Fronsac responded, it would make it easier for him to visualise a protective barrier around his sending, foiling any surprise attacks or wizardly eavesdropping while he was exposed. That was a risk as, aside from the necromancers, the Penullin army also had a contingent of 'normal' wizards in their midst, and if they had any real ability it was quite possible that they would also have seen my call to him shining like a beacon amidst the otherwise bleak emptiness of the bogs.

I felt a new and more powerful presence gather around me, bringing with it a clear impression of hard, sharp geometries. It was an impressive sending, and had I not felt the echo of Fronsac's magic within it I may well have felt a momentary twinge of fear. A moment later some of that energy poured into the circle I'd prepared, cutting off all traces of the outside world as surely as if someone had dropped a glass dome over me.

I opened my own defences just as cautiously until I recognised the touch of his will.

'Stratus?'

'Fronsac. We haven't much time. The enemy is preparing a powerful artefact, but I need you to read the runes upon it.'

'Show it to me, like you did the dungeons.'

I strengthened the flow of my sorcery, then invited him into the memories I had taken from the necromancer. I felt a momentary stutter in the flow of his magic as he separated himself from his sending spell, itself a feat of no little skill. I pulled him in and felt his reaction evolve from curiosity to horror, and then dread as I showed him what I had seen and felt. The connection between us shivered as his emotions distorted the otherwise predictable harmony of his magic.

'Stratus, I need to look at this more closely but, by the stars, if what I suspect is true then the doom of everything may well be at hand.' Connected as we were, I could hear and feel the fear that coloured his magic.

'Tell me.' I didn't need to project a sense of urgency into my words.

'Do you know what a spirit well is?' He sensed my confusion and sent the rest of his message in a burst of light and sound, leaving me reeling. I had underestimated his skills once again.

'I will find you once I know more.'

With that, he withdrew his magic and I felt powerful wards flare back into life as he vanished from my mind. I sat down, closing my eyes as I absorbed the information he'd passed to me in the light. I sat quietly and concentrated on my breathing until my thoughts calmed enough for me to reach out for the Songlines, sighing as their familiar harmony soothed the frayed edges of my will. I sent a pulse of it rippling outwards, seeking any trace of foreign magic or human minds. I felt it pass across the quiet waters, softly touching the creatures that lived and died amongst the pools and reeds, but finding little else. Part of me was relieved that no pursuit was underway, while the other worried as to whether their plans were too subtle, too human, for me to comprehend.

Either way, there was no one out there, so worrying won me nothing. I laid back so that my feet were warmed by the coals and I could once more look up at the stars, something I had always found comforting. I had thought that the import of Fronsac's revelation would have kept me from sleep, but I had barely begun to mull over the doom that hung over us all before sleep claimed me.

CHAPTER 20

THE STONE CIRCLE *that Navar had created as my new cage sat within what was little more than a glorified barn. No sunlight reached me for all the time I was within it, and the only glimpses I had were when the doors swung open in the mornings to admit him and the gaggle of apprentices and students that trailed after him, exuding excitement and a lust for the cruelty to come. And it was cruelty, although he called it an education.*

Whichever lesson he purported to use me for, whether it be history, geography or the sciences, it always ended with his favourite students being rewarded with the chance to unleash whatever spells they had been practising on me. He'd correct their technique and cast them himself and they'd cheer as I bucked and twisted under the impact.

Every day was a new torment. If I resisted, they wouldn't stop until I collapsed so as to punish me for my aggression. If I didn't react, they increased the intensity and frequency until I screamed to punish me for my contempt. If I screamed too much, they bound my throat with chains so that I didn't disturb their lessons. I bled so much in that first year that the sawdust covering the cold stone beneath the circle had to be replaced every few days. Every now and then the rage and hate that was festering in my heart boiled over and I killed one or two of the workers tasked with that unenviable task, at which point Navar would smash me into unconsciousness and the cycle would start over again.

Eventually, however, the rage that burned inside me reached a new peak and sharpened into a cold knife permanently wedged in my chest. I spoke when I was commanded to, ate what I was given, and performed like the circus attraction that they wanted me to be. Days became weeks, weeks months, and months eventually became years. The cruelty continued unabated despite my compliance, and actually grew more vicious as his students grew in knowledge and power and lost any last vestige of empathy for me.

You can learn to endure anything with the right motivation. I waited for my chance behind a facade of submission and a hide that was fast becoming more scar than skin. They took this to be a sign of my submission to their will, feeding their contempt and sense of entitlement.

I nearly bit my own tongue the first time that Navar stepped into the circle. I felt the pressure of the wards he wore and forced myself to remain as I was, my mask of submission firmly in place, all too aware that leaping upon him would squander the careless arrogance that I had paid so dearly to foster. I hid my frustration behind a show of cringing subservience as he approached, hating that I was in fact genuinely afraid of him. That was the first time I truly smelled the taint within him, although I had no reference for it then and ascribed it to some of the pungent oils and potions that they occasionally threw at me.

Everything changed a month later. The day before it happened I had taken a particularly severe beating from one of Navar's senior apprentices who had finally mastered a form of lightning manipulation and wanted to show off his newfound skill. It had ended with him and Navar vying to see who could throw me furthest across the arena. Navar had won after striking me so powerfully that I had actually pierced the veil that usually prevented me from touching the standing stones and cut my face on its sharp whorls, leaving me unconscious for the rest of the day and most of the next.

I had dreamed as I lay there. Normally my mind conjured memories of my life with Anakhara, offering me a blissful refuge from the chaos and pain of that existence, but the dreams that day were different. They began with me in a darkness that had lost all memory of light, gripped by a formless dread that grew stronger with every moment that passed. I spat fire until I could see that I was in a labyrinth of sorts, and so began to lope along its seemingly endless passages, occasionally spitting further gobbets of fire to light my way until I came to a great stone door. I knew that something terrible lay beyond it, and stood paralysed with fear as it began to open before me, the grind of the stone lost to the sound of the keening wail that rose from within.

I spat a stream of fire into the mist that hung within the chamber, but the cold within suffocated the flame, reducing the blaze to a mere candle's glow. But that was enough for me to glimpse what waited within the chamber as it swung towards me. It was a dragon's skull, glittering as if rimed in frost, its hollow eyes lit with a light as red as heart's blood.

'Stratus.' The voice that issued from it was little more than the echo of a whisper, but I knew that it better than my own.

Before I could reply, the skull sank away into the oily darkness, and I felt a lurch of vertigo as that same *featureless dark broke and rushed towards me in a great wave. I had not spoken my love's name out loud since the day Henkman slew her, but I screamed it as I woke there in my cage, my mind afire with remembered pain.*

My scream was met with a squawk of surprise. I had woken whilst Navar was in the pit with some of his cabal, and it seemed that I had just interrupted a discussion about the probable density of my bones. My mind hadn't quite caught up with my body yet, or perhaps it was the other way around. Either way, I jerked back in surprise in much the same way they did, except that one of the rear facing spines on my upper arms promptly skewered a red-haired mage who had been lurking to my side. He squealed as I shook him off and flopped about on the ground gushing blood.

Navar reacted with his usual measured calm. I felt and heard his magic snap into life, and a moment later a trio of hissing bolts slammed me sideways. The rest of Navar's cabal ran for the perimeter as I skidded to a halt. I felt Navar's magic quickening again, but more than that, I heard it.

I stared at him as I tried to understand what had changed, but he was paying little heed to whatever I was doing or thinking. He was raging at me, but I was paying as little attention to him as he was to me because I had realised that he was using magic within the circle. Within the ward stones.

The wards in my cage had allowed magic from the outside in, but had universally stymied any use of it within the boundaries. I kept retreating as Navar's magic lashed at me. I knew he was hurting me, and quite badly too, but at that point my mind was still racing ahead of the pain.

The wards in the stones had allowed me to sense the flow of magic in a very muffled and cursory way, but had effectively cut me off from the Songlines, making me deaf to the harmony that lies at the heart of all magic. But I heard echoes of it now as Navar set the air alight in his anger. Why could he could still call on them?

I waited for the next barrage to strike, then made a show of collapsing; I'd done a lot of it since I had met him, and I must have done a good impression as he ceased his assault. I lay as still as death, the twitching of my abused muscles adding to the quality of my mummery, and for once it seemed that luck was with me.

Their voices trailed away as they strode towards the doors but I didn't move. I was bleeding from several wounds, but thankfully it had only been Navar who had attacked me; had the rest of his students joined in I might really have collapsed and lost my train of thought. I quickly packed the wounds with sawdust once they had left and settled back into my original position. I took some time to calm my racing hearts and mind.

Only once I had some modicum of control back did I dare turn my thoughts back to Anakhara. What had I seen and heard? Was the dream some fever phantom brought on by the traumas I had suffered? I didn't feel ill; in pain, yes, but not ill. My mind was still my own, despite Navar's brutish efforts. Had it been the contact with the magic of the ward stones? It had to have been her.

I knew her voice, and it had felt like her. There was no coming back from death, but we had shared our true names, our Words, with each other. We had been attuned to each other's being at a level that not even the gods could know. Had that allowed her to reach out for me? I fought against the weight of the emotions that threatened to overwhelm me, digging my thumbs into my wounds until the pain made me gasp, forcing the memories back until it no longer felt like they would crush me. I held them in,

*caging the pain within my soul, and slowly the torrent
subsided until I felt stable enough to try begin digesting
what had just happened to me.*

*There was one constant to all of what had happened
that day: magic and sorcery, two sides of the same coin.
Magic was the key, both to understanding my vision of
Anakhara and to my freedom. I replayed the moment
I had sensed and heard Navar's spell sparking to life in
my mind a hundred times in an attempt to ascertain why
the wards hadn't reacted. The answer, when it came,
was as shocking as it was simple. All magic, whether the
formulaic approach that humans took or the sorcery that
flowed through me had harmony at its heart. Vibration.
Music.*

*And like music, it has many forms. Some musicians sing,
while others play instruments. Some of those use lutes,
others harps, and each has its own range of pitches and
resonances that it can achieve. The ward stones were quite
simply attuned to react to anything outside of the range
that humans operated in.*

*From the skills I had seen displayed by Navar and his
students I doubted that any living mage retained the
knowledge or skill to craft ward stones with sufficient
precision to target any specific source of sorcery. Thus it
made perfect sense that rather than try to target anything
that they didn't want, they would simply deny everything
except the one source that they were familiar with. I
listened to Navar's magic again in my mind, and smiled in
the darkness as an idea took root.*

CHAPTER 21

I woke not long after sunrise to find Crow nudging me with a stick.

I swatted it away. 'What are you doing?'

'Just being careful. No one's ever told me how to wake one of you before.'

The fire had been relit, and a sweet smell rose from it. I sat up and peered into the pit, where a lattice of sticks supported what looked like a number of very large spiders.

'You like crab?' asked Crow, sitting down opposite.

'I don't know. They smell better than they look, I think.'

I had once been forced to eat goblins in order to survive, and while it was an experience I had sworn never to repeat, it had given me a far broader perspective to how bad things could taste.

'Freshwaters aren't as nice as salties, but they'll do.'

As it turned out, I liked the crunchiness and sweetness of crab. Crow tried to teach me how to crack the shells, and laughed when I simply ate them whole. Like eating hooves and bones, the shells fed a growing need within me, and were all the more satisfying for it. He was even kind enough to give me the broken shells from his portion.

We set off towards the west soon after, and even though the ground sloped gently downwards once more, it stayed firm and more or less dry underfoot, letting us keep a good pace. The food and night's rest seemed to have revived Crow and, despite his fragile appearance, he neither balked nor complained at the pace I set. Even more surprisingly, he still found the breath to ask me more questions as we walked, many of which were variations of 'Where's your tail?'

I ignored him as much as I could, something made easier by the grave nature of what Fronsac had told me. He had heard reports of the Lance from pitifully few survivors of the siege of Aknak, but had never dared to believe that the stories were true. Their stories of torture had been common enough to be believed, but amidst these piteous accounts were several about the strange rituals they had been forced to participate in. These rituals had involved a descent into a great pit beneath the cathedral, where they were bound with silver chains and forced to chant and dance about a terrible artefact that had pierced the heart of the city and gradually sucked the lives from those who approached it.

It was the reports of this artefact that had put the fear in Fronsac's mind, or at least the placement thereof, for the heart of that city was the great cathedral, a monolithic structure that had been built over a grove that was considered ancient long before men lost their tails and started building houses. When the 'heart' was pierced a strange gloom had fallen across the city and the countryside beyond its walls, and Fronsac had felt the current of the Songlines change, their thunder subsiding as if somehow dammed or diverted, something they had yet to recover from.

I knew enough now to realise that the heart of the city was also what he called a spirit well, but what I knew as a node or nexus, a junction of the Songlines that ran through the earth itself, mirroring the invisible currents above. The Lance that had been driven into it had somehow broken the flow of the energies, and it clearly continued to do so. There were no living witnesses to this final act, and scrying did not work either; by his account the last wizard to try that had been found with his eyes burned out and his body a dried husk.

If the lances were imbued with the power to disrupt or even permanently damage the nodes, the implications were even more terrifying than Fronsac's worst projections. He was considering the matter from the academic perspective of a wizard, an approach I felt precluded an appreciation of the real damage that poisoning the Songlines with negative energy could do. They weren't the linear conduits for magic that wizards envisaged when they drew their very neat and impressive geometric charts, but an essential component of life itself. Like a worm eating an apple from the inside out, their corruption would silently spread throughout this world, undermining everything until all that was left was ruin and death.

A dead world. The very thought stirred nothing but revulsion in me, but what would it be to a necromancer? Was that the dream that greeted Navar Louw whenever he closed his rancid little eyes? In a world where death was the rule and life the exception, he and his kind would be gods. It was insane, but then so was he. I had seen and felt it burning within him on the day I bested him for the first time.

I PRACTISED MIMICKING *Navar's magical signature for the rest of the night, no easy task when the ward stones nullified any trace of magic, forcing me to rely on my own hearing and memory to perfect it. The signature was only* one part of his magic, and without the other components it was like knowing the song of a thrush and then expecting to be able to fly like one. Our bodies were simply too different for me to try and replicate his magic as a whole. He was a lute, whereas I was a drum. We could play the same tune but it would always sound profoundly different, and that difference was what the wards were targeting.

What I had been hoping for was that his signature would blind the wards to the nature of my magic long enough for me to draw on it, like a fanfare from a marching band temporarily blending the sound of all the band's musicians into an whole. That had not happened yet, so either I was off key or I had simply been cut off from the Songlines for so long that I could no longer summon the meanest spark of energy. If that was true, my best chance would lie with me imposing myself into his spell as he cast it, creating enough of an echo that I could draw his own magic to me, effectively stealing it away from him.

I had never tried anything like it, and had no idea whether it would work, and spent no little time debating it with myself. It was the kind of theory that my beloved Anakhara would have loved to debate. She had always been far more curious and adventurous when it came to sorcery than me. I considered it a function of our bodies, as natural as breathing or flying, but for her it was always so much more. I remember how exasperated I would get when she would lie in the nest in the winter months, constructing endless chains of glowing lights and binding them to the walls until it looked like we were sleeping on the floor of some strange ocean of light. She would rest her head on my chest and stare at me with that smile until I couldn't help but laugh and let myself be swept away all over again.

I reluctantly shook the memories from my mind and

concentrated once more on Navar's signature, sending it out in the fading darkness time and time again until at last, the doors swung open and the mages entered amidst a thick beam of morning light. My primary heart skipped with excitement and I had to force myself to remain calm.

Navar walked in front of his chattering coven, his staff tapping against the floor with every other step. It might have been the anticipation, or perhaps another side effect of the priests' crumbling enchantments, but everything seemed more vivid that morning. The colours were brighter, edges and shadows more sharply defined, the sounds crisp and clear. The mages took up their usual positions, their conversations tapering off as they set out their books and ink-pots for another day of dragon torture. Their scent was thick with excitement, which was similar to fear but not as heady an aroma. If my courage held and my theory was sound, all of that would be changing before the day was out.

'Good morning,' boomed Navar, silencing the remaining chatter.

'Good morning, Master,' the new mages chimed in reply.

'Before you stands, or rather sits, the infamous Beast of Nagath, also known as the Dead Wind. I would warn you against passing beyond the warding posts; while intelligent, this creature retains a feral streak and has already killed two students and injured several more.'

I heard their indrawn breath and could almost feel their attention sharpen as they regarded me with renewed interest and, I hoped, awe.

'However, sometimes the pursuit of knowledge carries risk, and we are all here because we have accepted that fact.' He was pacing along the perimeter now, trailing his fingers across the whorls carved into the ward stones. 'Now. Consider the histories you have studied, most notably the descriptions of the Night of Fire, wherein the scribe Castell describes the creature as "a vast shape with wings twice the length of a dromadar. 'For those of you unfamiliar with the term, it simply refers to a very common type of trading ship, the forerunners of today's clippers.' He turned to me. 'Beast, spread your wings.'

I hesitated, then complied. It gave me a chance to warm my muscles for what I hoped lay ahead.

'So. The beast before you, while undoubtedly the same as he was describing, is neither vast nor gifted with wings twice the length of a ship.'

Not for much longer, I thought, making sure that my smile did not reach my face. Navar was starting his lesson in earnest now, the topic being of course transmogrification. Or, 'how to trick a dragon into fitting into an enchanted cage'. A lesson which I hoped would shortly be followed by 'how to be killed by a dragon that is no longer transmogrified'.

I took a deep breath and exhaled slowly, calming myself. I desperately wanted to test my theory, but as much as I wanted to make that bid for freedom, I was also beset by a plague of worries about the possible consequences if my timing was off, or my theory was flawed. Should I build my strength and practice a bit more, risking further injury and humiliation at Navar's hand, or did I gamble everything there and then and save myself months, perhaps years, of further torment?

If I waited, there was a chance that familiarity and false kindness would become a more effective prison than these ward stones would ever be, quietly erasing my dreams and memories until I was little more than a cumbersome pet.

'Beast! Pay attention!' Navar's voice snapped me from my thoughts and I turned towards his voice.

'I asked you to extend your arm. Now do it.'

I obeyed, stretching my arm out to the side, then stared at him as he crossed the boundary and stepped into the pit. He was talking about measurements and compression ratios, but I wasn't paying any real attention.

He was in the pit, and my decision had just been made for me.

My heartbeat surged and my senses sharpened as they hadn't in the centuries of my imprisonment. A hundred scents flooded my nose and I could hear the soft crump of the sawdust compressing beneath his feet and my bulk, the rasp of turning pages and a dozen whispered conversations from the watching mages. I had to act now. This was the moment.

It was crucial that Navar used his magic while he was in the pit. I couldn't initiate any of my own, not while I was cut off from my sorcery. His magic was the spark my kindling needed. If he stepped beyond the ward stones before he cast, their nullifying field would most likely distort the tenuous connection I was hoping to create, leaving me exposed and quite likely never to have the same chance again, assuming of course that I survived the punishment that would follow.

Navar was close enough to rap his staff against the ridge that protected my forearms, hard at work talking comparative mass, his arrogance almost tangible. He was close enough that he wouldn't have had much chance of avoiding what I did next even on a normal day.

I twitched my arm inward, hard enough to rip the staff from his hands – I needed him to use his magic, not the staff's – and to send him sprawling another few precious feet away from the perimeter.

The students reacted with a sharp, indrawn breath, such a uniform reaction that anyone listening from the outside would have sworn that it came from a single creature.

Navar rolled to his feet, shock and anger contorting his face beneath its coating of sawdust. He reacted with all of the anger I had hoped to rouse, his face contorting as he called one of his electrical barrage spells into being. The sensory pits in my jaw felt the current of his magic swell. He snapped the spell into being and I vocalised his spell signature.

Too late. I knew I'd missed the timing as soon as I spoke it.

Lightning raked my shoulders, the intensity of it shocking. I had not realised it before, nor credited him with any real finesse, but it was clear that up until now he had been holding back as to what his full capacity was. The barrage rolled over me with several times more force than anything he'd unleashed previously. This was his full, killing magic. There would be no second chances after today.

I gritted my teeth and fought the pain. Once it might have crippled me, but as his magic had grown stronger, so too had my tolerance. Even so, I would not be able to withstand much punishment at that intensity. I had to stay sharp. He was drawing more magic, and it was a fair guess that his students would start defending their teacher at any moment too. His magic gathered, and I had to fight hard not to be distracted by the weird colours that were bleeding into his aura.

He loosed his spell, and I coughed out his spell signature.

Time seemed to slow. I felt something tug at my mind and heard a strange buzzing sound like a thousand ruptured wasp nests, then I felt it. Magic. Like desert sand absorbing the rain so long denied to it, I pulled the magic from Navar. Through him. I felt it course into me, both familiar and strange at the same time. It wasn't as pure as sorcery, but it was magic. Power.

I saw the construction of the spell unfold in my mind as it broke apart into its constituent parts before coalescing into the shape he'd crafted once more, but now under my control. And in that moment, I felt the press of his mind against my own, the touch of it cold and utterly alien, the thoughts that filled it a cacophony of gibbering and howling voices. It was gone as quickly as it happened.

I turned, pointed my arm at the standing stone closest to where his students were standing, and released his spell. A trio of force bolts flickered into being in my palm and flashed through the air. The first missed the stone and found one of his students instead, bursting him like a grape. The second and third struck the stone. It swayed, but remained standing; the wards anchored upon it rippled but remained intact, the dead student's blood sizzling against the now glowing whorls upon it.

Navar was circling away from me, his brows furrowed. I knew that I couldn't give him time to think, and so bared my teeth and lunged towards him, the very real desire to kill him making the feint entirely believable. He reacted by reflex, firing off another of his prepared spells.

I snatched the spell from him, his signature spilling from my lips with more confidence now. I channelled it along my arm and sent the energy whip he'd prepared snapping forward, wrapping its glittering length around the same ward stone I'd loosened with the force bolts. With a single, hard pull I ripped the menhir from the ground like a rotten tooth from a gum, almost crushing him with it.

Yellow-green lightning flashed and crackled between the remaining stones as the circle was broken, jagged lines of power discharging into the air and scything through his students. Chaos erupted around me, and amidst the smoke and flames I launched myself from the pit and landed amongst the remaining students. Using Navar's magic had left a slippery nausea in my gut, a shadow of the revulsion I had experienced when he'd used his mind control to move me into the pit, but I forced it away. This wasn't the time for introspection.

I hit the students with the full measure of my current strength, laying into them with balled fists, teeth and tail. I found Abyon amongst them, desperately trying to organise a defence. He soiled himself as I snagged him by the ankles and lifted him high.

'Time to die,' I growled, taking a leg in each hand.

I tightened my grip and, twisting slightly, pulled him apart from anus to ribs and tossed him aside to die in his own filth. They all screamed then, and kept screaming as I broke their bones and hammered them with my fists and tail, the smell of blood and faeces swamping the glorious scent of their terror. Hot lightning scored a hissing groove across my flank and I spun towards my attacker. Navar!

A dozen or so students stood behind him, their voices droning as they prepared their most deadly attacking spells. To reach them, I would need to enter the pit again, something that I wanted to avoid at all costs. Armed guards and yet more mages were pouring into the building from a side door. I couldn't risk being cornered, and as much as I wanted to even the score with Navar, it was nothing compared to my bone deep need to escape.

I turned and ran towards the doors, trampling a few more men before I smashed the doors open and stumbled out into the glorious warmth of the sun, protective membranes sliding over my eyes, muting the sudden glare. There were a dozen or so men outside the building, all staring at me with open mouths and wide eyes.

I didn't wait for them to gather their senses and instead turned towards the east and began to run. My muscles weren't used to this level of effort but I had to get as far *from the university as I could before they could organise a pursuit. I was perhaps a league from the university when I realised that I was free. The sun was shining, and I was running free.*

I threw my head back and roared at the glory of it, sending a nearby flock of fat little sheep running in all directions, bleating for all they were worth. I snatched three of the slower ones up and loped eastwards.

CHAPTER 22

THE CRACK OF a cane against my head shattered the memories and I staggered to the side, my fists coming up.

'Damn you, listen to me!'

I righted myself and stared down at Crow. 'What do you think you're doing?'

'By the gods, haven't you heard a word I've said?'

'No.'

'Look, damn you.' He thrust a bony finger over my shoulder, back in the direction of the Penullin camp.

The clouds, which had begun to disperse since the wizard's most recent assault on Falkenburg were now gathering over their camp again, their shapes twisting and rolling upon each other as if driven by hurricane winds from every side. A series of flashes illuminated the purple and green undertone of their mass from within as I watched. There was something mesmerising, and almost organic about the way they rolled over each other, and I felt the stirrings of something within me. I dragged my gaze away and stepped closer to Crow, blocking his line of sight to it.

'Don't look at it.'

He swayed but remained standing. 'What is it?'

'Nothing good,' I said, holding a finger to his lips to

silence the protest he was already forming. He swatted my hand away but kept his teeth together. 'That is the work of their necromancers. They are preparing a terrible weapon, and I fear our time to stop them is nearly spent.'

'What kind of weapon does that?' He turned and spat. 'And what can we possibly do?'

The urge to turn and stare at the cloud pulled at me, but I kept my back to it. 'We keep walking for now.'

'Where to?'

It was a fine question. *Where was I going?* Whichever way I turned there seemed to be more questions and enemies, with no answers in sight, only strife and doom. I had no doubt now that Navar's lances were the greatest threat, far more so than a lost prince, tainted paladins, and the fall of cities. A few dead humans weren't my concern, since they'd simply start breeding again as they always did once the dust settled, but if the power of the lances was half as catastrophic as I feared it could be, there would be nothing left to live or fight for.

I had no doubt that I could kill Navar, but killing him wouldn't be enough if the lances remained. I needed to end him and destroy his works and everything they represented. I had to break the lances' power, and to do that, I needed to understand their power in order to fight it.

'What's that about Aknak?' asked Crow.

'I was thinking out loud,' I said.

'Well, don't stop on my account,' he said, so I didn't. He was garrulous and annoying, but he was also good at listening, and there was nothing to lose given that he already knew my gravest secret.

'They used a similar weapon at Aknak. If I am to destroy it, I need to understand it, so I am of a mind to go there and do just that.'

'Aknak is a ghoul- and Penullin-infested ruin that glows at night, and is surrounded by an entire army. An army which, I might add, chooses to camp outside the city walls.'

'You know it then?'

'I know what I heard. There was a massacre when the city fell, but the way I hear it, the dead and buried are the lucky ones. Everyone who was there is dead.'

'Not everyone,' I said, reaching for my sorcery with new vigour. I had made a decision, and even though the challenges and horrors ahead remained daunting, having a purpose buoyed my spirit. I melded the sorcery into what I needed then released it.

'You know someone?'

'I do.'

'Who?'

'The last scion of Aethbert Henkman,' I replied. 'She was there, right to the last.'

He made a show of looking around. 'So where is this hero?'

'I must find and rescue her.'

'She a princess then?' he asked, cackling wetly and leaning on his cane as his bony chest shook with laughter.

'Not quite, but I'll make an exception.'

'Nice of you,' he said.

I ignored him and closed my eyes so that I could focus on the feel of my sorcery racing away from me, skimming across grass, and ponds, and the boulders that broke the ground like the bones of some great, buried beast. It passed over the myriad of small creatures hiding, feeding and killing in their own hidden world, making some of them pause and sniff the air in bewilderment. And then, when my hope and focus were both being eroded by distance and the cost of spreading my sorcery so wide, I felt a gentle tug against the rolling flow of the sorcery. I narrowed the spread of my net and swept it back through the area again. The trace was small, but it was all I needed. I knew where they had taken her from, so now I knew the direction they were heading in.

'That way,' I said, pointing to the south.

'South's a good a direction these days I suppose.' He started walking. 'Might as well get started.'

'You offer no protest?' I asked.

'Would you listen?'

'You are most astute.'

Where the terrain allowed we walked side by side for most of the day, Crow pointing out various edible plants and growing excited over a type of bird he hadn't seen for many years. He didn't press me with as many questions, and seemed happy enough that I answered the few that I did. It was actually fairly companionable despite the occasional swarm of stinging flies, which made it all the more disappointing when I scented men on the breeze. I slowed our pace and drew a deeper breath.

'There are men some way ahead of us. At least a dozen.' A dozen did not trouble me overmuch, but I also did not want to trigger a pursuit. 'We'll need to keep off the known paths,' I said. 'How well do you know this country from your travels?'

'Um. It's not really my patch, see. This close to the city, folk are spoilt by the choice of traders. Most of my work is further out, where a copper pot and a sharp knife is still a cause for some excitement.'

'You can make knives sharp again?'

'Not anymore. Those bastards took my stuff.' He spat into the grass, but without his usual venom.

'A pity. Mine could do with sharpening.'

He was strangely quiet for a while after that, but I

wasn't about to complain about that. I paid more heed to my surroundings now, and I kept our path amongst the wild hedgerows and ditches where I could. We were in an area that the Penullin forces controlled now, and while we avoided their ambush, that sort of encounter could draw unwanted attention. I set a careful pace, or at least I thought I had until Crow's strength gave out late in the afternoon. He'd abandoned the stolen robes when we had stopped for a rushed lunch and had seemed to recover, but by the time the sun was dipping towards the horizon his pace had slowed dramatically and his breathing sounded wet and throaty. He didn't protest when I picked him up, and dozed off as I carried him. He didn't weigh much, and I quickly caught up some of the time that his weakness had cost us.

I stopped sometime after the last traces of the sunset had sunk into the west and set him down in a small clearing I had chosen for our night's camp. He didn't wake, and I let him sleep while I sent out my sorcerous snares and drew in some small game that I quickly despatched. The previous night's meal had been enough to satisfy the debt I owed healing my shoulder but little else, and as a result I was positively ravenous. I set aside a portion for Crow, then set about eating the remaining game from snout to tail, leaving me sticky with their blood but feeling almost whole again.

So fortified, I was about to settle down for some well deserved sleep when I felt a painful, stabbing pain saw through my chest. I fell to my knees, vainly clutching at my breastbone, momentarily confused when I didn't find an arrow sticking out of it, for that is how it felt. The pain rippled through me in waves, but it was only when my sorcery woke in response to it that I recognised the sensation.

Tatyana was hurt once more, and grievously so if the healing enchantment was pulling so greedily at my sorcery. It pulsed twice more, pulling hungrily at my power, heedless of the pain that lanced through me.

The connection between us was an accident, an unexpected side effect of me having rushed to save her life after she was stabbed in the heart. I had worried when it pulsed this strongly before I left the city, but that paled in comparison to what I felt now. Until now, it had never drawn on so much of my sorcery, not even when that insect Polsson had set her on fire, and until that moment I had not thought to wonder what the full implications of having bound her to me might be. How would it feel if she died? What would that do to the enchantment, given that not even I knew the full scope of it? Would it keep drawing power even though she was gone, like a wound that would never stop bleeding? Another pulse hammered through me and, like the final blow that breaks a dam, I felt my sorcery respond to it with greater force, so much so that for a few brief moments the filament of energy that joined us materialised as a line of golden energy streaking towards the south, curved like a rainbow.

A rainbow. Rainbows have beginnings and ends, and as the glowing line faded I jumped to my feet and traced it across the darkening sky. She was not that far away, perhaps ten or so miles as I judged the curve and fall of it. The connection was still pulsing, but not as powerfully as before. Whatever had happened to her had stopped, for now, but the amount of energy she had drawn was enormous. If whatever had hurt her didn't kill her, the deficit of energy in her body once the sorcery had healed her wounds surely would.

I moved back to Crow and whispered a farewell into his ear, lacing my words with sorcery so that he would remember them when he woke. He had been kind to me, this wizened little figure with a face like a disappointed walnut, and I felt a stab of remorse at leaving him like this. I left him what food remained, as well as one of my knives, then turned south and coaxed my tired legs into a run.

CHAPTER 23

TEN MILES. ONCE upon a time I would have flown that distance with barely a beat of my wings, the warm air carrying me as if I was no heavier than a feather. Now those ten miles felt endless, and if I'd had the breath to spare I would have spent it cursing.

Some three miles from where I had left Crow the land began to rise towards a series of the dark ridges that only seemed to get taller as I forced myself forward. I liked hills and mountains, but I liked them more when I wasn't trying to run up them. My last meal was sitting heavily in my stomach long before my pace withered to an enthusiastic walk, the pitiless slope sapping the strength from my legs.

I could smell men on the wind as I entered the foothills and forced myself to stop and rest. I had no idea where the trail would lead me to, and I'd suffered enough to know that a little caution could go a long way. Once I had my breath back I moved off the path, making the most of my night vision to avoid loose rocks and the worst of the tough, spiky shrubs that carpeted the hillside. Sound carries almost as well as firelight in the dark, and I gave the guard posts a wide berth, moving around their camps quietly, the darkness and jumble of rocks providing ample cover for my dark hide. Whenever I slowed, the pull of the sorcery reminded me why I was forcing this pace on myself. Every mote of power that Tatyana was siphoning from me came with a price to be paid, even if she wasn't doing it of her own volition. I had been tortured by Navar and his kind before, but I could not imagine they were visiting the same upon her, not unless they intended to kill her outright. But then, I had yet to find the limits of human cruelty.

There was little to be gained by such imaginings though and I forced myself to concentrate on the road ahead. I passed two more sets of guards, both far more vigilant than those lower down the slopes, so much so that I had to use a little sorcery to distract them. Less than a mile beyond these I finally had sight of what the trail had led me to. I had been expecting a fortified camp or perhaps a castle, but nothing like what I saw before me. It was a fortress spanning the base of a towering cliff, but carved into the very rock. There were no walls to scale, only a single, recessed gate of black iron and a series of narrow windows. Some sixty paces in front of this was a stone palisade lit by numerous lanterns burning with the distinctive silvery light of a wizard's touch, and all but infested with soldiers and archers. Distractions and a midnight hide weren't going to be enough.

I settled deeper in the shadows between two boulders and watched the comings and goings of the soldiers. By my reckoning it was fast approaching the middle of the night, which didn't leave much time until the sun stripped away the darkness I was relying on. Below where I was nestled I heard a gang of men moving along one of the three paths that converged on the fortress, the wind carrying enough of their conversation for me to know they were tired and hungry but relieved to be back without having any wounded. I hunkered forward as they passed under my hiding place, listening with new interest. It seemed they were not alone in the hills and the patrols were more than just a precaution, for while the armies of Krandin had retreated, there were still smaller groups hiding in the hills and forests and making a nuisance of themselves. I watched as the patrol was welcomed back, and then shortly a new group of men marched out the same way the others had come, magically enhanced lights peeling back the shadows around them.

They were clearly expecting to be attacked, and it seemed a shame to disappoint them. I left the hole I'd been lurking in and followed them from above until they were out of sight of the fortress but not out of earshot, then gathered my sorcery.

The first of them died before he even knew it, the rock burning his head like an overripe fruit. The man had time to bark a strangled warning before my next projectile lifted him from his feet and flipped him backwards into the rock wall. They scattered towards what cover the broken rocks at the edge of the road offered. The next few rocks missed, but after the third man went down, one of the soldiers at the rear burst out of cover and began sprinting back towards the fortress. The handful of rocks hovering next to me vibrated in anticipation as I toyed with the idea of turning my sorcery on him, but I let him go. I wanted to kick the ant's nest, not simply kill a few ants. I released another pulse as several heads poked up from the rocks below, the energy flexing and sending a fist-sized shard screaming off the rock the man was hiding behind, sending them all back into cover. I turned to the last pair of rocks and finalised my preparations.

'Surrender or die!' I called down the slope, which elicited a barrage of cursing in reply. One the braver ones pointed the wizard's lantern towards me and I ducked behind a boulder as the silvery beam lanced upwards. I launched a couple of rocks down and was rewarded with a cry of pain as the light spun wildly away.

I turned back the way I'd come and made my way back around the hillside to where I could watch the fortress. The ants were swarming by the time I had settled back in between the boulders, and as I watched a group of about fifty ran back along the road, a pair of wizards just about visible amidst their ranks. I knew it wouldn't take them overlong to reach the others but it felt longer, so much so that I started wondering if I'd set my trap properly. Had I been too hasty? I had just resolved to go back when I felt the feathery ripple of my sorcery discharging and sighed in relief even as the sound of men screaming echoed along the roadway. A horn sounded from the palisade and even more men spilled from the fortress doors, not a few of them still fastening their helmets and belts.

I called my sorcery as I moved along the rocks, while their commanders shouted at them to hurry up. Once I was as close to where the palisade met the cliff face as I dared to go I released the construct in a single wave. All along the palisade the lanterns, both mundane and magical, flickered and fell dark in the wake of that wave, which really set the soldiers to shouting and a frenzy of horn-blowing. I rushed forward, trusting to the darkness and their night blindness to hide me, and launched myself over the wall.

The landing wasn't the best I'd ever had, but nothing broke so it wasn't the worst either. I could see the men closest to where I'd hit the ground looking towards me but didn't have time to waste. I turned and ran towards the still open gates of the fortress itself, setting my shoulder and weight as the sentries posted before them turned towards the sound of my footfalls.

I think the impact only killed the first of them, but I smashed through and suddenly my feet were sliding on smoother stone. I skidded to a halt and hurriedly swung the doors shut, another of Tatyana's favourite curses falling unbidden from my lips.

It took longer than I had expected for they were far heavier than I had imagined, forcing me to use another blast of sorcery to keep the soldiers back until I could get them shut. The lights inside the fortress flared back to life as I was straining to lower the equally heavy locking bar. Once it was down the gates would hold firm, with a fair proportion of the fortress's population now locked out. As a plan, it wasn't without its flaws, but it was a start.

One of those flaws was that there were still a fair number of soldiers in the fortress, at least a score of which were staring at me as the wizards' lamps flared back to life, reducing the shadows that had hidden me to a few narrow ribbons. I slapped my hand against the metal bar that held the gates and channelled a measure of power into it, shaping into fire as it flowed through me. I kept my hand in place as the realisation that I was a foe finally penetrated their bewilderment. They shouted threats and shook their weapons as they advanced past broken, faceless statues, but I stayed as I was until they were only a few paces away.

There was little choice but to charge them. I picked one at random and threw myself at him, batting his suddenly hesitant spear thrust aside and chopping my hand into the side of his neck a moment before my shoulder lifted him from his feet and sent him skidding across the stone. A sword bit my back, but I didn't stop. Another fell to my fists, then another. Ants were effective as a swarm, but not so much when they were separated and acting as individuals. They could still bite though, and by the

FIRESKY

time I pulled my talons out of the last of them the blood dripping from me was not all theirs.

I hurried through the single doorway that led from the chamber, pausing only to reassure myself that the locking bar was now fused to the doors.

200

CHAPTER 24

I RACED DOWN the stairs that lay beyond the far doorway and found myself at the head of a short but unexpectedly tall gallery supported by four square columns, the eroded carvings that covered them hidden beneath the soot of a thousand greasy torches. Two doorways were visible beyond the columns, and I moved forward cautiously, blood dripping from my still extended talons. The empty beds and scattered possessions told me these were the guardrooms that my gambit in the hills had just emptied and I moved along quickly as the sound of human voices echoed from the doorway on the far side of the gallery. My claws found good purchase on the textured columns and I scrambled upwards.

Torchlight flooded the gallery as a dozen men burst in not long after, spreading out to fill the gallery. The grey-haired man at the head of the little mob was shouting angrily for someone to tell him what was happening but they all fell silent as they jogged up the stairs and into the entrance hall. I remained where I was as a handful of men retreated into the gallery, their now drawn blades gleaming in the ruddy light of the torches they held. I didn't much care for the smell of burning pitch, but perched where I was between the crowns of two of the columns I had little choice but to endure the stench. As usual, none of them looked up, which suited my purposes. Several more of them entered the gallery, all armed to the teeth, but I waited until most were under me, before extinguishing their torches.

I fell amongst them in the ensuing confusion, snapping more than a few bones as I landed on them, my weight and speed ensuring that it was a very uneven contest. I lit my eyes and growled, stoking their fear and panic. Swords whistled and cut both air and flesh, and most of that wasn't mine. By the time the remaining handful of soldiers came running in I was the only one left standing, and apparently I was quite the apparition as two of them fled back to the entrance hall while the other three tried to run past me and deeper into the fortress. I killed one of these with a thrown sword but didn't bother chasing the others. I was built for strength and endurance, and the turn of speed that their fear lent them meant the effort would be wasted.

I headed up the stairs and to where the two men were desperately hacking at the lock on the fortress door. Their cries became quite pitiful as I approached. One launched a wild attack as I reached for him and I slapped him to the ground.

'Tell me where she is,' I said, lifting the last, whimpering figure by his mail shirt and pinning him to the doors. His squeals fell silent as he met my gaze and my sorcery lanced into his mind.

It took a few moments to tear through his scattered thoughts and token struggles before he told me what I needed to know. I crushed his neck and let him fall to the floor as I considered what I had seen and felt in his dying mind. The fortress was actually a repurposed temple, and the soldiers were limited to the entrance hall first two chambers. At the end of the second gallery stood a gate that only the wizards and their doomed prisoners dared to pass beyond. That was a relief in that it meant I wouldn't be wandering along miles of tunnels, but what gave me pause was the depth of terror that had bloomed in his mind when I had made him think about entering the inner chambers. Even his imminent death had not generated such fear, and as I saw it that could mean only one thing: magic. Or, perhaps more accurately, necromancy. I gathered up a pair of knives that were almost long enough to be small swords and headed back towards the gallery and the inner chambers that lay beyond.

I could smell the other soldiers where they had hidden themselves in one of the four rooms off the second gallery, but with their scent ripe with fear and little else I left them to their skulking. The centre of the second gallery was dominated by a gently bubbling spring that filled an oblong pool that had several more broken statues rising from the dark waters. Satisfied that I was alone, I paused to drink my fill and then rinse the worst of the gore from my face and arms. The nearest of the statues watched me with the remaining half of its face, and I wondered who or what it was supposed to represent.

The entrance to the inner chambers wasn't hard to find, for even without my night vision the smell of the rotting skulls stacked around it would have been a beacon. Beyond these lay an unlit passage, as dark as only a cave could be. These rocks had never known the touch of the sun and the bone deep chill that emanated from them felt ancient and hostile. I moved to wall next to the skulls and laid my hand on the rock as I reached out to the Songlines.

I smiled in the dark as I felt their echo almost immediately. This cave had been turned into a temple to man's insipid gods in what they no doubt referred to as ancient times, but compared to the age of the mountains it was barely the blink of an eye. Their rituals and magics had left little residue upon the uncaring rocks, and anchored to the bones of the world as the chambers were, they were still strongly connected to the Great Song and I gratefully absorbed some of that raw energy through the stone. So fortified, I set some protective wards on myself and stepped through the gate of skulls.

I hadn't gone very far before I began to appreciate that the cold pooled within it was sharper than the cold air of a cave should be. As a creature born of fire, little short of a blizzard should bother me, yet this made my skin prickle and I could feel an incipient shiver building within me. It was not unlike the touch of dark magic I had felt in Cardinal Polsson's dungeon and I carefully drew a sorcerous veil across my vision. The dim outlines my night vision showed me shivered and swam out of focus for a few moments, but once the transition passed I could not help but gasp at the sight that greeted me.

It wasn't the cold chilling me, but the touch of hundreds of disembodied spirits that swam through the air, each no more than the vaguest suggestion of a distended human face or skull. They hung and swirled in the air like leaves caught in a turbulent river, too weak to even control the direction they floated in and entirely mindless. They were drawn to the life burning within me like moths to a flame, gnashing their ghostly teeth whenever they were close enough. Like the moth's suicidal infatuation with flame, it was a deadly game they played. They were the barest imprints of whoever they had once been, held together by slender filaments of negative energy leftover from the separation of soul and body at death, and those that managed to siphon off some of my positive energy were destroyed by it, not that it stopped them from trying. I made to move along through them, but if anything the air seemed to thicken the further I went until they were numerous enough that it felt like I was walking through frozen cobwebs and I could no longer see the floor or walls through their pale shapes.

There were dozens of them gnawing at me now with their ethereal teeth, enough so that for every ten that melted away, at least one resisted the dissolution and instead seemed to grow stronger for it. I didn't care for that at all, and in a moment of haste made the unfortunate decision to burn several of them away with a flash of sorcery, overloading their wispy bodies with positive energy until they disintegrated into glittering particles. These burned holes in some but excited the others into a frenzy and they pressed in, their sheer numbers giving them momentum as they sawed at me with their unearthly teeth, burying their faces in my flesh where they could.

Unlike the soldiers who had been forced to camp here I wasn't afraid of dead men or their spirits, but even I was taken aback by the sheer density of the deceased that were emerging around me. It was as if someone had opened a gateway to the world of the dead, a thought that carried an unpleasant resonance given who Tatyana had been taken prisoner by.

I pushed the thought aside as the swarm closed in once more and dismissed the veil of sorcery from my vision. It had shown me what I needed to know but the press of souls was blinding me. They vanished from sight, but I could still feel them on me like a burning itch. The problem was that I didn't actually have a real idea of how to get rid of them.

My sorcery could destroy them, but it also fed them and, if these fools had indeed pried the world of the dead open, there was also a very real chance that it would also serve to draw even more of them to me. What was more worrying than any damage they could inflict was how they would latch onto any sorcery that I tried to use, sucking the energy away as soon as it materialised. I discovered this when I tried to reach out to Tatyana and instead only felt the cold intensify before the pulse of sorcery I had released withered and faded. I muttered a curse and pressed on, doing my best to ignore the incessant sensation of their spirit teeth gnawing at me.

The passageway that linked the inner and outer chambers wasn't very long, but any hope that it would bring some relief from the dead was short lived. The passage emptied into a large, pyramidal chamber whose walls were lined with yet more skulls, some of which were still gleaming wetly in the flickering light of the torches that were set amongst them. Fragments of bone littered the floor, giving it the look of a troll's lair. *At least it didn't smell as bad.* I smiled at the thought and walked on towards the narrow but dramatically decorated exit on the far side, bone snapping and crunching under my feet on every step. I was almost halfway across when a skull smashed to the ground ahead of me, followed soon after by two more.

I stopped and looked up, but even then I only saw it when it moved again. At first glance it resembled a gigantic version of the crabs that Crow had cooked, but then it scuttled down the wall and into the torchlight and I found myself staring at it as my mind fought the realisation of what it was. In the simplest sense, it looked like someone had melted a score or more humans into a single mass without any care for where one ended and another began. It landed with a jarring thump that sent more skulls tumbling to the floor and screamed pain and hunger at me from a dozen or more mouths.

I had seen many things in the aeons I had lived in this

world, but nothing had ever prepared me for such a thing. I was still staring at it like a village idiot when it started pulling itself towards me, its malformed legs folding in too many places and bloodied drool spooling from its many mouths. I could feel the pain and hatred emanating from it, but it was the touch of the dark magic that commanded it that finally broke my paralysis.

I threw myself back as a leg swung at me, the splintered bone that dotted it as sharp as any spear. The knives I'd been so proud of now seemed small and impotent, but I drew them anyway, yet barely had time to weigh them in my hands before its leg bent back on itself and smashed into me.

I felt the bony shards pierce my side, the weight of its twisted limb driving them deep. Several scraped against my own ribs, which thankfully turned them, but others drove into my gut and tore ragged gouges as the impact sent me rolling across the floor in a shower of splintered bone. It was only as I was laying there trying to remember how to breathe that I realised the creature didn't have a recognisable head, but did have a multitude of eyes, so it didn't need to turn to face me. It screamed with a dozen voices as it began moving again.

I pulled myself to my feet, teeth gritted against the pain that flared along my right side, eliciting another howl from it that I took to be disappointment. It scuttled forward, two arms unfolding from beneath the mass of its body. Where its legs were dotted with bone spears, these were positively bristling with them. I drew my sorcery to me, but it came sluggishly, the flow of it diffused by the press of unseen spirits that my blood had drawn. I summoned more of it, enough to burn its way through the spirits, giving the air a golden sheen for a brief moment.

The power settled inside me, but drawing amidst the multitude of spirits had taken too long. It had kept my attention for too long and before I could shape it that nightmare creature was upon me, a bony club sweeping my legs out from under me. It screamed and howled as more blows rained down, battering my arms aside and finally landing one that turned my world black.

The Private Annals of Tiberius Talgoth, Archmage

THE CRUSADE WAS soon underway, though from the pomp and gaiety that surrounded it you would think that all have forgotten that barely a year has passed since the beast transformed King Jorak and his army into so much charcoal. Aethbert has been given a sword by the Church elders, a potent weapon indeed, and now carries himself like a strutting peacock. It is quite ludicrous but also a fine diversion, letting me continue my research without disturbance amidst the camp followers that the crusade has attracted.

The discovery of the ruin of Jorak's army was however a potent reminder for the crusaders as to the nature of their task. I had not seen such devastation for a very long time. The dead lay in great heaps amidst the churned and scorched ground, their bodies little more than blackened caricatures of men, twisted into nightmares by the fires that burned them and turned their weapons into gleaming veins of melted iron and bronze.

The chill of death was imprinted on the land, a lingering frostbite left by the beast having forced so many souls through the gateway at once. The study of the lingering energies was fascinating, and it was my habit of working through the bitter watches of the night that afforded me my first glimpse of the beast.

I was quietly studying the rate of decay of the energies surrounding a camp girl's corpse when I became aware that I was being watched, a sensation I'd heard from many others but never experienced myself. I stood and, as if willing me to see it, the shadows to the east thinned and I saw the dragon sitting there, its head rising as high as my tower. Awe and terror gripped me as it spread its wings and, with a single gust of wind, took to the sky with the nimbleness of a sparrow.

Henkman issued his challenge the next morning, a magnificent spectacle of trumpets and flags. The priests used their parlour tricks to cast his voice as loud as that of a young god so that it filled the valley and I could almost see the glow of his belief shining from him and his men as he stood there, and perhaps for the first time I started to think that there was some worth in this new cult of his.

But then his challenge was answered.

A wall of wind struck the army like a hurricane, tearing the fancy pennants from their lances and silencing the trumpets. The dragon's roar hit us like a great tempest, a sound of such fury that the stones about us danced on the earth and several score horses went mad with the sound, bucking their riders and trampling many others in their bid to flee. The spirit of the moment was shattered, and I knew that the beast would be soon be upon us.

I moved up the slope, away from the massed ranks, ignoring the jeers of those I left behind. I'd barely begun the first of my spells when I sensed its approach, first by the drawing of magic and then by the growing cries of the men below. It flew over us with a speed I had never imagined possible, so fast that its gold-edged scales were a single, gleaming blur and not one arrow loosed by the archers found its mark. A wave of mist followed it, unnoticed by most below as they watched it flare its wings and rise towards the sun once more.

I saw it though, and I was trying to understand what it was as it settled across the archers with an oily sheen. They noticed it then, but it was too late. The mist burst into flame in a single roiling sheet of flame, as if the very air we breathed was ablaze. The sucking roar of the combustion was almost loud enough to drown the sound of two hundred men or more burning to death together.

The beast did not attack again, but flew over us with long strokes of its bat-like wings, a display of superiority that not even the dullest amongst them could fail to understand. The carnage of that one pass was astounding, and the swift passing of so many men filled me with raw power unlike anything that my experiments had yielded at that point. Perhaps my senses had been heightened by the sudden influx of so much energy, but I could see the energy surrounding the dragon, trailing in its wake like golden smoke. It was no spell, but seemed to be a natural product of its very existence, as if magic was part of its very essence, as if it were a source rather than a mere channel for it.

What wonders could I accomplish with such power? I knew Henkman would never retreat, so I had one more chance to make it mine and set to preparing my spells for the second attack with a new and ferocious urgency. The dragon was meant for me, and was too important to be slain.

CHAPTER 25

'IT'S ALIVE.'

The words were spoken in answer to the pained groan that escaped my lips as I realised the same thing. I wasn't sure I wanted to be, for the creature had not been kind to me. All I wanted to do was sleep, but now that my mind had stirred, the pain found its way in and made that all but impossible. My noise was clear, so I feigned sleep as best I could and tried to concentrate on the scents and sounds around me.

It didn't take a very deep breath to know that I was once more in the grip of wizards. The bitter, burnt spice odour of their magic was thick here, competing only with the oily stench of necromancy. That taint was more than just physical though and I forced myself to push through it, to try and sift out the smells it blanketed like a layer of oil upon cleaner water beneath. Men and women shared this space, at least two score of them, all afraid and several bleeding. There was food too, which cheered me despite the wounds oozing blood across my limbs and torso. The scent of the wizards strengthened as they approached me.

A staff cracked down across my face and dispelled any pretence of sleep as I lurched upwards, straining against the bonds that held me.

'So it is,' said a new voice to my right. He seemed tall from where I lay strapped to what I guessed was a repurposed table, and aside from having a pointed beard he was otherwise unremarkable as men went. He was wearing blue robes, the material shimmering in the cold light that filled the chamber. 'But then it was always resilient.'

Eight other wizards stood around me, forming a rough circle, at least half of whom were tainted with necromancy. No others wore blue or purple robes, which made the Pointy Beard the most senior of them. I frowned as the import of his words finally penetrated my fogged mind.

'Do you remember me now, Beast?' he asked, leaning on his ebon staff as he looked down at me.

There was something familiar about his scent but I couldn't place it, nor did I have any particular desire to do so. I didn't bother replying other than to sigh wearily for I was heartily sick and tired of men and everything that went with them.

'I think that's a no,' said another of the wizards, prompting a round of laughter from the others.

'You killed my brother,' said Blue Robes, shooting a glare at whoever had spoken. 'And I'm going to enjoy making you suffer until my Master arrives to take possession of you once more.'

'You all look the same,' I said, my voice thick. 'Tell me, did he scream?'

He cursed and lashed out with his staff, catching my jaw a solid blow but doing little real damage.

'I'll take that as a yes.'

'Brave words,' he hissed. 'For something that howled so piteously under our spells.'

A piece of the puzzle fell into place for me. 'So you were at the university.'

'Correct,' he said, baring his teeth in an unconvincing smile. 'And I would hear *your* screams again.'

'There's no time for these games. Leave it. It's not going anywhere and we have to complete the next binding in this cycle.'

It was the same man who'd spoken before, and Blue Robes looked as if he were going to lash out again but took a step back, his knuckles white as he gripped his staff.

'Watch and learn, Beast. Your fate will be far worse than theirs.' He turned and walked away, followed in short order by the other wizards, their murmured conversations too faint for me to make sense of, but then I had more pressing concerns than their mediocre spellcraft, including breaking free of whatever held me on this table.

I took a breath to calm my thoughts and then set about testing which parts of me hurt the most, something made harder by the strap holding my head down. Most of what I felt was painful but superficial, being scrapes and tears from the many disjointed mouths and clawed hands embedded in the spider-creature's malformed body. I was fortunate in that these had all been of human stock and so relatively blunt in isolation. The idea of my flesh being swallowed and part of that abomination was more sickening than the actual injuries, most of which had already stopped bleeding. The puncture wounds along my side were another matter. The pain of those was a steady throb, and I could hear the steady patter of my blood hitting the floor beneath me.

One positive was that I could no longer feel the spirits attacking me, but when I reached for my sorcery I found only a lifeless void waiting for me. I'd felt something like it before when Fronsac had toyed with the aftermath of the runic ward I had triggered, and it was no great leap of imagination to think that the wizards had set such a thing upon me now too. If Blue Robes had been at the

University when I escaped, then he would have no doubt how dangerous I could be.

That meant that until I could remove it, I would have to rely on my wits and physical prowess to break free, find Tatyana, and then kill them all. How hard could that be?

I strained against the restraints as I tried to see more of the chamber. My night vision had retracted, but they had set enough of their white lanterns here that it wasn't really necessary. The chamber was an irregular shape and, aside from the floor and a column that had been carved with complex geometrical patterns, largely unworked by human hands. Scores of glittering spindles hung from the ceiling like an inverted stone forest above us, but as pretty as they were, it was the wooden cage pressed against the far wall that my gaze was drawn to. Several wizards were clustered in front of it, and as I watched they dragged two squirming figures from the cage, the armoured figures before it moving aside, the pale light within their visors identifying them as powerful ghouls. They moved away but I had reached the very limits of the restraint on my head and lost sight of them.

Their wailing lasted a while longer, and rose to screams. I had heard enough screams in my time to know that these were born of terror rather than pain. That changed once the wizards began their spellcasting, the unintelligible but insidious chant echoing through the cave far longer and louder than it should have, the miasma of dark magic that stained the air thickening by the moment until I could almost see the gleam of it even without my sorcery.

I was working on moving my left arm to a position where I could apply some leverage to the manacle on my wrist when their spell coalesced. I held still as the screams peaked to something positively inhuman and abruptly ended.

I listened as several men approached and gagged as they drew close. They were still saturated with the dark magic, the metaphysical stench of it lodging my throat like a dry, un-chewed meal while the life-sapping chill of the negative energy tried to pull the very life from my flesh. How they were still alive and able to manipulate such power was a complete mystery.

'You feel it, don't you?' said Blue Robes. 'The power.'

I hid my curiosity beneath a veneer of boredom. 'A dancing bear in a fancy robe is still just another dancing bear.'

'I could pull the life out of you right now and there'd be nothing you could do to stop me.' His grip on his staff changed, his bloodied fingertips finding a pair of intricately carved symbols upon it, and a moment later the unearthly chill that clung to him sharpened considerably. He leaned the staff towards me and I couldn't help but gasp as that cold knifed into me as cleanly as any spear. His eyes narrowed as it pushed deeper. 'I could take it all.'

I swallowed the panic that wanted me to buck and writhe under his touch and forced myself to lay there unmoving.

'It takes more than a trinket to make you a wizard, little bear.'

The deathly shimmer around the staff faded and the cold receded with it, leaving behind a hollow ache. Blue Robes loomed over me, pale lips drawn back from butter coloured teeth.

'Brave words,' he said, reaching down and poking a finger into one of the seeping wounds on my side. 'But you can only fool yourself for so long.'

'Andros,' said a voice from somewhere behind my head. 'If he is here, do we need to keep the woman or can we use her?'

Andros. The sound of his name woke a memory, one

of my blood dripping into the sawdust while Navar's voice exhorted him to strike again, faster and with smaller gestures. I saw him then, those same lips pulled into the same sneer, his scent charged with an almost sexual bloodlust as he loosed spell after spell into me. He'd worn green robes then. I looked up at him as the memory receded, and I didn't need to see into his mind that he knew I'd heard his name and remembered him.

'No names, you idiot,' he snarled at the man behind me. He took a deep breath and released it slowly before looking at me again. 'But I suppose it makes no difference now. Don't go anywhere, we've got quite the show in store for you.'

So they did have Tatyana. At least I had got that right. I forced my head to the side as far as I could, enough to watch Andros directing two of the other wizards to fetch her from the cage. From the shouts and the flash of magic within the cage that followed it seemed that there was still some fight left within her, albeit that she was limp and still when they eventually carried her out and bade the ghouls shut the door once more.

I used the distraction to try to worm my right arm into a better position. That whole side of my body was stiffening and throbbing where the creature had clubbed and punctured me, but the finger he'd poked into me had reminded me that I was bleeding. And that same blood was pooling on the table, making the wood slick under me. Slick enough to reduce the friction and effort that stretching and moving my arm required. I flexed and relaxed the muscles across my shoulder and back, the motion slowly drawing the blood in under me, giving the little extra movement I needed to move my wrist into position.

I glanced back to the wizards but they were busy strapping the now naked Tatyana to a similar sort of table.

She looked gaunt, her ribs pressing against her skin and her hips standing out enough to cast their own shadows across the hollow of her gut. The healing had taken its toll on her, but the bloody mouth on the one wizard who'd had to fetch her was testament to the strength of her will.

I took a breath, then clenched my fist and began bending my wrist upwards. The manacle felt immovable at first, and indeed I would have struggled at the best of times to bend the curved iron out of shape, but the nails that anchored it to the table were another matter entirely. Once the first shifted, the next became that little bit easier. I kept watching the wizards while I worked on the nails, and while Andros occasionally looked over at me, he gave no sign that he saw anything untoward. The final nail on the manacle squeaked loose as they began dragging Tatyana's table towards me.

They lifted the table with a chorus of grunts and let it fall forward, the impact and tightening of the restraints that held her splayed to it jolting Tatyana awake. She moaned and shook her head, which now almost looked too big for her starved body, and finally looked up and saw me.

'You're alive,' she croaked. Her gaze dipped towards what had to by now be a pool of blood under my table, then back up. 'I think.'

'I've come to save you,' I said, which made her cackle.

'How touching,' said Andros. 'You made a friend. It almost seems a shame to kill her in front of you, but with you here she has become quite expendable.'

'Touch her and you'll wish you were never born.'

'You mean like this?' He stepped forward and punched her squarely on the side of the jaw, whipping her head back to thud against the table. Blood spilled from her mouth as it fell back to hang unmoving between her shoulders. He shook his hand and stared at me. 'Well? Come on.'

'You're going to regret that.'

'Oh shut up, you ridiculous, pointless creature,' he snapped, voice rising. 'You can do nothing but watch, and even that is at my sufferance.' He took a step closer. 'And you will watch. Look away or say anything and I will take your eyes. Do you understand?'

A thousand curses waited behind my teeth, but I kept them firmly clenched and the fire in my breast subdued. The terrible truth of it was that for now there was nothing I could do, not without endangering both of us. Once upon a time the idea of quashing the rage that demanded I tear him limb from limb would have been impossible to comprehend, let alone accept without a murmur.

'I understand,' I said, and if threatening tones could kill, his soul would have fled his body there and then.

'Good boy.' Now he turned to the other wizards who had gathered to watch. 'Prepare her. She will be the soul anchor.'

'It's too soon. She's too weak,' said one from somewhere to my left.

'Only physically,' Andros replied, slipping a hand under her chin and lifting her head. 'The spark within her burns steadily. See? She is already healing.'

Now it was my turn to stare, for it was true. The bleeding had stopped, and her jaw was straight again. Which meant that she was still somehow drawing energy from me, something that Andros and his rabble had not yet connected with me. Which meant whatever spell was blocking the flow of my sorcery was one-directional, and not a complete block. It was a weakness, even if I didn't yet know how to exploit it.

I watched in silence as two wizards came forward and began wiping the blood and dirt from her body with little gentleness. It did serve to rouse her though and she was soon shouting and spitting at them like a trapped wolf, and even managed to land a decent bite as they strapped her head back like mine was.

Her cursing fell silent as three others came forward, all wearing robes of a purple so deep to appear almost black and shot through with silver thread that glimmered and shone too brightly to merely be reflecting the light. They were chanting as they approached her, and I recognised the sound of it as being whatever had preceded the piteous screaming of their earlier spellcasting.

'Oh sweet Drogah, not that, not that,' said Tatyana, the venom in her voice replaced by fear for the first time.

CHAPTER 26

HER PLEAS WENT unheeded. Magic flexed and slid through the air as their chant continued, the strength that they poured into the complex sound of it attesting to long hours of practice and an almost careless confidence. Their spells held her immobile as the wizard in the centre bent and began drawing symbols on her skin.

It was only when the blood flowed across her pale, scrubbed skin that I realised he was cutting the symbols into her with a fine bladed knife. She gasped, and had their magic not held her I knew her back would be arching. I could feel the urge to use that rising somewhere in the back of my mind.

'Remember our deal, Beast,' said Andros from behind me in a soft voice. 'You move or protest, and I will take your eyes. The Master wants you alive, no more than that.'

He punctuated the threat by tapping a curved knife against my jaw. I wanted to rip free and grab him, but what if he wasn't where I thought he was? What then?

The wizards kept chanting, and the knife kept cutting until her skin was more crimson than white. Her gaze met mine as the wizard knelt to carve his markings on her legs and I felt her press against my mind. It was an uncontrolled sending, and I doubt she even knew how or if she was doing it, but it was undeniably her.

I recognised the echo of my sorcery within it and felt the ghostly burn of his knife lighting up my flesh. I couldn't help or offer any comfort though, not with their spell shackling my sorcery. Her mind bucked and screamed against mine, and I felt their magic sliding and pulsing its way into her, so cold that it burned more than the runes carved into her flesh. I could feel the power they were pouring into her shining out from those bloody cuts, and worse, I could feel something great and terrible responding to that light. Something that radiated a bottomless hunger than went far beyond the physical, the force of it so elemental that even she with no skill could sense and interpret its intention: *to devour and destroy*.

They had created the monster that had defeated me, and now they were seeking to create another, with her at the twisted centre of it. Tatyana had seen it being born, and the horror of that knowledge was close to breaking her mind.

In front of me the wizard with the knife stood and stepped back as if admiring his handiwork and gestured to four of the others. They moved in silently and lowered the table, giving me one last glimpse of Tatyana's terror-stricken expression before they carried her away. Towards *it*.

'It's a shame you're too heavy to move.' Andros' voice seemed loud and coarse after the sibilant chanting. 'I would have liked you to witness her rebirth, but then you'll still get to see her in her new glory soon enough. Wizards made the best anchors, so a natural sorcerer like her should be truly remarkable.' He patted my chest as he walked away to watch. 'Remind me to thank you for bringing her to our notice.'

I watched him without saying a word as the idea that they thought she was a sorcerer raced through my thoughts. It was because of this that they wanted to bind her into the monster that they were creating. As a soul anchor, something a wizard was suited to, most likely because they were attuned to the Songlines, and their flesh was used to the tidal flow of power that went with that. Except of course that she wasn't the sorcerer. I was, and I was linked to her. And that channel was open, as she'd already proved by her clumsy projection of fear.

If her terror and pain could reach me, so too could whatever else they levied upon her. Assuming I was correct, and I almost certainly was, I couldn't wait any longer. As soon as Andros was out of earshot I set about pulling the nails out of the table. The chanting and the noise from the other prisoners masked the squeak of the wood relinquishing its hold on the iron and with a grunt of effort and a few more drops of blood I finally pulled my wrist free. It was easier if no less painful after that and, by the time that one of the wizards noticed what I was doing I was already sitting up on the table and working the thick straps on my legs loose.

I was aware of them pointing at me, but, now that I could see around me, my attention was largely fixed on the abomination that hung from a series of platforms in the far corner of the cave. Four thick, pale appendages extended away from a central, oblong body that seemed largely composed of wet bone, and the horror of its appearance was only exceeded by the realisation that the scores of men that had been melted together to form that pulsating mass were still somehow alive.

Heavy footsteps dragged my gaze from it and I saw the ghouls lumbering towards me, their heavy armour rattling and chiming. With my sorcery still refusing to heed my call I would have expected them to hammer me with spells but even as I thought it I felt the answer press on my skin. The chamber had wonderful acoustics, something they had also clearly recognised, and everything they were doing was laid out and carefully staged to utilise that and amplify the effect of their spellcasting. The rising spell had even driven off the shoals of souls, masking the vitality that they sought.

And they weren't going to risk casting another spell while the ritual was ongoing, not if it was so important to them. From the size of the monstrosity they had created it must have taken a long time to fuse the victims that comprised its body. Weeks, at least.

Which was all very encouraging and helpful, except that it still left me facing off against two very powerful and heavily armoured ghouls with nothing except a pair of baggy trousers and several still bleeding holes in my side.

But I was a dragon, not some bewildered farmboy. I let my real teeth slide from my palate, the pin sharp points filling my mouth with the taste of my own blood as they emerged. I gave the wizards a bloody smile as I extended my ebon talons, pushing them out to their full length, extending the reach of my arms by half again.

The ghouls didn't care and didn't pause in their advance. Their maces flashed out with the speed of Tatyana's sword, belying their mass, and I felt my wounds tear as I jerked back. I drove my right arm out at the first of them but felt the tip of the talon rattle off the plate protecting its neck. I wasn't expecting it to ram its shield forward, nor the fiery burst of pain as the spiked bit in the centre cut a new gash across my hip. I stumbled back, into the path of the second ghoul's mace and could not stop the squawk that burst from me as the metal head clipped the side of my head and turned the world white.

I felt myself hit the ground, the wounds in my side flaring anew. I threw myself sideways, rolling desperately to avoid what I knew was coming. A mace crashed into the stone where my head had been a moment before and I swung my arm back. I couldn't get the talon in the right angle to pierce anything, but I grabbed its arm and kicked back with the powerful muscles of my legs, pulling it off balance. It fell heavily, spoiling the second one's blow, and I wasted no time in ramming a talon through the fallen one's visor, leaning my weight onto it until I felt the tip touch the rock beneath before twisting it free.

I was still standing up when the enchantments that bound the ghoul failed catastrophically and detonated in a flash of purple-white light that transformed its helm and head into a thousand spinning fragments. This staggered the second ghoul and I launched myself at it, punching a talon through one of its unarmoured knees. It may have been immune to pain and fear, but the mechanics of its body were still unavoidably human. It caught me with a weak blow from the mace as it fell, but I stamped on its arm and ripped the weapon free.

It stared at me with its egg-like eyes as I lifted the mace and brought it crashing down, ending the parody of life that animated its flesh. Forewarned, I hurriedly backed away before its head exploded in a similar fashion. Andros and the two wizards who weren't tied to the ritual were advancing on me and they didn't look happy, which only set me to grinning despite the new streams of blood coating me like a second skin.

'Time to die,' I called, my predatory teeth giving the words an unwanted lisp.

Their advance stalled as I began walking towards them, the gore-streaked mace held in a two handed grip. There were on the cusp of fleeing when the dark magic surrounding the monster pulsed and rippled through the cave, the sound of it setting my teeth on edge as that foul magic coalesced into a silvery web of energy. For a moment they hung in the air and I hoped that it was only a precursor to the core of the spell, but then the strands of it merged and arced into the now screaming Tatyana.

She thrashed as the energy poured into her, energy she had no way of controlling. Her name died on my lips as the energy swelled and burst from her and raced towards me along the golden filament of sorcery that joined us.

CHAPTER 27

THE MAGIC ENGULFED me in an icy sheath, rushing into my mouth and nose like frozen floodwater until I was sure I would suffocate. That might have been a mercy compared to the caustic sensation of it sliding into my flesh, carried as it was by my own sorcery.

I was helpless to stop it and the mace fell forgotten from my hands as scores of confused and terror stricken human psyches exploded inside my mind, howling and screaming in madness as the necromancer's magic began to dissolve them. *Us.*

That was the intent. They would take all those lives and make them one, subsuming the will of each and fusing them into a new whole, the component parts of which were entirely indistinguishable. I could feel that purpose radiating from the corrupt magic pulsing through my spirit and flesh, the discordant, squealing note of it acting like a surgeon's blade to separate my spirit from the flesh it was paired to.

But there was a false note to it. I wasn't within the necromancer's carefully calculated circles and geometries, nor had my flesh been prepared with runes to guide and amplify the spell. Tatyana was supposed to be the vessel for the gibbering mass-mind, not me. Like the pebble that starts a landslide, that flaw began to impact on the structure of their spell. Magic, even their tainted version of it, was a continuous flow of energy that spells channelled, and now parts of their spell were having more energy flowing through them than they had ever been intended to handle. The smaller, subsidiary components of the spell failed first, the surge of energy shattering the neat channels the wizards had envisaged and finding the next path of least resistance. It escalated quickly, and once it combined with the spell they'd cast upon me to dampen my sorcery there was no recovering from it.

I felt the flow of it stall and being to vibrate in new and unpleasant ways. The structure of the spell upon me was collapsing as well, but the failure was out of control. I felt my sorcery break through the dregs of the enchantment, but the joy of that reunion was short-lived. It was the final stress on the already volatile mass of energy and with a shriek, the necromancer's spell exploded, both in me and around me.

Shards of their magic scythed into me cleaner than any blade ever had, discharging their corrupted and incomplete effects into my flesh. I felt myself fly backwards but not the impact of my body against the table. The magic was burning through me, the shattered fragments carrying the intent to separate spirit and flesh into my body in ways it was never intended to.

My body was unlike anything the spell had been intended for though, and I felt the shards bite into the enchantments that bound me to this form, themselves already damaged from the all the years that wizards and priests had been experimenting on me. It felt as if iron nails, each still red from the forge, were being hammered into me, pushing deeper with every breath I took.

I felt the Songlines shuddering around me, flickers of raw

energy flashing into being amidst the ice blue flames that already sheathed me from foot to crown, making them burn brighter so that I lost all trace of the world beyond them. And all the while, those red hot nails burrowed deeper, melting into the old and broken magics bound to my very core. I fought it, but it was too little, too late, and fear bloomed within me as I felt the enchantments reacting. Any fluctuation, however small, would affect the flesh they were bound to, and they were being torn and twisted. Fear became pain as the discharging fragments set off a chain of reactions that made my flesh run like water and my bones bend like saplings before a storm.

AN UNEARTHLY KEENING noise reached me, and it was only when I had to draw breath that I realised that it came from me. I writhed on the ground as the great muscles of my legs warped and twisted, and my scream finally faded as the flickering magics closed around my throat. I gasped for air that had no longer had a clear path to my lungs, and lay clawing ineffectually at my neck and chest until the burning need to breathe gave way to formless darkness.

CHAPTER 28

THE UNFLINCHING BLACK I had fallen into eventually gave way to mere darkness, the fringes of it softened by the glow of stars so unfathomably distant that their silvery light had still not reached where I hung, finally free of pain and anger. It felt comforting. Safe. Perhaps I was falling towards those distant stars, a journey that would take a thousand or more of my lifetimes, but that was of no consequence here. I was free. I moved to stretch out my wings and felt something tighten across my back, the sensation magnified by the lack of any other feeling in my body.

I looked over my shoulder and saw a glowing thread that stretched away from me into the darkness behind. It tightened again, as if it were tied to something within me, and with the tightening I felt the ghost of old agonies brush my mind. I finally managed to grasp that gossamer line, and used it to turn myself around. The thread shone weakly, the vibrant reds and golds fading in places to grey, like cooling iron. It stretched away from me, as fine as a hair and as taut as a bowstring, all the way back into the heart of the deepest darkness. It shimmered as I touched it, a single note sounding amidst the silence. A fragment of sound, filling the void around me.

I looked over my shoulder, back towards the soft light of the waiting stars, but with my hands upon the thread their glow now seemed cold and impossibly distant. I hung in the darkness for an unknowable time, then finally put my hands upon the thread and began pulling myself along it, back towards the darkness.

There was no telling how long it took, but finally it loomed large before me, and even as I reached out a hesitant hand it seemed to swell and swallowed me almost greedily. I was falling once more, falling towards the greys and silvers of winter cloud, my body solidifying around me, bringing a thousand sensations with it, all of which tried to rush into my mind at once. Buried memories surged forth as I fought to regain stability, the strain of my extended wings pulling painfully across my back as they fought the thin winter air but finally the horizon became a level line once more.

Thoughts of distant stars faded, replaced by the sure knowledge that I was flying home, back to Draksgard, laden with food for winter. The winter wind was blowing from the north more often than not now, and there was a bite to it that my hot blood felt all too keenly. Most of the herds would have left the valleys already, moving south in search of the sun and grass that wouldn't be entombed in ice for the rest of the year. We were creatures of sun and fire, but we understood our place in the great cycle and winter had its own charms. It was a time for songs and stories, of sleep and renewal.

The whale-meat I had harvested from the great bays to the south and west would see us through the months ahead. It was hard work, and perhaps there were other ways to build our larder, but I liked the taste of them, especially those I'd left to mature on the salt flats for a few days. Even thinking about it sent a lick of drool oozing through my teeth and I had to force myself not to think about the salty, succulent meat cradled in my arms.

The landscape below me slowly changed, the savannahs giving way to forests and rivers as every beat of my tired wings brought me closer to home. The thought of being reunited with Anakhara fed new strength into them and I gained some of the height I'd lost amidst my daydreaming.

After what felt like an age, I saw the shape of Draksgard take form on the horizon, its fiery summit cloaked in rolling white cloud. I looked towards the sun, seeking her silhouette against the light; her eyes were keener than mine, and she loved nothing more than to swoop on me like a hawk surprising a dove. The anticipation grew, then faded as I drew closer to the mountain and found the sky empty. Perhaps she was pursuing a herd that had been too slow to leave, and was even now adding to our stores. It would be a fine winter.

I was too pre-occupied with holding the whale-meat steady as I slowed myself to land to notice the silence, and too close to it to smell the blood that soaked the ground at the entrance to the mountain. I announced myself with a roar that echoed along the valleys, knowing that there was no chance that she couldn't hear it. I smelt the blood as the echoes faded, and her scent amongst this sent a jolt of lightning through me. Dragon blood. Her blood, mingled with the iron and salt of mankind.

My tiredness fell from me like old skin and my sorcery hurled me into the sky with barely a thought. I bellowed her name over and over again, each cry louder than the one before, driving what creatures remained in the valley below insane.

I found the first of her scales in a clearing near the far neck of the valley, the golden discs dulled and wedged amidst a cascade of rocks. The scent of blood and discharged magic was thicker here, and the rocks were scorched and blackened in long stripes, a mark of her flame. I landed amidst the bloodstained rocks, forcing my racing mind to slow as I tried to make sense of what the gouges and blood were telling me.

The shallow graves that the jackals had already begun pillaging told me that it had been men who had brought this about. I could not fathom how men, so recently little more than fearful cave-dwellers, could have done such a thing, but worse than that was the realisation that if they had survived to bury their dead, then Anakhara could not have. She would not have suffered them to live, not when they had shed her blood. I stumbled along the mountainside in the hours that followed, my hide smeared with bloodied mud and my mind lost to a growing inferno of rage and grief. I would bring her home while their world burned and their rivers ran red. I would tear their cities to rubble!

YOU NEVER FOUND her body.

The voice that filled the valley wasn't my own. I staggered to a halt as the very walls of the valley flexed and rippled around me, the trees that still stood bending as if a gale bore down on them. I could see parts of them flaking away and vanishing into nothingness. I shook my head as the rage in my breast faltered. The edges of what I could see before me were blowing away like sand and I knew then that this wasn't real. It was a memory.

But this wasn't how it happened. The whales, the blood, the shallow graves piled with blackened flesh and metal; those were real, or had been. But not this.

You never found her body.

The voice was a whisper now, breathed close to my ear.

I spun, but the churned ground was empty save for a taut, golden thread stretching away into a nearby cave. I cut at it with my talons, but it refused to break.

The valleys rippled around me in time with the vibration of the thread, larger pieces of the mountainside shaking themselves loose and bouncing towards me while the colours of the world around me shimmered and began running together, draining from the slopes like ash washed away by rain. I felt the thread pull me towards the cave, and I knew then that only inescapable pain and grief waited within it. I roared my defiance and dug my claws into the bloody ground, but it too dissolved at my touch. I cried out as the last of it peeled away and the thread pulled me into the cave, followed by a landslide of bloodied earth that stifled my cries.

BLOOD. THE SMELL of it came to me first, or at least the awareness that I was smelling something. It was in my mouth too, thick and bitter, but my tongue was too swollen for me to spit it out. I blasted mud and worse from my nostrils and drew in a lungful of the moist and mud flavoured air until my thoughts were no longer fogged and distant.

My body felt wrong. *Broken.* I heard bones click and groan as I moved one arm, then the next, forcing dirt and rock away from my face. I turned my head, the sound of it a cascade of gristly noises, and spat dirt and blood from my mouth. My hearts lurched and staggered, then slowly settled back into a synchronised rhythm.

I laid there, simply breathing, as the fractured memories of what had happened attempted to arrange themselves into a single whole once more. I remembered the stars, the bloody valley where she had died, and a golden cord, but the images were jumbled, as fragmented as a dream after a sudden awakening. Which came first, and where was I now? Was I awake, or was this some new nightmare? It smelt and tasted too foul to be anything but real. The darkness had come first, I remembered that, and with that memory came what I remembered of the necromancer's spell.

The images in my mind turned, their rough edges meshing together into a new whole. Their magic had collapsed on itself, the purpose and intention to separate the spirit and restore the flesh warping and reacting with the enchantments laid so deep on my flesh. Phantom agonies flickered through my body at the memory, reminding me of the first time I had reshaped my flesh.

And as it had then, something had gone terribly wrong. Even laying immobile as I was, I could feel the changes in the pressure on my back and the unfamiliar play of the muscles as I tried to move arm and leg. More dirt and small stones fell onto my face, making me cough and splutter as they closed much of my breathing space. Why was I laying here in dirt that reeked of human blood and pressed by piles of broken stone?

The cave must have collapsed from the wayward pressures of their magic, burying me. My side was pressed against the table I'd been thrown against, a much needed stroke of luck in retrospect as it had saved me from being crushed or smothered outright. However, it didn't change that I had been buried alive and that the air was already thickening around me. I'd be gasping before long, my lungs demanding air with increasing but hopeless desperation, assuming that the hole didn't collapse before then, filling my mouth and nose with its earthy taste while the worms closed in to taste my cold flesh. This hole would be my tomb, and I would rot here, forever forgotten and alone. I would never find my love and bring her home.

I would never find Anakhara.

The thought burned through my fogged brain and made my limbs tremble and twitch as life returned to them. I had been forgotten and alone for over seven hundred years and had long since stopped caring whether anyone would mourn me, but I had sworn an oath in her blood and mine that I would never rest until I found her and brought her home. Then, and only then, could the worms have their feast.

I spat dirt from my mouth and bared my teeth as I fed the anger the thought had kindled, drawing the strength it lent deep into me until fear and exhaustion lost their grip on me. I braced a shoulder against the stony floor beneath me and began to push. This was a combination of soil and broken stone, a fractured mass rather than monolithic slabs and I'd barely begun cursing the birth of mankind when I felt it begin to shift. I snarled with the effort, barely aware that my draconic teeth had emerged of their own accord and had pierced my still human lips. I pushed, then pushed again until I heard and felt the rumble of the stone above me.

Angry or not, I knew my strength was finite and I reached out for my sorcery, more in hope than anything else, and that snarl became a bark of triumph as I felt the Songlines swell in reply. The flow stuttered for a few heartbeats before the final dregs of the wizard's spell were eroded and the energy flowed into me.

I took a moment to enjoy the sensation, then sent fine slivers of shaped energy worming their way into the cracks around me, letting them pulse with my heartbeat at first, every thump widening the gaps and voids between the heavier pieces by the tiniest measure. I steadily fed more power into it, until the slivers became strings and finally ropes that shivered too fast for even me to follow. The vibrations spread until the compacted earth around me rippled like the surface of a strange pond. I felt the pressures around me shifting and took a moment to gather my will, then increased the vibrations tenfold. The grip of the dirt around began to collapse, the tension between the stones and grains of soil lost. I released a single, more powerful blast of energy upwards, blasting a cone-shaped crater open around me in a geyser of broken stone and dirt lit by arcs of raw sorcery.

I stood in the newly created void, stretching out limbs that were no longer as smooth and shapely as black marble. The collapse of the necromancer's spell had ravaged me like some terrible acid, puckering my hide with craters and leaving seams of rough tissue where the skin and flesh had been stretched and left to set into new patterns, as if I were some wax idol that had been left too close to a fire. The muscles on my right leg were withered, the skin over them gnarled like bark and its girth barely that of a man's arm, but it was the twisting in my back that truly gave me pause. It felt as if two great knives had been stabbed into my back, one behind each shoulder, forcing me to stand and walk like an old man. I strained my neck as far as it could go but could see little more than a bulge of knobbly bone, the skin across it stretched as taut as a drum's.

MY TEETH WERE a mess too; I'd always had too many to fit in this small head but now it seemed they had all decided to try and share my mouth at the same time, tearing my mouth and lips to tatters and fixing my face in what I could only assume was a demonic leer. I tried forcing them back into my skull as I had before, but barely a third of them shifted, and even then the pressure and feel of them retracting was acutely uncomfortable.

His magic had collapsed part of the enchantment

binding me to my human form, and the stars only knew what might have happened had the transformation spell been intended for me directly, rather than Tatyana. I tested my newly deformed limbs, wincing as new aches and limitations announced themselves, but I was alive. I could still fulfil my oath, and if I had the chance to kill a few more men and save my friend, it was all the better.

I punched my curved nails into the wall of dirt and pulled myself from my almost-tomb, feeling clumsy and awkward but buoyed by an anger that was burning brighter with every moment. I was tired of humanity. *Sick of them.*

I reached the top without too much difficulty and was prying a loose tooth from my mouth when a wizard came stumbling out of the dark. He stared at me dumbly in the ruddy light emanating from his staff, and only managed a single step backwards before I sprang on him. I almost fell short as my withered leg buckled, but the combination of his surprise and my long arms let me succeed. I grabbed a handful of his robe and pulled him towards me.

He flailed desperately as I fell back into the hole, dragging him with me. As we crashed to the bottom, a wild blow saw him cut his fist on my jutting teeth. The scent of his blood drew an involuntary growl from deep within me and I felt the agony of the rest of my teeth scraping their way back into my mouth.

My vision went red as I tore into him, the savagery of the attack costing me a few of the more precariously protruding teeth on the edge of my jaw, but I had more than I needed and paid them little heed. The first gout of blood washed the taste of the dirt and filth from my mouth, waking my hunger anew, and I gorged myself on the warm meat and felt a new, more wholesome strength course through me. I'd been using my sorcery without decent food and rest in between, and it had taken its toll.

I felt much better after I'd eaten, and my mind was calmer. I stood and rolled my shoulders, testing the range of movement they now offered. The bulge in my back was pulling my right shoulder back, shortening my reach with that arm and narrowing the range of movement that didn't send sharp pains stabbing up along my neck. Taken with my shrivelled leg, it left me with a strange, bobbing gait, as if I was walking on a tilting floor. I wouldn't be sprinting anytime soon, but the leg could still thankfully hold my weight when I wasn't trying to leap about, and that would have to do.

I climbed out of the hole and paused, waking my night vision and tasting the air until I found what I was looking for.

CHAPTER 29

ONLY HALF THE cavern had collapsed, but from the deep, almost subsonic groaning within the walls and roof I suspected that would not be long in changing. Dust hung as thick as coastal fog in the air, making my night vision less than useful, and I was left to scramble across the piles of debris like the other survivors I could hear around me. I still had the advantage of a proper sense of smell though, and even with the dust and limitations imposed by a human skull I could pick out Tatyana's scent. She was on the edge of the rock fall, still half-strapped to the remains of the table.

One of the wizards sprawled around her groaned as I approached, and called out for help. That changed quickly when I loomed over him, kindling the light in my eyes for little reason beyond knowing how much men feared it. And fear it he did. His plea for help became a wordless squealing that lasted as long as it took me to raise my good leg and stamp down on his face.

It also attracted more shouting and soon after several beams of white light shot through the darkness, the choking cloud of dust smudging the sharp beams and giving me precious moments to crouch behind the splintered remnant of the table. So hidden, I sent a brief pulse of energy into the unconscious Tatyana, just enough to glean that she had suffered no new injuries beyond the trauma of being so close to becoming what the necromancers had intended. Something like that would not be easily forgotten, and providing she lived through what would come next, sleep was probably the best tonic for her.

The three beams of light converged on the table, and I heard Andros' voice call out from the left side, instructing the others to secure Tatyana. That cheered me, for as dangerous as he might be, I wanted to be the one to tear the life out of him.

The first of the wizards took shape behind the light and I shifted my good leg under me, bracing my foot against the floor. I could hear his breathing and the rapid beat of his heart as he moved into range. I offered neither growl nor roar as I rose from my cover, a black talon punching out ahead of me like a paladin's lance. He opened his mouth, probably to scream, but whatever sound he'd intended was silenced by the arm's length of talon that smashed his teeth back into his mouth and out through the back of his head. A quick twist finished it and my arm was already back at my side by the time his body hit the floor.

The blast hit me a moment later, exploding against my side with a crack of thunder and sending me tumbling back across the rubble with the breath knocked out of me and ribbons of flame dancing across my hide. I recognised the feel of Andros' magic. He knew I was there and had waited for me to expose myself.

'I see him!' Excitement made the second wizard's voice sound feminine, but didn't affect his spellcasting. I could only tense for the impact as his staff flashed with crimson light. The spell slapped into me, an almost wet sensation, and then burst into flame.

I like to think he heard my laughter over the roar of it. It wasn't mage fire, but rather the more natural sort that my body craved. I drank it in greedily and rose to my feet as the last dregs of it sunk into my skin. Andros was raging at him for being an idiot, which meant he wasn't casting a spell. I flexed my sorcery and returned the favour, using more energy than I really needed to. The blast scoured the flesh from the wizard in a torrent of wind and fire that sent him crashing to the floor as a blackened skeleton from the knees up.

I enjoyed the sight of it far more than I should have and was punished by another of Andros' spells hammering into me. This one threw me against one of the carved pillars, pain flaring from my misshapen shoulders as the newly formed bone was mashed against the unyielding rock.

'Where is your vaunted strength now, Beast?' he asked, the words almost lost in the ringing echoes of the spell and grinding of the roof above.

I flicked a shard of energy at him, blade thin and faster than an arrow, but he barely flinched as his renewed wards snuffed it out. I'd expected as much, but there was no harm in trying.

'Pathetic.'

I sent another three such shards at his face, each of which his wards defeated, but then I knew they wouldn't be enough to strip his defences. It did focus his concentration though. It's hard to pay attention to anything else when someone is throwing burning knives at your face.

'Enough of these games.' His staff began to crackle anew and I felt the pressure of his magic press against the dregs of my sorcery. 'When you wake, it will be to the Master standing over you. And then you will know true suffering.'

'This is getting to be a habit,' I said, offering a bloody smile.

It was enough to make him pause.

'Don't worry, he wasn't talking to you,' said a voice behind him.

He gave a choked gasp as Tatyana grabbed his hair and pulled him backwards. His eyes widened when he saw the knife, and he screamed when she slid the same knife I'd used to cut her bonds into him just above the groin, and then sawed it up through his guts. His staff fell from his hands and she kicked him away from her, the solid impact to the small of his back sending the first loop of his guts slithering from the gaping wound. His screams started in earnest then.

Tatyana's smile was entirely predatory as she watched him trying to stuff the mess back inside himself, sparks of magic flashing from his rings as his control fractured. She kicked him in the face for good measure before walking over to me.

'You magnificent bastard,' she said in a hoarse voice.

I didn't let the insult break my improving humour. 'It's good to see you too, my friend.'

I reached out to one of the smouldering lamps and re-lit it with a flash of power.

She recoiled as if I was about to take a bite out of her. 'God's beard,' she breathed, her hand held to her mouth.

'It would have been worse had they completed the ritual,' I said, struggling to my feet.

She didn't move, only watched me with her hand still pressed to her lips. 'Stratus, oh my god,' she said, taking a step away from me. 'What did they do to you?'

'I'm fine,' I lied, my tongue struggling to form the letters around the extra teeth in my mouth.

She stepped closer and rested a hesitant hand on the gnarled bands of skin that snaked across my chest. I couldn't feel her fingers as she walked around me; when she stepped behind me she gasped again.

'God's beard,' she said.

'Touch my back,' I said. 'I can't see what has happened there.'

She didn't speak, but I felt her hand follow my spine from my hips upwards. When she reached the midpoint the feel of it changed and the pressure became fainter. At my urging she poked and prodded, describing what she saw in a somewhat strangled tone. From what I felt and she saw, part of my backbone had begun expanding to its natural size, folding and squeezing the skin and flesh around them, making some movements impossible and most others painful to even attempt.

It was only when she touched the bulges on my shoulders that I finally understood.

The necromancer's insidious magic had wormed its way into the enchantment binding me to this form, eroding its foundations. Part of it had collapsed upon itself and my flesh and bone had begun remembering its true size and form in a way it was never meant to. I was lucky that it had stopped when it did because this chest would not be able to contain either of my hearts. The jutting spurs on my back were the precursors of my wings, the rapid growth of them at odds with the musculature and skeleton of a human body, leaving me trapped somewhere in between, like a monstrous hunchback.

'I don't understand,' she said, moving to stand before me again.

I nodded, and even that felt awkward. 'I'd rather explain it under the sun.'

'No argument there,' she said, raking her fingers through her spiky remnants of her hair. She moved over to one of the wizards who'd been brained by a falling rock, working quickly to divest him of his robes and knife while I listened to the mountain above us grumbling at the violent magics that had been unleashed inside it.

'I think you should hurry,' I said, watching as a stream of dust began pouring from a new crack. She looked up as a tremor passed through the floor, and without another word we both began moving towards where the entrance should be, her with the gait of a crone and me bobbing and shuffling like some grotesque crow, an image that the tattered remnants of my clothing did little to dispel.

I was at the portal before I realised that she was no longer with me, but rather at the cage of prisoners, beating her dagger against the lock. Her strength had been eroded by the tortures and forced healing of her body though, and even as I called to her to stop, she swayed and collapsed to the floor, leaving me cursing as I made my way back towards her and the screaming captives in the cage.

CHAPTER 30

IF EVER THERE was one certain way to make the injured or weak bitterly aware of their inadequacies, then walking up a mountain was surely it. It was Tatyana who was now waiting for me at the top of every rise, impatiently watching the splintered crags around us for signs of the Penullin scouts who had harried me so much since I carried her from the collapsing fortress. The hardships of the walk had at least begun to teach me what of my strength remained, albeit that it was a painful and frustrating lesson that made anything more challenging than a flat path a test of mental and physical endurance.

I let her worry about the men she was sure were hiding behind every other bush or rock and concentrated on my walking, constantly testing what my mangled leg could withstand. I was learning more with every step, discovering how my body had changed, and challenging myself to push at the limitations it now imposed. Moving constantly had already eased some of the stiffness, and I had adopted a loping stride that let my good leg do most of the hard work. It was ungainly, but quicker and less painful than the shuffle I feared I would be limited to.

We found a small alcove, little more than a scoop in the rock a few dozen paces off the goat trail we'd been following to rest as darkness settled across the hills and freed the stars above.

'How's the leg?' she asked, as she had every night since she had woken up.

It had taken three full days of natural sleep before she had woken after I'd pulled her from the collapsing temple-fortress, and even then it was only at my gentle probing. She needed to eat as well as sleep to recover, and to her credit she showed no signs of having lost her appetite.

THE CAVE I'D found for us wasn't much by comparison to the temple the mountain had reclaimed, and was barely big enough for us to lay side by side or stand up fully, but it was dry and well hidden. I'd had to kill the more persistent scouts who had been tracking me, but after leaving a score of their bodies displayed as gruesomely as I could imagine, their enthusiasm for the hunt had waned considerably. I'd used the time that had won us to find food, and after a few miserable rock rabbits I had finally managed to bring down a proud mountain goat, a fine ram who'd thought that standing on a rock a hundred paces away would protect him. The fall tenderised him nicely and we'd eaten our way through most of him before I'd judged us strong enough to continue on our journey.

I considered her question. How did I answer that? It was painful and ugly, and walking with it was completely undignified, but the half shape I was in was also morbidly encouraging in its own way, a reminder that my flesh still remembered its true nature.

'Awkward,' I said eventually, earning a grunt from her as she pulled a smoked sausage and two sorely deformed loaves from her pack, a gift from an over enthusiastic but careless scout.

'Best eat the fresh stuff first,' she said, moving off to the side with hers.

I laid down on my side and chewed my way through the sausage, enjoying the warming spices and snap of the skin, at least until another of my teeth tore loose and ruined it with a mouthful of blood. I spat the offending tooth into my hand and rubbed the blood from it.

'Would you like a tooth?'

'What the fuck for?' she said without turning.

'I thought they were considered good luck.'

'That's rabbit feet,' she said, rolling her shoulders and neck about with enviable ease.

I flicked the tooth over the edge of the trail and watched it vanish.

'Do you think there are more of them?' I asked.

'Who? The hunters?'

'Yes.'

'You killed scores of them, a whole cabal of wizards and brought down an ancient fortress. So yes, I think they're still looking for us.'

'You killed a wizard too, and it wasn't my magic that brought it down.'

'Semantics,' she said, waggling a hand at me. 'Everyone in this area is going to be looking for us, and next time they're not going to be so friendly. Now finish your sausage. I'd like to top that next ridge before full dark.'

I ate as quickly as I could and pulled myself to my feet with a frustrated groan. My muscles had cooled and stiffened again as I'd sat there, and it took perhaps half a mile of walking before the discomfort began to fade. The trail twisted its way through a series of shallow ravines filled with a tumble of rocks, the crystal fragments in them glittering like precious stones in the light of the setting sun.

I welcomed how the ground evened out a little after that, enjoying the respite it offered my aching joints. Tatyana moved off ahead of me to scout the area before the last of the day's light bled from the sky, and the time alone it offered suited me very well. The air was clean here, and for once there were no clouds masking the spread of stars above me. Had it not been for a body that seemed unsure as to when, rather than if, it was going to betray me I would have been tempted to spend a day or two languishing there, stretched out on the rocks to soak up the sun. I missed the touch of that pure, clean warmth reaching into the heart of me.

'Are you listening to me?'

'No,' I said, reluctantly opening my eyes. I hadn't realised that I'd stopped moving, or that I'd even closed my eyes.

'God, give me patience,' she said, looking up at the sky. 'I honestly don't know why I bother.'

'What were you saying that was so important?'

'That I think I know where we are, more or less. The great lump over, the one shaped like a sleeping cat, must be Trollmound.' She gestured to a badly eroded conical hill that the sunset had painted gold.

'It looks nothing like a sleeping cat.' I squinted at it. 'Perhaps a melted one.'

'Use your imagination. Anyway, if I'm right, there should be a path down where we can cut past in front of the paws.'

I grunted my agreement. The mountain really did look nothing like a cat, and I found myself wondering what it would look like from above, which in turn made the lumps on my back twitch in strange ways.

'There's good eating on a cat.'

'We are not having that conversation. Ever. Now, get moving.'

She walked off, stretching her pace as she drifted off the path to scout ahead, which suited me well enough. I walked on at my own pace, enjoying the relative silence, fresh air and sunshine, all of which had been denied to me for so long, both in my cage and under Navar's cruel ownership. I had promised myself that I would never again take any of them for granted and it was one that I meant to keep.

I spooled out a small amount of sorcery and sent gentle pulses of it into the link that joined her to me as I walked. The connection had felt different since we left the temple, not in any way that I could easily discern or label, but until now I hadn't dared expose her to even the smallest kernel of sorcery for fear of blunting her recovery. If anything, the link felt stronger. I no longer needed to concentrate to sense it, and even though she was out of sight, I felt myself drawn to where she was like a lodestone to a metal.

I watched the mote of energy I pulsed at her flash between us, just enough to illuminate the structure of what I was seeing but too weak to have any palpable effect on her body. The link was much the same as it had been before, and contrary to my expectations, it wasn't broken, only more definite. The magic that had burned along it had forced it to react, the imperative to maintain itself drawing power from my reserves even without my conscious thought and, like a broken bone that knits stronger than it was before, it had evolved into something far more robust. Even a small amount of power let me pinpoint where she was and, if I fed a little more energy into it, I could all but see what she was seeing.

I kept this to myself when I caught up with her some time later, the link leading me unerringly towards her, albeit up a steep and rocky slope, which I took to with no little cursing. My complaints ended when I found that it led to a nice little cave that was made even more welcoming by the small buck laying within it, a bowstring snare tight around its slender neck.

'You are remarkably resourceful, Tatyana Henkman.'

'I'm also remarkably hungry. Can you do some light?' she asked. 'I need to clean it.'

I obliged, keeping the orb small and tightly focused. She worked quickly with her knife. I could feel saliva making its way through my teeth and along my torn lips but was largely powerless to stop it. I pressed the light closer towards her so she wouldn't be able to see the damage.

'Can you, um, cook it with magic?'

It was the work of moments to dilute my fire construct to a point that would cook the meat without blackening it, at least her portion anyway, but she seemed inordinately impressed by the feat and it was nice to be appreciated for once. I tore into mine with great enthusiasm, having scorched it to a perfection that no human cook had so far matched. I did pause long enough to encourage her to eat some of the liver. Her body was still some way from recovering from her prolonged exposure to magic and needed the strength the organs would impart.

In turn she made me crack its bones and skulls outside, a display of fastidiousness that made me laugh given that she'd been wrist deep in its guts not long before. I didn't object though as it meant I didn't have to share. When I was done, she helped herself to one of the split bones and, by the light of my orb, she sketched out a rough map on the floor of the cave.

'See, we're here.' She tapped a broken nail to a mark she'd made amidst a series of curved lines. 'This is Trollmound. The cat.'

I was tempted to remind her that it looked nothing like a cat but simply nodded.

'If we keep west, we go around like this. But if we go through, it should bring us out at the edge of the Jemaa valley, and from there it's a straight shot to Aknak.' The bone rasped as she drew it across the floor.

'We should go around,' I said.

'Around? No. That adds days, and will put out us here.' She jabbed with the bone.

'That appears to be closer to Aknak,' I said.

She conceded this with a brief nod. 'Maybe so, but it's as flat as a blade out there. We'd stick out like wolves on a chicken farm.'

'Have you ever seen a troll?' I asked.

'What?'

'A troll.' I tapped a curved nail against the blob representing the cat. '*Trollmound*. It's fairly self-evident.'

'There aren't any trolls in Krandin.'

'So you've been there before?'

'Well, past it, but it's an old name. If there were trolls there someone would know about it.'

'So you would walk into a mountain your very ancestors named Trollmound, disregarding their every reason for doing so. Why record your history if you never learn from it?'

'Because it's the past. It was named that hundreds of years ago. Whatever lived there is long gone. Things change.'

'They do and they don't," I said. 'Remember who you are talking to.'

'There's no need to get all dramatic,' she said. 'And besides, we're going *past* it, not into it.'

'If they scent us, it won't matter. We'll never outrun a troll.'

'There are no trolls. Besides, danger makes life interesting.'

I chuckled at that. 'That sounds like something she would have said.'

'She being Anakhara?'

'Yes.' I hadn't realised I'd said it aloud. I stared out into the night. 'She was always daring me to do things. She used to enjoy racing me through narrow canyons, or diving deep into the ocean to fetch red and yellow rocks from the floor. She feared nothing.'

'Sorry,' she said. 'She sounds like an amazing person.'

I smiled at that. 'She was.'

'Do you miss her?' She clapped a hand to her forehead. 'Sorry. That's a stupid question.'

'More than the sun misses the moon,' I said. 'Once Navar is dead, I will continue my search.' An image of the valley where she'd died danced across my vision, the flies rising in great clouds from the churned and bloodied ground and the broken human bodies the jackals had already dug up. 'I'll take her home.'

And then I would join her. The thought came from nowhere, but I knew it was true. Once my oath had been fulfilled I would seal myself within Draksgard and begin my journey to meet her.

'Good, that's good,' Tatyana said in an odd tone, turning away and looking towards the glimmer of the north star. I followed her gaze and smiled. Soon, the seasons would turn and the constellation I knew as the Labyrinth would be visible again. The home of my ancestors, and the resting place of our fallen.

'We should move on,' I said. 'Such maudlin thoughts won't help our quest.'

'We'll rest up for a couple of hours. No point running ourselves into exhaustion.'

I needed no further encouragement and stretched out on my side, eventually finding a position that didn't strain or hurt some part of me. I closed my eyes and sank myself into the Songlines, weaving a measure of healing power through my lingering injuries. The corrosive effect of the necromancer's spell had left knots of scar tissue within me that were disrupting the flow of energy, making the already constricted flow of blood and energy into the malformed parts of me even worse. I fell asleep musing which part of me was truly deformed: the human shaped body, or those parts that had remembered it was a dragon?

When she shook me awake, my mind was rested but my body felt like it had just rolled down a rocky slope. At least my healing had done good work, and my lips and back had stopped bleeding.

'You groan more than the dead,' she said as I pulled myself to my feet and stretched away the terrible stiffness gripping my twisted spine and leg. I didn't dignify her comment with a reply and simply followed as she led the way back onto the trail with an easy dexterity. The walking helped though, and by the time that the sun parted from the horizon the worst of it had passed and I was moving as well as I'd managed the day before.

There were no signs of pursuit, or at least none that either of saw, although the steepness of the slopes meant we were going sideways more than we were forward, but by midday the worst of it was behind us, and what we both assumed was the infamous Trollmound was before us. From a distance it looked like the top of the mountains that formed the walls of the valley had been sheared off by some great sword and had fallen into a pile in the centre.

The walking was easier for some way after that as we made our way along the trail, both silent as the wall of rock that it led to, began to loom over us, its surface hard and imposing. The last few hundred paces were across bare rock, cracked and sharp, and bereft of any life. Not even moss or thorns grew there, and what I'd taken for a desiccated shrub revealed itself to be a discarded ribcage as we grew closer. I knew Tatyana had seen it when she started cursing. The shape was distinctive, but to be sure I snapped off a rib and rang my tongue along it.

'Human,' I said, tossing it aside. 'Dead less than a fortnight.'

'Well, shit,' she said, not looking away from the midnight black cleft in the rocks. 'You're telling me that there may well be an honest to god troll inside there somewhere.'

I walked a bit closer and took several deep breaths. Their acrid scent was unmistakeable, even after all these centuries. 'Just the one, judging by the scent.'

Her fingers tapped a beat on the handle of her sword. 'Can you kill it?'

'Anything can be killed,' I said. 'But not even I would be so bold as to try and beard a troll in its own lair.'

'That bad, eh?'

'Quite vicious, yes.'

And so it was that we found ourselves climbing the hills again. There was a prideful, bestial part of me that wanted to go back and match myself against the creature, but fortunately the common sense prevailed. The diversion had soured Tatyana's mood and she'd decided to range ahead of me, sparing me more of the muttering and cursing she'd been engaged in since we turned aside.

We walked throughout the remainder of the day and, aided by the lambent moonlight and a mutual aversion to camping in a troll's territory, we continued for some time after nightfall. The steep inclines of the previous day's walk were not repeated, which was a relief, although some of the steeper descents presented their own problems, and on at least two occasions it was only the strength of my arms and speed of my reflexes that stopped me from plummeting down the mountain. It was a pattern to be repeated over the three long days of walking that followed until, finally, we had our first view of the nice flat grasslands beyond.

CHAPTER 31

WE ATE WELL on our last night in the hills, courtesy of a careless brace of mountain hares. I ate until it felt like my stomach would surely burst inside me, relishing the crunch of the bones that I so craved, albeit much to Tatyana's evident disgust.

And yet, even with such a good meal inside me my sleep was fitful, plagued with strange dreams about magical nets trapping my wings and wizards hammering iron spikes into my head. They faded as swiftly as dreams do, only for shards of them to return whenever I settled once more. Eventually I gave up and sat watching the night dissolve into dawn while Tatyana snored behind me.

After a paltry breakfast we began making our way down along a mostly dry riverbed. What seemed to be rolling plains from above soon resolved into an uneven landscape that the tenacious grasses and gnarled shrubs that lived here failed to soften. The soil of the plains was thin, a bare scraping of dirt across the hard bones of the earth beneath, and it came as no surprise when Tatyana told me that the people who had lived here before the war took them had mostly been goat herders. She spoke of the cheese the area had been known for with such fondness that I began to yearn for it too, despite having never tasted or known of it.

The walking was at least easier now that we were away from the slopes, and it actually felt like we had made some tangible progress. Where we could, we followed the larger cracks in the land so that we were harder to spot if anyone was watching the area, which Tatyana assured me they would be.

We walked without pausing until sunset, heading towards a lone farmhouse that was the only real landmark in sight. I could smell ash and decay as we drew close, and a pulse of sorcery told me that there was no life amongst the blackened shell, at least nothing larger than field vermin. So forewarned, I eschewed Tatyana's suggestion that we crawl forward on our bellies, leaving her to curse my apparent stubbornness. She eventually gave up and caught up with me as I entered the house, which had been hollowed out by a fire that had burned with a steady but unremarkable heat. I nudged a charred ribcage and human skull from the ashes, but Tatyana stepped over it and out into the courtyard without a word, which intrigued me enough to follow her.

Three corpses waited in the courtyard. Two had been impaled on spikes as thick as my arm, the tips protruding from the armpit of one and the mouth of the other, the weight of their bodies having stretched their skin in grotesque ways as their bodies slid ever downwards. The third body was that of a child, and was roped to the side of an overturned wagon. The white of its backbone and ribs clearly visible amidst the tattered strips of flesh hanging from its back.

'Drogah have mercy,' she said, waving away the flies we had disturbed. She stood there a while longer, grinding her teeth before she then strode past me and back into the shell of the house, the scent of her anger at odds with the flat tone of her voice.

'We'll rest here for a few hours, then head east.'

I lingered in the yard, fascinated and appalled by the savagery contained within such a small place. I had no doubt killed children in the fires of my past, but never like this, not with such obvious but pointless malice and cruelty.

I eventually followed her in and cleared some of the rubble until there was a clear space for us to sit. I pulled out the wiry rabbits I'd managed to snare during our walk and asked her to skin them.

'You're going to eat?'

'I'm hungry.'

She shook her head but set to work with her knife. 'No fires.'

I grunted my disappointment as she finished with the rabbits and set them on a salvaged plank. I'd have preferred a nice hot fire, but I was adept at improvising. I spun the fire construct out and pulled it *through* the meat, rather than over it, then released it. I watched it carefully, curious to see how the meat reacted. I liked a good charring, but that was easy to gauge when you could see it. I pulsed the heat through the meat, spreading it evenly and it wasn't long before the smell of roasting meat rose from them in a gentle smoke, and I was gratified by how Tatyana's eyes widened in wonder.

'There,' I said. 'A hot meal, and no fire.'

'God damn you.'

I drew back. 'For what?'

'For tempting me with that damned meat. How can I eat after that?' She gestured towards the wall, but of course she meant the yard.

'They're dead,' I offered. 'Starving yourself means nothing to them.'

'Being right doesn't make you less of a shit.'

'But I am right.'

She said nothing but cut one of the rabbits in half and settled into eating the haunches. I was too busy trying not to drool on myself to bother with niceties of sharing and quickly set to devouring the rest, gulping the rest of the meat down in shreds. The first of my replacement teeth were almost finished emerging, and while they were strong and sharp, they were never meant for a human jaw and made chewing difficult. It would be the blackest sort of irony if I survived all of this only to choke to death on a mouthful of rabbit.

'How close are we?' I asked once I was down to the last few bones. 'To Aknak, that is.'

'Three days, moving cautiously. And we *are* going to move cautiously, do you hear me?'

'Yes. My hearing is fine.'

'How's your leg? I saw you were dragging it a bit earlier.'

'It's fine.' It was far from that, but I didn't need her sympathy compounding the worries that already dogged me.

'It's not fine, damn you,' she said. 'Do you understand how serious this is? We're miles from help out here. One misstep, and we're done for.' She waved vaguely towards the north. 'For all we know, Falkenburg has fallen and we're doing this for nothing.'

'I thought you were doing this for Lucien.'

She drew a sharp breath and exhaled it as an obscenity. 'You know I am, damn you.'

'Then focus on that and stop trying to damn me more than I already am.'

'That's not the point.' She gestured to the yard outside. 'Those poor bastards out there are. You see what they did to them, even that little girl?'

'My eyes are fine too.'

'That's not a patch on what they'll do to us. I'm not going to end up on a pole or flayed to death because your ego wouldn't let you move quietly.'

'Is that what you think?'

'You know it's true. Man or dragon, men are the same.'

I stood, gritting my teeth as pain fired down my back and legs. 'Do you think this is a product of my vanity? Look at me.' The words came out with the hint of growl behind them as the anger lit inside me. 'My back is bent and my body twisted as that of a cripple. My mouth is a bloodied mess, torn by teeth that I fear will not stop growing. My hands are clumsy claws and my leg alternates between being numb and alight with a stabbing pain that never goes away. Look at me, damn you. Look at me, at what has become of my glory, and tell me that I choose not to run and hide because of my *ego*.'

'I'm sorry,' she said. 'I clearly confused ego with self-pity.' With that, she stood with an ease that simply made my anger flare hotter and walked away.

A dozen responses crashed together in my mind, but none felt right and in the end I vented my anger against a fallen beam of wood, splintering it with my now clumsy fists. It would have helped too, had I not tried to hurl the remainder of it against the wall. I was halfway through lifting it when the strength of my arm was stolen away by a wrenching sensation across my shoulders that sent me to my knees, the stump crashing to the floor next to me.

How was I supposed to face Navar like this? I could barely move my head, and now couldn't even trust my own strength to throw a piece of wood. He would attack my sorcery first, so without my strength to support me, what hope was there? I pushed myself back until I could rest against the wall and closed my eyes as I slowed my breathing.

I needed to find a point of calm, to clear the anger and weakness clamouring within my mind. I turned my attention and sorcery inward, exploring my body as the deacon who had inadvertently saved me once had, but delving deeper than he had dared to. I needed to know what the magic had done to me. I drifted through my own body, the double thump of my hearts and the blow of my lungs comforting and reassuring in this otherwise silent world of merging colours and flashing nerves.

I followed my spine, and saw how the bones between my shoulders had grown, the largest of which was now many times the size it should have been, the very much inhuman mass of it pushing and against my ribs and trapping sinews and veins between them. It was a similar matter with the blades of my shoulders, the corners of each having thickened into cones that my wings would have anchored to, and the tip of the bone having lengthened and attached itself to my ribs, forming the framework my flight muscles would one day attach to. Those were meant for a dragon's body, not a man's, and so for now it had pulled my shoulders out of alignment and compressed other muscles and veins. My hands were as I saw them, the claws that curled from the tips having fused with my bones at the last knuckle of each finger. My jaw was a mass of teeth packed against each other, three score of them trying to emerge in a space that would barely fit half that many.

It was disheartening, and I brought my focus back to my mind and concentrated on the memory of my own real body, something which proved harder than I expected. It came together piece by piece, first into the shrunken size forced on me by Henkman's wizard, and then finally in my true size. For several blissful moments I could almost feel my wings again and the sensation of my muscles stretching to their fullest, but it passed as it had to, and I slowly felt the idea of that body crumple into the sad reality of the mismatched flesh that now encased my spirit.

It was still dark when I opened my eyes. Tatyana was sleeping alongside me, her leg hooked over mine and her head on my arm. I stretched out my sorcery and settled it across her. She had recovered well from the trauma the necromancers had subjected her too, or at least her body had; the scars upon her skin were thin and silvery, as if they were years old, but scars from such torture went deeper than skin and bone. There was still some residual scarring on her organs from the dangerous amounts of magic she had fed off, but nothing that a lot more rest and good, fatty meat couldn't fix. I twisted the pattern of the sorcery slightly so that it would deepen her sleep and gently eased myself out from under her leg.

I cursed the litany of aches and pains and snapping sounds that shot through my body as I stood up and made my way outside. The clouds were breaking up, and even though the moon was still swaddled, the stars shone brightly from between the widening gaps. I moved beyond the reek that hung in the courtyard and took several deep breaths, tasting the air. I could smell water close by, something that we'd been short of over the last day, and so began following the scent trail.

It made sense of course, for while goats were hardy creatures, even they needed water. The stream wasn't far off at all, and from the neat arrangement of stones I expected that some farmer had re-routed it from its source. I'd been hoping for something a bit more substantial, but it was clean and certainly better than nothing. I knelt and drank, which is when I heard the voices.

I didn't recognise it as a voice at first. It was just a moan that could have come from any manner of beast, but it was answered by what was unmistakably a man's voice.

Intrigued, I sat back and tested the air again and, helped by a friendly gust of wind, tasted the miserably familiar trace of armed men. It was fainter than I expected it to be, but then sound did carry further at night. I followed the trace of their scent, and perhaps a quarter of a mile further on, the smell and noise strengthened sharply.

CHAPTER 32

THERE WERE CLUSTERS of shrubs and thickets amongst the splintered rock that broke from the thin soil like broken bones. I kept behind these, moving in an awkward half-crouch, tasting the air regularly to ensure I would not be surprised by any guards.

I could hear them more clearly now too, and I risked bending a few twigs of the bush I was hiding behind. The ground ahead of me sloped gently downwards to a small dell surrounded by more of the same spiky shrubs and a handful of skeletal trees. One side was bordered by what was clearly a man-made pool, and it was from here that the small stream flowed away behind me. I counted at least two dozen men in the dell, most of whom were seated close together in the centre, and, with a little help from my night vision and superior hearing, I discovered they were chained together. The men on the periphery were their captors, and at least half were still awake and talking over a small fire that smelled of bread and lamb that was on the verge of spoiling.

The voices I'd heard belonged to two of the captors who, as I watched, continued to beat a man they'd bound to one of the stunted trees. I squatted a bit lower and watched.

'How's that feel?' asked one of them in a heavy Penullin accent, slamming the man's head back against the tree. I could smell the copper of blood on the air and, curious, watched as he proceeded to hit him several more times. After perhaps the sixth or seventh blow the prisoner sagged against his bonds, either unconscious or dead. His attacker stepped back and shook his hands, flexing them like I did mine.

'You shut him up good,' said his companion, hunching next to the slumped figure. 'Damn. He's still breathing. You're losing your touch.'

'The fuck I am. Let me get a drink and then I'll show you a trick or two.'

They stomped over to the fire, and I watched as one of the other prisoners crawled towards the slumped figure, but stopped when his chain clinked loudly.

'One word to him,' called a man at the fire, 'and you join him tomorrow morning.'

The crawling man returned to his position while his captors laughed. I looked from the fire to the slumped and beaten figure, unconsciously tapping the ground with my nails as I considered what I wanted to do. On one hand, they were nothing to me, but I was also curious as to who they were, and why they were out here, camped on goat droppings west of nowhere.

The braying laughter of the man at the fire finally made my decision for me. I didn't like bullies, and especially not loud ones. I woke my sorcery and spun something like a coat of shadows around myself, then began making my way to the tree. It was a slightly extravagant use of power, but with all that was happening to my body I thought I deserved it.

No one heard or saw me as I crept up to the tree. The bound man was indeed alive, but not by much. I wasn't a healer by nature, but between healing Tatyana and building my own body, I had a fair idea of what belonged where inside a human and how it should look, and both his face and ribs had dents where there shouldn't have been any. He was drooling blood just like I was too, which made me feel unusually sympathetic towards his plight. I closed my eyes and called my healing construct to mind.

When I had healed Tatyana, I had accelerated it by binding my blood to hers, the full ramifications of which were still unfolding, so I had no desire to do that again. But I had learned much more about men since, and with the benefit of a little more time to prepare than I'd had with her, I sunk the sorcery into him, and watched closely as the mote of energy expanded inside him, tendrils of golden light finding his veins and racing along them, repairing tears and pulling blood back from his tissues, easing the swelling and bruises. He stirred as his heart began to pump with new vigour and only my hand over his mouth stilled the moan as his eyes opened.

'Be silent,' I said. I felt him nod under my hand and slowly lowered it.

'Did Kegan send you?' he whispered.

I stifled an urge to hit him myself but instead simply covered his mouth until he remembered what being silent meant and nodded again.

'Close your eyes,' I whispered.

To be fair, they were still swollen and puffy so I had to assume he was actually doing it. I moved in front of him and leaned in close, guiding my sorcery to the bruising there.

'Open them.' He did so hesitantly, but I was close enough that all he could see were my own. My hand muffled his gasp as the light kindled in mine, my sorcery binding his gaze as I slid into his mind. His thoughts were jumbled and cluttered, most likely the result of his recent mistreatments, so I pulled my thoughts into a needle and plunged through it until I reached a less tumultuous part of his mind.

THERE'S A BOY *sitting on wagon, surrounded by more boys of his own age. Most of them are laughing and singing as sombre parents wave to them, but they're too excited to worry about their parents' tears. Years drift by and the boys are older, their ungainly bodies stronger and harder, burned by sun and inured to the lash their teachers dole out with little hesitation. Their days are long, their time spent hunched over ancient books and sweating in the yard under the fencing master's call. More time blurs past, and the boys are gone, replaced by stern men in hard used armour. The boy had prayed for war, for the great adventure, the chance to show his devotion to the god who has given him so much power. Yet now that it is come, he dreams only of peace.*

The city is already aflame when they arrive, the flames lighting the night sky and revealing the corpses that litter the fields around it, stacked six deep in places. Even in the dark the crows are at work upon them, as thick as flies on a summer's day.

They ride out as dawn breaks, but the enemy is waiting for them. Volleys of mage fire rain down on them amidst the storm of arrows, and several of his brothers fall around him, burned and pierced. Those who survive close up and form an arrowhead of their own. Although he cannot hear them, he knows that each man alongside him is singing the same Battle Hymn as they thunder ever closer to the enemy. He aims his lance at one of the men and knows that he will not miss.

When the tip of his lance is but fifty yards from his mark's breast, his horse screams and stumbles. The horizon vanishes over his head. Steel shod hooves slam into him, denting the plate he had spent so long repairing and polishing. He tastes his own blood and dust. He knows now that they were waiting for them, that they have ridden into a steel trap. He stands and draws his sword, casting his ruined helm aside. The charge is broken, and those who are yet mounted are being torn from their saddles with hooks. Horses scream and thrash all around him, kicking at anything within reach.

He gives his steed its peace with a thrust of Foe-Breaker and readies himself as the enemy surge towards him. He can't tell which are living or dead, so he stabs and cuts at every neck and unprotected joint. He has been taught well. He incants a prayer of vengeance as he fights, dismaying his enemies and letting his sword bite deeper, every stroke delivering a mortal word. For a moment, he feels the golden heat of hope within him, but it's torn away by the blast of magic that crushes him into the mud like an insect. Foe-Breaker is lost, and a club sends him into the darkness.

He wakes, stripped and bloodied, surrounded by his brothers. The shame of their capture silences them more effectively than the threats of the wizard's thralls who herd them eastwards, tormenting them with the promise of the unholy death that awaits them. He sings a prayer for hope, but they beat him before the first verse is complete. He feels ribs break, and knows he will die here amidst the goat shit and mosquitoes.

I WITHDREW FROM the paladin's mind as gracefully as I had entered it, but kept my hand over his mouth. I loosened my grip so that he could draw the deeper breath he would need, but kept it close to forestall any protests. I sat back and glanced over my shoulder but the captors were still braying laughter at each other and entirely ignorant of my presence.

I lifted a finger to my lips as I'd seen Tatyana do, and the man, the Paladin, nodded. His eyes followed my claw as I lowered it.

He spat a mouthful of blood. 'By God, what are you?'

'A friend,' I said, annoyed at how my jutting teeth made it so hard to pronounce. He looked over my shoulder and lifted his chin.

'They're coming back,' he said. 'There are too many. Just go.'

'Fine,' I said, stepping off him and retreating into the shadows. He was still staring after me when his captors arrived, one of them brandishing a knife with a tip that glowed yellow from its time in the fire.

'Well, you're awake. I'm impressed,' the knife man said, squatting down almost exactly where I had.

'Maybe they do breed them tough,' said the other man, who was still standing, his arms folded.

'Maybe,' said Knife, 'but they breed us mean. And mean always beats tough.'

'Judgement will find you,' said the prisoner, whose name I now knew to be Leopold.

'Well, damn, now I'm too scared to cut your eyes out,' said Knife. 'Oh, no, wait. I'm not.'

'Please, help me,' said Leopold, turning awkwardly and staring slightly to the left of where I actually was.

I shook my head in the darkness. What an adventure this was turning about to be, when paladins were beseeching *me* to save *them*. I hadn't sensed the coldness that spoke of a worm infestation within him, nor malice or fear, even when he'd seen me sitting on him. The last was really something, especially when I considered what he was and how I now looked. And it had been interesting seeing his memory of his spellcasting, which was less similar to a wizard's than I had thought it was.

Knife and his friend were looking over at where I was now too, and any lingering hesitation ended when he voiced that braying laugh again.

'Oh, so now your god's hiding in the fucking bushes? You're pathetic.'

'I'm not his god,' I said, lighting my eyes and casting my cloak of shadows out to either side of me, giving me the appearance of having a pair of ghostly wings for a moment. 'I am your death,' I added in a moment of inspiration.

He screamed like a maiden and launched himself backwards in a wild leap. His companion staggered and tripped over Leopold, and as he struggled to his feet the rock I'd pitched at him struck him square in the face with a meaty slap, snapping his head back.

Knife tripped over the legs of one of the men chained in the centre, two of whom abruptly sprang upon him in a clatter of chains and set to beating him to death. The other captors were rushing in now and I used their hesitation to ready my sorcery. In the state I was in I had no intention of fighting them directly.

I used a many-tailed whip of energy, a derivation of something Navar Louw had enjoyed tormenting me with, and cracked it at them. Nine strands of solid fire flashed out and wrapped themselves about the Penullin soldiers, whereupon I collapsed the structure of the whip and released the fire, which surged along the lines wrapped around them and exploded into yellow-white flame, transforming them into nine screaming, cavorting torches.

Not all of them died from the fire but the survivors were in no shape to fight back as I systematically crushed their necks. I left the chained men to struggle to their feet by themselves while I threw some more wood on the fire.

'Good evening,' I said, rolling my shoulders as best I could as the fire's pleasant warmth caressed my back. A pulse of sorcery took care of Leopold's bonds, and the men became far more animated as he staggered into their midst, bloodied but healthy enough, rubbing life into his arms.

'What are you? Who are you?' Leopold asked as he approached. The others followed him, their shackles clinking musically.

'I am Stratus,' I said, making the fire flare behind me. It was a nonsense, but it made me smile when they all flinched. 'I am a friend.'

I sent another pulse of sorcery flashing along their chains, breaking the locks and freeing them all in a stroke. I watched them stumble forward as the metal clattered to the ground, a storm of fire held in my mind.

'God has surely sent you to us, then,' Leopold said, dropping to one knee, 'for, by my word, we owe you our lives.'

'I assure you that your god has nothing to do with it.'

'A leaf does not know which way the wind blows it,' he said, standing once more and coming forward, his right hand outstretched in a familiar gesture. I gripped it as I'd seen others do. 'I look forward to hearing your story.'

'You seem remarkably calm, for paladins,' I said. Several of the others were standing watching me with the dead soldiers' weapons clenched in their fists.

He turned to look at them. 'My brothers and I have been upon a dark road,' he said. 'Our deliverance is unexpected, and that we treat our deliverer with such ill manners is a cause for shame that we must reflect on.'

The men behind him lowered their weapons at this, but I kept my fire in mind.

'Reflections are best done with a full stomach,' I offered.

He bared his square teeth in a broad smile that I didn't even try to answer. 'You would get no argument from us, Stratus.'

They quickly stripped the dead men's bags for any food and soon set to boiling a pot full of oats and sharing out the remnants of the bread and lamb that remained, talking quietly among themselves throughout. They were all watching me keenly, or at least when I didn't look back at them. The last time so many paladins had watched me so closely the night had ended with a city on fire and a lot more screaming.

The food worked its own magic though, and by the time that the last bowl was licked clean they had found other things to look at and were talking more freely. It was largely to do with who had been killed or injured, but this at least was more familiar.

The only one who was still paying me such close attention to Leopold. His eyes narrowed as he met and held my gaze.

'You're Stratus Firesky,' he said.

CHAPTER 33

'WHAT?' WAS MY eloquent response.

'That's your name, isn't it?'

'Yes,' I said. I would never deny my own name. 'How did you know that?'

'I saw it,' he said, pointing back at the tree he'd been tied to before tapping his head. 'Heard it. In here.'

Now that was interesting. I had not felt any intrusion on my mind, but then perhaps I had not been as careful as I thought. 'What else did you see?'

'Some,' he said, shifting closer so that none could overhear him. 'Enough to know that you are quite the enigma.'

His heartbeat was steady, faster than Tatyana's normally was, but not racing like one gripped by fear. His scent bore little trace of it either, but instead carried a strange, almost floral spice to it.

'We all have our secrets,' I said.

'That is true. But you, I think, have more than most.' He rubbed the bristles that covered his jaw. 'Stratus Firesky. I have heard your name before, yet I cannot remember the where or how of it,' he said.

I felt a small thrill pass through me. It was good to be remembered, even in such a threadbare way. 'It is an old name,' I said.

'Names have a power of their own, don't you think?'

'Indeed they do. What do you want of me, Leopold son of Sigmund?'

He masked his flinch well, and someone without my keen senses may well have missed it. 'You are a wizard, but unlike any I have encountered.'

'I think that much is obvious.' I clicked my nails together as I waited for him to continue.

'May I speak plainly?' he asked.

'Please do,' I replied, the words lisping through my jutting teeth.

'Your appearance is at odds with your deeds, and in other circumstances I fear our meeting would have been less friendly. Some of my brothers are struggling with this contrast, and only your kindness holds them back.'

'I thought you were going to speak plainly,' I said, looking past him to where perhaps half of the paladins were sitting and doing things to the weapons and armour they had stripped from the still smoking dead.

'I am not a wizard,' I said. *Was it for the hundredth time?* 'I am not a man either, but I sense you already knew that.'

He nodded. I had thought as much, for to glean my name from my thoughts was no accidental impression or moment of opportunity. It spoke of an education in such matters, and one that was more diligent than anything I'd encountered in the wizards whose minds I had looted on my path here.

'And your brothers will not lift a hand against me without your command, so do not insult my intelligence with clumsy attempts at flattery or intimidation. I have had my fill of both.'

His mouth straightened like a rope pulled taut, and when he spoke, his voice had lost its honeyed warmth, the soft tones hardening into something that may have intimidated a lesser mind.

'Very well then, Stratus Firesky. Why are you here, in these accursed lands? You have the miscast look of a demon about you. Why did you heal me and break our chains? Who are you? What are you?' He leaned closer. 'You will tell me. Now.'

There was a suggestion laced into his words, a hint of their magics. I gave a short laugh, the sound unpleasant even to my ears.

'So, this is how you would treat one you say was sent by your god? These are dark days indeed if a life debt is so quickly cast aside in favour of threats and parlour tricks.' I looked to the men behind him, then back again. 'I had hoped that you were men of honour, but it seems you have cast that aside and are content to live as oath breakers and thieves.'

It was the most potent insult I could think of for a paladin, and he recoiled as if struck.

'Our vows are unbroken. Our honour is our life.' A chorus of agreement rose from the men who were conveniently sat within earshot. He made to stand, but then sat down again, his heartbeat steadily slowing as he clenched and unclenched his fists.

'I apologise,' he said after a while. 'My words were hasty, and ill chosen. I fear this trial has taken its toll on me. On us.'

An idea kindled in my mind, and I put aside the carefully barbed insult I had been preparing. 'I too have been a prisoner at their hands. It is easy to lose sight of hope.'

His knuckles whitened. 'That it is. When our brothers fell, we let despair poison our faith. It has been hard to rebuild that what was lost.'

'I had no faith to sustain me, only anger.'

He looked up at me. 'We have that too.'

'Would you avenge your brothers?' I asked, leaning forward.

He bared his teeth. 'We would die for the chance.'

'Then perhaps your god has set me upon your path,' I said, hauling myself to my feet. 'Come. There's someone you should meet.'

I didn't need to look to know they were following me as I turned back towards the house, my smile hidden by the darkness.

TATYANA WAS WAITING for me just outside the courtyard, hidden from sight but not from my nose.

'They're friends,' I said as I stepped inside. 'Paladin friends.'

She stood up where she had been hiding behind a mostly collapsed wall, sword in hand, and walked over to me, although her eyes were solely on my dozen new companions.

'What the Hel is this?' she said, finally looking at me.

'Leopold, son of Sigmund. He's a paladin, and these are his brothers. In arms, not by blood.'

'My lady,' said Leopold, bowing low.

'Sir Leopold,' she said, inclining her head. She stepped forward and stared at him as he straightened. 'Leopold Sigmundsson? From Skeln?'

He straightened at this and looked at her with narrowed eyes. 'Yes, my lady. How did you know that?'

'My father ran the chapter-house at Balfont.'

'Balfont?' His hand rasped across his cheeks. 'That was Gerhard Henkman. You must be Tatyana Henkman! It is an honour to meet you,' he said, bowing again. 'Master Rawlings spoke highly of you.'

'He was too kind.'

'Then we're not talking about the same fencing master.'

They both laughed at that and the other paladins, who had formed a half circle around us, came closer and introduced themselves to her, something they hadn't bothered to do with me, which was almost hurtful, even if the gesture would have been wasted on me. I left them to it and circled around to the far side of the property where their scent didn't overwhelm everything, and took some time to taste the air. Dawn wasn't far off and I wanted some idea of what lay before us.

I found a sheltered spot downwind from the corpses and made myself comfortable, closing my eyes. I drew a measure of power to myself and began preparing the same scrying spell I had used at Falkenburg, taking care to include an extra thread that would warn me if I strayed too close to an active ward. The lurch of my perception detaching itself from my physical body wasn't as harsh this time, more of a falling sensation before I floated free. I looked down at myself and saw what Leopold and the others saw for the first time; a large, hunchbacked figure in a tattered cloak with claws for hands and a fanged nightmare for a mouth. I hadn't appreciated how much restraint Leopold must have summoned to talk to me so calmly, and resolved to try to like him more.

I turned away and let my perception rise like an invisible bird. The landscape was brittle and unwelcoming below me, seemingly one harsh summer away from giving up all hope and becoming a desert. I rose higher and began to swoop forward, first with great caution and then with greater speed when I saw no signs of life or movement. I was perhaps ten miles from where my body lay when I saw the patrol.

They were camped on top of a small butte that time and

weather had smoothed to a mere bump in the landscape. I counted thirty men as I circled it, and perhaps twice as many ghouls, most of them arrayed around the camp as a makeshift wall. I pressed in closer and caught a glimpse of orange robes, and approached more carefully. He was the only wizard there though, and if my understanding of their ranks was correct, he wasn't particularly strong. I couldn't even sense any wards on him, much less the camp.

I drifted away, rising higher as I did, until I had my first glimpse of Aknak. Like Falkenburg, it had been built upon natural high ground, but much of it was shrouded in a pearlescent mist that defied the risen sun. I didn't like the look of that at all, but it was without doubt the city we sought. The foot of the hill it sat on was a sprawling mass of tents and buildings marked with countless flags, and beyond this lay rank upon rank of tents and pens holding livestock, horses, and what could have been prisoners or simply more ghouls. I moved forward, but even this far from it I could feel a trembling in the Songlines, a low level distortion that forced me to concentrate that much harder on maintaining the structure of the scrying construct. I dared to press in further and that same trembling soon began to take on a vague pattern, nothing I could identify for certain but most likely a ward of some sort from how uncomfortable it made me feel. I pulled back, aghast at how much power it would take to cast, let alone maintain, such a large perimeter.

I swooped lower and studied the ground, noting the gullies and cracks, mentally marking the paths, all while quietly enjoying the simulation of flying that it offered. The temptation to do it over and over again was strong, but I didn't want to risk it this close to what was most likely a nest full of necromancers, so reluctantly turned and sailed back to my body.

I lingered above it, noting that a paladin sat nearby, watching both me and the lands beyond. Or perhaps he'd simply come to watch the sunrise. Curious, I floated past him and towards the house and pushed in through a gap in the rafters, from where I could peer down on Leopold and Tatyana as they squatted next to a crude map drawn in the ashes. The remaining paladins were either sleeping or praying, the sound of their chanting less annoying than I had imagined. They were talking about water and distance, which was entirely too boring for me to waste energy on.

I returned to my body and woke with a groan as the flesh closed around my spirit once more, the accumulated aches and pains flooding into my head anew. I pushed myself to a seated position, spat to clear my mouth and offered the paladin a quick nod of thanks.

'The land is clear for ten miles around,' I said. 'There's nothing, not even a mouse.'

'It's the rain,' he said unexpectedly.

'The rain?'

'It's come twice since we were captured. There's a foulness to it that poisons smaller creatures caught by it. I've seen them wither and die myself.'

'Interesting.' I paused as I was about to pass him. 'Are any of the men here from Kenwin?'

'No,' he said, not bothering to look at me. 'We're all from the north.'

'Good,' I said, choosing not to add *that means I don't have to kill you all.*

Tatyana stood as I entered the house and squeezed my arm. 'Sorry I snapped at you,' she whispered, then sat back down.

'Apology accepted.'

'We've been considering our options,' Leopold said,

glancing at her as he did. 'Although the truth is, there aren't that many. We're surrounded by enemy territory, with no provisions and a handful of weapons amongst us.'

'Water will be crucial too,' I added, and Leopold nodded his agreement.

'Exactly right.'

'My point remains,' said Tatyana. 'I've been trying to impress upon Leopold that we're not here as an army. We're here to get inside Aknak.'

He crossed his arms. 'And how are we going to accomplish that with no food, no water, no—'

'For the last time, there is no *we* here,' she said.

I peered at their crude map and scratched an X into the ash. 'There's a substantial Penullin patrol here, perhaps three hours on foot. Thirty soldiers and fifty ghouls, with a single wizard, mostly likely a necromancer assigned to herd the ghouls.'

'Are they coming this way?' she asked.

'No, but they have plenty of swords and food.'

'You're not serious,' said Leopold. 'We don't have the numbers or gear.'

'But we have him,' said Tatyana with a flash of teeth.

CHAPTER 34

I WATCHED THE sun rise while Leopold spoke to his men, still amused by the thought that they were supporting me. I had used pride as a weapon against paladins before, but never as a tool. It was fascinating to watch their preparations. Their prayers were more specific than I had ever thought, in so much that they were actual statements, rather than a jumble of sounds disguised as a language for the sole purpose of sparking a connection between the paladin and the Songlines. They still chanted them in a similar way to a wizard, but there were several other intriguing differences.

'We're ready,' said Tatyana, who had approached without me noticing.

'As am I.'

One of the paladins who was apparently very nimble led the way, ranging ahead of us to pick the best path, marking his way with patterns of stones since none there but me could follow the scent traces he left everywhere like a careless child.

We stopped some time after the sun had passed its zenith and took shelter in a small sinkhole. I settled myself in and sent my scrying construct into the air again. It was even easier this time, or maybe it was just my enthusiasm for the respite it promised from the muzzled hostility of the paladins and the toll the pace was taking on my twisted body.

I soared eastwards, back to where I had seen the Penullin camp and was heartened to see that it was still there, even if most of the soldiers were not. The patrol was easy to track given the way the dead dragged their feet and occasionally voided bodily fluids, and I soon found them. They were perhaps three miles from where we lay, moving in small groups while the herd of the dead followed, the orange flash of the necromancer's robes clearly visible behind them.

I returned to my body and quickly described what I had seen, which prompted a lively debate about whether it was better to take the camp and wait for their return, or to wait and attack the camp once darkness fell. It was interesting to hear the arguments for each, but the novelty soon wore off.

'We wait until dark,' I said.

'We are skilled in war, wizard. It would be better for you to defer to us on matters of battle,' said one of the other paladins, a bearded man with a terrific scar on the side of his face.

He'd made no secret about his distaste for me, and while the glares he'd been levelling at me all day were laughable, it had done nothing to improve my general mood.

'A claim that neither your face nor your recent imprisonment support,' I said.

'Watch your tongue, demon.' The words were a snarl as his face coloured with blood, apart from the scar, which now stood out even more.

'Or what?' I said, my voice creeping closer to a growl.

'Peace, please,' said Leopold. 'We have enough enemies already.'

I accepted this with a gracious nod while Scar grunted something noncommittal and possibly insulting. I ignored him and turned to Leopold.

'As I recall, your little array of cantrips include light spells, yes?'

'If our faith is true, we can ask Drogah to dispel the darkness around us.'

I suppressed a groan. 'Of course. And can he do that as soon as you ask him?'

Leopold flashed his square and very white teeth at me. 'His bounty and mercy know no limits.'

'As long as you're not a heretic,' added Scar. 'Like demons, heretics neither deserve nor receive any.'

I could smell his aggression, which in turn fed my own anger, but I forced it down once more. 'If you have nothing constructive to add, perhaps you should go look for a helmet.'

He scrabbled to his feet with a snarl, but Leopold was faster than him and pushed him back before he could do more than puff his chest out.

'Take a walk,' he said, and with one last look at me, Scar and two others made their way out of the sinkhole.

'My apologies,' said Leopold. 'He is a good man, but very passionate.'

'He's a prick,' offered Tatyana.

I smiled at that, then set out my plan.

WE MOVED INTO a position not far from the Penullin camp, but far enough that there was no chance of the returning patrol stumbling across us. The paladins huddled together to pray and do other paladin things, leaving Tatyana and I little to do but try and get some rest, although the hunger gnawing at me left little chance of that.

'Do you trust them?' she asked.

'No.'

'Not even Leopold?'

'I trust him least of all.'

She rolled over so that she faced me. 'Then why are you doing this? Why get involved with them at all?'

'Curiosity. And I have an idea, although you might not like it.'

'Tell me.'

'Their magic is different up close. I expected it was more closely aligned with wizardry, but the structure and tone of it is unlike—'

'I meant your idea.'

'Oh. They're going to keep the enemy's eye from us when we get to the city.'

'You're going to use them as a diversion?'

'That is the word. Yes. A *diversion*.'

'You're going to sacrifice them.'

I shrugged and shuffled into sunlight, enjoying the warmth on my skin. 'It is their choice,' I said, closing my eyes. 'And I am not the one who is lacing every other sentence with hidden compulsions.'

'What?'

'Surely you've felt it? How reasonable everything Leopold says seems, and how readily the others agree with him?'

'The *Aer Nephus*,' she said, rolling onto her back. 'The voice of the angels. That complete and utter shit.'

'So it has a name?'

'It's a powerful blessing, a gift.'

I snorted at that. 'It's a cheap trick.'

'God's teeth, did he use it on me? What if I told him you were a—'

'He tried, but I warded you against it.'

'When? How?'

Instead of answering I fed a little power through the link between us, enough to wake the dormant sorcery within her. I was careful to concentrate it on her senses rather than any sort of healing, making the colours and sounds around her twice as potent as anything she was used to.

'Damn you,' she said. 'Don't do that.'

'I thought it would be easier to show you.'

'Keep your damned magic to yourself.'

'Would you rather have confessed all to Leopold?'

'That's not what I meant.'

I opened my eyes again as I sensed the change in her heartbeat. 'Then what did you mean?'

'Just forget it, Stratus. Thank you for saving me from Leopold, even if you didn't bother telling me what you're doing to me and *my body*.'

'You're very welcome.'

I closed my eyes again and tried to focus on getting my own thoughts in order, and I must have succeeded because when I opened them again the day was a fading band of amber in the west and the paladins were rolling their shoulders and stretching their legs in a way I could never now hope to replicate.

'You're awake. Excellent. I was just about to call on you,' said Leopold. He was all but shining with vitality and, not for the first time, I was tempted to smash him in the teeth. Instead I made a show of dusting the dirt from my tattered cloak as I stood and joined them.

'I was not sleeping. I was preparing myself for the night's festivities.'

'Most excellent. We,' he gestured to the paladins behind him, 'are ready. Drogah has heard our prayers and stands with us.' He clapped a hand to my shoulder. 'We would ask you to pray with us.'

'Why?'

'So that he may grant his blessing upon you.'

'He would bless a nasty heretic like myself?'

'Do not joke about such matters, my friend.'

I considered this. I still doubted that their god was anything more than a manifestation of their collective imagination, a communal pool of willpower and intent channelled through their prayers, but it seemed churlish to say so now. Especially when it was that belief and the pride in their cult that would make them such an effective diversion. And, if nothing else, my curiosity had reared its head again.

'Well then, let us pray,' I said, and he clapped his hand to me again.

'You have some strength under those tatters,' he said as he led me into the circle the paladins had formed. Tatyana was there already, watching me with wide eyes and eyebrows that climbed midway up her forehead as I took my place. Leopold took my left hand, and gestured for me to take that of the man to my right, who nodded and smiled as I folded my fingers around his hand and let my claws rest lightly upon his wrist, as I had with Leopold. At the first hint of betrayal I'd strip both to the bone.

Leopold lifted his face to the sky and began talking in what I assumed was the language of priests. I'd heard snippets of it before, albeit mostly in the form of curses or cries for mercy, but didn't bother trying to decipher it. It had a pleasing cadence though, and I took a moment to settle a veil of sorcery across my vision, filtering out the harshness of reality until the men and rocks were vague silhouettes against the light of the magical currents that flowed through and around them. *Us.* All of the paladins were glowing brighter than men should, although I was pleased to see that Tatyana shone brighter still, the sorcery fused to her flesh reflecting and amplifying the energy the paladins were summoning.

I became aware of the power in the moment when I realised I was humming to the sound of Leopold's voice. It felt like I was standing in the sun on a summer's day, and by the stars, it actually felt good. The swirl of the Songlines around us had strengthened since I had first looked at it, but it was diffused, more like a mist than the stream I normally experienced it as. Glittering motes of it filled my lungs with every breath, and as I looked at Tatyana, I could see the glittering specks of it in her body too. I took a deeper breath, filling my lungs, and felt the energy inside me surge through my veins.

I felt Leopold squeeze my hand and I returned the gesture, a poor idea on my part given that I was paying more attention to my sorcery than my body. He cried out, and the swirl of the mist slowed and began to disperse.

I dispelled the veil from my vision and released my hold on the other's hands. Leopold was hunched over, rubbing at the hand I'd squeezed, but before I could do or say anything a crunching, crackling noise filled my head, swiftly followed by a deep ache in my chest that crushed any lingering euphoria from the blessing.

It felt like some invisible hand was crushing my chest, preventing my left lung from expanding. I reached out to steady myself and gratefully accepted a proffered arm, but the paladin who'd offered it was no match for my weight and we both ended up on the ground. The need to breathe was burning through my veins, but before I could even try to make sense of what was happening another hand touched my shoulder and I felt a spark of lightning flash through my body, breaking the paralysis that had gripped my chest. I took several greedy gulps of air and rolled off the unfortunate paladin who had fallen with me. He too was gasping.

I looked up at Tatyana, whose hand still rested on my shoulder.

'What the Hel was that?' she asked.

I accepted the hand she offered me with caution as I stood up, but she took it better than the paladin had. I took another deep, steadying breath, and was relieved to feel no trace of the mysterious pain.

'My body, I mean the enchantment, I believe it's reacting to external magic,' I said, more to myself than her. 'But not to my own.'

I looked across at the paladin I'd fallen on. Three of his brothers had their hands on his chest and I could feel the gathering of their magic as they incanted their prayer of healing.

'Thank you,' I called over to him even as I took a step back. He had tried to help, even if he'd failed, and that was something.

It took a bit longer before he and Leopold were well enough to move again, which did nothing to improve relations with them. Fortunately the imminent violence provided a useful distraction, and with the last of the light having drained from the sky it was time to move. We approached the camp with great caution, helped in no small part by having so few men clad in armour. In truth, Tatyana was the most heavily armed of all of them but she moved as nimbly, having tied strips of cloth to what overlapping armour she had, muffling the scrape and jingle that normally accompanied her everywhere.

The paladins split into two groups and moved out to either side of Tatyana and I.

'You ready?' she asked.

I called my sorcery to mind and considered the constructs I had prepared. 'I am if you are.'

'I have a sudden need for a pee, so I guess I am.'

'I don't understand.'

'Never mind,' she said, flashing me a smile as she tugged at a strap. 'I'm ready.'

'Then I'll begin.'

CHAPTER 35

I REMEMBERED THE layout of the Penullin camp from my scrying, so while myself and Tatyana approached the main cluster of the soldier's tents, the paladins swept out around us, and would attack from the other side once I had drawn their attention. My first idea had been to simply rain fire down on the camp, but Tatyana had impressed upon me the need to preserve rather than damage their equipment. They'd come up with a far more convoluted plan which I had simply refused to listen to, and in the end we settled on an improved version of my original notion seeing as the changes only affected their part..

I woke my night vision and moved up the slope until I had a clear view of the tents, then settled down and released the first construct, sending a score of sorcerous tendrils snaking through the air like serpents of smoke, each seeking the pulse of a living heart. Once they had all connected I spooled out the last component of the second construct and sent a pulse of fire along each connection, each of these just about visible to the naked eye as a streak of orange light.

It didn't work as well as I'd hoped though. Some of the trails had touched, merging or diverting some of the streams of fire, making some weaker and others stronger, so that the flash of heat meant to burn their hearts and kill them silently set some on fire and did nothing but scald others.

Screams and cries of alarm broke the night as the surviving soldiers burst from their tents. Some were dressed, some were burnt, but all of them were armed and angry. While they lit torches and spread out I watched the paladins rise from their hiding places and run up the final stretch of the slope on their flanks.

'Hold on tight,' I said to Tatyana as I put my arm around her waist. I didn't wait for her reply before releasing the wind spell, lifting us both high into the air in a spray of gravel and dust. The slope blurred under us, and as we passed the tents and milling soldiers we tipped downwards, landing close to their cooking fires. The second part of the spell woke, slowing our fall with another blast of air that scattered their pots and sent a cloud of sand and ash billowing out around us.

I released Tatyana as our feet touched the ground. She seemed to have taken the jump very well and wasted no time in opening the throat of a Penullin soldier while he was still shielding his face from the flying ash.

'A Krandin! A Krandin!' she shouted, and the Penullin soldiers turned on her as one, their answering shouts drowning hers out. They were streaming towards us when Leopold emerged from between the tents behind them, followed a moment later by the rest of his sword brothers. This was their part of the plan and I left them to it while I headed towards the herd of ghouls. They didn't need to be preserved, so the fire I had been nursing within me all afternoon could finally be released.

The dead were already lurching towards the sound of the battle, and the sudden flare of the paladins releasing their light spells behind me was clearly reflected in their dull eyes. I caught a glimpse of orange robes to my right just as I heard the sound of the wizard's spell discharging.

A bolt of kinetic force hit my side, and had it been properly focused, it may well have winded me or perhaps even cracked a rib, but he had rushed it and so weakened his spellcasting, spreading the impact until it was no worse than a man's punch. I wanted to capture him alive if I could, and so let him run off and hide behind his ghouls, as yet unmolested.

The dead closed in, their lines bending around me at an unheard command from the wizard. I stood where I was and let my sorcery flow into the fire construct while holding it close to me. I could feel the pressure building within me, and was forced to squint as flashes of energy bled into reality around me, momentarily painting the pale corpses reaching for me in vivid reds. I closed my eyes and released the fire, flinging my hands outwards in a sympathetic gesture.

The flame roared with its own voice as it rippled outwards, transforming from red to gold to white. It was mesmerizingly beautiful, the aftermath less so. The closest of the dead were dismembered, their limbs scorched off or simply ripped away by the initial blast, while others were scoured of skin and flesh, their body fats igniting so that they burned with their own greasy flame as they flopped about on the ground, while those furthest away simply stood there, seemingly unaware that they were on fire. The wizard hadn't escaped the blast either, and was rolling about on the ground trying to smother his burning robes, but from his wailing it did not seem to be a mortal injury.

'Drogah's angels have mercy on us,' said a voice behind me. A paladin stood there, smoke curling from his beard and hair, his chest painted red with steaming gore.

'I thought you were Drogah's angels,' I said, rising from my crouch.

He patted his beard and stepped back from the smouldering ghoul at his feet. 'We are his sword, his justice made manifest,' he mumbled, staring at me with bloodshot eyes.

Your kind killed the love of my life. I toyed with the idea of setting him alight and ascribing it an accident, but the fight with the Penullin soldiers had already come to its brutal and inevitable conclusion, and the flaming corpses had already drawn the attention of too many of the others.

Tatyana whistled softly as she and Leopold came to stand by me. 'You've outdone yourself,' she said. Leopold said nothing as he watched me.

I accepted the compliment with an awkward nod. 'They are predictable.'

'What about him?' She pointed her sword at the wizard I'd now dragged closer.

'He's mine.'

'He is a necromancer,' said Leopold. 'Our laws demand his death.'

'He is mine,' I said, showing him a few more teeth.

'Easy,' said Tatyana, stepping between us. She looked up at me. 'Are you, you know, going to do the thing?'

'The thing?'

'You know.' She took a step closer and whispered 'With his brain.'

'Ah. Yes, I am.'

'Right. I suggest you go do it somewhere out of sight.'

'What are you talking about?' demanded Leopold.

'I'm going to ea—'

'Interrogate him with magic,' Tatyana said, rudely interrupting me.

Leopold looked at her, then me again. 'Fine,' he said.

'Just be quick about it. We need to be away before dawn.'

'Yes,' said Tatyana. She glanced back at me. 'Make it quick.'

Since the bulge in my back wouldn't let me sling the still blubbering wizard over my shoulder, I took a handful of his robes and dragged him along next to me instead, leaving the paladins to start stripping the prisoners and the dead. I stopped a short way down the slope and squatted down next to the groaning wizard.

'Can you talk?' I asked, jabbing a nail into his blistered cheek to make sure I had his attention. He coughed and spluttered but eventually said yes.

He gave a short and incoherent scream when he finally saw me and made a quite pathetic attempt to escape, one that I foiled by catching his leg and dragging him back towards me, my nails sliding into the soft meat and making him thrash about.

'Where is Navar?' I shifted to the side, hoping that what breeze there was would blow the distracting smell of his seared flesh away from me.

'Who?'

'Your master. The Worm Lord. Carries a staff carved like a man's spine.'

'I don't know. How would I know?' He groaned and cradled his nicely burned right arm, the source of the aroma that was troubling me.

'You're one of his. Now talk before I start cutting you.'

'Oh fuck, it hurts!'

'Imagine how it will hurt if I burn the rest of you.' That got his attention.

'I'm just an orange robe,' he all but shouted. 'All I do is make lanterns and herd the dead! I've never even seen him.'

'So he has not implanted strange enchantments in your head?'

'What? No? I swear.'

'Excellent.' I grabbed him by the throat and pulled his face to mine, ignoring the feeble blows he landed. I woke my sorcery, the fiery glow of my eyes lighting his face with a soft glow. I felt his throat working under my hand, but neither protest nor scream could escape my grip.

I plunged into his mind, knifing through the fear and panic of our attack, beyond the tedium of herding ghouls for mile upon mile, constantly coaxing and forcing them into movement, their every touch making him gag despite his training. I pushed too strenuously and Aknak flew past me, forcing me to pull myself back through his memories, back along a column of soldiers and downtrodden prisoners, back past burned villages where bodies hung from trees like strange fruit, until finally the city loomed large before me again.

THERE ARE HUNDREDS *of prisoners at work all around us, hauling rock and brick to repair the walls broken in the first siege. I see how those that are too weak to continue are tossed or carried into ditches where they are left to die, either of exhaustion or suffocation as more bodies are thrown on top of them. Disgust and terror fill me, but I keep my face impassive and agree to everything, never questioning and never disobeying. Something worse than death happens to those who turn against him. The soldiers don't like me. They don't like any of us, but they obey out of fear of what happens to those who rebel. I keep saying sorry, but that just makes them laugh.*

I push a little deeper into the memories and faces and voices blur past me. *It is night, and the inner city is glowing with silver light that dances along anything metallic, jumping from man to man. The great spell has begun; the*

Gateway is opening and the dead are restless. I'm working hard to keep them together but the light draws them, as if they know what lies beyond it. I'm utterly spent by the morning, and for once I am glad to be going on a patrol. Eight more nights of that would burn the magic out of me forever.

I PULLED MYSELF from his mind, untangling my thoughts from his and blinked as the world came back into focus around me. The wizard was a limp, dead weight in my hand and I let his body fall back. A cursory check confirmed that his heart had stopped beating, which was perhaps the easiest death I could have offered him. A quick search of his body yielded little except a small purse of gold and silver coins which I tied to my own belt, more out of habit than any real need.

I left his body to what vermin remained in these blasted lands and made my way back to the camp which, to my surprise, was brightly lit with both torches and golden light emanating from the paladins.

CHAPTER 36

THE SURVIVING PENULLIN soldiers had been corralled in the centre of the camp, where they sat in a sullen silence while the paladins sorted through the pile of weapons and armour they'd taken from them. It all seemed bizarrely civilised given the amount of blood that had just been spilled, at least until I remembered Leopold's gift for lacing his speech with subliminal commands.

The man they'd set as a guard started as I moved into the reach of the light surrounding him but lowered his weapon before he did anything stupid.

'That's not a face I'll get used to seeing,' he said.

I didn't dignify that with an answer and made my way to where Tatyana sat by the re-lit campfire. I sat as close to it as I could, only edging back when the edge of my cloak started smouldering.

She had removed her boots and was sat with her pale feet extended towards the fire. 'So how'd it go with him?'

'The wizard? Well enough. He didn't know much, but I did manage to see something of the city.' She listened intently as I described what I had seen, then made me repeat it and asked enough questions that I was soon regretting telling her about it.

'What do you think it means, the great spell?' she asked

eventually.

I watched the play of light across the embers for a while before answering. 'I think it is no coincidence that this *great spell* is being prepared even as the wizards besieging Falkenburg are preparing a powerful ritual to infuse power into the same sort of Lance that sits in the heart of Aknak.'

'That's not good.' She didn't look away from the dance of the flames. 'What's a node?'

'A confluence of the Songlines. Like two or more rivers coming together.'

'Sounds important.'

'It is. The rivers.' I stared into the flames without seeing them as I saw Navar's plan unfold in my mind. It was reckless and once I would have thought it impossible, except that he had already done several things that I had once considered unthinkable.

'What about the rivers?'

It was Tatyana's voice, but there was another layer to it, as if another voice had spoken my name at the same time, but from a great distance. I listened, but it didn't come again.

'What's wrong? You started talking about rivers but then went off somewhere else. Without even blinking, which is creepy even by your standards.'

'The rivers,' I said again, making sure to blink as I looked away from the fire to her. 'That's the key, you see. The Songlines, that is the rivers, do not flow in a single, neat loop. They bisect each other, time and time again, surrounding the world like a net of sorts. Do you understand?'

'The rivers are a net?'

'That's right. Wherever they meet, they crash together.' I squeezed my hands together for emphasis. 'They're strongest where they meet, like waterfalls or springs, and closer to the material world. Aknak's node is on one such spring, and Falkenburg is another.'

'You've lost me.'

I stood and, in my mind, began pacing the length of my cage again. 'The nodes are powerful confluences, but they're also places of renewal. Their effect extends some way beyond where they meet, making the life that feeds them stronger in turn.'

'Still lost.'

'Suppose that someone poisons a river, but later on that river meets another that's just as deep and powerful. The poison will be diluted and while it may kill a few fish there, it would be washed away.' She nodded at this. 'But now suppose you pour more poison in every time the river meets another.'

'The poison won't be diluted?'

'Exactly. And it's not just the fish that will die. That water feeds the grasses and the trees, and in turn becomes the rain that falls wide and far, poisoning everything.'

'And everything will die.' She stared at her feet. 'So how do you stop it?'

I opened my hands and sent a flicker of fire dancing along my curved nails. 'You stop the poison and let the river wash itself clean.'

'That's obvious enough, but how do you stop the poison?'

'The lances are the source, like a viper's fangs hooked into the world's skin. They have to be broken.'

'I suspect that's easier said than done. I've seen what happens if you break magic stuff, and if these lances are that important, they'll be pretty powerful, right?'

I closed my hand and edged a little closer to the fire. The night was quiet apart from the popping of the wood and the sing-song sound of prayers somewhere behind us.

'I don't know enough about how they function, only that it needs to be done.'

'So what are you saying?'

'I'm saying I don't know what will happen. It could be nothing more than the dead falling over and a fresh breath of wind passing over the countryside.'

'Or?'

I spread my hands towards the fire. 'It's equally possible that the ground could open and swallow the city and its surrounds.'

'Oh great.'

'Or the entire city could explode, if the gateway is too blocked with traces of dark magic.'

'Even better.'

I paused. 'That was a jest, wasn't it?'

'Yes, damn it. God.'

'You don't have to come with me.'

'If I'm going to die it might as well be in an exploding city.' She lifted a gourd of sorts from a pocket and took a swift drink from it, wincing as she offered it to me. 'Any damn fool can die on a sword.'

It smelled of rank peaches, but I took a sip like she had. The fiery liquid scoured the taste of blood from my mouth in an instant, the fumes boiling up through my nose like the plume of a volcano and left me coughing and spluttering. 'Stars alive, what is that?'

'No idea,' she said. 'I found it in one of their tents and figured it smelled like hooch.'

'Hooch?'

'A distillation of the finest beverages the eastern valleys can offer.'

'You're not making any sense.' I took another sip and managed not to cough. 'It tastes awful.'

'That it does, my friend,' she said, taking it back and

risking another draught. 'Can we go for a walk? I've seen enough dead men for one night.'

'It is dark and there is not much to see,' I said, reluctant to leave the fire.

'There are stars.'

'I do like the stars,' I said. I stood as she did and walked beside her. She didn't say anything but simply walked along at a snail's pace, taking small sips from the gourd.

'That's the archer,' she said once we reached the bottom of the slope, pointing to a cluster of stars overhead. 'You see the arrow? It points towards the dawn.'

'I know it, but we called it the *reptákon*. In your language it would be—'

'The Scorpion.'

I cocked my head to the side and stared at her. 'Yes. The scorpion. What you call his bow is its tail. How did you know that?'

She shrugged. 'I don't know. It was just there, in my mind and my mouth.'

Curious, I pointing to another constellation. 'That is *Adamaster*. Do you know the word in your language?'

'The Giant,' she said, easing herself down on a tumbled rock and belching loudly.

'The Sleeping Giant,' I said. 'This is most interesting. Those names were rarely known, even in the golden age of the Shae.'

'The what?'

'You called them elves. Or sometimes fairies.' I rested my hand on her shoulder. 'The point is, it's a language that has not been spoken for a thousand years. There's no way you could know those words. I believe that the link between us is somehow evolving, and—'

'Can you just stop talking?'

'Why?'

'I just want to look at the stars.'

The irony of it made me smile. I leaned against a nearby rock and silently named those stars I could see while the other part of my mind recited dozens of questions and theories about how she had gleaned the knowledge.

'There's a nice hot fire up there, you know,' I said quietly.

'I thought you liked the stars.'

'I do, but there's a sky above the fire too.'

She sighed and passed me the considerably lighter gourd. 'I'm not squeamish about fighting and killing,' she said, her voice trailing off as she watched the cold blaze of a distant meteorite. 'But killing like that? Not for me.'

'Like what?' I said, my voice made gruff by the vile liquor.

'You don't know, do you?'

'I couldn't say, not until you tell me what you're talking about.'

'Them.' She pointed to the top of the hill where my fire was probably dying back. 'Leopold and his men. They're executing the prisoners.'

'Makes sense.' I took another sip and pointed to the north. 'Do you see that one over there? We call it the Great—'

She snorted and snatched the gourd from my hand. 'Never mind. I should have known it wouldn't bother you. So, carry on. The great what?'

I told her, then pointed out as many of the others that I could see, teaching her the names in draconic that she didn't know, while she taught me the names and ridiculous folk tales her people associated with them.

'Do you think Lucien is still alive?' she asked abruptly, interrupting my tale about how the moon was actually one of the Dreamsinger's disembodied eyes. 'I mean, they wouldn't do all that to capture him and then just kill him, right?'

I felt her heartbeat increase as I considered the question. 'No,' I said. 'I think he is still alive. Navar is a loathsome wretch, but he's a calculating and intelligent wretch. He will want to corrupt Lucien, not kill him.'

'So I can still save him?'

I clenched my teeth before the truth escaped my lips. 'Yes, I think you can. Life breeds hope.'

She sighed and stood up. 'Let's go back. It'll be done by now.'

She pointed out the constellations again on the way back, butchering their draconic names with her small and ill formed mouth, but I liked that she tried.

The camp was silent when we returned. The paladins were kneeling near the bodies of the now dead soldiers, who had been laid out in a neat row, their faces covered by squares of cloth, none of which did anything to hide the red that had bloomed along their hidden throats.

'What are they doing?'

'They're asking Drogah to accept the souls they've just freed from their human frailties.'

I waited for her to continue, but it seemed she wasn't trying to be humorous. 'They didn't seem frail.'

'Their sins, then.' She nudged me in the ribs and pointed. 'You see there, above their boots? The red bands mean they're under the wizards' command. It's a death sentence for any of them that get taken.'

'Redlegs,' I said, nodding. 'Victims of fashion, as Lucien would say.'

She barked with laughter and clapped a hand over her mouth as if it had startled her too. Several of the paladins had also turned to glare at us.

'Sorry,' she said, pulling me off to the side. 'That was entirely disrespectful and actually funny. There's hope for you yet. Now come, let's find some food.'

I didn't argue with that and set to emptying the tents around us. Dawn wasn't far off, and if all went well, by the following nightfall we would be at the walls of Aknak, and for that I would need every ounce of strength I could muster.

We scavenged a fair amount of food, although Tatyana forced me to share it out amongst the paladins as well, which struck me as wasteful given that they had every intention of dying at the first suitably glorious opportunity, but she was quite adamant about it and I eventually relented, but only after managing to tuck a length of smoked sausage inside my robes.

Leopold and his fellows seemed to be in a good mood as they wolfed down their share of the food and wine we'd found, and were eagerly showing off the armour and weapons they had stolen. I didn't point out that those same weapons and armour hadn't offered much help to their previous owners, reckoning that their false confidence would only make them more open to going along with my plan.

None of them interrupted me as I explained what I had in mind, and when I was done Leopold asked if they could have some time to discuss it, which I happily agreed to as it gave me time to eat the sausage without their greedy eyes watching me. I was feeling quite pleased with myself when they eventually called me back, and even more so when Leopold announced that my plan was a good one.

The final preparations didn't take very long, and by the time that the sun was more than a blush in the east we were already marching towards the city.

CHAPTER 37

IT FELT QUITE liberating to walk rather than skulk in holes and cracks like some rodent, and even Tatyana recovered her good humour and seemed to be enjoying the novelty of wearing the wizard's orange robes, much to Leopold's obvious disapproval.

We saw the first of the enemy soldiers shortly after noon, a troop of horsemen who had clearly seen us too as they turned and came riding up. I watched from under my hood as Leopold hailed the first of them in fluent Penullin, his words laced with friendliness.

There were some thirty riders, ten of whom dismounted to speak with him, or as I saw it, to listen to his charmed voice. Even though I knew what he was doing, I thought he was very convincing, and by the time they rode off again several of them had embraced him and sworn to meet him in the city for a drink that night.

'Impressive,' I said as I watched them ride northwards.

'Now you understand why Jean is working so hard to keep the peace with them,' Tatyana replied, idly picking at the end of the rope that supposedly bound my wrists. I was, after all, pretending to be her prisoner. 'Try and imagine a hundred men like Leopold telling the commoners that Drogah has decided that their king was not to be trusted.'

I grunted as I considered that. I understood his power and thought it a petty trick and an easy way to give cowards false courage, but if employed against men with no defence against it, it could be a powerful weapon. I'd used something similar in my own battles, instilling awe and fear in my enemies, but that had been a more an effect of my radiant will than a targeted assault with words and thoughts.

We encountered another such patrol with similar results mid-way through the afternoon. The leader of these riders directed Leopold to a fork in the road a mile or so distant which would lead us to the part of the encampment where the prisoners were to be interred. He didn't question why Leopold didn't know this already and rode away with a wave and a smile on his face instead.

Leopold swaggered over to us. 'He reckons it's about another six hours march to the city or so. If we push on, we'll get there sometime after sunset. We'll need to consider if we want the cover of darkness or to arrive pre-dawn and more rested.'

'Darkness,' I said. With my hide, it would be far easier for me to go unnoticed amidst the shadows than in the daylight.

'I agree,' said Tatyana. 'A camp that big, there's going to be a lot going on in the morning. It's better to hit them in the dark when everyone's tired and thinking about food and in no mood to chase after someone who might be just be lost.'

He scratched at his chin, then nodded his agreement and we set off towards the road the horseman had pointed us to. It was little more than a rutted track that had been widened by the passage of many men and marked out with strips of coloured cloth that I recognised from the camp outside Falkenburg, but it was at least straighter. The paladins summoned their light again, cleverly disguising the origin by casting it upon the hastily whittled branch masquerading as Tatyana's staff.

The city came into view shortly after, and it wasn't the size or bustle of the camp that brought us to a silent halt, but rather the silver-white glow that flashed and flickered in the mist draped across the city like a great blanket, filling the space between the towers and buildings in a milky radiance.

'God's teeth,' whispered Tatyana. 'We're going in there?'

I nodded, ignoring the crunch in my neck. 'Right into the heart of it.'

I could smell the growing tension in the men around me as the scale of what they faced grew more obvious. For my part, the camp's complete vulnerability to an attack from the air was painfully obvious, something that set the frustration and anger to gnawing away inside me again. I would have swept in from the west as the sun set, dividing the camp with a stream of fire, then quartered it with a pass from the north. The rising flames and smoke would sow confusion and denigrate what defence they could offer, letting me swoop again and again, more or less unmolested. I had done just that before, and I felt a deep sense of satisfaction that I could now at least remember where and when. I felt the scrape of my teeth against the inside of my lips and I realised I was smiling.

'What's so funny?' asked Tatyana, her voice bringing me back to the present.

'Just revisiting old memories.'

'You have memories of a city overrun with death-worshipping wizards?'

Images of cities in flames flashed through my mind, of streets clogged with charred bodies trapped inside red hot metal that they'd thought would protect them. 'Not exactly.'

'Well, shake it off. It's time to be my prisoner, you filthy animal.'

I lunged at her suddenly, fangs gaping, and she leapt backwards.

'You shit,' she said, dusting herself off.

'Remember that I'm a dangerous prisoner,' I said. 'If you get too close to me, I will bite you.'

'You wouldn't.'

'Oh, I will. You'll heal, remember?' Her smile faded. 'It will aid your mummery.'

What joviality there was faded as we drew closer to the outskirts of the camp. The paladins knew their time was coming, and they spent the last stretch saying their goodbyes and whispering prayers.

A score of Penullin soldiers stood waiting for us in the road, all fully armed and accompanied by a wizard in a robe that might have been yellow or green. Beyond them the road split into three paths, each of which vanished into the mass of tents and ramshackle paddocks that stood between us and the city proper. I tested the fake bonds that bound my wrists and found them loose enough to throw off with little effort, and even though the rope around my neck was just as loose, I really didn't like the feel of it and would have refused to wear it had the other end been in anyone but Tatyana's hands.

Leopold went forward, but the wizard waved him away.

'Come here, girl,' he called, crooking a finger at Tatyana.

'Fuck,' she whispered under her breath. She was still holding my neck rope so I followed after her, trying to look as I imagined a prisoner should.

'What's all this?' the wizard asked, gesturing widely.

'What does it look like? We're bringing a prisoner in.'

He grabbed a bundle of paper from one of the soldiers and stared at it. 'What's your name?'

'Sharon.' She folded her arms around her staff as he stared at her. 'The Orange.'

'Sharon the Orange,' he repeated. As he spoke, he clicked his fingers and the soldiers who had been watching suddenly straightened and took hold of their weapons. 'I've never heard of you. Whose class were you in?'

'You're certainly not in mine,' she said, earning a brief laugh from one of the soldiers.

'Where's your staff, *Sharon the Orange*?' His own staff flickered with sudden light as he activated a latent spell, and I heard the shuffle of the paladins spreading out behind me, something that the soldiers must have noticed too because the scent of aggression in the air strengthened considerably. They weren't the only ones either. I could see several more men watching from the nearby tents.

'I lost it capturing that,' said Tatyana, pointing at me. 'Do you think I'm carrying this fucking stick because I want to?'

'How convenient,' he said. 'Well, I'm sure you could cast something without it, yes? How about Jen's Pendulum? That's simple enough, even for someone with such a thick Krandin accent.'

I had woken my sorcery some time before we had arrived at this blockade, and as he issued this challenge I started reshaping the power I had called on into something less fatal than what I had first intended it for. I couldn't call out to Tatyana without ruining our ruse, so instead I sent a pulse of sorcery at her instead. I saw her twitch as it touched her, and a moment later she thrust her hand at the wizard, her fingers crooked like the claws of an arthritic eagle.

He stared at her hand, then burst out laughing. His laughter lasted as long as it took me to lift him a good six or seven feet into the air, at which point his laugh became a strangled cry.

'What are you doing? Put me down, put me down!'

I slowly rotated him in the air, sending a number of coins and papers falling to the ground, then gently set him down on his feet again. He staggered and just managed to catch himself on one of the soldiers.

'Satisfied?' asked Tatyana, lowering her hand.

'How?' he asked. 'How did you do that without a proper staff? You, an orange robe?'

'I'm gifted,' she said. 'Now, can we pass? It's been a long damn day, I've lost my staff and I just want to eat and sleep.'

'Yes, yes. So, who is that?' He looked at me properly for the first time. 'What is that?'

'Some sort of half breed,' she said. 'A *chimera*.'

Now they all stared at me, and I felt the wizard's spell take shape before he released it. It was a simple divination spell, nowhere near powerful enough to show him that what he was looking at was real. I woke my night vision and stared at him from under my hood as his spell washed over me.

'Goddess preserve us,' he said, lowering his staff. 'Where, no, how did you capture that?'

'There's a reason there's only twelve of us left,' she said.

He gestured to the guards around him. 'First squad stays with me. The rest of you escort that *thing* to the pen.'

'That's not necessary.'

'The Hel it isn't,' he said. 'I'm not going to be the one held responsible if that gets loose in the camp.'

And so it was that we entered the Penullin camp with an armed escort clearing our path and leading us towards the nearest gate into the city. The makeshift city of tents was far larger and more imposing up close, and even with the escort, we were stopped and questioned several times.

The guards escorting us ignored Tatyana entirely, but

soon fell into conversation with Leopold, who ignored their questions about which regiment he was from and kept asking them questions in turn. I was starting to feel the press of the strange magics that waited inside the city upon me, like a cold wind that I felt in my mind rather than on my skin, and so paid even less attention than normal to what he was saying.

As a result, I only became aware that things were not going as well as they might have been shortly after we started climbing the hundred or so stairs towards a city gate. It was dark by then, and the tent city was a torch lit mass on either side of us, hazy with the smoke of a hundred or more cooking fires. The soldiers stopped and turned to look at Leopold, who oozed with friendliness and camaraderie as he asked what the problem was.

'Enough!' said the first of them. 'Give me the name of your captain and regiment. Now.'

As he spoke the rest of them drew their swords, and in the case of the tenth man, lifted his crossed bow. Leopold looked to Tatyana, but the soldier spoke before he could. 'Talk to me, not the witch.'

'You are unworthy to speak the name of my captain,' he said, drawing his own sword in a flash of steel, his paladins following suit a heartbeat later.

The soldiers didn't hesitate. The crossed bow thumped and the first of the paladins was flung backwards, the top of his skull opening like a trapdoor.

His brothers leaped to the attack. There were no battle cries as they crashed together, only grunts and sharp gasps. To the soldiers' folly, they continued to ignore Tatyana, who used the distraction to untangle her sword from the harness beneath her stolen robe and then ram it into the armpit of the nearest of the enemy. He stiffened and fell, taking her sword with him. She stepped back hastily, but his death had taken the pressure off Leopold, who promptly felled another with series of short stabs of his dagger that were too rapid for me to count. He was quicker than Tatyana, which was saying something.

The fight ended quickly after that, but the damage had been done even before the first swords had clashed. There were cries of alarm all around us as the closest soldiers grabbed their weapons and began forming into a small, lethal mob. Leopold pulled the ropes from my wrists.

'Go, both of you.' He pointed his sword at the gates. 'Go kill that unholy bastard.'

Tatyana retrieved her sword and stopped in front of Leopold, laying her hand on his chest.

'Drogah shine upon you,' she said, then stood on her toes and kissed him.

He smiled as she stepped away, and I felt his magics stirring to life as he lifted his sword and touched the hilt to his brow.

'And upon you, my lady.'

'Farewell, Leopold son of Sigmund,' I said. 'Die well.'

Somewhere nearby a horn sent three short blasts into the night.

'Farewell, Stratus Firesky.' He grabbed my arm as I turned away. 'Tell me, why do you name yourself after that dread wyrm?'

I tilted my head as I met his stare. 'Because the name is mine, and always has been.'

I could feel his magic swell beneath his skin, a wave of it washing against my own, stronger than anything he'd baited any of his words with thus far. It was divinatory, and since it was the last chance he'd ever get, I didn't resist it this time and let him *see* me.

He looked at Tatyana, his eyes widening, then bared his teeth in a fierce smile. 'Henkman and the Dragon,

together once more. They will write songs of this day.'
His magic pulsed again and he pushed me away with
unnatural strength. 'Go now. Remember us.'

'We will,' Tatyana said, planting another brief kiss on
his lips. 'Go with God.'

I turned and began climbing the stairs, cursing my
withered leg on every other step. Behind us the paladins'
prayers sounded out, eleven voices chanting as one, and I
felt the sound of it defy the pressure of the magic radiating
from the city.

Tatyana raced up the stairs while I stomped and plodded
as fast as my legs would allow me. The gate was firmly
shut, and as she reached it a silhouette rose up on the
wall above and sent a heavy stone crashing to the ground
next to her, followed swiftly by a spear that spun away to
clatter down the slope.

I moulded a pulse of sorcery into the pattern for fire and
sent it arcing up onto the wall. I didn't hear it detonate
but the screams that followed it confirmed my aim was as
impeccable as ever. I caught up with Tatyana and, lacing
my fingers together, put my back to the wall.

'Go,' I said.

She took two steps back, then jumped towards me,
planting her foot in my hands. I flexed the twisted but still
worthy muscles in my shoulders and arms and lifted her
upwards. The wall wasn't all that high once you were at
the top of the slope that abutted it, perhaps two or three
times the height of a man, and my throw was more than
enough to put her on top of it.

I watched the paladins' battle at the foot of the stairs
while I waited for her to open the gate. I had expected
them to be swiftly overrun, but they were pushing the
soldiers back, their prayer-enhanced swords rising and
falling in golden blurs, their every stroke sending another

body to the ground, sometimes two. As I watched, one of the paladins burst into flame, the suddenness of it leaving little doubt that it was the work of a spell rather than a flask of oil or the like. The burning figure ran forward and threw himself into his attackers, the flames silhouetting the soldiers who hacked him to death even as he set some of them alight in his death throes.

The sound of bolts being drawn back broke the moment and I turned to see Tatyana's face in the small window set into the door.

'Push,' she said.

I did, and I made sure to close and bolt it again once I was inside.

CHAPTER 38

THE DOOR OPENED into a square and sparsely furnished room. A man in a Penullin cloak was currently lying face down in a slowly spreading pool of blood near the door, but aside from that it seemed perfectly unremarkable. There was another body sprawled across a narrow flight of stairs to the side, and from its charred appearance I guessed he had tumbled down from the wall after my fiery construct detonated.

I peered through the window of the door that led out into the city proper. The street beyond was gloomy and littered with scraps of wood, cloth and paper, but otherwise looked entirely deserted.

'Are you ready?' I asked Tatyana.

'No,' she said, wiping her sword clean for perhaps the sixth time since she'd opened the first door. 'I have a very bad feeling about all of this.'

'Their dark magic hangs heavy in the air,' I said. 'It is likely we'll face our death here.'

She muttered something in a language I didn't yet know, then shook her head. 'You're really shit at motivational speeches.'

'You would prefer me to lie?'

'Yes!'

'Everything will be fine.'

She cursed at that, but there was little venom in it, and shoved me towards the door. 'Let's just get it over with.'

That was a sentiment I readily agreed with, and so opened the door and stepped into the outer ring of Aknak, squinting against the arrhythmic flicker of the light within the low hanging cloud that crowned the upper levels of the city. It was brighter towards the centre of the city, and I had little doubt that it emanated from the cathedral that Navar had desecrated with the Lance. The feel of their alien magic was far stronger here, and within a few paces our breath was pluming in front of us as if we walked through a midwinter's day.

'Why's it so goddamned cold in here?' whispered Tatyana as she sheathed her sword, freeing her hands to rub some warmth into her arms.

Before I could answer, the light emanating from within the inner city swelled and brightened until a column of it shot upwards, momentarily connected city and sky before vanishing into the clouds and rippling outwards across the city. The air filled with a loud buzz and crackle as the first ripple raced towards us. It took me too long to understand what had happened, leaving no time to shout a warning as arcs of white light raced towards us between the buildings, several of which snapped out across both myself and Tatyana. The defences I'd prepared deflected the worst from me, but Tatyana was not so fortunate, and fell to the ground with a surprised yelp, swatting at the crackling sparks as if that would help in any way. She sat up as the pulse of energy raced away from us, clutching at her right arm and groaning. I could see smoke curling from where they had touched her, leaving patches of burned skin and milky blisters.

'Shit, that hurts,' she said. 'What the Hel was that?'

'I don't know,' I admitted. 'It didn't feel directed, like it was targeting anything. It may have been the Lance discharging excess energies.'

The healing construct had already woken by the time she was back on her feet and walking with me, and I ignored her mutterings as it expunged the fluid from the blisters and drew her skin taut once more. Aknak was not too dissimilar from Falkenburg in the way it was formed of three ascending levels with the ruler's residence at the top and centre, although its streets felt a bit wider. We were currently at the lowest and widest level of the city, once home to the markets and most of the common folk. The column of light had originated on the eastern edge of the next level, and so I began walking that way, keeping to the edge of the road where the shadows were more generous.

'Will that happen again?' she asked.

'Most likely. The node has been exposed and damaged, and although the Lance is powerful, I doubt it is enough to impose complete control. At least not yet.'

'Well, that sounds like something to look forward to.'

It didn't sound like a question so I didn't offer a reply. Instead, I hunkered down next to an abandoned cart and the frost-rimed body of the horse that was still harnessed to it.

'It's cold,' I said, rubbing my arms.

'Was it the ice that gave it away?'

'Largely, yes. I am fire born, so the cold does not normally bother me.' I scraped a swathe of crystals from the cart and tasted them, then spat the bitter meltwater out. 'But this is no mere chill.'

I fanned my sorcery out and let it spread, testing for any sign of life around us. At first there was nothing, not even a rat, but finally I felt the warmth of more living beings some way ahead of us, close to where the roads converged and rose to the next layer of the city. I was unwilling to waste my power and took a little extra time to pull it all back into me.

'Let's go,' I said, gesturing for Tatyana to follow me. 'There is no one here, not—'

I stopped and turned. Tatyana was still sitting where I'd left her, and didn't respond when I called her name. I knelt beside her and, with my hand upon her head, fed some power into my vision. She was colder than she should have been, almost as cold as someone who had fallen through an iced river.

I realised then that the chill that I felt was more than a side effect of the spell, it *was* the spell. As the Songlines carried the positive energy of life, so the necromancers' magic was powered by the cold, negative energy of death. Those powers had no place in this world, and the Songlines normally ensured that, but the spells being woven here had weakened their flow, allowing the negative energies to swell and encroach where life should have held sway. Their spell was summoning ever greater amounts of negative energy, enough to swallow the life and warmth the Songlines ensured, draining it from everything within its influence. It had Tatyana in its grip now, but I was a creature of the Songlines and, with one hand on her head and another over her heart, I sent a pulse of life-giving sorcery through her.

I could feel the two energies fighting each other within her, and so I pushed a little deeper into her mind. She was more adept with a sword than I would ever be, but this was a different sort of battle. The struggle within her had manifested in her mind, and I found her presence waiting on a shimmering street much like the one we were on now, surrounded by the forms of soldiers who were chanting her name and offering tankards of foaming ale as they beckoned her to take a seat on the benches alongside them. It would have been an enviably pleasant dream had the skull of the soldiers not been visible whenever a shadow crossed their faces. I could sense her fear at the sight of this, but also a strange longing and deep sadness within. It was a dangerous thought to hold onto while the vile magic wormed deeper into her.

I whispered her full name, and she turned to me and took the hand I offered. I fed another pulse of energy into her as we touched, but in truth her spirit did not need much encouragement to rise up again. Around us the soldiers blurred and faded into mist as the will to live woke within her once more. I carefully extracted myself from her mind but kept my hands upon her body, warming her flesh as she shivered back into full consciousness.

'Wait,' I said, watching as the unnatural blue that clung to her body slowly faded. 'The discomfort will pass.'

'Hands off,' she said, slapping mine away. She looked around and gasped, but there was nothing around us save an increasingly thick mist. 'What just happened?'

'They're opening the World of the Dead, and we're at the fringe of the spell...'

'What?'

'The cold that you feel is the touch of the void that waits beyond life.' I paused to rub a patch of ice from her shoulder. 'It was never meant to cross into this plane. Even the smallest touch of it has an endless appetite for the warmth of life. It will do what it can to erode what binds you to this world and consume that warmth. Whatever happens, stay awake.'

'This is death?' She waved her hand through the mist, which was slow to react to the movement.

'Yes.'

'Well, fuck.' She stood up and wiped her hands on the

padded tunic she'd slipped over her coat of rings. 'How're we supposed to even get to the damned church if we're walking through *death?*'

'Here,' I said, reaching into my robes and lifting out the medallion of St Tomas. Even in the misty half-light it gleamed brightly, as if I held it in bright sunlight, the blue stone in the centre glittering with golden motes. 'It will protect you from the worst of it.'

She reached for it, but then hesitated. 'What about you?'

If my teeth hadn't been in the way I would have smiled to hear her honest concern. 'My sorcery will protect me. Go now, take it.'

She did just that and, even as she sighed in sudden relief, I felt the chill press against me with a new hunger. I called to the Songlines and began drawing as much power from them as I could. There was a risk that a skilled wizard or nearby ghouls might sense it, but I needed the power. Without it I was just a crippled man with bad teeth.

'Are you doing magic?' whispered Tatyana. Her condition had improved considerably, and the shivers that had made her teeth chatter had all but vanished under the medallion's influence. One day I would sit and study its construction but that would have to wait for a better, peaceful time.

'Yes,' I said. 'Once we rise into the thickest of the mist I may not be able to replenish my power, so I'm absorbing as much as I can.' I could feel it slowly filling me. I had expected it to be sluggish and distorted, but the flow was steadier than I had dared to hope.

'Oh.' She stepped back and tilted her head. 'I can never tell. It's not very impressive.'

'Would you prefer it if I lit a candle and chanted?'

'Maybe.'

'Who were those men?'

She exhaled noisily and sat on the edge of a collapsed wall.

'You saw them too, eh? Fourth company. My men.' She stood and walked over to the other side of the road and back again. 'You see that building down there? With the broken chimney?'

The building she pointed to was little more than a pile of frost-rimed stone and broken wood sprinkled with shattered glass, but there was indeed a chimney.

'That was an inn. Our inn. We used to eat and drink there every other day, and when the end came, that was one of our rearguard positions.' She shook her head and laughed.

'Why is that funny?'

'The place was falling down around us and Fraser found an expensive bottle of wine. We stopped long enough to drink it.' She sat down again. 'It was our last drink together.'

I thought about what I had felt in her vision. 'They were your friends.'

'Friends are people you say hello to at the market.' She looked back towards the ruined inn. 'We bled and died for each other. They were my family.'

I felt the magic within the city swelling again, but before I could do more than turn towards the centre, several twisting bolts of white light flashed into the clouds where they remained for several heartbeats, squirming like the tentacles of some great sea beast. The flickering light threw strange shadows across the clouds, the swirls and eddies taking on the appearance of several enormous skulls looking down on the city below.

'God's balls! Did you see that?'

It was reassuring to know that it wasn't my imagination running riot, and as the bony visages dissolved into formless vapours again I heard, and felt, a strong vibration from the distant church.

'Brace yourself,' I said, reaching into my newly gathered sorcery and hurriedly forming a shield.

The glow brightened in the east, then rippled outwards once more, arcs of lightning racing from building to building ahead of it, their touch cracking wood and stone in bursts of dust and ice. I put my hands to the ground while Tatyana crouched and put her arm over her head. The cold, scything energy struck like a summer flood, washing over me in a loud tumult, biting and pulling at my flesh, but I let the worst of what my shield couldn't deflect flow through me and discharge into the ground. Tatyana held the medallion before her like an offering, the stone at the centre flashing like a sun trapped within the thickest ice.

We both stumbled forward as the pressure against us abruptly vanished.

'Wow,' was all she said.

I grunted my agreement. The pulse had cleared some of the mist away, but it was already rushing back, thicker than ever, a white wall that swallowed shape and sound entirely. My skin prickled as it enveloped us anew. The flow of the Songlines had slackened as well, but I was able to maintain the contact as we began moving forward again.

Tatyana insisted on going first, which made some sense as she had a fair knowledge of the city. The mist continued to thicken around us until it was as if we were walking through thick layers of cobwebs. The sound and flashes of the light across the clouds was muted as well, although the afterglow of these seemed to linger for far longer than it should have, an effect that played havoc with my sight, as I imagined it did with hers.

The chill had sharpened considerably too, but I refused

to use more of my sorcery to counteract it. The dark magic was oppressive, but I would need every mote of energy I could muster for what lay ahead, and wasting it on an illusion of warmth seemed supremely wasteful.

Now and then the mist billowed around us, as if stirred by the passing of something unseen, a sibilant whisper trailing it, as if something was trying to say my name with its dying breath. This happened several times, and the gap between Tatyana and myself grew smaller with each pass.

'Do you hear it?' she whispered when we were but a pace apart. 'The voice?'

'Some of it,' I said.

'It keeps saying my goddamn name.'

It didn't sound anything like her name. 'It's just the wind,' I offered.

'The Hel it is.'

Despite this protestation, she started moving forward again, her sword held unwaveringly over her shoulder, the blade beaded with droplets. We both stopped as a metallic scraping found its way through the mist ahead of us. The sound was brief and muffled, but I waited as she did, and not long after it came again. She kept her sword raised as she padded forward, moving remarkably quietly despite her armour and spare knives. I copied her as best I could, my bare feet soundless on the stone below. Several darker shapes began to materialise in the mist ahead of us, and it did not take much wit or a large nose to recognise them as ghouls. Unlike most I had seen, these were actively pacing back and forth, the pearly glow of their eyes marginally brighter than the mist as they swept their gaze back and forth.

Several of them slowed and looked in our direction, and Tatyana quickly pulled me back a dozen or so yards, letting the mist swallow them entirely.

'I count at least a dozen, possibly fifteen,' she whispered, her lips brushing my ear. 'I can't tell if there are more behind them.' She squinted into the glowing mist. 'Wait here.'

She was gone before I could say anything, vanishing within a few paces. I could hear the drip of water from somewhere, and the occasional scrape of metal from the dead lurking ahead of me, but little else, and all the while more mist flowed down the street, too heavy to be anything remotely natural. Pearlescent bands of it coiled around me like fish in a stream, thick enough that I could feel its passing against my skin.

Stratus. The voice was barely the echo of a distant whisper, but it was all around me. *Stratus.* Light flickered in the distance, the brightness muted to a soft, throbbing glow as it passed over me. I brushed the frost from my face and slowly turned around, but it was a pointless gesture. I might as well have been standing in a pail of milk.

The light throbbed again, and some of the mist before me seemed to drain away, leaving me standing before an immense, tapering skull with a small pair of horns over the hollow eyes. I knew every contour of that head, and what strength I had abandoned my legs as the truth bit into me. I clung to the wall, unable to look away from the skull. From *her* skull. I reached for it clumsily, but the image drifted apart before I could even close my hand, and I fell to my knees as the mist closed in once more.

Her spirit was out there, somewhere. I had vowed to bring her home, to send her into the fire as our kind had always done, but after almost a millennium I was no closer to finding her.

I would never find her, so why was I still fighting and suffering? If I surrendered, we could be together again, and surely that was more important than any vow sworn in the grip of blinding grief and rage?

She would surely not judge me ill for wanting to join her. I was so tired of grief, pain, and bloodshed. All I had to do was unbind my sorcery and let it drift out into the mist. I would fall asleep and wake in her arms, and it would be such a grand, soft end to this long bitterness.

I didn't feel my knees touch the ground, nor did I notice when I bowed my head.

CHAPTER 39

I OFFERED NO resistance as the cold slid deeper into me, its chill touch soothing away the pain of the muscles that lay twisted across my malformed back, replacing it with a kind of bliss. It didn't even feel cold anymore. I couldn't feel much of anything if I didn't try to move, so I didn't.

'Soon, my love,' I whispered as my name sighed from the depths of the mist once more. 'Together again.'

I wanted to smile but I couldn't. I could almost see the shape of her inside the mist, not the terrible visage of the skull that I had glimpsed before, but alive once more, her scales flashing like liquid gold as she soared and banked through the air for the sheer joy of it.

I WAS FLYING through the wide valley that formed the approach to Draksgard, the summer sun shining brightly and the thermals holding me aloft more than my wings were. I saw Anakhara ahead of me and called to her as I flew closer, eager to tell her of the strange and terrible dream I'd had, but she turned away, her wings beating hard. I followed as she sped along the valley, low enough that the wind of our passing set the apes in the tallest trees to howling and filling the air with thousands of rainbow hued birds that we disturbed from their nests.

Our shadows flashed across the great river and I beat my wings harder, the sour taste of fear in my mouth. Ahead of us lay the hill I had seen in my dream, the hill where she had died. I called to her to her to turn back, certain that something terrible would happen if she passed over it, but she only looked back at me and began a steep dive. I powered through the air, not caring how the muscles in my back were tearing, desperate to reach her.

She was almost within reach when the blood began to well out from between her scales. Her wings faltered and her dive became a wild spin, a cloud of blood trailing from her body like smoke. I screamed her name and she turned to look at me with hollow eyes. '

'You promised,' she said, her voice bursting into my head. 'You promised to find me.'

I screamed her name as she hit the rocks and exploded into a crimson torrent that poured down the hillside in a dozen bloody waterfalls, leaving no body.

THE VISION FADED into featureless, billowing white, leaving me upon frozen cobbles rather than bloodied grass, my arms outstretched towards nothing.

Find me, the mist whispered and I could only answer with a groan. Pain was needling its way across my body, a reminder of what waited for me if I did not lay down again. Part of me wanted to do just that, but the spell was broken. The peace it had promised was a lie. If I broke my oath, the vow I had sworn while painted in her very life's blood, how could I ever stand before her and hope for forgiveness?

I clenched my jaws shut and felt my jutting teeth scrape and tear at the inside of my mouth. The pain was a distant thing, but the heat and taste of my own blood was immediate. I clenched my jaw anew, driving the tallest fangs deeper into my palate until the pain and heat of my blood melted the ice encasing my mind. I could feel nothing but the pain, nor taste anything but my own blood, and I felt that dark part of me stir to life, that well of rage that had once terrified even me. It was the Beast within, and it fed on pain and despair and offered only anger and hate in return. It had fuelled me for this long and, by the stars, it would see me finish what I had started.

I fed it until its anger let my blood run hot once more, then gathered my legs under me, hooked my claws into the nearest wall, and slowly stood, a snarl rolling from my bloodied mouth. It hurt, but I offered all of that pain on the altar to my ancient rage, and rather than weaken me it made me stronger. I felt my hearts pump with new strength and spat a mouthful of blood to the ground, where it hissed and steamed.

'I'll find you,' I said, and the mist around me rippled as if fanned by an unseen wing. I reached into my reservoir of power and was relieved to find that while the cold had stopped me from seeking it, it had not yet siphoned it all away. I drew on a small measure of it to drive off the lingering effects and heal the small wounds that were gnawing at me.

'Stratus.' Another whisper from the mist, but this one I heard with my ears, and a moment after I felt the familiar touch of my own latent sorcery.

'Over here,' I said, and a moment later Tatyana seemed to solidify next to me.

'God's teeth,' she said. 'What happened to you? You look like a ghost.'

'I'm fine.'

She opened her mouth to say something but I grabbed her arm and pulled her towards me. The sword still hit her, but I could see that it was a glancing blow, barely enough to cut her thick jacket. The ghoul stepped forward, giving a definite shape to the dark outline that had warned me of his presence. More shapes loomed in the mist behind him, their eyes pulsing with the same white light that surrounded us.

'Shit,' she muttered, pushing me back too.

'They must have followed you,' I said.

'Piss off,' she snapped, jerking her arm from my grasp. 'I wasn't the one mewling like a baby.'

She stretched forward with sudden grace, her legs and arms straightening together so that her sword flashed across the gap between us and the ghoul. The wickedly sharp point found the unprotected underside of its jaw and disappeared into the mottled flesh. The creature fell to its knees and toppled sideways as she yanked the sword free in a spray of a thickened fluids. Its sword rang from the cobbles like a bell, eliciting a moan from the rest of the dead.

'Take my hand,' she said, grabbing my wrist before I could move. 'Stay close.'

She pulled me away to the side and, as much as I wanted to warm myself with some honest violence, I followed without protest. After what felt like an age of scrabbling over slick rubble and clusters of timbers that had been snapped or burned, we stepped through a badly damaged archway and into a passage littered with fallen debris, one that was almost too narrow for us to stand side by side in.

'What is this?' I asked.

She traced her fingers across some angular writing scratched into the closest bricks. 'A couple of years ago you'd have been up to your knees in kwai standing there. Now it's just a shortcut.'

'Who's Kwai?'

She patted my shoulder. 'What, not who. It's a leaf that some people liked to chew. And before you ask, it's sort of like a wine that you chew rather than drink.'

'And it grows here?'

She laughed and began walking up the slope. 'No, they sold it here. Now, if I'm right, we'll come out near the Forester's Arms. Another old haunt.'

I acknowledged this with a grunt and kept walking, the voice I had heard in the mist louder in my thoughts than whatever it was she was telling me about the inn. It wasn't anything I had ever experienced before, yet I knew it was Anakhara's voice, or at least part of it was. It had been a whisper, the words croaked and twisted, and yet I had known it was hers the moment I heard it. But where had it come from? My mind had not spared me any torture in the long centuries of my imprisonment and, in the worst years, the words *what if* had caused me more lament and misery than anything a human had ever done to me.

I had buried the memories of her deep inside me, insulating me from the raw pain that they alone had the power to evoke, but never in that time had I heard her voice other than as it had been on our last day together.

So why was my mind torturing me with such awful, ghostly whispers now? Was it some strange symbolism that the basest, most ancient part of me had summoned in a desperate gambit to stoke my will to live? And what of the dream that the Beast had shown Tatyana when it could not reach me?

A hand slapped down on my chest and I blinked away the remnants of that dream, the echoes of that awful voice fading and being replaced by Tatyana's less melodic tones.

'...some goddamned attention. This isn't a stroll in the park.'

'I was thinking about her.'

'This isn't the time to get mopey. Do you see that?' She pointed to the left of the street the alleyway bisected.

'A wall?'

'Gods,' she muttered, pushing me forward. 'Wake up, would you? Look, down there. You see the light?'

Since my neck wouldn't turn that far I edged forward until I could see past the corner. The mists were thinner here, perhaps pulled to the lower levels of the city by their not inconsiderable density, and the glow from the cathedral was far brighter as a result. The road tapered downwards to the left, obscured in places by rubble from the ravaged shops and houses along it. There were a number of tall poles set along it, and after a moment of squinting I made out the human shapes tied to them. Some hung by their necks, others from grotesquely distorted arms. Several of them were still moving, their legs twitching as if they were still trying to escape and had not yet realised they were dead. There were several dozen ghouls milling about along the length of the street below them, all of them clad in armour and carrying weapons, some of these rattling and sparking as they were dragged along the ground.

Beyond this mob a large building straddled the road, the archway beneath it and the two windows above that giving it the aspect of a crude but unhappy totem. Both windows shone with a steady yellow light, the warm colour vivid amidst the monochrome of the city they overlooked.

'What is it?'

'That's the middle barracks,' she said, moving up next to me. 'Right up until a few months before we moved in it was the headquarters for the city guard.'

'Why are you excited by this?'

I felt her try and squeeze my arm. 'Because the city guard also ran the gaol. There are hundreds of cells in the rock beneath the south tower.'

I thought about that. 'You think Lucien is in there.'

'It makes sense, doesn't it? Where else would you keep dangerous prisoners?'

'Perhaps.' I turned to her. 'You understand that he might be dead already? This mist is like poison.'

'I saw. But he's not dead.' She tapped her chest. 'I would know.'

'Such hope is dangerous.'

'Hope is everything.'

'Then you can hope for both of us. What about them?' I pointed to the dead in the street. 'There's no mist for us to hide in here.'

'We move through the shops,' she said, pointing to the side. 'Most of them have storage yards and back doors. If we keep it smooth and quiet, they'll never know we were there.'

I looked towards the glow in the east, then back to the guardhouse. It was likely that I would not survive the destruction of the lance, so perhaps it would somehow count in my favour if I saved the prince. He had been a friend to me when no others were, and such debts carry their own weight.

'Very well,' I said. 'Let us go find your prince.'

She flashed a smile. 'Thank you.'

The dark magic pressed down on me as we stepped out of the alley, but the cloying touch of the mist was at least considerably lessened. The air felt charged, as if a thunderstorm was gathering, but there was nothing clean about the feeling.

We made our way through the first abandoned shop and into the next, where we came across a scene of slaughter. Three soldiers lay atop one another, their bodies stripped and mutilated, the bloodied shreds of the blue sashes they wore around their waists the only hint to their identity.

The bodies of a fat man and two women lay nearby, both fully dressed but slain with equal savagery. It wasn't their wounds that made us pause though, but that they, like the figures hung in the street, were still moving.

'Drogah have mercy,' Tatyana breathed as the topmost soldier reached towards us, his hand waving weakly. He sagged back, and for a moment another face briefly pressed up against the skin of his gut, as if he had swallowed someone whole. She took a step back, then another when the face reappeared, the mouth working soundlessly.

'What the Hel is that?'

'I do not know.' I drew a knife and, before she could say anything more, slashed it across the face as it pushed against his belly with even greater vigour. White sparks flashed from the cut, followed by a brief flash of cloudy light that quickly faded.

'Goddamn it, Stratus!'

'Interesting.'

'No, not interestingl! Just leave it alone and let's get the Hel out here.'

'They're not ghouls,' I said, wiping the blade on the fat man's clothes. 'I think they have forced a gateway open.'

'A gateway?'

'A portal. A door.'

'I know what it means. A gateway to where?'

I watched as the fat man's generous gut rose and fell, as if something were trying to stand up inside him but didn't yet have the strength to. She bit her hand as she saw it too, then looked at me with owlish eyes as the realisation struck.

'The World of the Dead,' she breathed. 'You were serious.'

'Yes.' I poked at the slit in his body. 'The gateway opens when a spirit passes into the void, but it seems these men's spirits have been trapped in between, holding the gateway open, allowing other spirits to drift into this world.'

'Their souls are doorstops?'

'Yes,' I said, pleased that her grasp of the matter was improving.

'This is too much. Let's go,' she said, shoving me towards the next door, and I didn't argue. As fascinating as they were, examining the bodies wouldn't get us any closer to our goal. We made our way through two shops, one of which had been gutted by a magical fire, moving with great care when little more than a single wall separated us from the ghouls. Even without purposefully waking my sorcery I could feel their presence, the sound of the enchantment boiling within them like the buzzing of a thousand trapped hornets.

The deathly chill had strengthened them and sharpened whatever senses they had, and as we discovered, any movement or sound drew their attention. We inched our way forward between the brittle remains of coats and boots that a wizard's fire had ravaged, and almost made it to the gap that would take us to the prison when it found us.

It arrived soundlessly in the way cats do, but that did not last very long. I barely had time to point it out to Tatyana before it started a wretched wailing, a gasping sound made worse by the wounds that were still obvious in its icy coat. The dead in the street answered its mewling with moans of their own.

The cat staggered forward as Tatyana inched closer, then gave one last wail before she kicked it in the head, which promptly snapped off and bounced off the wall. It was too late though. The first of the ghouls burst through the remains of the doors, a nasty looking axe in its hands, and I hastily raked my claws across its eyes.

I doubted it felt pain, but the instinct to protect the eyes is too deeply embedded in every creature that ever lived for even death to entirely erase. It flinched backwards, raising the axe to knock my hand away. If he had been a living man I might have torn the great artery in his groin open then, but instead I slapped the side of the axe, knocking it away from me, and punched a black talon through its forehead.

More were already crowding the doorway and climbing through the window as I ripped the talon free. Tatyana chopped at the arm of another that was reaching for her, but despite its arm being split from knuckle to elbow, it barely slowed, forcing her deeper into the shop. I narrowly avoided having my face parted by a butcher's cleaver as the fire-damaged frame collapsed under the combined weight of the ghouls tying to climb through it.

Several of the creatures fell over as the supporting wall crumbled, stalling their rush. I paused only long enough to stamp down on the nearest helmeted head before following Tatyana out through the gap and towards the guardhouse, where I found her working her sword loose from the skull of a persistent ghoul, the bone squeaking noisily as she sawed it from side to side.

'Let's go,' she said as she flicked the worst of the gore off against the wall.

'Wait.' I knelt next to its body and, curling my claws into its skull, wrenched the crack in its head open even wider.

'What—'

A pale tube unfolded from the red mess within, a luminous maggot larger than a man's thumb. It rose from the wound like a seedling eager for sunshine but the glimmer of light beneath its thin skin was rapidly dimming. Moans and the sound of weapons scraping stone warned us that we had no time to linger. She slashed at the pale mass with her sword, releasing a horrid stench, one foul enough to penetrate the dampening effect of the mist. We hurried from the house mere paces ahead of the ghouls and raced towards the looming shape of the guardhouse.

CHAPTER 40

THE DOOR WAS locked, but only with metal and wood, neither of which resisted the sorcery I used to manipulate the primitive mechanism. I kicked it open in the same heartbeat, sending the man behind it sprawling. I pushed through into the room before he or anyone else who might have been lurking there could recover.

I really shouldn't have been surprised to see six more soldiers within, seeing that it was a guardhouse, but I had begun to think we were the only living creatures in the city. Tatyana charged in behind me, providing enough of a distraction that I could step in and slam the door shut before the ghouls could scramble up the stairs.

Something flashed in my peripheral vision and I felt a sword bite as I threw my arm up into its path. It hurt, but the wound was shallow, unlike the slashes my raking claws opened across my attacker's face. He staggered back, reaching for his scored face in shock, and so didn't even see the punch that ended him coming.

The five remaining soldiers charged in and began hacking at us in something close to a frenzy. I shielded my face with one arm, my teeth set as their blades bit and gouged me, the strokes too many and too quick to counter. There was no space for fire, and barely enough for me to follow where Tatyana was. I extended both talons and threw myself at the closest of them, heedless of the swords that flashed out as I gave them an opening. The man I lunged at managed to knock one talon away, but the other found his throat and he fell to his knees, choking on his own blood.

I turned and the soldier on my left tried to punch me with a spiked gauntlet. I swayed to the side, then lunged forward and sank my teeth into the meat of his forearm before he could withdraw it. I jerked my head to the side like a terrier with a rat, tearing a fistful of meat away. He fell away screaming as the third man stabbed me in the back. I felt the sting of it piercing my stretched skin, then a dull rasp as the blade scraped across the malformed bone that had sprouted around my wing nubs.

I lashed out blindly as I spun and caught his helmet with the edge of my talon, ringing it like a bell. It wasn't enough to really hurt him, but it was enough to distract him and Tatyana's knife opened his throat a moment later.

He was the last of them. Five men were sprawled on the floor, the warmth and scent of their blood rich and welcome after the bland nothingness that hung outside. The sixth was holding the blade of the sword that Tatyana had pinned him to the door with, coughing blood and mewling 'No, no, no' as if it would change his fate.

I was bleeding from a dozen wounds myself, some of them deep enough that I had no choice but to set my sorcery to healing me before my vision greyed out even further. Tatyana picked up another sword from one of the fallen and was peering past the edge of the door that led into the rest of the guardhouse.

'Are there more of them?' I asked her, clenching and unclenching my left hand as a rather nasty gash across my back knitted together.

'Can't see any.'

I turned to the man she'd pinned to the door like an insect. Driving a sword entirely through a man in armour was an impressive feat in itself, but she had also done it hard enough that sufficient of the blade was buried in the wood to support his weight.

'How many more of you are there?' I asked.

His reply was to spit a mouthful of blood at me. In return, I kicked his feet away from under him, sending his full weight onto the sword. His scream was sudden and piteous, and I waited until he got his feet under him again.

'How many?' I asked.

'A platoon,' he gasped.

'Penullin platoons are a score, so another fourteen on top of these,' offered Tatyana. She poked him with the handle of her new sword. 'Any mages?'

'You ungodly bitch.' He gave a strangled sob. 'You've killed me.'

I slapped the handle of the sword and his words ended in a screech.

'Focus,' I said. 'Tell the truth and I will spare you.'

He gave a wet sounding laugh. 'I'm dying.'

'You are, but it doesn't have to be that way.' I let a few arcs of raw sorcery flash across my fingers. 'Are there any wizards?'

A bout of coughing wracked his body, and even though I thought him mere moments away from death, he fought to draw more breath, to cling to life however painful and terrible it was.

'Two,' he said between mouthfuls of blood.

'My money says at least three then,' said Tatyana.

'Three is manageable,' I said. I ripped the sword out of his chest, sending him crashing to the floor to die at his own pace.

'So much for sparing him.'

'He was already dead.' I tossed the sword aside. 'I am surprised he could even stand, let alone speak at the end.'

'The power of hope,' she said.

A grunt was my only reply to that as she led us out into the hall that would bring us to the stairs leading to the floors above. There were dungeons below us too apparently, several levels of them cut into the rock that the city had been built on, but she was convinced that a captured prince would not be held in such mean conditions, and the voices we could hear from the floors above supported her idea. The speakers sounded angry as they called out threats and warnings in guttural Penullin. We moved on as quietly as we could, and with my injuries knitting nicely I siphoned some of the energy away and set about preparing some defences against the wizards. Just in case.

The building was wider than it was tall, but fortunately most of the space was utilised by shelf upon shelf of books and scrolls, with whole rooms dedicated to them alongside chambers for the senior guardsmen and sheriffs appointed to pursue various crimes. It was amongst these chambers that we stumbled across more of the guards and both wizards.

The wizards had sensed our approach, but in turn I had felt the sudden pull of their magic as we rounded the corner. It was enough for me to push Tatyana out of the way a fleeting moment before a hissing ball of fire flashed through the space where her chest had just been. The fire ball obliterated a portrait on the wall with a sharp crack and flash of superheated air, and a second exploded across the shield I had just prepared. It felt like I'd been kicked by a large, burning mule, but the core of the spell was deflected and expended itself in the ceiling rather than me.

Six guards rushed forward as the sound of the detonations faded, but they weren't quick enough.

My sorcery didn't require a staff or wand, and as such the first they knew that I had killed them was when the fire burst into being around them, scorching their skin blacker than mine and setting their hair, beards and clothing alight. Their screams were shrill before the fiery air cooked their lungs and throats, and within a few strides they had all fallen, their bodies convulsing as the fire burned ever deeper.

The wizards cast a wall of shimmering light behind them as they fled, their robes pulled high, but I used my sorcery like a knife and cut the filament of energy that powered their shimmering little wall, forcing it to collapse upon itself.

We pounded down the passage behind them, or at least Tatyana did. I followed as quickly as my leg allowed. I saw one of them turn and thrust his staff at her; a thunderclap sounded and she flew back past me, skidding and tumbling across the floor, wreathed in smoke and flame like a clumsy demon. This and the dismayed gasp that escaped me seemed to embolden them, for the second wizard stopped and turned towards me too.

I stepped over Tatyana's groaning form and threw my own shield up around me as they released their spells. The first, a translucent pulse of kinetic power, careened off my shield and into the wall opposite, blasting a hole the size of a barrel through the wall. The second wizard thrust his staff towards me, giving me a moment's warning of the angle of his attack, and I tilted the shield against it. The ball of white fire he'd launched at me struck it at a sharp angle and streaked back towards them, scorching the floorboards as it skipped along across the floor and promptly detonated at the feet of the first wizard. It wasn't a direct hit, but it was enough to hurl him bodily into the wall and leave him laying there, insensate and smouldering.

I threw a knife at the second wizard as he tried to understand what had just happened. He tried to dodge it, and may have succeeded had I not put a pulse of sorcery behind the throw that both accelerated it and steered it into the centre of his chest. It punched through his breastbone with enough force that only the knob at the end of the handle was visible as he crashed to the floor, dead without another sound.

I looked up and down the passage. Their deflected spells had started two large fires, but fortunately the smoke had already begun to escape through the hole in the wall. I hurried back to Tatyana, who was alive and twitching as the healing construct repaired the damage. It was unfortunate that she'd been hurt enough to wake it so soon again, but there was no other choice at this point. I left her to it and hastened over to the wizard who'd been blown from his feet.

'A blue robe,' I said, squatting down next to him. Shards of bone were protruding from both of his legs, one of which was folded beneath him in a way that left little doubt that he'd never dance again. 'Perfect.'

'What are you?' he groaned.

'Where is the prince?'

'Prince?'

I stuck a claw into one of the raw wounds and wiggled it about, which set him to howling.

'Prince Lucien Stahrull.' I leaned forward until my face was mere inches from his. 'And do not pretend you have the courage to withstand what I will do to you if you lie to me.'

'One floor up,' he said between gasps.

'Very good. Now, when does your Master arrive?' It looked like he was going to laugh so I set the tip of my claw in his earhole and pushed it in until it met something solid, which quickly silenced him. 'Why is that funny?'

'Stratus Firesky,' he said, baring his bloodied teeth at me.

'You know my name?'

I felt a shiver in the air, as if something I could not hear was roaring nearby; it passed quickly enough that for a moment I thought I had imagined it, but then the wizard stiffened, his back arching violently.

'In life and death, I serve.' His words started as a whisper and ended as a scream.

My hand was still against his face, and I felt his skin shift under it, not so much tearing as dissolving. Behind me, the newly conscious Tatyana gasped as his skin and flesh sloughed off his bones, transforming him from a man to a gleaming skeleton quicker than the telling of it.

I moved back as the blood flowed back towards his bones, then rose into the air above his body and spun itself into a glistening globe that took on the aspect of a human face.

'Stratus Firesky.' A new voice bubbled from the bloody head, wet and gasping, but I recognised the cadence. 'In the end, the Beast always returns to its master.'

'I will be your death, wizard.'

Wet laughter bubbled from its lips. 'I am death, you fool.'

I looked at the head through my sorcery and saw the hair-thin streams of bluish light that coursed through it like puppeteer's strings, rising and stretching away towards the east. 'I am waiting for you.'

The cords flashed once and, as they vanished, the head fell and exploded into a shower of blood, the ripples of it spreading and lapping around my feet. I stared as the ripples spread and settled. *I had seen that before.*

'God above,' Tatyana said from behind me in a hoarse voice. 'Was that him?'

'If you mean Navar Louw, then yes.'

'Ow, fuck,' she said, pulling herself to her feet. The padded coat she'd donned was blasted away across her chest, the edges of it still smouldering. I was impressed that she'd recovered so quickly, but I caught a glimpse of glittering blue light from within the mail shirt she wore beneath and smiled. I really liked that medallion.

'At least you're not cold anymore,' I offered.

'Piss off.' She picked up her sword and came to stare at the steaming mound of flesh at my feet. 'He's really here, isn't he?'

I nodded. 'In the cathedral.'

'Shit.'

'Shall we go?'

'Well sure. Let's just go find the Worm Lord. And I'm fine, thank you for asking. It feels like I tried to catch a burning catapult shot with my tits, but really, I'm fine.'

'Good.' I helped myself to the knife on the wizard's belt to replace the one I'd used. 'Also, I can smell Lucien. Upstairs.' My nose at least had benefited from the shifting of the enchantment.

She hurried off without another word, her heartbeat thumping and I again found myself trailing after her as she strode towards the stairs, her sword held in both hands. Footsteps sounded from the floor above us, but she didn't slow until she was halfway up to the flat bit in the middle.

'They know we're coming,' I said.

She carefully peered around the corner of the staircase but flung herself back as one of the fat arrows from a crossed bow smashed into the wall behind her, burying most of its length in the old wood.

'Come on up,' called a voice from above. 'There's plenty more where that came from.'

I was about to ask her to move out the way when another arrow buzzed past and slammed into the wall, close enough that it lifted several strands of her hair in its wake. With my back bent and twisted and my leg aching, crouching on the stairs was simply intolerable and what remained of my patience swiftly evaporated.

My sorcery filled the pattern for fire in my head, the familiar shape and heat of it a comforting certainty as I pushed her aside and edged higher until I could see over the top step. The archer was behind an overturned table but was still winding back the string of his bow, which gave me more than enough time to finalise the shape of the fire. I glimpsed five or six human faces staring at me from behind other furniture.

They disappeared from view as I released the construct. It caught the archer as he turned to run down the passage, flaying his back to the bone. The wind blew their barricade apart and the fire that followed rushed through the gaps before blossoming into a flame that raced across the walls and ceiling like floodwater. The men dove for cover, but the fire greedily pulled the air from their lungs. I extended my talons and moved in as the primary bloom of flame collapsed into smoke. Killing those that had survived was easy, and more of a mercy than a necessity. When the last of the screams fell silent I could hear more men coughing from behind each of the four doors that were set into the walls.

'Lucien!' shouted Tatyana, racing up the stairs, her scarf pressed to her face. 'Lucien!'

The smoke made it impossible for me to find his scent, and as it was unlikely that I'd recognise him by sight I left her to investigate the rooms. I busied myself with the nearest of the charred soldiers, quickly gorging myself on the blackened meat, pausing only to spit out the tattered remnants of his clothing that threatened to choke me.

Tatyana found Lucien in the last cell, disturbing my impromptu meal with an urgent shout. I wiped my face on the soldier's cloak and hurried over. I ran my nails across the wood and listened carefully as I tapped it.

'Step away from the door,' I said. Normally I would have simply kicked it open, but with only one good leg I opted to barge into it with my shoulder, letting my weight rather than my strength do the hard work. My estimation of its strength was accurate and on the second attempt I smashed through it, splitting the door from top to bottom and stumbling into a cell that was certainly more comfortable than anything he'd offered me in the palace. The floors were laid with wood, and there was a raised bed piled with blankets. I caught a glimpse of Lucien before Tatyana threw herself into his embrace, but he seemed healthy enough.

I dusted splintered wood from my shoulders and, ever curious, released a pulse of probing sorcery. I felt the wards hidden beneath the floorboards buzz and flicker, and since they were still embracing and paying me no attention, I used the distraction to explore the pattern hidden beneath. It was a series of wards, rather than a single complex creation, which was a blessing and a curse in that it was easier to break, but more likely to react badly if I broke it in the wrong place. It would take time to unravel and understand it, time that we no longer had. I couldn't sense the stored energy that an offensive ward would normally carry, which was somewhat comforting, and the power it was drawing was minimal at best.

I raised a shield around me and, taking a deep breath,

broke the chain of wards. The silver light shining out through the gaps in the floorboards stuttered and went dark, and a moment later Lucien cried out and staggered to the side as if struck, and may have fallen had Tatyana not caught him. She lowered him to the bed, where he clutched at his head and groaned through clenched teeth.

'What did you do?' she said over her shoulder.

I stepped closer and looked down at the prince, who was still groaning and holding his head.

'Hold him,' I said, and to her credit she did not protest. I put my hand on his forehead and sent a pulse of sorcery through him. I felt the resistance of bound enchantments slow the energies, and felt him shuddering under my hand as I increased the flow of power, overcoming their resistance. Tatyana leaned forward and kept his arms pinned against his chest.

I looked down at him through my sorcery, concentrating until all I could see was the glowing outline of his body and the red gold of life pulsing from his heart. I followed it through him, seeing the recently healed injuries from swords, knives and magic and, finally, the dark shape nestled within his head. The red glitter of his lifeblood dimmed to grey as it passed through the mass. The worm twitched as I watched, every movement eliciting a groan from Lucien. I pulled the energy back into myself and straightened. Tatyana sat back, not looking away from him.

'Is it, you know...' She gestured to his head.

'Yes. It's right about here.' I tapped the left side of his head.

'Can you do anything? Use your magic to remove it?'

I considered that. The ward under the floor had clearly been linked to the worm and not much else, which went some way to explaining the negligible power that it had been sending out. But why? The worm was a physical thing, and had only needed a glass of wine to find its way into him. It was feeding on his life, and yet now seemed to be struggling to survive even though his state of being had not altered.

'Perhaps,' I said to Tatyana. 'It seems weak, like a newborn pup.' I pinched Lucien's nose until he stopped his groaning and focused on me. 'Hello, Prince.'

'Stratus? Is that you?'

'Yes.'

'By the gods, you look perfectly hideous.'

'Perhaps you could paint my face later.'

His smile became a grimace as the worm flexed. 'Not enough paint in Krandin,' he managed through clenched teeth.

'Perhaps.' I knelt on the floor by the bed. 'I need you to focus now. I want you to think about Fronsac. Do you remember him?'

'I'm a prince, not a simpleton.'

'Everyone is entitled to an opinion. Now, focus on him, and only him. Remember his voice. Keep him fixed in your mind and look into my eyes.'

I lit my eyes with a flicker of sorcery, drawing his gaze to them, and pushed my mind at his. When I tried something similar with his brother, the wards imposed by the court wizard had expelled me within moments, but now I found myself amongst Lucien's thoughts with barely a token resistance. They were jumbled and confused, with fragments of dreams mixing with memories of myself and Tatyana and much more, the colours and sounds muted, in a similar way to what the mist had only recently visited on me. I gleaned enough to know that he hadn't even heard the commotion outside the cells; whoever had broken through Fronsac's outer wards had done so with no little cunning and subtlety and left him in an almost trance-like state, weakening his will.

I marshalled my concentration and pushed deeper, beyond the fitful dreams and fantasies that had driven coherent thought from his head.

Think of Fronsac, I pulsed at him, and around me his thoughts stirred sluggishly and darkened as half formed fragments touched and drifted apart again. *Fronsac.* I continued to pulse it at him, and slowly the fragments began to hold together for longer. Blurred suggestions of the wizard took form around me, dissolving back into mist before drawing together again, their lines a little sharper and the grey giving way to a little more colour with each attempt until even I recognised Fronsac. A tremor passed through the mind around me as the mists retreated, revealing a vista where Lucien sat sharing a mug of ale with him at an inn before melting away to them debating fiercely in the wizard's chambers, then both of them arguing with Jean, and finally to Lucien and Fronsac sitting upon the palace roof as Fronsac instructed him in astronomy.

I felt his concentration growing, and with it the first strains of the ward that I was seeking. It was a powerful enchantment, set deep within the prince's mind and not so easily eroded. *Fronsac, Fronsac,* I whispered at Lucien, and the images around me sharpened considerably. I saw Lucien step out of the palace, standing tall in his armour of war even though fear was eating at him like a cancer as he walked towards the paladins he was to lead from the city. I saw Fronsac beckon to him from a side door, and he made his way to the wizard, who grabbed him by the arms and stared into his eyes.

'Be careful out there, Lucien. There's something rotten in our midst.'

'You'll protect me, won't you?' asked Lucien, laying a gauntleted hand on the wizard's shoulder.

'You know I will. But spells can only do so much.'

'I'll be fine. There are still good men amongst them.'

'Who'd hang us both if they knew the truth.'

'I'll come back,' said the prince. 'Look after Tata while I'm gone. Tell her I'm sorry.'

'I think the mysterious Stratus will keep her safer than either of us.'

A paladin called Lucien's name from the courtyard before he could reply to that.

'Let us pray he remains our ally. I must go.'

'Wait.' The wizard placed his fingertips on Lucien's forehead and spoke a word, and the memory cracked apart and began to fade. But I remembered the word and repeated it, filling his mind with echoes of it. I felt it reverberate deeper in his mind and settle into a steady pressure that began to rise and strengthen with every whisper of it.

I RELEASED HIS mind and sat back. Lucien blinked and rubbed at his face as if waking, then suddenly squeezed at his head. 'Oh god, it hurts. Argh!'

'What did you do?' shouted Tatyana, rubbing ineffectively at his arms.

'I woke Fronsac's wards.' I was fairly sure that was what I had done, but it wasn't the time or place to try and explain the vagaries and dangers that came with toying with the spells of others. 'Just give him time.'

Lucien groaned again as a thin stream of scarlet broke from his nose and snaked across his jaw.

'Is that supposed to happen?'

'It's not unexpected.' Which wasn't entirely a lie. 'The

wards are suffocating the worm, and I fear it will not die without a struggle.'

'Can't you help him?' The blanket she was holding to his nose was rapidly turning crimson. 'Please?' Her eyes glittered as the spent magic and strength of her emotions kindled the spark of sorcery within her.

Navar was here in the city, waiting for me, and given what was at stake, the power that I had should not be wasted on another meaningless human life. I opened my mouth to tell her just that, but the words would not pass my lips. Instead I found myself sitting next to the prince and laying my hands on either side of his head.

'Are you sure you want me to do this?'

He looked up at me and I felt him give the slightest of nods.

'As you wish,' I said. I adjusted my hold on his head, aligning my fingers, then released my sorcery, sending arcs of energy springing from finger to finger, filling his skull with the golden light of the Songlines.

CHAPTER 41

I FELT FRONSAC'S wards flicker to life, but they were not yet completely restored, and my power flowed through the gaps it had yet to close like sunlight penetrating a forest canopy. I had not shaped the power I was filling Lucien with, but had simply focused my intent on driving out the dark magics that ensconced the worm, trusting to the purity of the energy I was channelling to do what was necessary.

The sound and feel of Fronsac's magic were familiar enough to me that I could identify and guide my construct around it, but anything else was fair game. I saw imprints of Lucien's memories as the sorcery coursed through his head, dislodging forgotten memories of castles and palaces, food, and dances held beneath glittering ceilings and starlight. Lucien was a child of summer and a fool, but he was a happy one, and despite my misgivings I knew then that everything he had ever offered me had been given without malice or hidden intent. I wanted to curse him for making me like him, but instead I narrowed the focus of my sorcery and let the magic burn its way through the dark spells that clogged his mind, smothering his song and his inner light.

I felt the doubts and fears embedded within those spells

turn their poison on me, but the light of the sorcery showed them for what they were, rendering them powerless and setting the worm within his brain to thrashing. I had not been so close to a whole one before, not like this. The depth of Fronsac's wards and spells seemed to have stymied the necromancers' attempts to lay the full weight of their spells and enchantments on it yet, leaving it vulnerable. I wrapped the squirming monstrosity in a sorcerous sheath to still its thrashing before it damaged something in Lucien's brain and rendered him a drooling idiot.

Once it was held fast, I formed my sorcery into needles thinner than a hair and pierced its body, steadily driving them deeper, seeking its core. It was a dumb thing, entirely devoid of thought beyond the instinctive need to feed and entirely defenceless without the spells of others to protect it. I sent a mote of golden power into its body and watched as that part of it discoloured and died, much as flesh would at the touch of raw necromancy. I was about to dissolve it into nothing when I sensed a change in it, an agitation that wasn't there before. I tightened the protective barrier around it and watched as the grainy gel of its body began to glow with a faint white light that quickly stretched out into a feathery tendril that pushed against my sorcery. It was too weak to penetrate the shield I had imposed, and too primitive to disguise what it was: a cry for help, the blind mewling of an infant seeking its mother.

I pushed my sorcery deeper into its viscous body and filled it with the power of the Songlines. It shivered once, then fell apart from the inside out, decaying into a greyish ooze that I guided to Lucien's nose before I slowly retreated from his mind.

I sat back and steadied myself as reality reasserted itself around me. Lucien was coughing and gagging next to me as the now dissolved body of the worm oozed from his nose; the smell of it was quite something, and I doubted he'd have much use for his nose for several weeks.

'God's teeth.' The words were muffled behind the hand Tatyana held to her mouth. Death was food and air to these creatures, but they had had been alive once. Necromancy could mimic but not create life, not even something as simple as a worm. I spun out the cry for help that it had generated and listened to its wordless tone over and over again. The intent was unmistakeable. Something had imprinted on it, something with the power to infuse a living thing with the ability to manifest a spark of death's cold energy and live.

'WHAT DID THEY call it?' I said, more to myself than either of them.

'Who?' groaned Tatyana, who had covered the bloody sludge in a blanket to try hide the stench of it. Lucien was sat on the edge of the bed, his head cradled in his hands, blood dripping from his nose. *His nose*. There was something about the nose.

'Do you remember the man in the birdcage?' I asked.

'The man? You mean under St Tomas?'

'Yes. That's it.' I closed my eyes and saw the dungeons in my mind again, the cold bodies laying in the darkness with worms fattening in their skulls. '*Bloodseed*. He called it the Bloodseed.'

'Yes,' croaked Lucien. 'They spoke of it... They... They...' His voice trailed off and he abruptly began to weep.

'They what?' I prompted him, but he seemed intent on watering the floor. 'Come now. You're a prince of Krandin,' I said, lacing my voice with the dregs of the power lingering about me. 'Yours is the blood of kings, descended from the Firstborn. Stop mewling like a scared child.'

He lowered his hands and looked at me, and for a moment I thought he was going to succumb to his misery once more but instead he stood up and wiped his face with the hem of his shirt. 'They called it the Bloodseed.' His voice was a croak. 'They fed it to us, all of us, even the dying. It was inside them.'

'Inside who?' Tatyana said, her voice a hoarse whisper.

'The necromancers. They had tattoos on their bodies and faces, all sorts of spirals. They held us down.' He took a deep breath and exhaled it as an entreaty to his god. 'One of them pressed his mouth to mine and, Drogah help me, pushed something into it. Like a tongue, but longer. It pushed upwards.' He bent over and vomited noisily across his feet. 'I felt it crawl into my head. Oh, my god.'

I felt another piece of the mystery wriggle into place. I didn't know the how of it, but I was starting to understand why. The worms in themselves were nothing but a tool, a way to integrate death within the living. It was a similar thing to what the goat-faced wizard had done with the metal ward in the seneschal's camp. Their victims accepted the worms, however unwillingly, and as they grew into their living flesh the line between one and the other became blurred, until the thoughts that were projected into the worms would be as their own. It was a fiendish way to create an obedient army, one that could survive and even thrive in the presence of death.

'It's inside them. They incubate them,' I said, more to myself than them. Tatyana muttered something but didn't stop rubbing Lucien's back, at least not until Navar's voice boomed from the skies outside, loud enough to send dust raining from the ceiling and make Tatyana's sword rattle across the table it lay upon.

'Stratus Firesky. Come to your Master.'

I could feel the spell he had woven into it wrap around me, and if he had spoken the whole of my name I may not have been able to resist; as it was I had to dig a nail into the soft of my arm to stop it from swamping my thoughts.

'Sweet mercy,' said Lucien, gripping Tatyana's arm and starting out the narrow window. 'What is that?'

She answered for me. 'The Worm Lord.'

I stood up and shook the remnants of his spell off. 'It's time to end this.'

'You can't do this alone,' Tatyana said, slipping out of Lucien's grip. 'You can't fight that.'

'I have to.'

'How? He has an army of the dead out there and god only knows how many goddamn wizards. How can you fight that?'

'With claw, fire and cunning.'

'Don't be glib. It's suicide and you know it.'

The scent of fear in the room had strengthened, and while they were only human, I felt the same sensation crawling through my gut.

'This is not your fight, Tatyana. Take Lucien and get out. Once this begins their eyes will be on the east. Go west.'

'The fuck it isn't. Krandin is my home, and you're family now.' She tapped her chest, right over her heart, and I took her meaning.

'As you said, it might be suicide. But you swore to see him home.'

Lucien stood and stepped forward. 'Krandin is my home too.' He lifted his chin and squared his shoulders. 'I would be worthy of the blood that flows in my veins.'

It was a grand gesture, even if the vomit and blood smeared across his chin diluted the effect. I looked at him closely but could sense no trace of falsehood. However, before I could speak, more voices rose from outside the cells alongside the one that we stood in, the words somewhat muffled by the walls.

'I am your man, my prince. I would stand with you.'

'And me!'

'My sword and my life are yours!'

Tatyana looked about, then stepped out of the room, and I followed her. Faces were pressed to the bars of several of the other rooms, and as they saw us they reached out.

'We are yours, my prince.'

'Paladins,' I said, unable to hide my dismay. Was I never to be free of them?

'They were taken with me,' said Lucien. 'They fought like lions.'

'They're all infested,' I said. 'You cannot trust them.'

Lucien spun to face me. 'I know you don't share our faith, and by god, I know you haven't seen the best of them, but I have. I believe in Drogah's mercy and the courage of these men.'

The sound of weapons hacking into wood echoed up the stairs, a rapid and incessant beat.

'I do not know what manner of creature you are,' called the man in the closest cell. 'But I would give my solemn word that I will serve Prince Lucien to my dying breath.'

'The word of a paladin means less than nothing to me,' I replied. I pointed to Lucien. 'Swear it to your prince, upon the blood of the Firstborn that fills his veins.'

They all did then, their voices overlapping in their eagerness to swear their lives to his service. Once they were done, I smashed the locks open with a borrowed axe. I would need every morsel of power for what lay ahead and didn't want to waste a mote if I could help it. There were seven of them, which they seemed strangely pleased with as it echoed some legend of their order. They quickly stripped the dead of anything useful as we made our way back to the doors, which by then were almost in splinters and would long since have collapsed if it wasn't for the iron bands holding the wood together.

Three of the paladins had retrieved long weapons that looked like the bastard child of an axe and spear, and these three put themselves ahead of us as the doors finally collapsed. Then, with loud cries to Drogah, they began cutting and stabbing the dead that forced their way through the doors with exemplary violence, exulting in every thrust and cut they delivered. Had I not been on the way to my own death I might have marvelled at the deft skill with which they used such cumbersome-looking things. They pushed the dead back, quickly finishing off those that stumbled, but there were even more waiting in the street below.

Lucien began shivering as soon as the mist oozed in through the open door and I grabbed Tatyana's arm and pulled her over, thrusting her against him despite their protests.

'Stay close to him,' I said. 'Keep touching him, no matter what happens.'

His shivering eased as she clutched his arm, and from her lack of argument, she understood my meaning. Sharing the medallion would weaken the protection it offered, but it was better than nothing. It was more interesting to watch how the paladins reacted as the mist wrapped around them. They slowed as the cold energies began siphoning their energies, but then stopped and shook their heads as the effects touched on the worms inside them. Two started bleeding heavily from the nose, but all seven were clearly in pain, clutching their heads or grinding their teeth together. The worms had been surrounded by the same dark magic in the cells, but perhaps the intensity of what hung in the streets was too much for them, like a day-old baby being offered meat rather than milk from his mother's teat.

And yet, as the paladins hacked their way towards the bottom of the stairs, their long axes separating arms from torsos and splitting heads like old fruit, their cries of pain faded and their movements steadily became smoother and faster once more. One of those with the bloody nose faltered, falling to a knee as blood began to well and flow from his ears and eyes as well as his nose and mouth. The others helped him back to his feet and gave him back his fallen sword. He limped over to Lucien and said something I couldn't hear, and then walked to the front of our little war-band and began chanting, his voice slowly gaining strength.

At first I couldn't hear the words, but as the other paladins took it up too I finally began to understand. It was something I had last heard a long time ago: the death-song of the faithful, a plea to their ancestors and their god to witness their courage, and swearing eternal allegiance to the brothers who stood by them. Their forebears had once sung it as they marched to fight me, but I had not paid that much attention to it then, other than as a way to track their progress. The paladin was bleeding profusely, but he marched into the gathering ghouls without hesitation, and kept singing and cleaving right up to the moment that a particularly large ghoul split his head with a shovel.

Tatyana was staying close to Lucien, wielding her sword one-handed which, as she quickly demonstrated, was no obstacle to her despatching stray ghouls who managed to avoid the paladins' steel. I stayed back as well, making the most of their presence to continue preparing my sorcery for my own trials. One or two ghouls stumbled out from side streets and alleys, but they were alone or in pairs and easy enough to stop. Breaking their necks wouldn't 'kill' them as such, but it left them unable to do anything but snap and claw at the cobbles. Even Lucien helped end a few, his sword finding eyes and throats in the openings that Tatyana created.

Another of the paladins fell before the road was cleared, his neck slashed to the bone by the wild backswing of an axe. He slew the creature who killed him even as death bore him to the ground. Their death-song drifted into a prayer as the last of the creatures fell and they stood there, steaming in the mist as they gulped in lungfuls of the cold air.

Ahead of us the road rose and disappeared towards the steady throb of Navar's spellwork as it rose into the sky like a strangling vine, robbing the world of all colour and leaving only shadows and the pearlescent glow of his magic. I wasn't alone in stopping to stare at the column of swirling light as it dispersed into the churning clouds.

'At least we don't have to worry about directions,' muttered Tatyana, pulling Lucien closer to her as another shiver passed through him. The medallion was helping him, but he was only getting a portion of its protection. To his credit, he uttered no complaint and instead bared his teeth.

'Let's go kill the bastard,' he said, offering me a fierce grin. 'Wizards bleed.'

'Wizards bleed,' I agreed, and without another word we set out once more, unaware of the new nightmare that was about to descend upon us.

CHAPTER 42

IT MOVED SILENTLY despite its great bulk, and with the dark magic pressing down on me I didn't feel its approach either. The first warning we had was when it sent a shutter crashing to the ground as it lowered itself down the side of a nearby building, its bone claws sinking into the brick as if it was soft wood and not stone and mortar. I could do little but stare at the impossibility of what I was seeing as it raced down the side of the buildings and landed in the street with a screech of claw on stone, sending a tremor through the ground with its great bulk.

It was another of the necromancers' abominations, even larger than the one that had bested me in the mountain fortress, and staggeringly hideous. It scuttled forward with a speed that belied its bulk and reared up on multi-jointed legs until it stood more than twice my height. It shrieked from a score of mouths, and lashed out with a knotted limb that looked more like a huge, muscular spine than anything else. The blow smashed one of the paladins to the ground, the bony hooks that dotted its length piercing him in several places. He screamed as it lifted him into the air by those hooks and swung him in a short, vicious arc to dash his head open against the cobbles. Multiple mouths opened along its body and it screamed my name with six tortured voices, the unearthly sound sending a chill down my spine.

'By the stars,' I breathed, the sheer impossibility of its existence warring with the growing urge to flee or fight.

The four remaining paladins shouted the name of their god and launched themselves at it, an act of such mad courage that it broke the spell cast by the monster. It answered their challenge with a piercing shriek of its own as it turned to face them, that massive spine lashing back and forth, a glancing blow from the hooks opening a terrible gash in one of the men.

Tatyana screamed as well, and I felt the sorcery within her jolt to life as she charged forward, her sword at her shoulder, the point levelled at the creature. Lucien staggered and ran after her, his sword raised too. Shamed by my hesitation, I followed them, hastily summoning the sorcery that had slipped from my bewildered mind.

The wounded paladin died before anyone could reach him. Perhaps drawn by the heat of his blood, or simply the promise of an easier kill, the creature sprang upon him. His sword carved a crescent in its hide as he fell, but it didn't seem to notice or care and pressed its malformed body down on his. Three smaller arms unfolded from a crease in its breast and tore at him with blackened claws that ripped divots of flesh from his writhing form, slowing only to stuff the bloody meat into the mouths clustered at the centre of its body.

The remaining paladins fell upon it, hacking at it with renewed savagery, their swords gleaming with the thick, rank fluids that burst from it. Tatyana charged at it and plunged the blade into its torso like a lance, the blade bending as it struck bone within. It shrieked and rose from the eviscerated paladin, its mouths still blindly snapping at the strips of meat that hung from them. Tatyana was flung backwards as one of its arms lashed out, shredding what remained of her thick jerkin but fortunately not the coat of rings beneath. It drove the paladins away with a series of vicious swipes, then shook itself like a wet dog, spraying fluid everywhere. I could see the mist clinging to its wounds, binding them as surely as I used the Songlines to heal my own.

I shouted 'Get back!' loud enough for the paladins to hear, and they edged backwards, batting its flailing arms away with their swords.

It rose up as I stepped towards it, and again screeched my name from its many mouths, something I would sooner die than ever hear again. I knew I had little chance of avoiding that bony whip and so instead lunged forward as it attacked. I felt the barbs along its length bite into my skin and I grabbed onto it with all my strength before the beast could rip it back and flay the skin from me.

I threw myself forward as it charged at me. Its body looked soft and bloated, but as it crashed into me I realised that I had underestimated it. The layers of coarse, saggy skin hid the mass of bone that enclosed the core of its body, and from the breathtaking weight that slammed into me there was clearly a lot of it in there. The arms that had scooped the guts from the paladin now unfolded once more, the shovel-like claws glistening with his gore.

I released the wind construct as the claws reached for me. The compressed wind roared as it flung us both into the air. I had braced for it, but the creature hadn't, and I heard its limbs crack and snap as we shot into the air. I clung to the whip as the creature flailed and shrieked, then twisted so it was beneath me before I released the second part of the spell.

The wind smashed us back down into the cobbles like a hammer, but I was on top of it and my weight was firmly on top of Tatyana's protruding sword. Bone cracked deep within it as my weight was transferred to the angular point of her sword. I felt the blade bend, then straighten as the point burst through into its body, saving me from being impaled on the handle. Undead flesh was still only flesh, and steel was steel.

A great gout of black fluid burst from several of its mouths as the metal slid deep beyond the bony cage. It shrieked and flailed, desperately trying to right itself with broken arms. I grasped the handle of the sword with both hands and with a roar of my own, I sent a bolt of sorcery along the blade and into its very core. If I had thought its bestial shrieks loud before, the noise that rose from it must surely have been heard across the city and beyond.

The paladins rushed to join me, their baritone prayers a welcome counterpoint to its bestial screeching as they plunged their weapons into it, hacking and chopping its flesh while I sent pulse after pulse of sorcery into it, the golden light burning flesh and breaking the enchantments that bound it to this mockery of life. After what felt like hours it gave one last shudder and lay still. I stood and staggered away, binding the residual energies to staunch the blood flowing from the uncounted gashes across my ribs and back.

'Drogah's beard,' said the paladin to my left, his words punctuated by him gulping down mouthfuls of cold air. 'We had heard rumour of such creatures but never gave much weight to them.'

'This is the second I have met, and the first I have bested,' I said between my own gasps.

He shrugged and spat a gobbet of blood onto its body. 'Drogah has only seen to challenge us this once so far.'

I looked across at him as I worked the last of its hooks from the underside of my arm. 'What are your names?'

'Our names?' He gave a rough laugh. 'You ask this *now?*'

'Because such courage should be remembered.'

He stood and offered me his hand, which I ignored. There was no way that he could take my weight.

'I am Norak, and this is Sir Konroi.'

'I will remember.' With my death imminent I felt I could say it with some certainty.

'We would count it an honour.'

Behind him Tatyana gave up on trying to pull her sword from the already rotting carcass and took up one of the fallen paladins' weapons instead. 'We should go,' she said, pulling the extremely pale Lucien against her side. 'Before he sends another.'

That was good enough for me. I wanted to die with my hands around Navar's heart, not eaten by some misshapen pet of his. We waited for Norak to kiss his fallen brothers and whisper some platitude their corpses could not hear then hurried towards the silvery glow that had swallowed the rest of the city.

THE CHILL SHARPENED as we pressed on, but the healing I'd been forced to do helped keep the worst of it at bay. The mist was thinning as the road climbed, pulled ever downwards by its own weight, leaving us to advance through a city cloaked in ice that glimmered like a sea of gems beneath the eldritch light that lit the sky. The air was still, and cold enough to freeze the spittle on my lips and leave my breath suspended in the air long after I had passed by. Lucien was pressed tightly to Tatyana and the two paladins were whispering their prayers with increasing urgency as the dark magic burrowed deeper into them with every breath they drew in. For my part, I knew *he* was watching.

I had touched his magic once, and had even stolen some of it, and, with every step closer to the pulsing light that sheathed the cathedral, the memory of it grew clearer. We were close. Ahead of me the paladin named Konroi stumbled and was caught by the other. He struggled to his feet, but the crimson that fell from his nose was stark against his pale skin. Norak supported him and they kept walking. I glanced at Tatyana, who was also supporting much of Lucien's weight.

'The air feels so heavy,' she said. 'Like I am wading upstream rather than walking.'

That was a fair description of what I had felt since we set foot in the city, except that rather than wading upstream I was walking up a waterfall littered with icy shards that would reward any lapse in concentration by impaling my soul.

'You should turn back.'

'I'm not abandoning you. I gave my word. We all did.'

Lucien shivered as he turned to me. 'Blood of Kings,' he croaked.

'You're fools,' I said, shaking my head as they straightened and began walking forward once more.

Metal clattered against stone as the paladins, who had continued on for another forty paces or so ahead of us, both collapsed. To my surprise, I found myself moving to their side.

The one called Konroi was twitching and making strange barking noises, both of which intensified until they abruptly stopped and he sagged into my arms. Before Norak could even give voice to his dismay, Konroi's body glittered with amber light and a glowing mist was drawn from him. I could feel the radiance of it against my skin like the touch of sunlight breaking through winters gloom.

'My god,' breathed Norak.

A moment later it rose upwards, faster than an arrow but not fast enough to outpace the hissing arc of pearlescent energy that flashed from the pale column of light that was now a constant presence in the east. It wrapped around the amber glow and began pulling it back into the column of murky silver.

Norak was on his feet, screaming, and even I was utterly transfixed as Konroi's still squirming essence was sucked into the column, where its glow was washed away like blood in a stream.

'My god,' repeated Norak. 'Blessed Drogah, guide him home.'

Tatyana and Lucien said nothing as they dragged their gaze away, but I could taste their fear in the air.

'It's not too late to go back,' I said.

Norak gritted his teeth and shook his head. 'He must pay for his sins.'

'Stop wasting your breath,' said Tatyana from behind me. I wasn't sure who she was talking to, but it seemed to have settled the matter. Norak began walking with new strength, perhaps fuelled by hate alone judging from the curses he was stringing together as he walked. Ahead of us the pulsing light shifted and settled into a steady glow as we drew level with it, enough so that the silhouette of the cathedral could be seen in the centre of it. Faint echoes of screams and half formed words filled the air, first coming from one direction then the other, growing louder every time an arc of magic snapped from the column to dance along the hoary bones and gravestones we were passing through.

I could feel the pulse of magic in the air now, buffeting my skin like the wings of a thousand unseen birds. Norak was struggling as he caught up to me, with patches of his skin already turning black and beginning to flake away as if he were made of ash.

'My death is close,' he said.

'It is. That you are even here to say that is testament to your strength.'

He accepted the compliment with a nod. 'I would have liked to die in battle.'

'You may yet have your chance,' I said, pointing towards the flicker of shapes moving amongst the gravestones closest to the cathedral. As I watched, another arc of light stabbed into the ground, the afterglow offering the suggestion of a screaming face before it faded. All across the graveyard the soil had begun to rise and fall, almost as if the ground were breathing, but that image was lost as soon as the first skeletal hands broke through the surface and began to paw at the frozen ground. Scores of corpses were pulling themselves from their graves, the rents and holes in their rotting bodies lit by the cold light of the souls that had stolen them, obedient to some unheard signal from the necromancers within the cathedral.

Norak was whispering a prayer, and with my own muttered curse I laid my hand upon his shoulder and sent a pulse of sorcery through him. I could neither heal him nor aid his faith, but anger and hate were boon companions of mine and I lent him a spark of it, fanning his own anger and need for revenge into a new flame. He stood straighter and didn't seem to notice the blood that had begun to leak from his nose and ears.

'Thank you,' he said. He turned to Tatyana and Lucien. 'May Drogah protect you.'

'And you,' Tatyana replied through clenched teeth, her cheeks gleaming with ice.

The dead were gathering into a mob, forming a barrier of dead flesh between us and the cathedral grounds, silent apart from the clack of bone and patter of the pungent fluids leaking from their soiled flesh.

Norak rolled his neck and raised his sword, and began to chant as he moved ahead of us, his voice gaining strength with every other word. When he was but a few yards from the herd he raised his sword, which shimmered and then lit with a honey coloured light as if fresh from the forge.

I raised the veil of my sorcery as he charged into the front rank of the dead.

'He shouldn't be alone,' said Tatyana, her free hand straying towards her sword.

'No,' I said, grabbing her wrist before she could touch the handle. 'Lucien needs you.'

She pulled her hand away but didn't take another step. The power that Norak had imbued the sword with drew my attention once more. It wasn't coming from the Songlines; they felt impossibly distant and even I would struggle to draw power here, and I could see no connection between them. In the end it was the golden sheen of it that gave the answer. It wasn't magic that made the sword so deadly to the dead, but his own essence. His life energy. The undead would crave the heat and sensation of life, and Norak's sword was a beacon, drawing them to him. He was using that same positive energy as a weapon though, for even though they craved it, the touch of it was as deadly to them as the touch of death was to the living. Norak was hacking and stabbing his blade deep into them, disrupting their hold on this world and the flesh they had stolen. Every touch sent the souls screaming back into Navar's vortex, but also stole away a mote of his life. The blade was already starting to dim.

'Whatever you're going to do, do it now!'

Tatyana's voice shrieked into my thoughts and the delicate traceries vanished from my vision.

'Go!' I called, pointing to a space between two of the spires. I had no idea what lay there, but it was a step closer to the nexus of the dark magic. She charged ahead, felling several of the slower dead who were shuffling towards the doomed paladin with quick sweeps of her sword. Lucien stumbled along behind her, clinging to her arm but alert enough to take the arms off a lurching corpse that rose from behind a gravestone.

I followed them, working as quickly as I could to reinforce my own wards. I could barely sense the Songlines here anymore, and certainly not in a way that would allow me to draw power from them. Everything I was doing was being fuelled from my own all too finite reserves of power.

I didn't see the standing stones until I passed them, and then barely had time to utter a curse before the full weight of the magic that waited beyond them fell upon me like a mountain.

CHAPTER 43

IF IT HAD felt as if I was walking up an icy waterfall before, now it felt like that waterfall had redoubled in volume and ferocity. I staggered backwards and fell as my heel caught a gravestone. I hit the ground hard; it felt like the pressure was going to hammer me into the frozen ground like an oversized nail. The standing stones I had blundered past acted to contain and channel the power that bled from the broken nexus, and I had blundered into the midst of that rampant energy like a blind fool. The sound was almost worse than the pressure, a pulsing drone that resonated deep within me, making it feel like each of my bones was shivering independently of any others and my teeth were loosening in their sockets. There was no end to it, no break in which I could marshal my strength and find a way through, just the unbroken cacophony of a hundred spells woven into one and the psychic earthquake of two worlds colliding.

I tried to pull myself up, but the droning was in my mind, the unending rhythm of it pushing my thoughts from my mind. I couldn't even remember how to lift my arm, let alone fight back. Something glittered at the edge of my vision, a piercing blue mote like midwinter ice struck by the sun. It grew closer and I fought to raise my arms to fend it off, but I felt them being knocked away and could do nothing as the glittering shape fell onto my head.

A wonderful heat spread through me as it struck, a wave that began at my forehead and pulsed through my flesh, throwing off the crushing grip of the magic, if only temporarily. I didn't question the sudden reprieve and hastily woke the defences I had been preparing, shaping them to meet the new danger as best I could. The weight of the magics fell upon me again as the heat passed, pressing at the wards I had set. Arcs of pain shot through my head as I fed more power into them. I felt them buckle inwards, but by the grace of the stars, the structure was sound and they held.

I sat up to find Tatyana and Lucien slumped beside me, delicate feathers of frost already covering their bodies. Her arms were outstretched, and on the ground next to me lay the medallion I had given her, the stone at the centre still glowing as if lit from within. I snatched it up and felt the pressure in my head ease again. It was a powerful tool, a hidden weapon against whatever terrible magics Navar could, and most certainly would, unleash upon me. I pushed their bodies off me and weighed the artefact in my hands for a moment as I gazed down at them. They were surely as good as dead, and even if they somehow survived this, Navar and his cabal would make short work of them.

I had intended to say goodbye to them, but instead I found myself pushing the medallion under Tatyana's armour and laying Lucien across her.

'I'm a fool,' I grunted to no one, and pulled myself to my feet. The dead had finally overcome Norak, or perhaps he had simply spent the last of his essence, and the remnants of the horde were now shuffling towards me. They no longer had the numbers to overwhelm me though, and I set upon them with my claws, shredding the dry, icy flesh like kindling or twisting their heads from their necks. The exercise warmed my blood and helped shake off the worst of the chill. Tatyana and Lucien were just about on their feet by the time I felled the last, albeit that both looked like drunks who had woken in a snowdrift.

'Thank you,' I said, but she barely nodded. The medallion had restored them, but they were only human, their bodies unused to absorbing the magic it radiated. I cursed under my breath as I siphoned off yet another measure of my sorcery and, with my hands on their heads, pulsed it into their bodies, driving out the lingering lethargy and will-sapping residue of the magic that was eating at them. They recoiled as if struck, but I held them fast until I was satisfied they were lucid once more.

'Thank you,' I repeated, and this time Tatyana flashed the briefest of smiles.

'And thank you,' she said in a hoarse voice.

'He killed them all,' said Lucien, peering at the mound of broken bodies that marked where Norak had fallen. The dozen or so on top were my handiwork, but I decided not to labour the point.

'It was a good death. Impressive even, given that he was dying anyway.'

Lucien looked up at me, then clapped me on my arm. 'Aren't we all?'

I tilted my head as I considered this. 'I'm starting to like you.'

'Who could resist?' he said, picking his sword up from the ground and scraping the ice from the handle. 'I would have such a glorious death too.'

'Be careful of your wishes, my prince.' I gestured to the outline of the cathedral that loomed over us.

'When this is over,' said Tatyana, moving up next to us, 'I'm going to get drunk for a week.'

'Me too,' said Lucien. 'And I'm going to lay in a bath for a day. And I want to sing.'

'That sounds fine,' I said. *How long had it been since I had sung anything?* I shook the maudlin thought away.

Nothing further was said as we made our way towards where I expected the doors would be, the lines of the cathedral growing more distinct as we moved closer. The pressure of the magic changed as we climbed the frozen stairs, pulling where it had once pushed and crushed, hungry for the life within us. I fed yet more power into my wards and bade Tatyana and Lucien move behind me as I pulled the cracked doors open.

A wave of light and sound burst out like water from a broken dam but it quickly abated, and I cautiously stepped into what remained of the cathedral, probing for hidden wards and traps. The cathedral was little more than a roofless shell, the walls seemingly only held in place by the heaps of spoil piled against them and the arcs of magical energy that linked the enormous spirals of runes carved in each wall. The floor had been gouged away as if dug by some gigantic beast, leaving a steep sided pit, the centre of which was marked with three triangular standing stones. As I watched, these pillars seemed to swell with silver light, the runes carved upon them glowing as bright as a sun before the light pulsed upwards, feeding the pillar that had drawn us here.

I moved forward cautiously, still wary of hidden wards or ambushes, but found none. Was he that arrogant that he thought me no threat? I dismissed the thought and concentrated on keeping my wards intact. A slip this close to the heart of Navar's power was likely to be fatal.

I paused at the edge of the pit and stared down at the

patch of absolute darkness that sat in the centre of the standing stones. The churned ground was marked with the tracks from many pairs of feet. It seemed that however unwelcoming the pit appeared, it had no shortage of visitors.

'We're going down into the black pit of death, aren't we?' said Tatyana as she moved up next to me.

'Yes.'

'Oh good.'

Lucien looked down into the pit and quickly stepped back. 'Maybe we should wait here. Rearguard and all that.'

'No,' I said. 'My sorcery has all but faded from you already, and the medallion will not be sufficient to shield you from that.' I gestured to the column of light coalescing above the ruined roof and the stray souls that fluttered around it like grotesque moths. 'It will pull your essence from you, leaving your hollow body to be ridden like a puppet by whatever wraith sees it first.'

'Oh.' He stared up at the twisting column and somehow managed to grow even paler. For a moment it seemed that he was about to faint or bolt, but Tatyana pulled him closer and whispered something into his ear. Whatever she said seemed to work, because he straightened his back and lifted his sword-point from the dirt with what I thought was an overly dramatic sigh. 'Let's just get it over with.'

With that inspiring speech complete, I set off down the slope. Strangely, the intensity of the droning magic lessened the closer I came to the standing stones, a fact that I welcomed rather than questioned. The stones were huge, at least twice my height, and each was tightly bound with three thick bands of golden wire. The glow from the runes incised along their length was too bright for me to see past, and almost bright enough to cause permanent damage if I looked too closely. Tatyana and Lucien came sliding down

the slope behind me, their arms held in front of their faces
to shield them from the glare.

'It's three steps ahead of you,' I said, then stepped into
the void.

CHAPTER 44

I HIT THE ground hard enough to drive the breath from my lungs and fill my nose with the scent of blood, and then suffered the indignity and not inconsiderable discomfort of both Tatyana and Lucien landing on top of me. For several terrible moments it felt like I had forgotten how to breathe, but at last their weight shifted and I sucked in greedy breaths of the cold, damp air. Tatyana and Lucien were still groaning when I pulled myself to my feet.

The hole was directly above us, easily thirty paces up, and I guessed that Navar and his cabal had used their magic to descend, something I might have considered had I stopped to test how deep it was. What was more interesting was the narrow and very roughly hewn staircase that rose towards the hole from *beneath*. From the mortar and rocky debris around us it seemed that it had been blocked up and sealed at some point, hidden for countless years until his wizards blasted it open.

The chamber we had landed in was a smooth hollow, the dark walls laced with a glowing network of crystal veins of varying sizes, some thicker than my torso and others no wider than my fingers. They stretched across every surface, each pulsing with the same silver-white light that lit the sky above the cathedral. Some were pulsing at a different pace, something I found disorienting, and I couldn't help but think of them as pale throats swallowing the glow. Or perhaps vomiting it out.

The one thing they all had in common was the direction of the pulses; the veins merged and thickened towards the end of the chamber, lighting a smooth walled tunnel that curved away deeper into the tainted earth.

I moved closer to one of the veins and cupped my hands over it to dampen the glow. It was a seam of fairly normal crystal; they all were, which made sense. Crystals like these often formed where Songline nodes touched the earth, although perhaps it was the other way around. Either way, they helped dilute and disperse the raw power that seeped into reality around them, carrying the spark of life deep into the ground, enriching the earth for some way around it and surrounding the node in harmony, something that was now being distorted and turned against itself. At least here the pull of the negative energy was diffused through the veins, blunting its intensity and making it marginally easier for me to think of something besides holding my wards up.

I helped the humans to their feet and waited as they tried to make sense of the alien vista they found themselves in. I gave them a few moments, then ushered them towards the curving tunnel. The walls here had been painted with multicoloured pictograms of great bison, antelope and lions, and occasionally a group of stick figures carrying spears and bows. Taller figures stood here and there, and one entire wall was taken up by the spindly scratches of human writing, at least where the creeping damp had not swallowed it.

'What is this?' wheezed Tatyana, tracing the outline of a human with a stag's antlers framing its head.

'I've seen pictures like this before,' said Lucien, lifting

her fingers away from the drawings. 'They're from the elder races. These are of exceptional quality, and quite ancient.'

'Relatively speaking,' I muttered, turning my attention to what lay ahead. By my reckoning, the tunnel was turning away to the north, almost following the curve of the rocky cone that Aknak was built upon. We passed more walls decorated with similar glyphs, and occasionally human skulls that glittered with coloured stones and gems embedded in the age-darkened bone. After what felt like miles of walking I felt a change in the pressure of the magic, and soon after the slope of the floor began to even out.

'We're close,' I said.

'Shit,' was Tatyana's eloquent response. 'Is he here?'

I touched one of the throbbing veins that zigzagged across the wall, ignoring the painful sting of the cold energy and concentrating on the magic resonating within it. It didn't take long for me to pick out the familiar and still unpleasant tremor of Navar's spellcasting amongst it.

'Yes,' I said, barely aware of how I wiped my hand on what was left of my clothes. 'I can feel his magic in the air and stone.'

'Shit,' echoed Lucien. The long walk had helped him recover some colour, and he seemed more lucid than he had since we freed him. He took a deep breath and blew it out in a sharp breath. 'The Hel with it. I'm ready.'

'I'm not fond of goodbyes, so just promise me you'll kill him,' said Tatyana, laying her hand against my face. 'Whatever happens, just promise me that.'

'I will kill him,' I said, returning the gesture. 'Stay behind me if you can.'

I turned and began walking again, repeatedly sliding my long talons from my forearms, ignoring the sting as they pushed through the skin between my knuckles. I heard Lucien gasp at the sight of them, but that was all. I slid them in and out a few more times, desensitising myself to the discomfort and ensuring that the muscular sheaths that propelled them were warmed and ready to react at an instant's notice.

The air stirred as I followed the curve of the passage and I drew a deep breath of it through my nose. I hadn't smelled much aside from frozen corpses and old blood since we entered the city, so the scent of crushed grass came as enough of a surprise to slow me. Grass, and air that wasn't stale. I took another breath, but this one carried the more expected odours of the dead and the burnt spice aroma of necromancers. And Navar.

His scent made my gut clench and my hearts surge like I hadn't felt for some time. Excitement and anxiety swirled within me at the prospect of facing him again; time might have taken the brightest edges off the memory of the pain he had inflicted on me, but the sense of helplessness and despair that I associated him remained strong, and would only fade once he was well and truly dead.

The curve of the passage lessened and gave way to a straight stretch some twenty paces long, beyond which it opened into what looked to be a wide clearing of some sort. I could hear, and feel, the drone of the magic more distinctly now. It was a chant carried by a dozen or more separate voices, the cadence bound together by a strange thumping vibration. I edged along the final stretch, then stepped out into the clearing.

I HAD EXPECTED a cave, but instead found myself stepping into a truly enormous, egg-shaped cavern, the top of which had fallen away or been sheared off by some ancient impact, leaving it open to the sky above. The floor of the cavern was covered with what must once have been lush growth, fed as it was by the silvery curtains of water that trickled over the rim of the cavern and the life-giving glow of the node that had pulsed like a heart in the confluence of the crystal seams. A large, wooden figure lay off to one side, a number of axes and swords buried in its trunk.

This then was the secret that lay at the heart of Aknak.

It would have been glorious once, before Navar and his cabal of necromancers descended upon it. Now the gardens were little more than frozen mulch, and a dozen stone monoliths had been driven in amongst the crystal outcroppings that dotted it, creating an outer perimeter. The runes on the stones were bright with silver fire, and the same cold flame raced along the golden wires joining them. Inside this burning perimeter were two concentric rings of chanting necromancers, and in the centre of these stood the Lance.

It had been driven into the very centre of the crystal seams. Sheets of coloured light flashed and flickered above and around it, swelling and then collapsing into a single, twisting ribbon that looked like fire but moved like water, lashing back and forth like a trapped serpent. The Lance itself was blurred and hard to focus on, and as the chant pressed in against me I realised that it was continuously vibrating, the almost insectile buzzing of it indelibly woven into the necromancers' chant.

The rings of men stood unmoving as they chanted their strange spells in harmony with the shrill buzz that the Lance was giving off. It wasn't the sight of them that made me stop, nor even the six enormous, heavily armoured ghouls that turned to face us with mathematical precision.

I was staring at the man in black robes who stood before

the glowing Lance, his strident voice ringing clearer than any other.

Navar Louw.

As I watched, he lowered his arms and turned towards us, his eyes glowing with the same silver fire. He lifted a hand and pointed at me, and a moment later the ghouls began to march forward in perfect lockstep, their iron helmets filling with the same cold starlight and their broad bladed swords rising.

My talons slid from their sheaths and I felt Tatyana's heartbeat increasing.

'God save us,' she said quietly, and I tasted her fear anew. 'Death Knights.'

'Sweet Drogah save us,' Lucien said, his voice a whisper.

As expected, his god ignored his entreaty entirely and the death knights continued march towards us.

'Back to the tunnel,' I said. Neither of them hesitated, and I walked backwards, watching the knights as they followed us. They were monstrous, each of them at least as tall as me and even broader in girth, their size buoyed by their heavy, rune-inscribed armour nailed to their bodies. They were ripe with dark magic and I could feel the pull of it as they came closer, moving with a strange predatory grace that belied their weight.

They slowed as they entered the tunnel behind us, but only enough to move into a staggered formation. All that bulk and their long blades left them unable to come at us in anything more than single file, and even then they quickly filled the confines of the tunnel. I reached for my sorcery and shaped it into a coruscating bolt of electrical energy that grew in power as it materialised, agitating the air around it until the entire length of the passage glittered with arcs of suppressed power.

I planted my feet and unleashed the bolt at the death

knights. I expected the runes on their armour did a lot of things, but metal loves lightning even more than it likes fire. The bolt struck the first of them like a battering ram, hurling him backwards. The power leapt from knight to knight, bouncing from armour plate to armour plate and back again, searing great funnels through their flesh as it climbed towards their bell-like helmets. I fed another lash of power into it and howled in victory as their helmets melted into slag and the crackling energy continued to burn its way through the flesh and bone beneath. The four knights at the front collapsed as the lightning dissipated, their limbs kicking uncontrollably and steam rising from where their armour had melted into their flesh.

The pair at the rear escaped the worst of it, and given time they would no doubt have recovered and been back to their full deadliness, but that wasn't something I was going to allow.

I pushed my way through the smouldering carcasses and charged into them, but despite the damage they had suffered they were faster than I could ever have imagined, and I felt the hard impact and burning rasp of a blade as it caught my right shoulder and cut its way down to my elbow. It happened too quickly for me to feel any pain, something that would change very soon, but for a moment his blade was down.

I rammed my talon upwards along his breastplate and into the grey flesh under his jaw. I straightened my legs as I drove upwards, the hard tip breaking through his palate and bursting up into his rotten skull, whereupon I released a bolt of raw sorcery along it and into the centre of his being.

I wrenched the talon out and pushed him into the path of the last knight. He staggered half a pace forward before his head exploded inside his helmet, sending bone and blood gushing from his visor. The last knight pushed the body aside and lunged for me.

I twisted aside but his blade followed and still managed to open a gash across my hip. I threw myself at him as he pulled his sword back. I wasn't fast, but I hoped he wasn't expecting me to attack. I pushed in as close as I dared, grinding my talon along the sword to keep him from raising it. It was too heavy and strong for me and my withered leg to knock down, but that was not my intention. I just wanted to be inside the reach of its arms and too close for it to block the talon I rammed through its visor. I gave it a blast of energy and kicked myself away from it just as the ruined enchantments in its head vented themselves in a corona of white light and shrieking metal.

'Drogah's balls,' said Lucien in a hushed voice as the echoes faded. 'That was incredible.'

He was staring at me as if he'd never seen me before, which I suppose was fair seeing as the only time I'd fought by his side was the night he had drunk a stupendous amount of ale.

'This is only the beginning,' I said as I wiped the gore from my talons. The stench of their already rotting bodies was less offensive than the magic animating them had been.

'Did you know he could do that?' the prince asked in the same tone.

'Something like it, yes,' Tatyana replied.

'We have a chance with that kind of power, don't we?'

Her gaze darted to me before she pulled him close again. 'There's always hope.'

Hope. I couldn't remember the moment when hate had finally eroded the last of whatever hope I had once held. Hate, like anger, was constant and reassuring. It didn't falter, nor could sweet words undermine it. Hate was strong, and had given me the strength to endure long after hope had abandoned me.

'Stay behind me,' I said, the words emerging more as a growl as I stalked back into the cavern, my hearts beating hard and fast and my chest filled with the uncomfortable flutter of fear. It was time to face Navar.

CHAPTER 45

I STEPPED OUT into the cavern and directly into the path of a well-timed fireball that hurled me into the wall.

It felt like I'd flown into a mountain. My clothes were little more than burning shreds, and the skin of my chest was charred and raw, the flesh glassy and curling with smoke. For the second time that day it felt like my entire torso was being crushed in an invisible fist when I tried to breathe. The wizard who had hit me was shouting at Navar now, or was it the other way around? I knew I should be more concerned about it, but it was difficult to concentrate.

I gritted my teeth and looked up, wincing as the cavern spun and tilted around me. I saw the wizard, a half-starved creature with a long and unkempt beard, lifting his staff once more. A dark red light glimmered around the end, like sunlight glimpsed through blood, and the whining in my head sharpened to a painful pitch as he lowered it at me. I tried to pull what was left of my wards into place, but they slipped away from me. I had no defences other than to try to shield myself with the thick meat of my arms.

The sound stopped as I lifted them. I lowered them and looked at the wizard, but his attention was fixed on the sword protruding from his chest. He fell to his knees, mirroring my current pose, and let the now smoking staff roll from his twitching fingers. Blood welled from his mouth, drenching his beard, and a moment later his unfinished spell burst his head with a silent flash of crimson light.

I sucked in a painful breath as the pressure on my chest loosened, then another. The cavern stopped spinning as the air hit my lungs, and I felt reality snap back into focus a heartbeat later. Ignoring the painful pull of my scorched and blistered flesh, I pushed myself to my feet as Navar floated towards me, his cape flaring out around him and his bone staff clutched in his iron gauntlets.

I shot a glance over my shoulder and saw Tatyana sitting with her back to the wall, the smallest movement of her chest telling me that she yet lived despite the burns that blackened most of the right side of her body. It was, of course, her sword that had slain the wizard and saved me, a debt that I hoped I would have the chance to repay. Lucien lay sprawled awkwardly next to her, the edges of his tunic burning with a steady orange flame.

'Pathetic.' The word rolled across me like thunder. He had stopped not twenty paces away, his robes slowly swirling around him as if he stood in a river, his eyes burning pits of silver within his hood. Behind him the rest of his cabal maintained their chant as if I wasn't even there.

I could not look away from him, not even if I had tried. I could feel the power brimming within him, and it almost took more strength than I had not to step back from him.

'Yes,' he said, his voice becoming that of a man once more rather than a god. 'You feel it.'

'I'm here to end you.' My voice was a child's compared to his, and he roared with laughter.

'You? And is this the mighty army you have brought

to help you?' He tilted his head and I felt his magic flex, almost lazily, lifting both Tatyana and Lucien into the air. She screeched as her burned skin folded and stretched, but Lucien seemed entirely insensate, his limbs swinging limply. 'A prince and a failed paladin. A *woman*.'

'Fuck you.' Tatyana spat the words at him, a remarkable effort given the pain she must have been in.

I gasped in naked relief as his gaze switched to her, while she stiffened as if struck. I felt his magic ripple as he studied her.

'Interesting,' he said, spinning her in the air as if she were an insect caught in a web. 'Is that your handiwork?'

'Let them go,' I said.

'I don't think I will,' he said. 'Not until I've peeled every secret from her flesh.'

His hand twitched and they were thrown against the nearest wall, where they fell in a tangle of limbs, unmoving and silent.

'Now, did you really think that wearing that suit of skin would save you from me? You're a shambles. Look at you. Too pathetic to maintain even one enchantment, but you dare to walk in here and challenge *me?*' His voice rose in volume as he spoke, the tone hardening and bringing with it a rush of unpleasantly painful memories. 'Look upon me, wyrm. Look!'

I squared my shoulders and faced him, my claws and sorcery held ready. He rose another yard into the air as the space around him glimmered and shone, and I could not help but take a step back as he flexed his power. It was staggering to behold. He had been quick and strong when I was his captive, but the strength he now brought to bear was of an entirely different magnitude; it was as if a wolf cub had grown into a cave bear. I could feel the mere promise of it curdling reality around me.

'You begin to understand,' he said, lowering himself to the ground. 'It is not too late. Come, you know that you cannot win.' His voice softened. 'Surrender yourself to me, and we can rule this world together.'

His words were a baited hook, and had Leopold's fondness for using the same trick not recently hardened me to it, I might have succumbed to its false promise.

I spat a gobbet of blood and phlegm at him. 'Surrender to you? A charlatan who has mistaken brute force for actual talent? You're little more than a cruel child who thinks himself strong because he has pulled the legs from an insect.'

I doubted it was the reaction he expected, as for a long moment he simply stared at me, the light in his eyes dimming.

I took the moment to release the fire I had been furtively preparing. It flashed between us and struck him square in the chest, where it burst and rolled over him, shrieking tonelessly as it sucked in air and bloomed into its full intensity. I roared as it enveloped him and walked forward, my claws twitching in anticipation.

I had crossed half of the distance when the flame simply winked out of existence, leaving Navar standing in front of me, entirely unhurt. The only sign it had ever happened was that his staff was cracked, which gave me some hope, but he tossed it aside with a careless gesture and raised his hand. I felt his magic shift around me, the touch of it cold and oily, and a moment later the air in front of him rippled and coalesced into another staff. This one was slightly longer than the other, and wrapped in strips of glittering grey leather that weren't so much tied to it as *part* of it.

'You will learn your place, wyrm,' he said in the same calm tone of voice he had always used before visiting his cruellest punishments upon me and, the stars forgive me, I felt the cold hand of fear crawl through my gut.

'You think yourself a match for me? For *me*?'

I ignored his ranting and instead used the time it gave me to get my focus back. I was ready when he levelled his staff and sent a whip of energy uncoiling towards me; it seemed that he had not given up the needless affectation of gesturing with his tools.

I leaped out of the way of the whip and sent an experimental bolt of lightning arcing towards him. He didn't even blink as it fizzled away a yard or more from him. Instead, he smiled that same sickening smile and spun his energy whip out once more, but this time with two coils of energy.

I dove out of the way as they lashed the ground where I had stood, opening two sharp furrows in the earth. I had barely got to my feet when a bolt of kinetic force smashed me backwards into the crystal-lined walls, the jagged minerals tearing a swathe of skin from my back. I hit the ground as hard as I had the wall.

The arrogant bastard stood there, simply watching and waiting as I clawed my way back onto my feet, clinging to the wall until my vision righted itself.

'Come then, do your worst,' he said, holding his arms open. 'Let us see if your bite is as vicious as your bark.'

I wasn't about to ignore an invitation like that. I pushed the pain away and raised my fists, and with a roar that blew his hood back, I unleashed what power I held. A bolt of lightning as thick as my leg flashed between us, smashing into his wards with a boom of thunder that I felt in my bones. I fed the lightning as it writhed and burrowed around the edges of his wards, seeking their weaknesses, and amidst the eye searing flare of it I glimpsed sparks of red light as it began collapsing his wards.

Hope swelled within me, then faded. Despite the nexus of the Songlines being so close I could draw no more power than I held within me, and the bolt eventually stuttered as my reserves rapidly emptied themselves. The final arc of energy vanished, leaving only the memory of it in my vision each time I blinked.

Navar was still standing. His clothes were smouldering, but there he stood, his hands on his hips and his laughter filling the cavern.

'Is that all that you have? A bolt of lightning?' He took a step forward and I matched it with a step back. 'The human body was a novel idea,' he said in that same calm tone. 'I had not appreciated your cunning, and I will admit you did have me flummoxed at first. But then I heard a story about one of my pets trying to heal a strange man not twenty miles from the university.'

He uttered a swift incantation and invoked a ball of red energy that looked remarkably like crystalline blood. He tilted his head, then thrust the staff forward, sending the glob shooting towards me, fire sparking within it. I threw myself sideways and it splattered against the rock behind me, melting several inches of the surface to glowing slag in mere moments.

'I thought you wanted me alive,' I gasped, circling around him, desperate to win some time.

He gestured, and a bolt of shimmering energy slammed into me. The wards that I had managed to erect deflected a measure of it but it still hit my gut with the force of a catapult shot, emptying my lungs of air in a loud huff. My priorities suddenly shifted from evasion and planning to simply getting air back inside me.

'I did, at the beginning,' he said, now circling me while I gasped like a landed fish, three gleaming bolts of power hovering over his shoulder, awaiting his command. 'I thought your power would be so much easier to mould if it was freely given. A mistake my master warned me of, and one I have no intention of repeating.'

His master? I had no more time to wonder about that. The first of the bolts brightened and blinked into motion. I braced for the impact against my wards, but they parted like old papyrus and I felt his magic smash into my ribs, breaking several and sending a wave of nausea rippling through me.

I fell backwards against the spiky surface of the wall, the taste of blood in my mouth and the ground as unstable as mud under my feet. I could feel his magic burning into my flesh, *through* it, the touch of it as foul as it was corrosive. But it wasn't only burning my innards, it was also mixing with my sorcery, burrowing into it like a predatory worm from within me. I cried out at the unspeakable horror of the sensation, clutching at the wound like an animal.

I didn't see the second bolt fly towards me and only knew it had struck when the world suddenly spun into a coloured blur that only stopped when I hit the ground a dozen yards away from where I had been. I tried to stand, but my leg folded and I fell again. I pushed myself onto my elbows and watched as Navar strode towards me, the final bolt glittering next to him and his teeth bared in a predatory smile.

CHAPTER 46

'YOU SHOULD HAVE surrendered when I gave you the chance.'

I spat out a mouthful of blood and teeth. 'You're an abomination. I'd sooner die.'

'And die you shall,' he said, squatting down next to me, his scent choking me with its strange ripeness. 'But in case you had not noticed, death is not the end, not anymore.'

'You're playing with forces you cannot understand.' The numbness was fading from my broken leg, giving way to a rising tide of pain that would soon drown me.

'How sad that here at the end, you still don't understand that power is all that matters.'

'I will never serve you.' If he would only stray a little closer, my claws could reach his throat. I had nothing else to offer. I tried to shift my weight but stopped when a bolt of white hot pain shot erupted from my leg, stealing the thoughts from my head and reducing my vision to shades of grey.

He was smiling as I sagged back. 'You already serve me, and you will continue to do so.'

I looked at the grey leather wound around his staff and the milky veins that bound it.

'Do you recognise it? You seemed so upset after I cut it from your wing.'

I felt something fall into place within my mind. I remembered the pain and confusion I'd felt, waking in the prison he'd built for me, my wings hacked by knives and saws and hanging in bloody tatters. *That's* why he could resist my magic, and why it felt like his was weaving into mine; he was channelling it all through my own skin. Skin that his foul magic was keeping alive. Fighting him with magic was like fighting myself, only I was feeding him with it.

'I see that you do.'

The veins swelled and I felt myself being rolled onto my back as if by a giant hand, one that didn't care how my cracked bones shifted and made me scream in agony. He stood and loomed over me.

'I don't need your body, not all of it. Perhaps I'll carve a staff from your bones and bind your soul to it. You shall serve me forever. Master and servant.' His eyes began to glow as he gathered his power once more. 'I shall rule this world forever.'

Blood red light arced from the staff and pierced me like the claws of a giant hand, lifting me into the air and pinning me against the wall, the impact lost amidst the sharp agony of my broken bones sawing into my flesh. I could feel those unearthly claws pressing inward, filling my own veins with ice.

I knew there was something I had to do, but my thoughts were slipping away from me as the coldness spread deeper into my pierced chest. A voice in my mind was whispering to me, promising me peace if I would only stop fighting, that it was all for nothing. All for nothing. I felt my body jerk as Navar sent another bolt of his bloody energy through it, pushing the claws deeper, but I hardly felt this new pain.

'Die, damn you.'

Stratus Firesky.

I forced my eyes open and my head back to stare at Navar. He was saying something, but I couldn't discern the words.

Stratus Firesky. My scream became a gasp as my name was whispered into my ear, the draconic syllables reverberating deep within me. The fog that had gathered at the edges of my vision thinned and I drew a breath as the world around me swam back into focus again. Navar was talking at me, his staff alive with coruscating power, but I wasn't listening to him.

It was *Anakhara*. It was impossible, but there was no mistaking it. It was *her* voice. Was she waiting for me? I tried to call to her, but my mouth was full of my own blood and all I could do was cough it out. Navar raised his staff, his power flowing through my stolen flesh as he fed more power into the spell that was sucking the life from me and replacing it with something other. *My flesh.*

I spat more blood and forced myself to take a deeper breath. An idea took shape in my mind, as fragile as a butterfly caught in a tempest, and I threw everything I had left within me into nurturing it. Pain and ice pressed in from all sides as Navar sensed the shift within me, and I screamed as his magic burrowed deeper into my being, sapping my remaining strength, threatening to force the idea back into a darkness it would never again rise from.

It was a hopeless battle. He had a nearly unlimited supply of power at his disposal and I could feel the weight of it descending upon me. I sucked in a desperate breath so that I could say her name once more before I died, but before I could mouth it I felt the focus of his power shift, the unending stream of it faltering. Like a drowning creature seeing the surface, I thrashed against its grip, kicking and clawing with that last mote of life, surging upwards, desperate for one last breath.

The glare of his magic was almost blinding as I forced my eyes open. I was still pressed against the wall by a writhing mass of pale energy, but he had turned away for a moment, distracted by a smaller figure. I squinted against the glimmering light and saw light reflecting off steel as the figure darted forward. *Lucien?* Navar swatted him aside, sending him and his sword spinning away, end over end.

I reached within and grasped the idea in protective hands, breathing life into it as I would a dying ember. I felt a change within me as it grew and lit a new warmth inside me, blunting the frozen claws of Navar's power. I drew a deeper breath as the cold within me eased, then another. I could feel my broken bones scraping against one another, the torn flesh around them shifting. Knitting.

Navar's power flexed anew and I was thrown across the clearing to tumble across the frozen ground and smash into the wall. It hurt, but I had suffered worse. I gritted my teeth and, with a groan that became a growl as strength found me once more, I pulled myself to my feet. My newly knit legs shook like those of a newborn gazelle, but by the stars, they held.

'Enough games!' Navar shouted. 'Die.'

He raised the staff and a dozen bolts materialised in the air around him, each as long as an arrow and gleaming with the unbridled power of his killing magic. He lowered the staff and they flashed forward as one, each burning as hot as the sun and as sharp as a fractured diamond.

They broke against my skin, hissing into nothingness like rain upon a fire.

'Impossible!' He screamed the word loud enough to shake a storm of condensation from the roof of the cavern. 'I command you to die!'

Another dozen bolts rose and sped towards me, and

once again they shattered against my skin. I extended my fighting spikes and bared the jagged mass of my teeth as I limped towards him.

He uttered a string of guttural words and loosed a pulsating beam of violet light at me. There was nothing I could do but close my eyes and trust the fragile construct that I held so carefully in my mind. His triumphant shout died as the light faded and I walked forward again, my hide blistered and smoking.

'No!'

His hubris and pre-occupation with loosing such powerful magics was a fatal combination. I was unsteady on my legs, but I was still moving forward while he stood there, unmoving.

'Anakhara!' I bellowed her name at him as I leaped forward, both arms punching towards him for additional momentum. I felt my leg crack anew under the sudden pressure, but by then it was too late.

He staggered back, but my arms were long, even without the black talons that added another third to their overall length. The same black talons that now pierced his chest like twin spears.

My falling weight bore him to the ground, the impact driving my talons through the rest of him so that I felt the tips grind into the stone floor beneath us. I threw my head back and roared as loudly as this body would allow me to while he screamed and flailed beneath me. I bent forward and buried my teeth in his face, gouging grooves in his bones and bursting his right eye beneath before I ripped my head to the side, tearing most of his face away. He shrieked, the sound barely human.

He tried to swat at me with his staff, but it was a feeble effort, and I spat his own face back at him in reply. He lost control of his bowels when I leaned forward and gnashed my teeth together, and in that moment more than any other I knew that he was *just a man*. A man who had forgotten that I knew the sound of his magic, and who had bound his magic to *my* flesh.

I put my mouth next to his ear and whispered his mistake to him. I gave him a few heartbeats to understand, then ripped my talons out of his chest in a spray of ruby blood. He rolled into a foetal position, coughing blood and trying to clutch at his wounds with arms that quaked and shivered. I took my time preparing the fire I would end him with, savouring the spectacle of his agony.

Once I felt the pressure building at the back of my throat I pinned his shoulders to the floor and vomited my fire bile over the length of his body. I had been nurturing it for some time, constantly regurgitating the rocks I had taken from Fronsac's alchemist, leaching every ounce of the minerals from them. It was still a weak and diluted mix, and so took far longer than I remembered to ignite, giving him some time to realise what was about to happen.

'No!' He clutched at me with claw like hands. 'I'll tell you where she is! Don't!'

I stared at him, but whatever hope either of us felt in that moment was lost as the bile finally ignited, sheathing him in yellow flame. I hunkered over him as he screamed and thrashed, holding him down as the fire gained strength and burned downwards, the flames flaring up anew as the fats beneath his skin ignited. I drew in the scent of his death like the sweetest incense and laughed as his soul went to whatever Hel awaited it.

Navar was dead.

CHAPTER 47

CASTING A COMPLICATED and powerful spell is a dangerous business, more so when there is more than one wizard involved. A total commitment of mind and spirit is needed to maintain the harmony of the magic that has been summoned, with any significant imbalance likely to create a reverberation that would only worsen the longer it was allowed to continue.

The cabal that Navar had assembled to weave and control the forces bound to the Lance numbered twenty, and between them they had woven an intricate lattice of sound and intent, binding the raw power of the Songlines and channelling it into the predatory vortex of the Lance through countless layers of eldritch runes and enchantments. It was, in simple terms, as if all twenty of them were holding a single enormous pot of molten metal above them. Provided they all stood calmly and supported it, they were safe and Navar could pour the 'metal' into the shape he desired. That fine balance also kept them from coming to his aid as he burned and screamed, as much as any of them may have wanted to.

But now he was gone, and his brain and whatever else had writhed and crawled within it had boiled to a black mass inside his charred skull. The iron grip of his will had perished with him, and was no longer there to guide and shape the swelling magics they were gathering. The harmony of their spell had begun shifting even before the fires had finished their work on his corpse, subtly at first, but at their heart humans are creatures of fear and distrust, and as I rose from the smouldering ruin that had been their master, that same fear began to leach into their magic.

The steady pulse of crystal veins dimmed then brightened considerably, growing until a blinding arc of light flashed from the end of the Lance and struck one of the wizards, instantly burning the flesh from his bones with a sharp crack that was felt more than heard. The pulsing light stuttered and I felt their fear ripen within the magic that suffused the cavern. Their great pot of metal was overfull and becoming steadily more unbalanced with every passing moment.

I hurried across to where Tatyana and Lucien lay. She was badly burned, her flesh punctured with dozens of metal rings from her blasted armour, while blood frothed and bubbled from Lucien's mouth. They were alive though, which was far more than I had expected, and I dragged both to the mouth of the tunnel, clenching my teeth against the sawing pain in my leg. It was unlikely that they would survive the coming conflagration, but they at least deserved a chance, however remote.

Another of the sharp cracks sounded in the clearing, and then two more in quick succession. I stepped out, squinting my eyes against the now blinding light beaming from the crystal seams and saw the bloody skeletons where three more wizards had been. As I watched, one of them abandoned the spell and sprinted towards me, but as he ducked under the golden wire binding the stone pillars a blast of light from the nearest pillar cut him in two. I couldn't hear his scream as his legs walked away from him, but I imagine it must have been quite shrill.

The discord within the cavern was growing exponentially. The remaining wizards were desperately trying to fill the gaps left by the dead men, but they could not do both that and restore the harmony. I edged back into the tunnel as another of them was transformed into bloody chunks and steaming bones. This was too much for the others, and like the first crack in a dam, the great energies they were trying to contain broke free and rushed back along the channels that had summoned them, which in this case was their bodies. Such unworthy vessels had no chance of containing even a portion of such a deluge. Few had a chance to scream before they were explosively unmade by the energies, filling the cavern with a scalding red mist.

The light stopped pulsing and swelled ever brighter while a whistling shriek unlike anything I had ever heard filled the cavern. I felt it pull at me, a sharp and cruel sensation, but I sunk my claws into the mud and bound what sorcery I had left into deflecting it; there was no chance of resisting it head on. It felt like my bones were going to shatter, and not a few of my teeth cracked as I clenched my jaws against the pressure and noise.

The light flickered, and suddenly it was gone, the cacophony replaced by the tinkling of the small waterfall that tipped from the top of the cavern. I pried my claws free and rose to my feet, slowly realising that I wasn't dead. I held fast to the walls until I was confident that my bones had not in fact been transformed into jelly. The crystals were flickering arrhythmically as I staggered forward, beyond the now dark stone pillars. The golden wire had melted away and several pillars had shattered, but the runes on the Lance were still lit with the same white light. The air was colder than it had been before, and the spirits gathering around it were thicker in the air, each trailing light behind them like tattered gowns.

The enchantments upon the Lance didn't care that Navar was dead, nor that the wizards were now little more than an assembly of rapidly freezing bones. The complex enchantments embedded within it had been woken and they would continue to pollute the Songlines and hold the gateway to the world of the dead open while power still flowed through the node.

The dissolution of the wizards' magic had been one thing, but they were only manipulating the discharge from the Lance. To end it I would need to break the magic bound to it, and like any enchanted item, doing so would release its power in a single catastrophic discharge.

I ignored the souls that gathered around me like little nibbling fish and walked closer to the Lance, pausing only to kick a wizard's charred skull from my path, sending it bouncing across the frozen ground. It rolled until it came to rest against the enormous wooden figure that lay at the edge of the cavern, its position marked by the cluster of swords and spears embedded in its back. I was curious about it, but my priority was the Lance and how its now undirected magic was filling the cavern, coating the crystals in a feathery dusting of ice crystals and thickening the air into a milky fog. Reality here was already warped by the presence of the node, and given enough time the pervasive pressure of so much death could well erode it entirely.

I took a deep breath and bent my will to fashioning two sets of wards. The first was for me, as protection against what lay ahead, and the second was to deflect what was coming from the tunnel where Tatyana and Lucien lay. I could still feel the spark within her valiantly trying to heal her wounds, but once I perished it would only be a matter of time before it winked out.

I rolled my neck, releasing a frightening amount of crunching noises from my twisted back, then hobbled forward. It was like entering a blizzard, and as I passed the ring of bones that had quite recently been a cabal of wizards I felt a scrape against my arm. Then another. The spirits were coming at me in greater numbers, their distorted faces more distinct with every step I took, and I watched one dart forward and latch onto my arm with hollow teeth; my blood shone like gold as it shook its head and burrowed deeper. I swatted at it, but my hand passed through it. More souls pushed in, their faces peeling back to reveal rings of translucent teeth.

As before, it wasn't my blood they sought, but the life within it, and the sorcery I thought I had shielded myself with was a beacon to them. These weren't the mindless shoals I had encountered before though. More bit into me, nipping viciously at the back of my legs and neck, pushing their mouths harder against me with every mote of life they sucked from me. I swallowed the urge to lash out at them and concentrated on lifting my feet. One step forward, then another.

My body was anchored to reality, as was the physical body of the Lance. I could feel the souls drawing the life out of me but the pain of their attacks was a hidden blessing. Pain was familiar and fed my anger, and anger in turn fed my strength. Swarms of milky shapes crowded in on me, biting and clawing in a frenzy so that no patch of skin wider than my hands was left intact, and my life and my blood were streaming away in red and gold ribbons around me.

My outstretched hands touched something solid. *The Lance.* A dozen souls flew at my other arm as I fought to lay my hands upon it, savaging it to the bone, but my anger had lit the fire within me and I roared my defiance even as they tore pieces from me. I set both hands upon the shaft and my roar turned into a scream as the full might of its terrible, fell magic flashed through me.

THE RING OF light that marked the boundary between life and death receded to barely a pinprick of light as I fell through the gateway and into a darkness broken only by the luminous shapes of men and beasts, thousands of them, that swirled around me. I somehow knew then that they were the spirits of those I had slain in my life. Of the spirits of the men, some were laughing, some weeping, while others screamed and cursed my name. These I ignored. The animals were wiser and simply watched with soft, dark eyes as the circle of life was completed, then slowly faded from sight. I no longer felt the cold as I fell, for it was part of me now.

My body shattered like glass when I hit the barren plain that waited below. There was no pain, not even when the pieces reassembled themselves once more. All I felt was disappointment, for I still wore the body of a man, although at least no longer one as deformed as the one I had died in. The spirits who had chased me were drifting away, and at last I was alone.

A desolate plain stretched out around me, featureless and flat in every direction, visible only by the pale, watery reflection of the gateway above that glittered like a lone star. I waited, perhaps for a moment or for many years, and when nothing happened I began walking. I could barely feel my body as I walked, and with no change in the land around me there was no way to tell how far or for how long I had walked. It may have been moments, or perhaps it was years. I tried to sing as I walked, simply for the sake of hearing something, but while I could feel the words upon my lips, the sound vanished between my mouth and my ears.

At some point I became aware of another light, a faint glimmer ahead of me, but I had no memory of when I had first seen it. I kept walking, and could not tell if I was getting closer to it, or if it was drawing closer to me.

Eventually I came to a point where the ground fell away in a sharp line from horizon to horizon, as if cut by an impossibly large knife, leaving only a spar of rock barely as wide as my shoulders arcing away over the impenetrable blackness below. The glow came from the other end of this delicate bridge, a golden sheen that held the promise of something better. I set out across the bridge, my torn arms held out at my sides for balance at first. Behind me the bridge fell to dust as I passed over it, but I felt no sense of danger. When I reached the midpoint, I found that I could see what lay ahead. Where the plain behind me was desolate, the land in front dropped away into a series of sunlit valleys and canyons, each filled with rivers and trees. I could feel the soft, welcoming warmth of it from where I stood, and I felt my icy skin crack as a smile found my face.

I started walking again with new energy, but I had barely taken my fourth step when I felt a cold wind upon my back. I turned and nearly fell from the bridge as the darkness coalesced into a huge and terrible shape that hovered above me with the sound of iron chains rattling across bone and the leathery thump of wings wider than the sails of a dozen ships, the wind threatening to tip me into the hungry darkness.

'Who are you?' I said, my voice barely a whisper. 'What do you want?'

The dark shape reached out and grabbed me, and I screamed at the terrible pain that spread through me at its touch. I fought against its grip and felt pieces of my hands falling away, but its grip was loosening. I could feel the promise of the Shining Lands against my skin as I eventually broke free and staggered away from it, clinging to the rocky spur with chipped and broken claws as I dragged myself closer to the warmth and light. I was so close.

'You promised, Stratus.'

My strength and anger vanished at the sound of her voice. I turned and stared into the darkness that wreathed her.

'Anakhara?'

I felt a tremor pass through the great shadow, and a moment later two great, fiery eyes opened, basking me in a cold light.

'Come back, Stratus.'

'Oh my love,' I said miserably, unable to do anything but stare up at the writhing shape of her. The warmth of the Shining Lands called to me, but the promise it had held was empty, for she was not there.

'I failed. My strength is spent, and my body is broken.'

'Hope endures where hate cannot.' She drew closer, her shape almost recognisable amidst the shadows that cloaked it. I felt her hands cup me once more and I could not help the cry of pain that burst from me. 'You are my hope. My last.'

Bone and iron creaked as her tattered wings extended and beat down. I saw the bridge and the light of the Shining Lands vanish below me. I wanted to hold her, to ask forgiveness, to hear her voice, but the pain of her touch burned through me like acid, tightening my throat and driving all other thoughts from my mind. With every beat of her wings the Shining Lands grew more distant and the glittering star that was the gateway grew brighter and the pain more profound. As we drew closer I saw that the cloud that surrounded it was a great press of tormented souls, swirling like a tornado in their desperation to return to the world of the living. They shrieked in dismay and fled at her approach,

'Bring me home, Greatheart,' she said, and threw me through the gateway.

MY EYES SNAPPED open and the pain and cold redoubled as life surged back into my dying body, my hearts suddenly forcing blood through veins that had started to collapse and empty. I might have screamed, but I had done so much of it recently that I no longer noticed. My hands were still clutching the Lance, and seemed to have melted into it. My body was a mess of torn skin and exposed bone, my blood frozen around me as if I had risen from a crimson lake. The souls that had stripped my life from me like razorfish now turned back with newfound hunger as they sensed my reawakening. I saw their gleaming teeth and greedy human eyes and felt the hate and anger within me rising.

'Go to Hell!' I snarled, not so much swallowing the pain as embracing it. I bent my legs and gathered my strength. The souls swarmed towards me, shrieking their unending hunger as I straightened my legs, my muscles straining as I tightened my grip on the Lance. It shifted in my hands, the movement sending a shockwave through the cavern and throwing the tide of the predatory spirits into disarray. I worked the shaft back and forth, using all the strength I could muster. It was a powerful artefact, but its physical presence was its one real vulnerability. I could not break the enchantments but, by the stars, I could break *it*.

Streams of raw magic shot into the air as I worked

it loose. I felt them tearing into me, but I simply didn't care anymore; all I wanted to do was destroy it. I pulled the Lance sideways, my still frozen muscles tearing with the effort, and with a squeal of metal it began to bend. The first of the runes, those closest to the folding metal, touched each other, disrupting the circuit of power and sending a spray of sparks across the cavern, each potent enough to melt the rock they landed on. The flow faltered, weakening the next rune.

I ripped the Lance from the ground with a roar and brought it down across my knee, mashing more of the runes together as the metal folded even further. A quickening shiver passed through the Lance as incandescent magic leapt from rune to rune, almost blinding in its brightness, adding another layer of blisters to the lacerated mess that used to be my hands. The touch of death still hung heavy on me and I could see the pale circle that marked the gateway to the beyond. I marshalled the last of my strength and hurled the crumpled Lance through it before it could detonate.

CHAPTER 48

Before

THE MEN WHO had slain my Anakhara were careless in their jubilation. It had taken many long days for my mind to return to me, days in which I did little but roll in the mud her blood had soaked into and sing my pain at the stars. But eventually that grief had settled into a cold rage, and I had taken to the skies once more, following the wide trail left by her killers.

I found them on the savannah under the light of the new moon. I rose high into the night sky and roared my challenge loud enough that herds in distant lands bolted. Many of the men below were driven mad by the sound, but it would not save them. It would not save any of them.

I swept over the camp, belching a great stream of fire to add to their disarray, then set upon them with claw and tooth. I could have burned them all, but I wanted to feel their deaths. It took several days to hunt them all down; none could hide from me, but even when I was red with their gore my rage was not remotely slaked.

The hardest part of it was letting some of the paladins' escape, especially their leader, the insect named Henkman. It was he who had gathered the crusade that had slain

Anakhara, and his death should have been long and terrible, but instead I had found myself circling his campsite and watching him eat and drink. I consoled myself with the knowledge that his death had simply been delayed, and that when it came I would be the last thing he saw.

The paladins had fled the destruction of their army, striking out towards the great mountains to the north and east with scant need to whip their steeds, who could smell me on the wind. I enjoyed the terror it instilled in them, even more so when one threw its rider and sent him crashing to his death from a mountain pass. I flew from peak to peak, watching them, and once there was only one path left that they could take I flew on ahead and found myself in a wide, lush valley, at the heart of which rose a castle unlike any I had seen before. The walls were high, but it was narrow and tall, the towers too slender to hold more than a handful of poorly fed archers.

This then was the lair of the archmage, Talgoth by name, who had been so instrumental in felling my beloved. I had hoped they would flee towards him, and they had. They would all pay the price for their collaboration soon enough. I waited for the paladins to enter the castle, then set about my work.

The valley was secluded, protected from foul weather and war by Talgoth's magics and the fang-like mountains that surrounded it, but it was not safe from me or my fire. I fell upon the first town I found in the deep watches of the night and burned it to the ground. Soft and coddled by the wizard's protection, they could barely muster a dozen warriors. These died first, burnt into a single mass of black bones and iron, and the rest I crushed with my tail or rent asunder with tooth and claw. I retreated to the mountains for two days, replenishing my fire and letting the word and terror spread from the survivors, then struck again. It was not long before the fields were marked by streams of terrified refugees flocking to the castle.

Once the lands were as black and empty as my heart I announced myself to the wizard by perching on the nearest crag and filling the valley with my roar. His answer was to send a score of men mounted on enormous eagles to attack me. They were fast and quick in the air, but the feathers of giant eagles were as flammable as any other and it was less than a morning's work to send them all spiralling to their death.

I burned all traces of life from the eastern ramparts, then began smashing my way to the heart of the castle. Arrows rained down upon me, and scores of wizards filled the air with their cruellest spells, but my hide was as iron and my sorcery proof against anything their primitive command of magic could muster. My rage and thirst for vengeance were overwhelming and I was still convinced of my own strength, a mistake that would cost me dearly.

A few dozen more of the archmage's minions died as I barged my way through into the central courtyard, the last battleground before I could penetrate Talgoth's sanctuary and crush him. I expected to be greeted by panic and a barrage of magical attacks, but instead I found myself facing a full regiment of paladins in gleaming armour, arrayed in neat ranks and their weapons and armour lit by powerful runes and spells. It was a trap, of course, but behind the shining ranks of Drogah's favourite warriors stood the men whose continued existence was an insult to the life and memory of my beloved Anakhara.

Archmage Tiberius Talgoth and Aethbert Henkman.

It was the Archmage's rectangular symbol that was embroidered into the flags that flew from the battlements, and stamped into the base of every blade and arrowhead that had gouged my flesh. The twin serpents over the eight pointed star, a form of his secret name rendered in the script of the mages.

'Wyrm! Beast! I, Aethbert Henkman command you to surrender, in the name of most holy Drogah!'

His armour had been cleaned and now shone as brightly as any golden bauble I'd ever beheld, but it didn't take much effort to sense the potency of the protective wards that had lurked beneath its gaudiness. He held out a hand, and a shorter and somewhat less splendid figure handed him a sword.

'Behold Sep Duain, the Dragon Slayer! Surrender, or it shall end you too this day.'

I'd had men brandish outlandish swords at me before, men who'd died under my claws and teeth shortly after, so I doubted it would help this fine peacock either, however much it glittered and shone.

'Give me her body and that wizard, and my vengeance shall be done,' I lied, and from the shifting of the men in the courtyard I guessed that they hadn't been expecting a reply.

'The archmage is under the church's protection.' He pointed his fine sword at me. 'You have been declared an abomination, and your death shall cleanse these lands. For is it not written that...'

I hadn't burned my way across the continent to listen to him giving a sermon for his own benefit, so as soon as he pointed his sword at me I had started reshaping my sorcery. Their armour would no doubt be proof against fire and impact damage, but lightning loves metal like a dragon loves meat. I woke my sorcery and reached out to the Songlines for the power to complete the deadly construct, but my will hit an invisible force and like an arrow shot into a rock wall.

The paladins stood unmoving while I gawped at the sky

above me like a fool. Such a thing had never happened before. And worse than that, the same spell was now pressing down on me, smothering my sorcery entirely. It was impossible.

'In the name of Him most high, smite the beast!' Henkman's voice jolted me from my puzzlement.

The paladins closed their visors and began marching towards me, their weapons held ready. I brought up a good mouthful of fire-bile and sprayed them generously, and yet of the score or more I had sprayed, barely a handful succumbed, the flash of the detonation searing their eyes and the superheated air cooking their lungs as they inhaled. The wards and oily sealants on the others' armour protected them, and I backed away as they came marching through the blaze, only to feel myself come up against that same barrier once again. I spun around, but there was nothing there at first glance, but then I felt the buzz of the shield-dome that Talgoth had dropped in behind me while that damned paladin had distracted me. It didn't take much imagination to realise that this was an extension of what had foiled my own spell. There would be no escape by air until the wizards died.

Killing the paladins was the only real option left to me. These were the best of them, so I couldn't afford chances or half measures. I drew up all the bile that I could, and rather than trying to kill a swathe of them, I targeted just enough to give me some room to manoeuvre. I spat it in a steady stream, which allowed me to adjust my aim. Their visors had been open before they'd charged, so those hinges would be their weak spot. I sprayed them at head height, relying on both the pressure and volume of bile to dislodge enough of the protective oil smeared across them. The results were better than I'd expected. Bile splashed through breathing grills and trickled between the warded plates before igniting, and as I had hoped, the fire-dampening wards were all crafted on the assumption that the fire would be on the outside of their armour.

The full dozen that I had targeted fell to the ground or staggered out of formation, screaming as they clawed helplessly at the seals on their armour. The flames went out shortly after, extinguished by one of Talgoth's minions, but the damage was done and I had the room I needed. And not too soon either; even as I extended my claws the rest of them closed in.

The battle that followed was a bitter, bloody thing, claustrophobic in its intimacy. The paladins swarmed over me, each of them crying out to their god and fathers as they hacked divots of flesh from my body. Their armour was tougher than I had expected, and I was forced to break each one individually, giving their comrades more time to saw and hack at me. By the time I had slain all but the two champions I was a torn and bleeding wreck, and only my innate stubbornness was keeping me from being overwhelmed by the pain and blood-loss from so many wounds. Anakhara would have suffered much as I had, but rather than stoke my anger, it only brought on a deep sadness that I had to fight to dislodge.

Talgoth and his pack of mages were still concentrating their magic on maintaining the wall of force blocking my escape, but I had little doubt that they had some nasty surprises set aside as well. I was in trouble, and was starting to understand the depth of it.

The two heroes were circling me now, coming at me like hounds baiting a bear. Their weapons were cruel, but they knew that I was still a deadly opponent too. It was then that I felt Talgoth's magical wall shift slightly out of alignment as one of his robed minions collapsed. The shield's integrity wavered.

I glanced over to where I had felt the disturbance and saw that part of it had collapsed, revealing a narrow gap that led out to the battlements and the sanctuary offered by the sky beyond. I wanted to take the chance, but the opening was too narrow for my bulk.

Even as I thought this, Henkman cut a vicious gash in my leg with Sep Duain. I felt, rather than saw, my flesh yawn open, and I knew that even if the next blow failed to cleave the bone or the artery that ran along it, I would not have enough time to heal it before the blood loss rendered me insensible. I had to escape!

I scooped up a pair of corpses and hurled them at the champions, forcing them back. I charged towards the gap, howling at the star-bright agony that flared in my cut leg. I reached out for my sorcery in desperation, throwing every iota of my remaining strength into the attempt, not caring that it would leave me with nothing, for if I didn't, I was doomed. I felt it respond with an alacrity and force that I was too grateful for at the time to think suspicious.

I wrapped myself in bands of magical energy and willed myself smaller, the pain of my wounds becoming one with the pain of my twisting, shrinking flesh. I told myself that it was only for a moment, just long enough to reach the battlements and the sky beyond.

The illusion vanished the moment I set foot in the cage, but I was too wrapped up in my escape to notice it until my face hit the bars on the far side, the sound of that impact almost indistinguishable from that of the gate slamming shut behind me.

'Now you are mine, my little lizard,' I heard Talgoth say a moment before the runes embedded in the cage flashed to life and paralysed me while his laughter filled the air.

CHAPTER 49

THE MEMORY DISSOLVED into meaningless slivers as I felt someone lift me from the ground. With my returning consciousness and awareness that I still lived came the pain of the countless wounds I bore, but I barely had the strength to groan.

I forced my eyes open and looked at what had lifted me, and confusion and wonder silenced my groan. It was a wooden man of a sort, one half as tall as me again and crudely fashioned from a solid tree trunk. The bark had been stripped, leaving a honey-coloured wood decorated with hundreds of fine carvings and polished to a lustre by age and long exposure to the raw magic of the nexus. As it moved I saw the spears and swords that jutted from its back.

'You are the guardian,' I wheezed at it.

A head that was little more than two smoothed crystals for eyes and an axe gash for a mouth tilted towards me.

'Wouldnae beest thee?' it said, the voice oddly piping and wheezy for all of its bulk. The sound of the old human tongue sounded strange after all these years, but I recognised it easily enough. *Who are you?*

I considered the question carefully before replying, opting for honesty. 'Ae emm thist wyrm Stratus ep Skeyfeir.' *I am the dragon called Stratus the Skyfire.*

It seemed content with that, insomuch that it set me down on the ground next to the smouldering hole left by the Lance. The crystal around it was cracked and dull, much like the guardian's eyes.

'What do you want of me?' I said. It took me an age to remember the words, and longer to fight the waves of dizziness and pain that threatened to pull me back into a dreamless and potentially eternal sleep.

'Sing,' it said.

'Sing?' It stared at me with its dull eyes but clearly had no inclination to repeat itself. 'I can't,' I said. I looked down at the weeping gash in my side. 'My sorcery is spent and if I move my hand I think the rest of my guts will spill out.'

Wood creaked as it took a step forward and pressed its crude, blunt hands against my head. I felt a pulse of magic, soft and green, wash over me.

'Sing,' it said again, then slowly crumpled to the side like a puppet whose strings had been cut.

I closed my eyes and concentrated on the wisp of power it had given me. It was the last vestige of its power, as ancient and gentle as the place it had guarded since before men first descended from the trees. It reminded me of summer prairies, of crushed grass and the cry of river eagles hunting. I inhaled deeply, and smelt flowers and honey rather than decay and blood. I focused on that, and amidst the hum of the bees and birdsong that came with it I heard the pattern.

I hummed it at first, finding the pitch of its magic, then slowly put more breath into it. Pain flared from my cracked and broken ribs but I focused on the idea of the eagles swooping across an emerald grassland and gulls wheeling over cliffs, and somewhere in that moment, I heard the echo of something waking.

I concentrated on that sensation and the agonised mass of my body slowly shifted to the back of my mind. I tilted my head back and raised my voice, putting all of my breath into reminding the crystal of the song that still echoed somewhere deep within it. I felt the sound pass through the crystal and the countless connections embedded in the earth around me, and then the echo returned, stronger than before. I kept singing as the echoes chased my voice, and with every return the gap closed and the scent of summer and sound of wind across the eagle's feathers grew more distinct.

And then the echo caught my voice and became one with it. I opened my eyes as the first glimmer of golden light shot through the cavern. Another followed, and like the sun rising, the nexus woke beneath me, filling the cavern with amber light as the Songlines reconnected. I could feel the force building, pushing against the remaining barriers imposed by Navar's foul magics, and it felt like I was standing in a great basin waiting for an ocean to fill it once more. I opened my arms wide as those final barriers splintered and pure, unadulterated power flooded into the cavern with the roar of a thousand waterfalls.

I opened myself to it entirely and felt the response as I sang my true name. There was a distortion in the reply, a corruption caused by the broken enchantments that bound me, and I felt the nexus try to correct itself, to scour that imperfection even as the Songlines washed the taint of dark magic from the node. The power swelled around me, then *through* me. It felt as if a chain was being pulled through the length of my body, rubbing and scraping my bones as it went, rupturing my flesh as the enchantments were broken.

I screamed, but there was no stopping what I had so carelessly begun. The Songlines didn't care for my pain, only that the discord within me was removed. The power of the node stripped the tainted flesh from me until I was a raw and quivering thing and then began to reshape my flesh into what my name compelled it to be.

NIGHT HAD FALLEN by the time that my senses returned to me, although the soft light that filled the cavern made it seem as if it were dawn instead. I yawned and looked around, only to stumble in surprise when I realised that I was looking down at the cavern from somewhere twice as high as I remembered my head being. I shook my head to clear the fog from it, but the cavern spun around me wildly and I fell to the side, my disorientation complete. I lay there with my eyes shut, just breathing, letting my balance find itself once more.

As I did, I became aware of the press of my hide against the thawing ground. I could feel every pebble and, in some places, bones and fallen menhirs beneath me. I breathed in deeply, and rather than the death and stench of sweet spices that had filled it before, I could taste rain, good earth, and crushed grass. And men. No, not just any men: Tatyana and Lucien. The impossibility of their survival fired my curiosity and I opened my eyes and made to stand up, only to drive my snout into the mud like a peasant's plough. My neck kept bending, and I was sure I was falling over, but I wasn't.

I shook the dirt from my face and steadied my stance as I looked down at myself for the first time. At my thick arms and legs, with knees bending back the way they should, and at my proud, horned snout and my tapering tail.

I was whole again. The man's body was gone, and I was remade. I stretched my wings out and almost laughed when I saw that they too were strong and whole. Even my claws had returned, although they, like my newly remade scales, were softer than they should be. I stretched languorously, enjoying the feel of my great muscles stretching as they hadn't for almost a millennium. With every breath I took the memories of my human body were slipping away like a dream forgotten in morning's light, and I let them go without hesitation. I shook myself and stood there, simply laughing at the sheer joy of being *me* for some time before I lowered myself and peered into the tunnel where the now diminutive bodies of Tatyana and Lucien lay.

She was sprawled where I had left her, her burned hands still clutching the medallion which, from the look of it, had destroyed itself in its attempts to shield her from the intensity of the magics that had been unleashed when I broke the Lance. Its destruction had wounded her, but the remnants of her armour had saved her from the worst of it. Lucien was the one I had expected to see reduced to bone or ash, but instead he lay across her legs, his arms still crossed over his face, as if he had fallen while standing over her. It was a ludicrous notion. As brave as the little summer prince had been, even without the broken bones he'd suffered at Navar's hand, no mere mortal could have withstood what had been unleashed here, not without protection.

Curious, I reached for my sorcery and felt it respond with alacrity. I closed my eyes and summoned it to me, and for the second time that night I laughed as I felt the power of it flow into me. I had been made whole again in both name and flesh, and with that, the last impediments that had choked the flow of the Songlines into me had been washed away.

I flexed my will and felt the mountain shattering potential of the raw power I now contained rise at my command. I released it and looked back at Lucien, who now seemed so small and frail. I raised a veil across my vision and looked closer. Fronsac's wards had been broken by what the boy had faced here, and as my gaze penetrated his flesh and will I saw what the wizard had been hiding all this time. Lucien was as I was, a sorcerer, the rarest of gifts offered by nature. The first kings had all been sorcerers, so his blood ran true indeed.

I felt the mote of healing within Tatyana reach for me, but rather than feed her the healing power it wanted, I gave both her and Lucien the gift of sleep. They would need food more than magic when they awoke, but more importantly, I was ravenous, and the long suppressed and irresistible need to hunt and soar amongst the clouds was on me.

It was no hard thing to leap for the top of the cavern, which was now far closer than it had been to me as a man, although it did take a bit of manoeuvring to wriggle out without catching my wings on the edge. I stretched them out a few times, reacquainting myself with the feel of my flight muscles and making sure that they were ready. I called my sorcery to me with as much ease as drawing a breath and wove my wind spells with glee. And then, turning my head towards the pearly crescent of the moon, I launched myself into the night sky with a cry of triumph that set the animals of the army encamped around the city walls to rearing and screaming in terror.

I laughed as the ground dropped away beneath me, the sheer euphoria of flight washing every other thought and concern from me. I had worried that I would not remember how, but nothing could have been further from the truth. My blood thundered through my veins, all but glowing with renewed vitality and power. I drew a deep lungful of air and shouted my name for the sheer joy of it. I hadn't expected any reply, and none answered me. The skies remained mine alone.

I felt the welcome strain of muscles I hadn't used in an age pulling across my back as my wings lifted me higher into the night, up through the clouds until only the stars were higher than me. The un-breathed air at that altitude was cold, but it was a clean, fresh sort of cold rather than the insidious, choking kind that still clung to the city streets. I banked and descended, looking down on Aknak and the glittering pinpoints of firelight that surrounded it. It had seemed so imposing when I first approached it and had dominated the landscape, but from the sky it seemed like nothing much at all. I swooped lower until I could watch the camp without exerting myself. They were agitated, like bees whose hive has been kicked, but ripples of Navar's death had yet to reach them. I smiled in the darkness at the memory of his death, but it faded as I recalled his dying words. *I'll tell you where she is.*

That and the vision of her that I had experienced on the other side of the gateway had watered the seed of hope within me. Could it be that she was alive? But if she was, how was it that she had crossed to the World of the Dead to bring me back? And yet, if she wasn't, would she not have wanted me to join her there?

Unless she was both. The thought was almost enough to spill me from the air. I had seen so many impossible things already, so was it really so unthinkable that she was both, a living creature so corrupted by dark magic and Navar's worms that Death no longer sought her? If she was, could I purge her as I had Lucien?

The miles slipped away under my wings as the thoughts ran through my head in maddening circles, and it was only the familiar complaint from my gut that pulled me back to the present. My brooding thoughts about death and burning eyes in the dark faded as the idea of food reasserted itself and I tipped my wings into a descending turn that sent me drifting downwards in a long spiral, luxuriating in the caress of wind rather than stone, seeking out farmlands as yet untouched by the war and the fat sheep and cattle tucked away in as yet un-ravaged pastures.

I smiled again when I found the pastures, and roared into the night for no reason beyond the thrill of seeing the panic that scattered the herds below. I wanted them to run, and run they did. It took several attempts before I started getting the timing of my swoops right, but once I did, the feasting began. I burned them and gorged myself on their fat little bodies, and with each that I gulped down I felt real strength return to me, a solid and comforting kind rather than the hollow approximation that sorcery could offer. Like healing, strength drawn from sorcery had a price that needed paying, one that only grew the longer it was delayed. I hunted, if that was what you could call my rampage, until dawn began to colour the skies.

I gathered up a cow and a handful of sheep in my claws and returned to Aknak. I dropped my bounty and a dead tree through the cavern roof before following them down, slowing my fall with an expert snap of my wings. I broke the tree apart and kindled a good blaze before using my sorcery to skin and gut the beasts. It was perhaps a scornful use of such sacred power, but I remembered the mess I'd made trying to do it by hand the first time and didn't want to waste the meat. I set the meat to roasting on the embers before I carried Tatyana and Lucien nearer to the fire. Lucien's injuries were many, but now that I understood what he was I could stoke his natural healing through his own gift. Once he was on the mend I did the same to Tatyana, speeding the healing that she needed, but gently so as to soften the price she would need to pay for it. I retreated to the side of the cavern and spun an illusion of shadow around me as they began to stir.

Lucien woke first, springing to his feet immediately and patting his body as if worried parts of him were either missing or on fire. Then he went to Tatyana and helped her into a sitting position before unfastening what was left of her armour and tossing it aside.

They clasped hands as they looked around the cavern.

'Hello?' called Tatyana.

'Hello,' I replied. They flinched as my voice rumbled through and filled the cavern. I'd forgotten that each of my lungs was now bigger than the whole of my human body had been.

She stood, and Lucien followed her a moment later. 'Stratus?'

'You're a hard person to kill,' I said. 'You both are.'

'I didn't know you were trying,' she said, and I chuckled at that, the sound echoing around us. 'Where are you?'

'I'm here,' I said. 'Though you may not recognise me.'

I felt her fluttering heartbeat gather pace. 'What do you mean?'

'Showing you is easier than explaining.'

She was staring at me now, although she would have seen nothing more than a wall of featureless black. 'Then show us.'

'Are you certain?'

'God's teeth, just show us. Dithering isn't going to change anything.'

'As you wish.'

I let the illusion fade as I stepped forward and stretched my wings wide, turning so that the fire could catch the red that chased the midnight hue of my scales.

She rubbed her eyes and stared at me, her mouth falling open, while Lucien fell to his knees and began sobbing like a child. I folded my wings and turned so that she could behold me in my full glory, then settled myself down on the opposite side of the fire, my chin upon my forearms, watching them.

She didn't say anything for a long time after that, not even after she accepted the roasted mutton I passed her. Lucien wiped his face but, like Tatyana, simply continued to stare at me while he chewed, and I began to wonder if my undiluted magnificence had addled their senses.

Fortunately the combination of succulent mutton and the gut-hollowing hunger that only a healing spell created worked together to pull them from their unblinking reverie. Lucien was a more difficult proposition. His natural sorcery had long been repressed, and having it woken here, at a nexus and in my presence, was no doubt doing all manner of strange things to his mind and body.

'Eat, Prince Lucien,' I said, startling him into a state resembling wakefulness. 'What you are feeling is the quickening of your gift. It will pass, but you need to focus your thoughts, and for that you will need your strength. Feed your body.'

I laced my words with a small amount of compulsion, and he lifted the meat he'd been gnawing on and fell upon it with renewed enthusiasm, tearing into it like a winter-starved wolf until fats and juices ran down his chin. Seeing it was enough to reawaken my own hunger and I devoured the half-charred cow, hooves, horns and all.

While I picked the bones from my teeth I let the healing construct with Tatyana finish its work on her body, and by the time she finished her mutton and loosed a belch that would have startled a troll, her burned skin was flaking away, revealing the new and healthy pinkness below. If she noticed, she gave no sign.

'I never imagined you would be this magnificent,' she said, wiping her hands on her torn trousers and walking towards me warily. I couldn't help but straighten my shoulders at that. After so many years of being squeezed into a cage and bodies that weren't truly my own I *felt* magnificent. I tilted my head towards her so that she could stroke my snout with hands that were now smaller than my teeth, quietly marvelling at how helpless she now seemed compared to how vital and strong she had felt when I was human.

'Can you breathe fire now?' she asked as she walked alongside my body, the touch of hands incredibly ticklish on my newborn scales.

'No,' I replied, watching as her shoulders sagged. 'But I can fly.'

CHAPTER 50

THEY ONLY STOPPED screaming once I adopted a level flight just above the clouds some way to the south. I skimmed over the tops of these, twisting the vapours into spirals as I passed, enjoying the feel of the sunlight penetrating far beyond the warmth it spread across my skin. Tatyana and Lucien sat at the base of my neck, what little weight they carried spread across the wide mantle of scale that protected it.

I had bound them to me with ropes of condensed air so that there was no way that they could fall off even had they wanted to. Of course, I hadn't told them any of this, so the shrieking that had accompanied every other wingbeat was largely my fault, but then if I was to be ridden like some common steed gaining some amusement from it was only fair.

'CAN YOU HEAR ME?' she shouted, again completely unnecessarily. The bindings also extended to providing a buffer against the chilling effect of the altitude and windspeed, with the added benefit that we could converse at normal volume. And enjoy every shriek.

'I can hear you,' I replied, 'There's no need to shout.' I couldn't smell her, but the skin contact we shared was more than enough to tell me that she was quite emotional.

'This is amazing! How did you ever survive being locked up in a cage?'

It was a good question, and one that deserved an honest answer. 'I'm not sure that I would have, had your ancestors not employed priests to send me into long hibernations every few years. Looking back now, they were a kindness, even if they had been intended differently.'

'I'm sorry, Stratus.'

'We both are,' shouted Lucien.

I felt her shift her weight. 'I hate them for what they did to you. All of them.'

Coming from a Henkman, that was a touching sentiment. 'Thank you both.'

'So what happens now?' asked Lucien.

A slightly desolate laugh escaped my lips. 'For these last few years I only ever thought about killing Navar. I never expected to live past it.' I paused. 'And, had it not been for you, young prince, I would not have. Your reckless, stupid courage saved my life, and for that, I owe you a debt that I intend to repay.'

'Wait,' said Tatyana, 'What stupid courage?'

As I angled my wings and sent us knifing through the clouds, I told her about him leaping to my defence against Navar, smiling to myself as she berated and praised him in turn. The sun had thrown a golden sheen to the patchwork of lands below, and the path of the war was a blackened strip easily seen amidst the otherwise autumnal shades.

'It's so beautiful,' breathed Tatyana.

'Where are we going?' Lucien asked.

'I'm taking you home, to Falkenburg. Navar is dead, but his minions are readying another of the accursed lances. I cannot allow them to complete his quest.'

I heard him mutter something, and then Tatyana burst out laughing, a raucous cawing that was so absurd that it made me laugh too.

'What is so funny?' I asked, shaking my head at the absurdity of it all.

'Don't,' said Lucien. 'I promise I'll never call you Tata again.'

She laughed at that. 'He said he has nothing to wear.'

'Damn you, woman.'

I was still laughing at that when the remaining towers of Falkenburg came into view, and soon after that the dark mass of the Penullin army besieging it. I circled both, wide enough to avoid the clouds of smoke hung about the city, but low enough to see how the fields around the walls were churned and littered with the wreckage of war. I banked and tightened my spiral, setting the men upon the walls running in what looked very much like panic, sounding trumpets as they tried to elevate their siege bows.

I send a pulse of sorcery towards the cluster of towers that marked the location of the palace and felt Fronsac's wards flare into life. I did it a few more times as I hovered about the city, my wings fanning the smoke into curling whorls until I was sure I had his attention. I spoke his name, infusing it with a lick of power, and projected it towards where he was surely waiting, much as I had when I had once called to him from the swamps.

'Go back to the shadows, wyrm!' His voice boomed at me in response, the command he had woven into every word breaking against the sorcerous shield I could now maintain without fear of depleting my strength.

'You owe me a pie, wizard.'

I felt his spell waver, then flicker into new, probing form. I lowered the shield, enough to let him see me. 'Stratus? This cannot be.'

'No trick, spellweaver. I gave my word and am here to keep it.'

'Oh my giddy gods.'

I tipped my wings and dove towards the city, the screams and blaring trumpets that announced me reminding me of another time and place, but rather than filling the streets with flame and death, I slowed and made a game of flying sideways through the streets and around the towers, tilting this way and that so that those who had not fallen into the dirt could see the prince and Tatyana howling on my back.

I hovered over the palace for a few beats, then landed in the muddy square where I had once watched Tatyana demonstrate her skill with a sword. We didn't have to wait long before several doors banged open and a score of soldiers reeking of fear and awe filed out, their swords and spears held in quaking hands. Never one to be outdone, I flicked my tail across the cobbles, sending a shower of sparks into the air that made them flinch as one.

I felt the touch of Fronsac's magics press against mine and turned as he stepped out into the square. His wards still burned brightly, but they dimmed as I lowered myself to let Lucien and Tatyana leap off without harm.

'By the gods,' he said, running forward to embrace Lucien and pulling Tatyana closer when she hesitated. I helped myself to a trough of water while they embraced and tried to talk louder than each other. Eventually Fronsac disentangled himself and walked towards me.

'Stratus?'

'You look like a tramp.'

He lifted his stained robes and let them drop. 'It's been a rough few weeks.' He rubbed his beard. 'Reading about the Dead Wind is an entirely different thing to seeing him in the flesh.'

I inclined my head at that.

'I should have known. It's a name burned into this

Kingdom's history, but I never thought...' He fell silent and shook his head. 'I would have never thought it could be true. How? How did you come to be here, in this city, as a man? Can you do it again? How did you do it?'

'That is a conversation for another time.'

'But I have so many questions.'

'So it seems.'

He took a step closer. 'I felt something in the ether last night, a surge in the Songlines unlike anything I have experienced before, enough to leave two of my apprentices on their backs. Was that you?'

'It was.' I leaned closer to him and was impressed when he didn't flinch. 'Navar Louw is no more, and the Lance of Aknak has been destroyed.'

'Sweet Drogah.' The soldiers around us had a similar reaction, and soon after the intensity of their fear weakened. 'The Worm is really dead?'

'Unless he's found a way to thrive as a burning, headless skeleton, then yes.'

He leaned on his staff and looked up at me. 'I do not know what to say.'

'I keep my word,' I said. 'Although you could tell me where to find more alchemists.'

'Alchemists? Whatever for?'

'Can you help me?'

He opened his arms. 'Of course. You—'

'Give him anything he wants.' I turned as Prince Jean emerged from another door. He and Lucien met in a frenzy of backslapping and not a few tears, and I felt my opinion of the fat little man creep up a notch. He seemed genuinely pleased to see his brother and it pleased me to know it.

'What is it you need?' asked Fronsac, moving closer. I told him, and he sent a soldier off to fetch ink and parchment. While we waited for his return Jean joined Fronsac in examining me, neither of them saying much as they walked along the length of me, occasionally reaching out to touch my scales, their eyes wide. The soldiers, on the other hand, were becoming more boisterous with each moment that passed without them being crushed or immolated. Several of the braver ones patted me as if I were a horse or faithful dog, but I was in a good enough mood to tolerate it.

Soon enough though, Fronsac had his ink and wrote many things on the parchment while Jean and Lucien clung to each other, talking in low but urgent tones.

'Give it to Tatyana,' I said when Fronsac finally offered the parchment, which seemed to surprise them both. 'I can't read your scratchings.'

'Do you want me to read them to you?' she asked.

'You can read while I fly,' I said. A broad smile flashed across her face and she leaped onto me without hesitation, pulling herself up using the smaller ridges along the back of my neck.

'I will be back as swiftly as I can be. Hold the city,' I said to Fronsac.

'We will.'

'And hold onto that fine hat, wizard.'

'What?'

I released my wind spell and launched myself into the air, sending all in the square rolling across the dirt with my laughter ringing in their ears.

'Tell me where to go,' I said to Tatyana as I made my way out of the city, enjoying the challenge of twisting through the narrow streets, the wind of my passing tearing shutters open and canopies from their frames.

'North, to Bucksburg.'

'Directions will suffice. The names mean nothing to me.'

'Oh. It's about a day and a half's ride, on the northern bank of the river.'

A day and half's ride. I smiled at the thought as I climbed to just under cloud level. I could already see the town on the horizon and spread my wings to enjoy the glide.

'It all looks so different from up here,' she said sometime later. 'So small.'

It didn't sound like a question so I kept my teeth together and started a gentle descent.

'It must have been strange for you, seeing it all from, you know, down there.'

'Strange at the very least,' I said. 'Terrifying at its worst.'

'I'm sorry you got to see us at our worst.'

'Seeing the worst makes it easier to see the best.' I pointed to the town. 'We're nearly there. Where should I land?'

She gave a strange laugh. 'There's a square right in the centre that should be big enough.'

'You like to make an impression,' I said, circling over the town and resisting the urge to roar and send the townspeople scurrying for cover.

'It's petty, but I'm really going to enjoy this. These bastards refused to provision us the last time we came through here.'

'I think I understand.'

The town square was indeed large enough, and mostly empty, with all but the most stubborn inhabitants having fled. I hovered over it, the downdraft of my wings sending several abandoned wagons and carts rolling across the cobbles, as well as a few mesmerised gawkers. I released the roar that had been tickling my throat as I landed, sending the few men remaining in the square bolting for their homes, much to Tatyana's amusement. She slid from my neck and landed neatly in front of me as I folded my wings away.

'Wait here,' she said, patting my snout then yelping when I snapped at her fingers.

I helped myself to some of the spilled produce as I listened to the commotion rising from the streets beyond the market. Her heartbeat was steady and she didn't need healing so I wasn't particularly worried. I could see faces staring at me around corners and from windows but it felt good to be looked at.

The sun had climbed a bit higher by the time that she returned, pushing a handcart while a portly man in a splendid hat decorated with feathers walked beside her, the sound of his heartbeat audible before I even saw him.

'Stratus Firesky, may I introduce Dominic of Bucksburg, the mayor of this fine town.' I lifted my lip, revealing my fine teeth to the mayor, who shrunk back. 'Mayor Dominic would like to know how we're going to pay for the damage and these fine rocks you've requested.'

I leaned in closer and spoke in a rumbling tone that I knew he'd feel as much as hear. 'By not burning his town to ash or feasting on his succulent flesh.'

The man whimpered and fled as fast as his thick legs could carry him, which was a pity. Those heavily marbled limbs and round gut really would have been immensely satisfying. Tatyana fairly crowed with laughter as she pushed the cart up to my side.

'So,' she said, wiping her eyes, 'what do you do with these now?'

I overturned the cart and picked through the collection. At least half of it was useless, but the other half were of a decent quality. These I swallowed whole, one after the other, taking care to ensure they went into the right stomach, while Tatyana watched with wide eyes.

'You ate them,' she said when I was done. Several filthy

children had gathered behind her and were watching us, occasionally screeching at each other.

'Where is the next town?'

She shooed the boldest of the children away as she took out Fronsac's parchment. 'Umm. I think it's due west from here, a small village perhaps. I've not been there.'

With that, she climbed onto my back while I prepared my wind spell. I was nearly ready to leave when a stone hit my nose. It was neither big nor thrown well, but my nose was sensitive. I rounded on the culprit, a tall boy with ropey hair, and grabbed him before he had taken more than six strides. Men always underestimated my speed, and he was no exception. The boy squealed like a burning pig and squirted his mess out through his trousers as I lifted him from the ground, my claws dimpling his belly.

'Stratus, don't!' called Tatyana, and from the tone of her voice I believe she thought I would really soil my palate with such an unworthy creature. Of course, it also drove the boy to new heights of terror and he promptly went limp in my hand. I had intended to simply crush the life from him as a lesson to the others, but I stayed my hand and dropped him into a horse trough instead.

'The next to lift a hand against me will burn,' I said, amplifying my already powerful voice a hundredfold, sending the animals and weak minded in earshot into paroxysms of terror, the scent of which I drank in greedily. Satisfied, I launched us into the air, scattering the children like dolls.

'For a moment there I thought you were really going to do it,' she said as I swooped westwards, the wind singing across my out-swept wings.

'I was only going to crush him, not eat him.'

'Seriously?'

'Quite. They owe their lives and town to you.'

She didn't say anything after that until we found the next location, which was indeed a small village, the inhabitants of which fled into the surrounding marshlands at the first sight of me, something that improved my mood considerably. We collected three more lots of minerals before the sun began sliding into the west and sent the shadows snaking across the landscape below.

'This last one is quite far,' she said. 'North and east, four days ride at least, but it's a city.'

'I like flying by night,' I said. 'Especially on nights like tonight, when there are no clouds. We used to fly from dusk to dawn in summer, drifting on the thermals and naming the stars we saw.'

'I can see the reptákon rising in the east,' she said a while later, her voice almost too quiet to hear, and I turned to smile at her.

'You have good eyes, my friend. You see that one over there? That we named the Centaur. Do you know this word?'

'I do. It's a chimera, half man and half horse.'

'Did you learn that when you trained as a paladin?'

'How did you know that?'

I twisted through the air in a tight loop, making her yell, then evened out again. 'It was something that Navar said.'

She grunted. 'It's more disturbing that he knew that.' She sighed loudly. 'But yes, I volunteered.'

I was content to listen and hummed an old tune that a bard had once composed about me as the darkening lands sped by beneath us.

'I did quite well as well. Maybe too well. The week before the oath-taking, when the head of each order came to the school, they were so condescending that it made me sick to my stomach. Sick and angry. I got into an argument with one of their recruiters.' She paused and fidgeted against my neck. 'It turned into a fight. A nasty one, once he took umbrage at being beaten by a girl.'

'You killed him.'

I took her silence as confirmation. If I closed my eyes, I could almost see the images in her mind. A blurred circle of shouting men and kicked up dust, the taste of blood and anger in her mouth. A single word resonated strongly amidst it all. *Witch*. Even thinking it made me bare my teeth, and I shook the images from my head and found she was still talking.

'And I was supposed to be grateful for that! As if those bastards would have done so much as boo if *he'd* actually done it to me. Of course, my father was livid. He hadn't wanted to me to join in the first place, and now he'd have to offer a large dowry to convince anyone to put a son in me. I walked out not a month later.'

I settled a veil of sorcery across her as she muttered on, infusing her with a sense of calm and letting the anger that the memories had woken bleed off. Her cursing slowly subsided into melancholy and we flew on in companionable silence until the lights of the city grew visible in the distance.

CHAPTER 51

IT WAS SHORTLY before sunrise when I landed in a dark and muddy field no more than a mile from the city walls, my approach silent enough that the only creatures that noticed our arrival were a few field mice and the disappointed owl who had been hunting them. Tatyana slid off my back with a groan, and set about stretching herself this way and that. It seemed the romance of flying upon a dragon had been rubbed away by the uncompromising seat my scales offered. Once she had finished complaining she tucked Fronsac's list into her pocket and headed off towards the city with a wave and a promise to return before sunset.

I bid her farewell and, once I was alone, set about finding some food for myself. I liked farm animals; they were generally well fed and trapped in handy pens, and it wasn't long before I was savouring some roast pig. I generally tried to respect sorcery by not using it to hunt, but since I'd killed the pig with a well-placed bite I felt justified in using a touch of it for the roasting. I scooped the offal out for the jackals and crows. Unlike most animals, crows didn't seem to mind my presence and their raucous cries soon filled the air as they set upon their breakfast and perched on my horns. I listened to the crows bickering for a while, then hunkered down for a nap, satisfied that they would warn me of anyone approaching.

When I woke, I was surprised to see that the sun was dipping towards the west already, and I rose and stretched lazily before turning my attention to the path I expected Tatyana to use. She'd warned me that it was a large city, and likely to take her some time to find the authorities, so I was content to wait a while longer. I gave her the benefit of the doubt until the last crescent of the sun was sinking below the horizon, whereupon I lifted my head and tried to find her scent, but all that came to me was the trail she had left that morning. None of the crows had seen her either, and something about that set my teeth on edge.

I closed my eyes and reached out with my sorcery, tracing the healing spell within her once more. In its new form it was easier than it had ever been and I knew without putting much power into it that she was active and moving about quite quickly. Perhaps she was hurrying towards me, but even as I thought that, I felt her distant pulse quicken and the connection flare with a surge of emotion. *Anger*. I knew it too well to mistake it for anything else. It wasn't long before I felt a sudden flare of the healing construct activating. She was hurt, not seriously, but hurt nonetheless. I sat up and fed more power into the construct, enough so that I could get an impression of what was happening.

My vision blurs as they pull something over my head. Others are holding my arms. Shouting around me, calling me a spy and a witch. Their fists fly and pain flares in my ribs and stomach. I taste my own blood.

I spread my wings, spooking the crows into flight, and once they were clear I released my wind construct, driving me into the sky with a blast of compressed air that tore the nearest hedges from the ground. I rose higher into the air with swift strokes of my wings, and it was not long before the city was spread out below me. Unlike Falkenburg with its natural slopes and high walls, this city was built on the flat of the plain, and was a low sprawling mass of wood and stone buildings that gave the impression that becoming a city may have taken it by surprise.

I spread my wings and caught the column of warmer air that rose from the city, circling it like an eagle as I worked to marry the sorcerous trace of Tatyana's healing against the layout of the city below. By the time I had fixed her location in my mind the unmistakable signs of panic were spreading in the streets below. I woke my night vision and found myself baring my teeth while my hearts pumped with renewed vigour as hundreds, if not thousands, of squirming figures clogged the streets, the taste of their fear rising with the warm air.

I dipped my wings and swept down, low enough that I passed by the windows of the tallest cluster of buildings, my tail smashing chimneys and balconies to rubble as I twisted between the rooftops, slowing at the last minute to settle in a muddy square outside the ramshackle building that hid Tatyana. I released the roar that had been building since I sensed her pain, my sorcery painting the sound with the rage and hate that festered within me as it echoed through the streets, sending a storm-cloud of panicked birds into the air and setting every animal and not a few humans in the city to howling and bleating. Those in the streets fell to the ground screaming for their mothers and gods.

I crossed to the building and, ramming my claws through the windows, I flexed the great muscles of my arms and ripped the entire front of the building away. Timbers and glass rained down around me and revealed a gang of men clustered on the lowest level; Tatyana stood in the middle of them, her mouth bloodied and her armour missing. One of the men had an arm around her neck, and a knife in his other hand. Most of the other men were shouting and screaming, drowning out whatever he was saying, not that it mattered to me.

Metal loves heat, and I was fireborn. It took less time than the taking of a breath to melt his knife; it pulsed with an orange light and dissolved into its molten state, burning through his hand as if it wasn't there. He screamed louder than the others then, and was still screaming when Tatyana rammed an elbow back into his face, sending him sprawling, whereupon she stamped on his throat, silencing him. The others stood frozen in terror, unable to do more than scream the same things over and over.

I beckoned her towards me and, once she was safely in my grasp, I sprayed a jet of fire-bile into the building, burning the others where they stood and sending a plume of orange flame and black smoke coiling into the air.

I lifted Tatyana onto my shoulders as more men spilled from the neighbouring buildings. I swept the flame across them too and they scattered, several of them burning like torches. A sweep of my tail smashed the rest of the building to kindling, sending a fountain of sparks high into the evening sky.

'Enough, Stratus,' Tatyana called, but the sight of her torn clothes and spilled blood had ringed my vision in red. *I could still feel their hands squeezing me, my strength stolen away by their numbers, their stinking breath choking me.*

My fist pulped several more men, and my tail whipped once more, sending another building tumbling into the street in a cascade of smashed wood and stone. I swung my head around, ripping the roof from another with my crest of horns, then threw my head back and roared again as smoke and blood filled the air.

I launched myself into the air, scattering more of the burning timbers, and rose to hover above the city. The streets were clogged with fleeing humans and the mean walls bristled with soldiers trying to bring their all too few siege bows to readiness.

'Stop, damn you!'

I turned and looked at her. 'You are blood to me. Your enemy is my enemy.' I bared my teeth. 'And my enemies die.'

'And they're dead, damn it. Look what you're doing!'

I looked down at the fires burning below and shrugged. 'But they hurt you.'

'God's teeth, Stratus, I get hurt for a living.' She took a deep breath and exhaled slowly, then patted my neck. 'God help me, I understand the sentiment, but enough! You're doing our enemy's work for them.'

'Are you certain? I can follow the scent they have left on you and destroy their bloodlines if you wish.'

She didn't answer immediately. 'That's almost as terrifying as it is tempting. But no. Watching them burn to death was enough.'

'As you wish.' I circled higher before they could ready those bows. 'Did you get the stones?'

'Really?'

'Yes.'

'No. I was too busy getting jumped by those bastards.'

'That's disappointing.' I dipped my wing and swung to the east.

'Where are you going?'

'I recognised the shape of the river, and that mountain over there, the one that looks like a hunchback.'

'So? Where are we going?'

'You'll see.'

It took a few more miles for me to start remembering all of the landmarks and to re-orient myself to the gentle pattern of the Songlines, but the memories soon came back.

'Hold on,' I said, and began the long, curving dive towards the bog that I had sought. The wind was blowing towards us and even from a good distance the unmistakeable rotten egg smell of the bubbling grey waters rose to my nostrils. If anything, it seemed even larger than I remembered it.

Even though I knew the sun was rising, it was as if I was descending into a strange new world inhabited by shapeless, gurgling creatures. I sent an orb of light ahead of me to guide me through the vapours, and finally found a spit of dry land, an island amidst a gently bubbling sea. I settled down upon it as delicately as I could, the wind spells I used to control my descent dispersing the sharp smell for a few precious moments before it closed over us once more. I maintained the binding spell on Tatyana, loosening the bonds that held her slightly but ensuring that the fumes didn't burn her lungs, or worse, make her vomit on me.

'Wait,' she said, 'is this Rotlung Bog?'

I shrugged my folded wings. 'In my tongue it's *Kraz Gur*. The Fire Waters.'

'And what are we doing here exactly?'

I turned to look at her. She looked quite comfortable perched where she was. 'The same thing we have done all day. If I am to face my great enemy and free my beloved, I will need every tool and weapon at my disposal. First amongst these is fire.'

I smashed a fist against one of the spherical rocks on the edge of the rocky shore of the island. It cracked and fell open, revealing a glinting yellow mass within. 'This place is rich with all that I need to produce fire-bile.'

'Fire *bile?* Are you telling me that dragon's fire is actually vomit?'

I nodded.

'Well, that kills a little of the romance.' She rubbed her face. 'Does it hurt?'

'Only if I don't control the stream. It doesn't care what it burns.' I picked up the cracked rock. 'This shouldn't take very long.' I bit into it and began to grind the soft rock into a bitter paste.

'Wait, wait, wait. What do you mean by if you are to face your great enemy and free your beloved? I thought Navar and her were both, you know, dead.'

I swallowed the powdery mass, gagging at the bitterness of it, then lifted the other half. 'Navar is dead, of that I have no doubt. But he is not the one I was speaking of.'

She slid down along my wing, towards the knuckle, an uncomfortable sensation but one I chose to tolerate. 'Slow down. Are you telling me there's another goddamned necromancer out there?' She stopped suddenly, gripping the curved thumb that protruded from the junction of my wing knuckles. 'And Anakhara? Do you think she might be... alive?'

I watched her as I chewed the last chunk of brimstone into something that wouldn't get stuck halfway down my throat.

'I've been thinking about it more often that I had, forcing myself to face the most bitter memories.'

'And you think she might really be alive?' she said, abruptly sitting down.

'I believe she is. Climb back up and I will tell you.'

'We're done here?'

'Yes.' I could feel the stones grinding together inside me, the strong acids in my secondary gut leaching the minerals from them and changing as they did so. I was glad to be away from the bog, and took several lungfuls of clean air to blow the last vestige of the stench from my nose.

'Are you going to tell me or not?'

'Patience, Tatyana.' I swooped down across some neat fields and helped myself to a few sheep, then landed on an isolated mound some miles away where I skinned and set about roasting them with no complaint from her. We ate heartily while the sun chased the shadows from the lands and then I told her about the archmage Talgoth, the cunning fiend who had trapped me, and the fragments of Anakhara's voice that I had been hearing, giving me strength when I needed it most.

'If he could trap me, he may have done the same to her. It would explain why I have never found her body, only scales, teeth, and blood.'

She was silent as she watched the light bleeding into the eastern sky. 'We have to find her.'

'We?'

'Your enemies are my enemies.'

I flashed my magnificent teeth in a smile and stood up. 'Speaking of which, it is time to return to Falkenburg.' She ran up my arm and vaulted onto my neck. 'It is time for me to keep my word to your prince.'

I STEADILY GAINED height as I flew back towards Falkenburg, enough so that the Penullin army was a dark spot on the landscape below me.

'What are you going to do from here?' asked Tatyana.

'Fall,' I said, adjusting my position slightly so that when I did drop, I would be hidden in the glare of the sun. I could feel Tatyana's excitement radiating from her, and quietly bound wards around her that would deflect arrows and the like before I began my dive.

'What do you mean, fall?'

Her question became a shriek as I folded my wings in

and began plummeting towards the army. The dark spot began to expand rapidly, the single mass of it gaining definition as the distance between us vanished. The silvery light radiating from the mages' tents was the first detail that I saw, and from that point of reference the rest of the camp was easy to understand.

I flared the fins on my tail, steering me towards the bulk of the tents and slowing me enough for me to extend my wings without breaking my shoulders. The soldiers looked up as one as they snapped out but it was too late for them to do anything but gawp. I clenched my throat and felt the pressure of the fresh bile press against the back of my mouth, a strange but familiar sensation. I tilted my head and spat a stream of it as I skimmed across the camp, the wind of my passing tearing tents loose and making their flags and pennants snap briskly, spreading the bile in my wake. I tilted my wings and revelled in the strain on my flight muscles as I pulled myself up in a climbing loop; I was almost at the apex, looking down at the camp, when the bile ignited.

A line of flame the colour of molten gold sped across the camp from east to west, billowing outwards as the wind of my passing dispersed droplets of it, spreading the carnage. I had spat extra as I passed over the wizards' encampment, and roared in delight as more than half their tents disappeared in a roiling mushroom of orange flame.

Now the alarms sounded, a wild cacophony of bells and trumpets that drowned out the screams of the dying. I twisted through the air as Tatyana howled like a wolf upon my back, then made another pass from north to south, quartering the camp. A handful of arrows chased me, but none found their mark. Fire bloomed below me as I fell towards the camp again, sweeping my wings back and forth and spreading the fire even further.

A beam of violet light speared towards me from the wizards' tents, followed by flashing rain of fiery bolts, each bursting against the shields I had set. I raked their remaining tents with sorcerous lightning, then swept down, spinning my body as I landed so that my tail whipped through the air, the bony end pulverising several of the slower wizards, dead before they hit the ground. I could feel the unearthly presence of the Lance throbbing within the one tent that wasn't on fire, but with my sorcery at full strength and its power not yet fully woken I didn't hesitate. I tore the tent away and sprayed the cluster of wizards within with bile. They had enough time to think about fleeing before it ignited. Those few who had escaped the spray scattered, tossing their staffs aside and fleeing as fast as their legs and robes allowed. All but one.

This one strode forward, his purple robes smouldering, and sent a beam of killing energy at my breast. Typically for his kind though, he gestured with his staff, an affectation that gave me warning of the attack and its direction. I angled my shields and felt the energy scrape across them, an impressively vicious blast that could have done some serious harm had I been the dumb animal he clearly thought I was. My hands were still busy crushing the life from a few of the survivors, so I lunged at him with my head, a risky option but there were few other men here who I considered a real threat. He tried to leap away, but his legs tangled with those of a half-burnt wizard who was still thrashing about next to him. He screamed as I snapped my jaws shut and drove at least eight teeth through his torso, the snap and crunch of his ribs eminently satisfying. His scream was choked off by the blood that fountained from his mouth.

I twitched my head to the side and bit again, severing both his legs, then tilted my head back and swallowed the rest of him.

I twisted around, scanning the area for others of similar courage, but the rest had fled or died, all aside from one yellow robed wizard lying on the ground screaming for his mother. I pushed more energy into my shields, then plucked the Lance from the air, gritting my teeth against its unpleasant, greasy feel. The chill of death was already thickening around it, but the spells that would wake its full potential were not complete and it was nowhere near as powerful as the one Aknak had been.

I bent it twice upon itself and tossed it into the middle of the Penullin camp, where its enchantments failed catastrophically and consumed fully a quarter of the camp in a blast of pale light, dragging scores of panicked men and animals through into the world of dead before the energies dispersed and the gateway snapped shut again.

I charged the nearest concentration of soldiers, laying into them with my claws and tail, something which men always forgot to watch for. I whipped it forward, scything their legs from under them, then pounded them into the ground with my fists and feet.

I was still killing when I heard more trumpets, a different note from the Penullin horns. I launched myself into the air, the blast of air scattering burning debris and bodies. A column of horsemen and foot soldiers were charging from Falkenburg, the blue banner of the royal house flying next to the symbol of the paladins. I hovered and watched as their charge smashed into what remained of the disorganised army, their swords glittering with reflected firelight as they chopped down every man who didn't wear the blue.

The end was not long in coming. The Penullin army was in disarray and large mobs of their soldiers threw down their weapons, while on the outskirts small groups of cavalry charged down those who tried to flee. The trumpets blew again and a great cheer went up from the soldiers of Krandin.

At Tatyana's bidding I circled over the cluster of blue banners, making the paladins' horses rear up and whinny loudly, although not one of them bolted. Another cheer went up as I came around for a second pass, and this I answered with a roar of my own before fanning my wings and heading back to the city.

The Private Annals of Tiberius Talgoth, Archmage

To MY SURPRISE, Henkman retreated from the dragon's territory, whereupon he set about calling for reinforcements while the priests argued about who was to blame for their god not smiting the creature. I left them to their blathering and used the additional time to prepare my spells.

Once Henkman had whipped his newly swelled army of crusaders into a suitable religious fervour we set out towards the battlefield once more, newly reinforced with great siege bows and a gaggle of mediocre wizards who kept their distance from me.

Henkman radiated a supreme confidence as we approached the valley and arrayed ourselves in a clever new formation that would make it difficult for the dragon to kill so many with a single breath. At noon, when the symbol of their god shone brightest in the sky, he bellowed his challenge again, buoyed by the priests' magic.

It did not take long before the dragon answered his call with a roar that turned many men's bowels to water. The blocks of infantry and archers took up their staggered positions on the valley walls, and the great arrows on the siege bows gleamed with the enchantments his wizards had laid upon them.

The beast arrived with a clap of thunder and flash of fire,

and his neat plans were torn asunder. The archers loosed arrows until their fingers bled and the siege bows thumped like great machines, the crews working themselves to the point of death, but their efforts only seemed to enrage the dragon more as it moved from formation to formation, burning and scattering the brave fools who thought swords and arrows could stop such a creature.

I kept far to the side as I began my casting, trusting that there was enough death in the valley to keep the creature busy. Finally, my spell was ready, and I cast it out into the valley, exulting in the perfect symmetry of the net as it expanded and fell across the beast's sail-like wings as it passed overhead.

It gave a shriek like a scalded cat and crashed to the ground, wiping out an entire regiment of spearmen as it thrashed and roared. I could feel it turn its magics against me as it fought my spell, and had I not yoked my apprentices into sharing the magical load it would have been my brain liquefying, not theirs. With each of them that fell, the strain on my mind became worse, but then Henkman rallied his paladins and they fell upon the creature with their enchanted swords. Its attention shifted away from me and I sealed the spell and set about the next, working feverishly before Henkman and his idiots could kill it.

I had never imagined that there was so much blood in the world. The valley was thick with death when the beast finally succumbed to a combination of its wounds and my spellwork. The cheer that rose from the survivors seemed thin and weak after its great roaring. I drew in the energy that so much violence had released as I waded through its scalding blood, relishing the power that filled me.

It was immense, easily thrice the length of a warship even without its muscular tail, and quite beautiful where it wasn't cut and maimed. Some of the men had already hacked scales from it, believing that the iridescent golden shimmer on their edges was precious metal, but had swiftly thrown them aside when they saw that it was nothing of the sort. Henkman was standing on its tapering head, his sword held to the waning sun as a prayer of thanks tumbled from his lips.

It was surely a stirring sight for his ragtag band of survivors, but I was more interested in the flicker of raw magic I sensed within its skull as he cast a blessing upon his stalwart band.

The beast was alive, and the relief that my spell had worked was enough to convince the men around me that I was also giving thanks.

I remained with the fallen creature when darkness and fatigue sent the survivors retreating to the camp to grieve or celebrate as the mood took them. The numbers of the dead and the extreme violence of their deaths had opened the Gateway wider than I had had experienced and I drew the energy into me until I was almost drunk with it. Holding so much negative energy was dangerous of course, and I could already feel it gnawing away inside me but I focused on the promise of what the dragon's power offered. If I succeeded, the risk would be repaid a thousand times over.

I spun my final spell in the grim watch of the night, binding the creature with chains of runes, the strain of it such that blood rose from my skin like sweat. At last, it was ready, and I watched in such terrible fear as the magic enveloped the beast and sped it away to the prison I had prepared. I laughed even as I sank to my knees in exhaustion.

It had worked. The she-dragon was mine.

CHAPTER 52

FRONSAC MET US as I settled down in the same muddy square as I had used before, striding out from the nearest door, a great smile splitting his beard.

'You did it! By all the stars, that was magnificent! I had read about such things but I never dreamed to see it for myself.' He raced towards me, then stopped, lowering his arms. 'If I had any idea of which part of you to hug I swear I would do it.'

'It is the thought that matters,' I said, dipping a shoulder so that Tatyana could slide off.

She was blackened by smoke but entirely unharmed, and to my surprise and Fronsac's, she raced forward and embraced him heartily.

'I want to scream and laugh,' she said, still crushing him to her. 'It was incredible!'

He eventually disentangled himself and they both stood there grinning at me like fools while I scraped charred meat from my arms.

'Are you waiting for me to say something?' I asked.

'No,' said Fronsac, shaking his head. 'I was just feeling this moment sinking into history. People will talk about today for centuries.'

I grunted. 'Maybe for a few years. Men are quick to let

truth slide into myth. The only ones who will remember will be bent-back wizards.'

'I could live with my journals being read and studied for a thousand years.' He took a step closer. 'Speaking of wizards, did any escape?'

'It's hard to crush every insect.'

'There was one amongst them. Ludvig, their leader. A purple robe, and the most dangerous of all.' He gripped her arm. 'Tell me they're all dead.'

'Was he blonde? Forked beard?' asked Tatyana.

'Yes,' said Fronsac. 'He killed my sons. I'll not forget him.'

'Oh, he's dead,' she said.

'Did he die badly?'

She smiled. 'The worst kind of consumption.'

He looked at her, then at me, his brows furrowed.

'I can regurgitate him you if you don't believe her,' I offered.

He watched me for a moment, then covered his mouth with his hand. 'You're serious,' he said.

'It wasn't pretty,' said Tatyana, who laughed and clapped him on the shoulder. 'Smile, mage. It's a good day.'

'It is, isn't it?' he said, his smile reappearing amidst his beard. 'Novstan is routed, my sons are avenged, and the princes are even now accepting the salute of the army. Lucien is their new hero, and it looks good on him.' He approached me and laid a hand on my forearm, his skin as pale as marble against my obsidian hide. 'And you are free.'

'It is a good day, and I am pleased for you. Both of you,' I said, sitting back on my haunches so that I didn't have to look down on them. It seemed a strange perspective now, but perhaps I had simply been a man for too long. 'But I have one more battle to fight.'

'You mean to destroy the northern army too?' asked Fronsac, moving to lean against the rim of an old barrel. Tatyana simply sat on my forearm, straddling it as she would a horse.

'Tell him,' she said, tapping her heels to my arm. 'He might be able to help.'

It was unlikely, but I understood her intention. 'I must seek out and destroy Navar's master.'

'You're a crap storyteller,' said Tatyana.

'How so? This is what I must do.'

'Where's the drama?' she said, waving her hands about. 'The epic tale of you rescuing your long lost love and exacting bitter revenge?'

'Stop, both of you. What are you talking about?' asked Fronsac. 'What master? What revenge?'

'Stratus believes his mate is being kept as a prisoner by some ancient wizard who helped my ancestor defeat it.'

'Defeat *her*,' I said.

'Sorry.'

'Talgoth?' asked Fronsac, standing up. 'You're talking about Tiberius Talgoth?'

I tilted my head. 'You know his name, but not mine?'

He waved the question away. 'I was inspired to read the rest of *Henkman's Chronicle* last night. You do mean him then?' He paused long enough for me to nod. 'He had a brilliant but twisted mind. He has been dead for centuries though.'

'Like me?'

'Yes, but you're a *dragon*, Stratus. A wizard, even a brilliant one, is just a man. I know of no spell that can heal time's touch.'

I stared at Fronsac as his words echoed in my mind. *I know of no spell that can heal time's touch.* No spell could, especially if the person casting it was as steeped in death as the archmage would be after so many centuries of exposure to its energies; all that dark magic would nullify the positive energies required to heal and grow. They would need help from someone who was their equal or greater in strength to pull enough energy in, and to keep pulling it in, for while time could be slowed or held back by a constant flow of rejuvenating energies, it would only ever stave off the inevitable.

Time was an impossibly intricate element to try to bend to your will. I had once tried to keep the last of the unicorns alive after a virulent plague had decimated their kind, and it had worked as long as I maintained my concentration, but after several decades I had become distracted and, like a bent sapling suddenly released, time had corrected itself. The poor creature died within a heartbeat, suffering a torment I didn't dare to imagine. To keep a flow of energy going for a period like we were talking about was an unimaginably difficult task with a cost to match, both to the one who was maintaining it and to their target. Anakhara had always had a masterful control of the Songlines, and had ever been stronger and more skilled than I ever could hope of being.

'He lives,' I said, my voice dropping to a whisper while I struggled with the enormity of the thought. 'As does she. I feel it, here.' I laid my hand across my primary heart.

'Stratus, what you're talking about it is impossible. There has been no sign nor word of Talgoth or another dragon since you were captured. The *Chronicle*—'

'I tell you this, he is the architect of your misery, and Navar was but his mouthpiece. Tell me, does your precious *Chronicle* speak of another dragon?'

He closed his eyes for a moment. 'Yes. When they, that is Henkman and his crusaders, first approached Nagath it describes an encounter where, and I quote, *a great beast, as sleek as a lion and chased in gold, rose from the north and laid waste upon us with fire and claw.* It was slain by Henkman.'

I bit back the growl that the image stirred within me. 'Is that all it said?'

I felt his magic stir lazily, but it was directed inward. *'The beast was commanded to the earth by the Archmage Talgoth, whereupon the courage of the paladin shone forth and he smote it with mighty strokes of his god-given blade. It fell with the coming of night, and by the morning sun, its gruesome body had fallen to ruin, leaving only a lake of blood as evidence of its sinful existence.'*

I bared my teeth as any remaining doubts were removed. I knew the words weren't his, but it was enough to fan my anger into a new flame.

'Tell me, am I chased in gold, and does it feel as if I am likely to melt into a lake of blood overnight?'

He hesitantly touched my snout, running his hands along it and patting the bony ridge that ran along my cheekbone.

'The archmage took her,' said Tatyana from my arm.

Fronsac stepped back and sat against the barrel once more with a sigh. 'Forgive me if this sounds cold, but are you sure? About her body?'

'Yes. We are not blood drinkers, to be melted away by a ray of sunshine.'

'You really believe she might be alive?' he asked.

The words were on my tongue, but a sudden fear of saying it out loud and somehow dashing the fragile dream of it being true kept them there.

'She's alive,' said Tatyana.

Fronsac looked at her, then at me. 'How is that possible? And why?'

I closed my eyes and woke my sorcery, pulling the power

I needed to replenish my energies from the Songlines with a thought, then turned all of that power to Fronsac, holding it back at the last but letting the weight of its potential fall upon him. He slid back across the cobbled yard as if pressed by a great wind, his wards burning brighter with every passing moment as the surfeit of power bled into them.

I pulled it back and he staggered forward, leaning heavily on his staff, his eyes glowing with a golden light that took some time to fade.

'By the stars,' he breathed, staring at his hands as if seeing them for the first time.

'Power,' I said. 'That is the how and the why. It has ever driven men mad, either by the lust for it, or the fear of others having it.' I sat back once more. 'You count sorcerers as the most powerful and dangerous of all those with the gift, but what they can wield is limited by their mortal flesh and human mind. We are born of the elements and the Songlines themselves.'

Fronsac took a deep breath and let it whistle out between his teeth before replying. 'But if he has such power, if he has somehow enslaved a dragon, why have we not seen it? Why would he need a cat's paw like the Worm Lord?' He stopped and slapped a hand to his forehead. 'Oh god. Not Worm. *Wyrm*.'

I let the additional power I had drawn drain off into the yard and surrounding buildings as I considered this, smiling as various pots of flowers and herbs bloomed anew around us, cutting the stink of the mud with fresh scents.

'I have seen glimpses of his rule, both in visions and memories stolen from the dying, enough to know that he hoards his power for himself like a miser does coin. Everything he does is with the sole aim of increasing his power. He will not care for me having thwarted his plans and wasted the power he had invested in Navar.'

'You think he'll change tactics?' asked Tatyana. 'Maybe bring that power to bear?'

'It's possible. Perhaps he has another champion who he will empower.' I rolled my shoulders. 'Which is why I do not intend giving him the luxury of choosing. Come the morning, I will begin my journey to his lair.'

'You mean we,' said Tatyana. 'I'm with you to the end.'

'No, my friend, not this time. Good fortune and St Tomas' jewel kept you from the worst of what Navar offered, but what lies ahead would be certain death for you.'

'It's my decision.'

'No. I admire your bravery but again, it would be certain death for you.'

'I think he's right, Tatyana,' said Fronsac as she stood up, anger clouding her scent. 'If what I just felt is any indication of what Stratus must face, then there is no charm or spell that could protect you. It would be folly of the worst kind.'

She shrugged off the hand he moved to lay on her shoulder. 'It's my decision!'

'So be it,' I said, and didn't miss the surprise that flashed across her face. 'But equally, it's my decision that I shall not carry you. Come with if you wish, but you will need a considerably faster horse.'

She gaped at me, the surprise melting into anger as she mouthed words that never left her lips before abruptly turning on her heel and marching from the square, slamming the door behind her hard enough that the handle fell off. I felt her presence receding deeper into the palace, and surprised myself by feeling slightly disappointed that she didn't turn back, but then I had laced my words with a compulsion in an attempt to diffuse her emotions.

'She may not forgive you for that,' said Fronsac, surprising me again with his deft touch. I thought I'd been quite subtle about it using my power. 'Even though I understand it was only for her own benefit.'

'I'd rather have her angry than dead.'

'You're rather fond of her, aren't you?'

'She's the closest thing I have to family.'

'Of course.' He moved along my flank, occasionally running his hands across my scales and muttering to himself. I watched him, but since he wasn't using his power I left him to his examination and only spoke when he had completed his examination and stood before me once more.

'Does Lucien know?' I asked.

He stopped as suddenly as a man spying a viper at his feet. 'Know what?'

'That he's a sorcerer.'

He leaned on his staff and gave a low laugh. 'I didn't even consider that you would know.' He lifted his head and looked up at me. 'No, he doesn't. No one does. I suppress it.'

'And siphon his power.' He clearly hadn't expected me to know that, and his surprise was such that I saw the glimmer of it ripple through his wards. 'Which makes me wonder for whose benefit that is.'

'It's not like that,' he said, straightening. 'I feed the power that bleeds from him back into the same wards, keeping them sound even if we are apart. It's not a strong gift, and he has never felt it.'

'You are twice wrong there, my friend. He feels it, even if he only knows it as the *blood of kings*. Which is more accurate than he knows, since the Firstborn had the gift too. And think on this. He resisted the necromancers in the heart of their stronghold, faced Navar alone, and he survived the backlash of both the collapse of the Lance's spellwork and the awakening of the nexus. His power is growing. No mere wizard or paladin could have survived any one of those things.'

'But you—'

'No, Fronsac. What powers I had available were solely bent on keeping me alive.'

He sat back on his barrel. 'A sorcerer and a prince. It will change everything, if he survives.'

'He's a prince, not a charcoal burner's son, locked in a cell and fearful for his life. His gift is already woken, and he has you to guide him.'

'This isn't going to sit well with the Church.'

'I'm sure they will find a way to take credit for it.'

He gave a short laugh that carried little humour. 'That's so accurate that I'm not sure whether to laugh or weep.'

'You're rather fond of him, aren't you?'

For a moment, he said nothing. 'He's a friend.'

'Of course.'

He laughed at that, then stood. 'Talking to you is a dangerous business, and I must go. Tell me, is there anything you need?'

'Fire,' I said, after a moment's thought. 'A normal fire, with wood preferably. It will help harden my scales for what lies ahead.'

'I will arrange it. Will we see you again, if you succeed?'

'I do not think so, not for some time. If Anakhara is there, she will need me.'

'I hope she is, my friend.' I felt his sincerity ring in his words.

'Thank you, Fronsac.'

He bowed deeply and kissed my snout before hastening from the yard. He was true to his word too, for soon after a throng of nervous soldiers appeared, each carrying armfuls of firewood, and I bade them stack it in a pyramid. Once they were done and had retreated behind their doors once more I lit it with a small lick of bile and curled up around it, drawing the smell of pine and cedar deep into my lungs before I fell into a deep and restful sleep, the kind that I hadn't experienced for decades.

A CHORUS OF screams broke around me when I opened my eyes again, and for a several terrible moments I feared my adventures had all been a dream and I was still in my cage, rattling around the countryside for the stupid and ignorant to poke sticks at.

There were more screams as I sat up, shaking the fog of sleep from my mind as the place and time took shape around me again. I was still in the courtyard, still free, and the sun was shining down on me and the numerous men and women who were now pressed against the walls.

'What do you want?' I asked the closest of these, a woman reeking of overly sweet rosewater that failed to hide the sweat and fear that slicked her body. She shrieked again and stumbled back while the tall man next to her stepped forward hesitantly, as if expecting me to snap at him, a not entirely unrealistic fear to have.

'I am Lord Trott of Dunhallow,' he said in a piping voice more suited to a child.

'So?'

'Prince Jean gave us leave to come and see you.'

'Then see me.'

I stood up, which made Lord Trott stumble backward thrusting his woman before him like some sort of offering, either by accident or by design. I ignored them and the other gawkers as I stretched my back and legs before fanning my wings out and tilting them towards the sun, letting its gentle heat warm the membranes while I considered what lay before me.

I was assuming that Talgoth still lurked in his hidden valley, and despite the unpleasantness waiting at the end, I was actually looking forward to the long flight needed to get there. Flying this way and that with a human perched on me was one thing, a novelty, but to properly soar in complete isolation with only the sun for company was a different prospect entirely.

'Do you breathe fire?' Trott's thin voice crept in at the edge of my thoughts, and I would have continued to ignore him had he not decided to poke me with his stick.

'I'm talking to you, beast.'

'Arek, don't.' The woman's voice.

'Nonsense. This thing is chattel to the crown and I am of the blood.'

'Listen to your woman, insect,' I said, my words tapering off into a growl. The handful of other gawkers there echoed her statement, and for a moment, it seemed their entreaties had helped him recover his wits.

Then his cane cracked across my claws. 'Rubbish. It's a beast like any other and I won't be spo—'

I had suffered countless torments in the centuries I had been caged. I'd had all manner of foulness thrown or spat upon me, but the worst had always been those who had wanted me to do something, to perform for them like some toothless and broken dancing bear. Sometimes they succeeded in goading me, and I would throw myself at the bars, teeth flashing, shattering their bravado.

It happened now, without me really thinking about it. A snarl and a lunge, and then the screams. But that part of my mind had forgotten that I was myself once more, and that there were no bars anymore. My mouth was suddenly full of meat and blood and the square rung with the screams of men reduced to a primitive, bestial need to flee.

The meat my fangs had pierced flailed weakly and I snatched my head sideways, the ridges on my teeth sawing through gristle and sinew, sending an arm and head flopping and bouncing across the cobbles before I swallowed the rest in a single, convulsive movement. He was dead anyway, and I was never given to wasteful ways. Trott's wife was still standing before me, her side painted in crimson as I fed power into my wind construct. I braced my legs and leaped into the sky, leaving the courtyard and its tumbling, mewling occupants behind as I powered upwards.

CHAPTER 53

I FLEW THROUGHOUT the day, high enough that the land was largely featureless beneath me and only the glint of lakes and the toothy ridges of the highest mountains hinted at the shape of the ground below. I descended as the air began to cool with the coming of night, the thinner air adding an unpleasant edge to the strain that was already sawing at my flight muscles. The Archmage's domain had been a long, hard flight the first time I had attempted it, and that was with strong muscles that hadn't been twisted and bent for over seven hundred years.

I landed near a small lake amidst a forest, startling a few dozen waterbirds into flight. I winced as I folded my wings back, the ache I felt then foreshadowing what awaited me the next day. I drank my fill, and with neither the inclination nor energy to go hunting, I used my sorcery to pull a good-sized stag to me from the nearby woods for my dinner. It was healthy and full of life, and the taste of it finally scrubbed the lingering tang of the stringy nobleman from my palate. Sated, I stretched out, savouring the feel of grass under me and the soft, sweet smells and sounds of the forest around me. For the first time in an age I felt in harmony with the natural order of things, so much so that I found it difficult to sleep despite the day's exertions.

Instead I amused myself by trying to guess the patterns of the bats that swooped across the water, eating their fill of the countless flying things that lived near the water's edge, enjoying the simplicity of it.

I slept eventually, and woke sometime after dawn, shrouded in a cool mist that covered the lake, an idyllic start that lasted as long as it took me to move and feel the stiffness and pain that lurked in every part of me. I slumped back down again and waited for the sun to climb high enough for its heat to soothe the aches away, summoning and eating a few hares and such to while the time away. Sunlight and fire both healed in their own way, but without the price that using sorcery would have imposed, something that the Henkmans had noticed early on in my captivity and went on to use as leverage for my compliance.

I shook the memory away as I stretched out in the sun. The Henkman dynasty was finished and the last of them now had my blood flowing in her veins, a delightful twist that no one could have seen coming. I stared out across the water, struck by how silent and alone it felt without her here with me. I knew that I had made the right decision, for bringing her with me would have been an entirely selfish act, a realisation which in itself was quite eye opening for me. I would never have countenanced such a thought in the years before.

Once the sun had worked its secret magic and my aches had faded I rose into the air and resumed my journey, gliding on the rising air where I could. I didn't climb as high as the day before, choosing instead to enjoy the natural beauty of the lands below as I flew.

That lasted for another three days, and the point where I reached the outer reaches of Talgoth's dominion. It was a gradual transition, and I only became aware of it sometime after the forests began to thin beneath me, their canopy reducing to skeletal fingers grasping at the sky. The stretches of grass between these faded from green to brown and eventually to a grey that made it look as if the world was covered in a fine ash, the uniformity only broken by empty riverbeds and the gleam of bone here and there. My shadow flicked across the remains of towns and villages, their squares empty and the houses blackened by fire. I glided lower, the air growing progressively more sour, and swept my sorcery ahead of me. I felt no trace of any living thing of note, and hastily rose once more, seeking sweeter air.

I flew over such devastation for another day before I eventually saw something apart from my shadow moving across the landscape. I circled the dust-cloud I had spotted and saw it was a train of six large wagons, each drawn by teams of yoked men rather than cattle or horses. That alone woke my curiosity and I spiralled lower, watching closely as they stopped when my shadow passed over them, the chains of men in front of the wagons immediately prostrating themselves on the ground. The others, who I took to be their masters, formed into a rough square, neither fleeing nor screaming, which really piqued my interest.

I renewed my protective wards as I banked in and landed in front of the square, fanning a great cloud of dust and grit into them to foil the aim of any hidden archers. Apart from a few hacking coughs from within the cloud, my arrival was met with silence. Once the worst of the dust had settled three of the men slowly approached me, their heads bowed. The first of them called out in a language that made no sense to me and I called on a measure of sorcery, letting it do the work of deciphering his babbling. I felt the warm pulse of it settle on me just as he finished whatever he was saying. I had missed most of it, but assumed that it was something akin to 'hello great dragon, please don't kill us'.

I toyed with the idea of eating one or two of them, both to curtail any ideas they might have about trying something stupid and because I was getting hungry, but in the end I chose to simply wait and see what they did next. I was hoping they would offer a tribute of meat and spices, saving me the trouble of tearing their wagons apart to find some. The nearest of these three envoys slowly lifted his head, but then dropped to his knees when he saw me watching him.

'Oh, great one,' he intoned, the words forming in my mind a heartbeat after they left his lips. 'Mighty goddess, we pray our tribute is worthy and for your forgiveness at being so late. The sands were deep and our slaves weak. We shall slay them if it pleases you.'

As much as I enjoyed being feared and respected, there was something about his manner and the smell that surrounded him and his fellows that set my teeth on edge. I reared back with a hiss as his words sunk in, making him scrabble backwards. *Goddess?*

Besides the most obvious protest that their powers of observation were sorely lacking, the most immediate thought that came to mind was that they had seen a dragon before. A female dragon. But that was impossible, unless the even more impossible was possible. Could it be that Anakhara still flew these skies?

'Tell me of your goddess,' I said, the words taking on a hollow echo around me as my sorcery changed them. They stammered useless snippets of an answers in a way that swiftly eroded my patience. I wanted answers.

'Speak!' I bellowed the word at them, the command I had bound to it pushing them into the grit.

They didn't answer but instead mewled and, by the stars, several soiled themselves. With a roar of frustration I smashed my fist down onto the nearest envoy with enough force to blow his guts out of him from both ends. Now the screaming and fleeing began in earnest, both from the men before me and the slaves gathered around the wagons, who were leaping about madly, their chains ringing and rattling. I ignored them for now, for not all of their masters had broken free of the terror that gripped them. These few cowered as I advanced on them, frozen by fear and awe. One by one, I asked them the same question, and four more of them died a miserable death until one at last found both a voice and spine.

'She is the Deathbringer!' he screamed. 'She is bone, and iron, and flame!'

He screamed anew when I lifted him from the ground, but fell silent as my sorcery lanced into his head and hollowed it out, drawing his memories into my mind even as it scourged the life from him.

THE WIND HOWLED across the hilltop as we waited, every face turned towards the sky and the clouds that boiled across it. We were silent, but the prisoners weren't. They knew she was coming and most were begging us and the gods for the mercy of a swift death. Those that weren't were crying or simply staring into the darkness beyond the torches, perhaps imagining they were somewhere else.

I could feel Suzanna's gaze upon me but couldn't bring myself to look at her. She called to me again, angry now. I would know that tone anywhere; it had chased me from the house enough times. She hadn't used it since the night of the Choosing, and then only briefly before the shock set in. I kept my eyes on the clouds and tried not to listen to how that familiar anger was being eroded by fear.

'She comes!' called another voice, and all our faces lifted

to the sky as a flash of lightning silhouetted the dragon against the clouds. I felt the strength leach from my legs at the sight of its tattered hide, and the bread I'd eaten that afternoon rose up in my throat again.

'Stand firm,' said a voice behind me. Stefan, steadfast as ever, his voice betraying nothing of what he must be feeling with his daughter staked next to Suzanna. 'Stand or we all die.'

The creature shrieked, the sound seeming to miss my ears and echo directly in my head, as if it the hate and pain it carried was meant for me alone. I no longer felt shame about pissing my pants when I heard its voice. None of us did, because it happened to all of us.

A cold wind washed across the hilltop as it swooped around us, snuffing several torches, the chains that trailed from its wings singing before it slammed down onto the earth with a terrible weight. It shrieked again, the sound impossibly loud, and I felt the bloodseed within me expand in response, sending a bolt of pain lancing down my neck. I staggered, but didn't fall.

The dragon's gaze swept across us, the silver light within its eyes chilling my skin as it passed over me. It hissed as it gathered the chains of the damned, not even looking down as it stepped on the baker's son, crushing his spine and skull under its bony tread.

'One more,' it said in a voice like two blades being drawn across each other.

Fat Uther didn't look so pleased about being elected the Speaker then. His trousers darkened both front and back as the men pushed him forward.

'Fifty souls were demanded,' he said, fear giving him the voice of a young girl. 'Fifty were given.'

I didn't see it move, but suddenly Uther was in its hand, his eyes bulging like a toad's.

'Fifty,' the dragon said, the sound cutting into me. Suzanna was screaming at me now, telling me she loved me and to please help her and, Drogah help me, my legs carried me several strides closer before the cold that surrounded the dragon stole my strength and sent me stumbling to the ground. I screamed that I loved her and the dragon's head whipped towards me, that terrible, soul corrupting light pinning me where I stood as surely as any lance.

It would kill me now, as it had all the others who had dared defy it. I held my breath as I waited for the bloodseed to burrow out of my skull, and wondered whether it would be more painful if it came out of my nose or an eye.

It watched me, that cruel, lipless maw tilting like a crow's, and the light of its eyes suddenly dimmed. It looked away and a moment later, an icy wind snapped across the hilltop and it was gone, rising into the lightning chased sky, dragging Uther, Suzanna and the all others to their doom.

HIS BODY TIPPED from my hand as I sat back. It felt as if a great rope was wound about my chest, stilling my breath and making the blood thunder through my head. Anakhara was *alive. Alive!* I saw her again as I closed my eyes, grief piercing me like hot knives as I saw the cruelties that had been inflicted on her. Chains and hooks pierced scales that were once as black as jet and chased with golden veins, the hide between a fine tracery of scars and weeping sores. Her eyes were gone, replaced by crystal orbs, and her lips were shredded tatters that would never smile again. I barely noticed the men scattering and fleeing around me as I gave voice to the despair and grief swelling within me.

I screamed her name until my throat refused to make another sound and hurled myself into the air, raw sorcery propelling me upwards until the air was too thin to fly and the blue of the world curved away beneath me like a drawn bow. I hung there, weightless and numb, until the madness loosened its grip upon me and I remembered how to breathe again. I folded my wings and fell back towards the ashen fields, letting the anger at what she had suffered cauterise my grief.

By the time that I found the wagons again the rage was a furnace within me, and something of it must have bled out, for the men scattered at the first sight of me. It wouldn't save them. I killed the slaves first, stopping the wagons, and a single pass was enough to set them all aflame. My claws and tail accounted for the rest, wherever they fled; their trails were obvious in the lifeless sands.

I ate my fill from the charred bodies, taking care to avoid their infested heads, and when I rose into the air once more it was with a new heat in my breast. I turned towards the rotten heart of Talgoth's empire and sped onwards.

CHAPTER 54

THOUGHT AND REASON began to return to me when I sighted the foothills of the mountains that formed the outer border of Talgoth's heartland. The sky beyond them was dark, and as I flew closer I began to comprehend the scale of the unnatural clouds that rose over the whole of the mountain range, as if he had bound a thousand hurricanes into one. This then was his outer defence. He'd had something similar in place the first time I had come here, but nothing on this scale, testament to how his power had grown.

At least this time I had the advantage of knowing what to expect, so I slowed and took some time to prepare some protection for myself, binding the names of the winds that I knew to me like armour to deflect the most violent gusts. I drifted in the sunlight, recovering some of the energy I'd spent in my furious flight here, then picked a point to enter the mass of clouds. It didn't really matter where I went in as they extended as high and as far as I could see.

There was no way to avoid the maelstrom. All I could do was hope to keep flying in the right direction and not lose sight of the horizon. If that happened, I was lost. My strength would eventually give out and I would be torn apart like a gull.

I roared my challenge at the uncaring cloud and entered

a world of madness. There was no time and no light within the cloud barrier, only darkness, howling winds, and the near constant booming of thunder, deep and loud enough to make my bones rattle within my flesh. The air pressure around me swelled and fell away with no discernible pattern; I dropped thousands of feet, wings beating uselessly while the power of my wind spells was instantly dispersed by the dozen or more hurricanes battering me from all directions. Sudden updrafts slammed into me like invisible fists, throwing me upwards again, tumbling through the sky with my only thought being how to prevent my wings from being torn from me.

Lightning flashed in the darkness with eye searing brightness, briefly revealing the night-black filaments of dark magic that ran through the clouds like a puppeteer's strings. Hailstones as large as catapult shot and as sharp as caltrops hammered at my scales, chipping their newfound hardness away, forcing my eyes shut and drumming against the membranes of my wings, forcing me to fold them in lest they be torn and shredded. Up and down lost all meaning as the full fury of the imprisoned storms was unleashed on me. Fear and uncertainty were washing my bravado away with every passing moment. My concentration was slipping, and the potency of the wards that were deflecting the worst of the storm's power were slipping away with it.

A shard of ice smashed into the side of my face and sent me spinning, and stupidly I opened my mouth to give voice to my pain. Sleet and hail instantly blasted into my mouth and throat, choking me and sending a sharp spike of agony into my mind, and with that the last of my wards evaporated. If I had thought the storm loud before, now it became a cacophony, the sound of it like the world's ending. I couldn't fight it, nor could I ride it out. I folded my wings in, hugged my arms and chin to my chest and fell, holding only to the hope that the stars would let me hit the ground without too much damage.

I WOKE TO pain, cold, and a lungful of water. But I was yet alive, there was solid ground under me and I knew which way was up, so it was a victory of sorts. I pushed and clawed my way out of the icy torrent I was laying in, just far enough that I could cough, vomit water and even occasionally take some air in. Once the worst of that had passed I concentrated on pulling the rest of me out of the water, temporarily grateful for how the cold had numbed the injuries I'd taken from the fall, some of which looked quite terrible.

The stream was deep but narrow, the bed it ran in a sharp-sided crack where part of a mountain had been split away by ice. It was too narrow for me to have landed in cleanly, and the wounds in my hide and the fractured bones I could feel were testament to how I had been thrown against the mountain and slid down, the flinty edges of the shale cutting dozens of deep furrows in my flesh as I did. I pulled myself onto a shallow ledge and tried to tally my injuries, but blood loss and the persistent cold were fogging my mind, making cohesive thought as slippery as a greased eel.

I had to do something, but what was it? Something about a screaming woman. Perhaps I should sleep. Things are clearer after a good sleep. No! Why not? Not sure. It's getting warm now, so much better. Was I looking for someone? It's raining too much. Go to sleep. Sleep.

And sleep I did, the constant raging of the storm and shriek of lightning fading into the background. When I woke, it was again to pain and confusion. I was shivering uncontrollably, each shiver tearing a little more at the livid wounds that marked me and setting my cracked bones grating against each other. I licked the wounds that I could reach; it was all that my fogged mind would allow me to do. I don't know how long I lay like that, panting and licking at my injuries like some common beast, but eventually the exertion began to generate some warmth, and with that a basic level of coherent thought returned to me, enough that I could take stock of where I was and what shape I was in. The storm had relented, perhaps due to the lack of a clear target, but the riverbed remained a deep and dangerous crevice to my right, effectively leaving me trapped on the ledge, at least until I was strong enough to leap to the other side.

I reached for my sorcery, intending to employ it for healing, but two things happened. First, I heard an immediate rumble of thunder and saw the clouds darken overhead, and second I felt a yawning void where the Songlines should have been. Even here, clouded by the Archmage's construct, I should have been able to feel a sliver of it, but they were *entirely gone*. Perhaps I should have expected it, given what even Navar's magic had accomplished, but this was a complete void, not just a mere absence. I pushed at it, ignoring the grumbling in the skies, but all that I sensed was an emptiness, like a river that had been dammed at its source. I stopped trying, and noted how the clouds seemed to thin out again. I tried it twice more, with the same result.

That was it then. The storm effectively hunted by magic. *Cunning.* If I could fly without relying on any sorcery, I might be able to keep low and break through the barrier before it could close on me again. It wasn't much of a plan, but it was a start, and I scraped away a few loose rocks and made myself a bit more comfortable on the ledge.

I wanted to hoard the sorcery that remained in my reserves, but as I saw it, having it wasn't much use if my body gave out. I slowly wove it into a healing pattern, stopping whenever the storm reacted, and eventually found something like a middle ground where I could use it without the fear of attracting a lightning strike. I settled it across me, then closed my eyes and tried to concentrate on my breathing while the magic did its work. I had waited centuries for my vengeance, so what were another few days? If nothing else, it gave me more time to imagine all the ways I could kill Talgoth when I finally got my claws on him.

Eventually though, the tears in my hide were sealed under fresh new scars and my cracked bones had bonded once more. I was stiff, cold and very, very hungry, but the hunt was back on. I stretched as best I could, took a few deep breaths, and launched myself from the ledge with a growl. I barely made it to the far edge of the ravine, and for one terrible moment I thought my grip was going to tear loose and sending me plummeting into the icy depths yawning behind me, but my claws held. I stretched out my wings and leapt. The air was thin, and it took a thousand feet or more for me to level out, but the same sharp, steep valleys of the mountains that had hurt me before now worked to my benefit.

There was a pleasant ache in my shoulders and chest by the time that I had gained enough height again to rise over the jagged peaks. I could see the inside curve of the storm barrier now and was more than glad to leave it behind me.

And so I began my descent into the heart of Talgoth's domain. It was still dark here, but it wasn't the forced darkness of the storm but rather the more natural gloom of sunlight that had been made to fight its way through cloud and mist. There was still life here, despite the death that the Archmage seemed to surround himself with, and I followed the trails that man and beast had left until I came upon the first village of his lands. I had thought that it would be a poor collection of hovels, but instead found it to be far sturdier and inhabited by several families who kept dozens of lovely fat herd animals. I was not in the mood to waste time trying to scare them away and simply landed in the middle of the village, collapsing several houses and whatever was inside them. I ignored the screams and protests as I helped myself to half a dozen goats, a full churn of butter and an amazingly obese man with a feathered hat, presumably their chief. I was too hungry to pass up the soft bounty promised by his jiggling stomach, although I took the precaution of gutting him first so as not to ruin the creamy saltiness of his fat.

One or two enterprising males shot at me with their bows, but a lash of my tail left them bleeding their life into the dirt. The rest of the inhabitants fled, so I took the opportunity to check that my fire bile and reflex were ready; I wasn't disappointed. The bile burnt fast and cleanly, and after the coldness left by my passing through the storm the feel of a real fire against my hide was glorious. I lingered there until the houses burned to ash, helping myself to whatever foodstuffs I could find, including a small barrel of treasured whale oil. Sated and refreshed, I endured the indignity of a running launch and, muscles straining as I gained height once more, I continued my journey.

There was a long stretch of featureless scrubland between the village and the fortress, a good few hundred miles. I flew steadily, chasing my shadow at a decent pace but without tiring myself. It was quiet here, unnaturally so. Nothing stirred except dry, dead things that the wind toyed with in a desultory manner. Such was the unbroken monotony of it that scores of miles passed by without me really being aware of their passing, nor of what was bearing down on me.

I didn't see them until it was far too late, and even when I did it took me precious moments to shake off the stupor that had settled on me. By the time my almost hypnotised brain matched the outline of the wyverns to their cat-like shrieks they were on me. There was no time to wonder how they were even here. The first slammed into my ribs and vanished with a scream, having broken its wing in the mistimed attack.

But the second and the third hit me like thunderbolts, digging their eagle-like talons into the soft membranes of my left wing, collapsing it and sending me into a deadly spiral. The rest of the flock were following us down, waiting to strike after the impact rattled my senses and, they hoped, left me too injured or stunned to defend myself.

But I still had time, though not much. I stretched my neck through underneath my wing and clenched my chest muscles in. There! I lunged as soon as the move brought the rump of the first wyvern within biting distance. Wyverns were a bastard breed, a misbegotten experiment in solitary reproduction by those who had come to this world before Anakhara and I had. They lacked arms and looked like nothing more than the overly large offspring of bats and swamp lizards, and as the one in my mouth had just discovered, the price of their unmatched aerial dexterity was a lightweight frame and leathery skin rather than the robust skeleton and hide of a true-born.

I bit down and felt its pelvis collapse. It shrieked in agony and, as I had hoped, tried to flee; its talons tore my wing as it yanked them free, but with it gone I could bring the rest of my wing into view. I couldn't reach the last one, but I didn't need to. I spat a thin stream of bile into the wind, and a moment later the spin we were in sent the wyvern through the centre of the dispersing stream, gobbets of it clogging the miserable creature's nose and mouth. Its yip of confusion turned into an almost human scream as the bile combusted, burning its skull out from the inside as the wind pushed the fire up its snout. It spun away streaming smoke but the ground was now rushing up at me in a blur. My teeth squeaked as I clenched my jaws and fought to tilt my wings enough to widen the arc of the spin I was in, flattening the angle I would hit the ground at and turning what would have been a bone breaking impact into a tumbling slide.

Dead grasses and sand exploded around me, filling the air with a fine dust that I would be digging out from between my scales for decades to come if I survived. The dust-cloud was a blessing though, for it hid me from the rest of the swarm for precious moments, giving me a chance to clear my senses.

I could hear them calling out as they followed the trail I'd left, swooping down from alternate sides, their razored claws extended and eager to find my flesh. Given the unnatural absence of the Songlines in the area, I was still loathe to tap into my inner reserve of sorcery for fear that I wouldn't be able to replenish it before I confronted the Archmage, so this fight would be with teeth and talons.

Their hunting calls rose in pitch as they saw me, then faltered as I leapt into the air to meet them. The first died with the fighting talon of my left arm rammed entirely through its chest, splitting both spine and heart. As we dropped back to the ground I lashed my tail into the second, the knotted bone and horn catching another under the wing and smashing its ribcage. The others broke off and circled me, suddenly unsure.

That's when I felt it. After the absence of any type of

magical presence, the sudden pulse of dark magic that stabbed through the air was staggering in its potency. I felt the force of it tug at my own sorcery, but this time I wasn't the target. As one, the wyverns' shrieking ended, and I saw their eyes darken from amber to black. With blood streaming from their eyes and nose from the force of the compulsion that had crushed both their fear and free will, they attacked in a swarm of teeth and razored claws.

CHAPTER 55

THE REMNANTS OF the flock bore down on me as one, attacking with wild abandon and scant care for their own protection. I could still feel the thrum of the dark magic coursing through them, a discordant vibration at the edge of my hearing.

I managed to sweep my wings out behind me to protect the soft flight membranes, but then they were upon me, squirming and climbing and biting in a frenzied melee. They shrieked piteously all the while that their claws and teeth were ripping and biting into me, heedless of the blood that streamed from their snouts and eyes.

I snapped at any wyvern flesh that came within reach of my mouth, my teeth stabbing through their supple hides and flesh, but they kept fighting even when they should have been dead twice over. A pair found the softer skin under my arms and bit deep, shaking and spinning like swamp lizards taking a gazelle, trying to tear the wounds wide enough to thrust their heads through. I roared in pain and clamped my arm down, holding them steady long enough to bite down on the back of their necks, but even then I had to all but sever their heads before their thrashing ceased.

This took time though, time enough for the others to try

to nip under my belly and bite at my groin. With one arm incapacitated by the two half-decapitated creatures that still hung from my ripped flesh, I stumbled backwards then rose up. Enticed by my apparent weakness, the remaining wyverns darted forward, jostling each other as they raced for the softer flesh that was suddenly exposed. I wasted no time and belched a jet of fire bile across them as they grouped together. It ignited when they were mere yards from me, the flash of its detonation scalding even me and robbing them of their senses entirely. Their shrieking ended as they opened their mouths to draw in breath and swallowed the superheated air, cooking their lungs. Magically-induced frenzy or not, it was a mortal wound. They died before they could even turn in my direction again.

I felt the dark magic bleed from them, and hoped that whoever was behind the spell had felt their pain. I pried the remains from under my arm and reluctantly drew on my sorcery to heal the wound, just enough to stop the bleeding and seal the skin. The remaining scratches and bites were largely superficial by my reckoning, and were already scabbing over.

I examined one of the wyverns whose neck I had broken, wrinkling my snout at the residual stink of dark magic that lingered in its flesh. Like the others, it was fine boned and lean to the point of being gaunt, and even in death its features looked feral. Its lipless jaw was disproportionately heavy, and its teeth were close enough together that at first glance it looked to have a beak. I closed its jaw, and the teeth aligned perfectly, just touching. It was no wonder the bites had hurt as much as they did, and I was grateful that I had taken the time to harden my scales, even if they were nowhere near as strong as they had once been. If they'd fallen on me when my skin was still soft and pliable they would have torn pieces off me like a swarm of razor-fish flensing a whale.

I had only seen such perfect teeth on one other creature, and my stomach clenched painfully as that thought sunk in. *These were Anakhara's offspring*. She had once thought of them as an abomination, and now she was spawning her own. I stared into the distance, to where the citadel waited, wreathed in its unnatural shadow and, for the first time, the thought of being reunited with her filled me with dread rather than joy.

The smell of the dead wyverns was foul and the touch of their cooling flesh even more so now that I knew their provenance. I threw their bodies aside and scrubbed their blood from my hide with handfuls of sand. As soon as my wounds were knitted together I took to the air once more, snorting the last of their stench from my nostrils.

I didn't have far left to fly, but the sight that greeted me as I burst through the final ring of mist that surrounded his fortress stole the very breath from my lungs. His castle, once a tall and delicate looking creation of pale towers and hanging gardens, now hung in the air over a huge pit in the heart of the valley, the rock that clung to the underside giving it the appearance of a great, rotten tooth.

I could feel the pull of the dark magic that radiated from it intensify as the mist fell away from me, its touch more caustic than anything Navar had ever brought to bear upon me. I retreated into the mist and felt its power lessen, like the touch of the sun being lost behind a thick cloud. I wasn't about to go any closer until I had a better sense of what I was dealing with, and so banked in a long turn around the citadel, keeping within the mists as I noted the decrepit state of its physical defences. The battlements that I remembered as being proud and lined with rows of chanting wizards were now fallen into ruin, with a bare handful of towers marking the pitted remnants of the walls. Slowly and carefully I extended my metaphysical senses, probing the magic that pulsed through the air. I fanned my wings out and hovered as I trickle-fed some of my sorcery into my sight, turning what I had felt via my sensory pits into visible images.

The citadel hung there, pulsing like the heart of some terrible god, but instead of arteries and blood, it throbbed with a darkness that swallowed whatever light that it touched. Shadowy tendrils laced the sky around it, weaving and writhing like headless snakes. I looked upon the monstrosity and knew then why I could not feel the Songlines in this place; they had been entirely corrupted, the power and life that they carried now drawn directly into the citadel, where some terrible spell of unspeakable magnitude siphoned the life from them and sent out something poisoned in return. This was what I had feared Navar would attempt at the nodes at Aknak and Falkenburg, but advanced to a far greater scale than I had ever dared to imagine.

It was a chilling and sobering sight, and the anger and hate that I had worn so proudly now seemed meagre and pathetic. To go against such might was beyond folly. Talgoth had nearly defeated me when he'd had but a fraction of the power that now flexed and throbbed in the skies before me, so what chance did I have now, when he commanded a power that could corrupt reality on this scale and harness the power of death itself? I relied on the Songlines for my strength, and he had stripped them away, so how could the strength they gave me prevail? The power that hung in the sky before me had not even been purposefully gathered and was simply the reflection of spells that he had already cast.

If I went against such might in open battle it would take

a bare fraction of it to turn me to ash. It would be a grand, but brief and utterly hopeless gesture. It wasn't despair that made me admit this, but logic. To attack him with tooth and claw was to die, and given his command over death, that was the least of the evils that would be done to me.

Even as I watched, the clouds bubbled and twisted, forming themselves into a face. I didn't recognise it, but I knew the voice that rolled from it. It had haunted my memories and dreams for half a millennium. *Tiberius Talgoth.*

'I can feel your fear, lizard.' His voice was as monstrous as his lair, and his mocking laughter boomed through the skies like thunder and sent sheets of rocks tumbling down the mountains around me. Twisting chains of dark magic were spreading out from the citadel, branching off again and again, becoming a net as wide as the sky and as black as the emptiness between the stars.

'I know your true name, *Stratus*. You cannot defeat me.'

I felt a stab of real fear as he pronounced my name in perfect draconic. And while some part of me had expected it, the sense of betrayal that followed the fear was so powerful and intimate that I nearly fell from the sky there and then. Only Anakhara had known how to truly say my name, and she had given this most intimate of our secrets to *him*. Despair fought with grief for the opportunity to tear my hearts from me.

I could feel my name reverberating in the dark net that was reaching for me, woven into every unnatural fibre of it, binding me to commands that I would not be able to defy, not when they were attuned to the very core of my existence. Like the staff of my skin that Navar had wielded, it would defy my every defence, turning whatever sorcery I pitched at it back against me, but this time there would be no chance to turn the tables on him. With no viable defences, flying into the source of his power was madness, and worse, stupid.

I pushed back against the sorrow and fear that he was drawing from me like a glutton savouring his next meal. I turned my attention inward, gathering my most precious thoughts, feelings and most powerful memories and locking them away deep inside a corner of my mind, burying it deep, beneath countless layers of meaningless chatter and bodily functions until they were entirely gone from my waking mind. That done, I gritted my teeth and braced for what was to come as the net closed in around me. I could have fled, but to where? Stopping Navar would have slowed the spread of Talgoth's dominion, but within the walls of that fortress there could be a thousand more like him waiting to do their dark master's bidding.

A terrible coldness preceded the net, a freezing air that had no place amongst the living. Like the blood-fiends of old, its touch quickly leached the life and vitality from my flesh. I could feel it wriggling its way into me, every tendril of it resonating with my name, a thousand insidious voices commanding me to surrender, to obey, to fall, to succumb. Neither my wards nor my sorcery offered any hope of resistance, and through it I felt an echo of Talgoth's triumph as it closed around me, trapping me more completely than his original cage of iron and steel ever had.

Then it began to contract, the commands digging into me like barbed hooks as it drew me towards the pulsing depths of the citadel and whatever loathsome fate awaited me.

CHAPTER 56

THE COLD BECAME unbearable as the net drew me through the maelstrom surrounding the castle and into a cavern deep within the rocky fang that it was perched upon. Dark magic saturated the place, and I felt my sorcery being siphoned out and consumed by the raw toxicity of my surroundings. Everything here bore the mark of Talgoth's iron mind but then it was his will that drove the magic that seethed in this place, and its strength was monstrous as his nature.

The net retracted and melted away into the smooth walls of the cavern, leaving me shivering uncontrollably while scores of globes set into the walls began to glow with a dull red light that did nothing to disperse my initial impression that this place was a disembodied heart. The cavern was enormous, big enough that I could have flown within it, and entirely empty if you discounted the almost palpable intensity of the magic that pressed against me. A pair of heavily engraved doors took up most of the far wall, the wards set into them powerful enough that I could feel them prickling against my skin even at that distance.

The magic stirred around me like an oceanic tide, and I felt Talgoth's presence swell within it, his need to dominate preceding him like a wave. My skin blistered at the touch of his magic and I didn't resist as he twisted me this way and that, pulling at my wings and examining like a careless child with some colourful insect. His full regard was on me, choking me with an irresistible, smothering intensity. Corposant energy crackled across the walls and my skin as his energy filled the cavern.

And then, when the concentration of power felt like it would surely crush me into the stone, I felt the touch of something distant draining the power away from the cavern and absorbing it all, drawing it back into itself.

'I had forgotten that you existed.' His voice filled the cavern as his will clamped shut around my mind, crushing it under an avalanche of raw power. I realised two things then; the first was that, like Navar, he relied on brute strength over finesse to accomplish what he wanted, and the second was that he had enough brute strength to do just that. There was nothing that could stand against such power.

'Your power is paltry, but I shall take it for my own anyway.'

It took everything I had to push back the crushing weight of his presence.

'No'. My voice was a croak, but nonetheless it echoed through the chamber. He had not expected resistance, or that I could voice it. Pain bloomed in my head, a terrible agony as if lances had been driven through each of my eyes and were now grinding their way through the bone, seeking my brain.

Talgoth's laughter drowned out my scream, the sound of it eating away at my sanity.

'You think to resist me? You are something to scrape off my shoe, nothing more.'

His power was colossal, but he used it as a blunt instrument, all of it directed in one direction. Perhaps it had been too long since anyone stood against him, long enough for hubris to take hold within his fevered mind. I felt him drawing more power to himself. It was a strange, shifting sensation, and amongst the unnatural tone of his magic I heard a false note. It made no real difference, for the power was flooding into him nonetheless, and I only had enough time to register that, for all his might, he was still flawed, but then his will crushed me to the floor in every sense of the statement.

I felt my remaining essence fragment under the impact of his magic like a glass cup struck with a hammer. My thoughts became jagged, incoherent slivers and I fought to stay conscious as his will crushed mine with all the subtlety of a landslide. He wouldn't stop now, not until I was utterly destroyed, and with a cry I drew the tattered remains of my will together and triggered the collapse of my remaining wards. I hadn't expected them to actually keep him out for more than a heartbeat, but he would have expected something and now he would feel them shearing apart. I had no strength to brace myself for the backlash of destroying my own wards, but that particular agony was lost amidst the ongoing rape of my mind and body.

I was dimly aware of my body thrashing about as he wrenched control of it from me, carving any vestiges of my will away with no little brutality, and the only blessing was that his control was so sudden and overpowering that I could no longer feel the pain. I released my thoughts an instant before he snuffed them out entirely, sending my essence retreating back within the small part of me that I had hidden away, my own secret mind fortress, while his presence swelled within me.

I forced any consideration of how foolish and reckless my plan was from my thoughts. What was done was done.

I had sacrificed my power and my body to bring Talgoth within reach, and fool's hope or not, there was no coming back from whatever happened next.

When enough of my splintered will had gathered, my sense of self finally woke again. I had feared that it would take too long, that he would ruin my body in the time that would have passed, but if I'd still had control of my lungs, I would have sighed in relief. My preparation had been hasty, but Talgoth's assumption of victory had been hastier still and he was still crowing about his capture of 'the last dragon'.

Convinced that his triumph was complete, he was not shielding his thoughts. The part of him that he was projecting into me was all but shouting them out every moment, such was his arrogance. I still had to be careful, but with patience and a subtlety his human mind couldn't hope to replicate, I began to worm my way back into my own body. I was an echo of his own thoughts, a silent ghost shadowing every unguarded thought and action, each of which carried a fragment of his magic. They had to, for powerful or not, my flesh was attuned to my name and my song, not his. To maintain hold upon it meant he had to keep using his magic.

The first days were both the hardest and the most productive. He controlled me now, and he harvested what he wanted to from my brain, no matter how secret or intimate a thing I had once thought it to be. I could not refuse, for my name and his strength compelled my flesh. I could not so much as blink without his express permission, but for every pause or distracted moment, the secret part of me padded around the edge of his mind, gathering the crumbs of power he left behind. It was hard – because his arrogance meant he was incapable of admitting he didn't have the acuity to be able to move me like he wanted, so he just used brute force – and productive because the brute force meant he was careless with his power, providing more scraps for me to cling to. Which was fortunate, because what I feared most came to pass far sooner than I thought it would.

I knew something was afoot, because after days of a reduced presence, when Talgoth returned to me I felt a sense of agitation and excitement around him. I sensed the pressure of the carefully prepared spells that he began weaving about both my body and himself. He still made no effort to hide his thoughts and, compelled by a dread curiosity, I carefully burrowed into the spells. These I discovered would bind me to him, and him to me, but there was another element to it as well, something of enough import that it made the traces of him vibrate with longing and excitement.

It was something he called the Vortex. I pried at his stray thoughts as much as I dared, but whatever it was, all I could glean was that it was something that Anakhara was involved with, and that it was immensely important to him. I wanted to know more, but my limited abilities left me unable to do more than brush against his thoughts and time was not on my side.

It was not long after that his presence flooded the chamber, his will pushing into my body like a hand carelessly thrust into a too small glove. My body shook and trembled as he flexed his will and took command of my limbs. He'd done this before, gleefully, but now he moved me through the citadel with more than his usual clumsiness, the almost palpable excitement radiating from his mind distracting him and sending my body crashing into pillars and walls. I watched as my body stumbled past silent legions of ghouls and scores of necromancers whose awe he drank in as we passed them.

And then we were alone in a dark passage lined with uncounted thousands of skulls, each carved with silvery runes that lit as we passed them. This was the approach to the Vortex. I could feel his impatience mixing in with his growing excitement. The hall of skulls ended in a great portal which, as far I could sense, was made entirely of gold. He slowed as we approached it, his spell cycling to a new intensity that forced the ghost of me further back into the depths of my brain but I fought to hold onto the visions I was siphoning from him. There were no runes carved in the arch; there was no point, for gold is a pure element, and more of a foil for magic than running water ever could be.

I felt his spell discharge as he all but threw my body through the archway. No magic could pass through the nullifying effect of that much gold. My body stumbled into what I took to be the Vortex with the clumsy grace of a newborn foal, my balance and bodily functions controlled by the most basic part of my brain. The gold hadn't done me any favours either, and had stripped me of whatever little power I had managed to steal away from him.

The Vortex was a hollow at the bottom of the castle, an enormous egg-shaped cavern lined with precious crystals joined with jingling silver chains, and the walls covered with countless thousands of deeply incised runes. The floor of the cavern ended in a large circular void, revealing the crystalline centre of the pit that the castle was suspended over. I should have known that he would have built his seat of power over a node, but there was no time to think on that now. The Vortex was alive with energy, and even through the distorted vision I was seeing it through it was both glorious and terrible. The Songlines were still alive here, but their energies were harnessed and trapped within the crystals that lined both the Vortex and the shimmering crater below us.

No single crystal could contain such power, but the rune-carved chains connecting them redirected their power, cycling it through the clusters to spread the burden. More wires ran between each of these, linking other crystals into a network more complex than the rings of a mail coat. These wires flickered with a hundred shades of violet and black as they siphoned the golden energy of the Songlines and twisted it into something dark and tainted. All of these chains and wires lead to a single, large crystal that descended from the centre of the roof like a mammoth's tusk, the length of it shining with an eldritch light.

A dozen finer chains, some of gold and others of silver, led away from this tusk and towards my Anakhara. I had seen her through the drovers' eyes, but that was no preparation for seeing her now for myself. The chains pierced her flesh, carrying the tainted energy into her very body, and hundreds of tokens were embedded in her scales, either on hooks or carved into them and filled with molten silver and gold.

She rose as my body staggered to a halt, the chains clanking and the crystals that now served as her eyes flaring with light. I felt both energies surge, arcs of gold and purple light racing from chain to chain and leaping across the crystals in a pattern that was too fast for the eye to follow, and a moment later I felt Talgoth's presence knife into my mind again. I knew that it was an important moment, and that I should be prying into how I could use the dampening effect of the gold to my advantage, but the sight of her was too much for me.

My concentration slipped, and I felt Talgoth's attention turn on me. He had finally seen through my ruse. *It was too soon, too soon!* Love had damned me once, and now it was going to kill me forever.

He flexed his power and it closed around the ghost of

me like a fist. I tried to squirm away, to vanish back within the parts of my brain that were too deep and alien for him to follow me into, but he was as single-minded as ever and his power lanced deep and carelessly, cutting me off. My anger and desperation were pitiful compared to the force he held me with, and it was all I could do not to drown in the contempt that radiated from him.

'*You think you're so clever, Stratus.*' His projected thoughts struck me with the power of a falling mountain. '*I am the master of Death. Did you really think to fool me with such a pitiful charade?*'

I knew that it had, but that was no comfort. I had been so close to unlocking his magical signature, so close! If I had only had a little more time I was sure I could have stolen his magic, as I had Navar's.

'*The game is at an end. I am not without mercy though. I will let you watch your beloved as she carves your soul from your flesh and feeds it to me. Too long have I been held captive by this mortal shell. I shall wear yours, and I then shall rule this world forever.*'

He let me see again, and I watched, mesmerised and helpless, as a fell light kindled within Anakhara's lifeless eyes, matching the fiery glow that lit within the runes burned into her once beautiful flesh.

'What is your command, my master?' Her voice, if that was what it was, was flat and cold, and I couldn't tell whether it I heard it through my ears or as a mental projection.

'*This beast still lives. Take its name into yourself, then bind it to me. Its body shall be as mine. Use the rituals of Sharnak.*'

'Your will be done, my master.' A pause. 'That ritual will require both bodies.'

I felt his annoyance scrape through my mind. '*Very well.*

Hold the beast here.'

'Your will be done, my master.'

I felt that strange, faltering note once more as Talgoth withdrew from my mind, a sensation almost as awful as him entering it. I felt the origin of the force he was holding me with pass between them, and then, for the first time in a millennium, Anakhara and I were alone together.

I threw everything I had into breaking free of the force he had bound me with.

'*Anakhara!*' I screamed her name as best that I could as an extension of that struggle. Her iron studded skull turned towards me, tilting slightly to the side. I redoubled my efforts, heedless of the strength it was costing me. It would all be for nothing if I couldn't reach out to her.

I felt her extending her will through the connection of the bindings that held me, and its touch was as cold and lifeless as her voice was. If Talgoth's touch was unclean, hers was positively corrosive, leaching the emotion and thought from whatever it touched, stripping everything down until all that was left was the kernel of life and energy that connected to it a living thing, and she quickly and ruthlessly absorbed that small mote too.

Her attention was killing me more effectively than either Navar or Talgoth ever could, and I wondered whether this was what he had done to her, and if she even knew that she was doing it.

'*My poor Anakhara.'* At least here, with her in my mind, I could communicate directly with her.

SILENCE. Her command was as hard as steel but I fought against the compulsion it bore with a strength borne of desperation and a hopeless love.

'*I have missed you more than the sun misses the stars, and the moon the sun.'*

As I sent the thought towards her, I infused it with some

of the memories that I had hoarded within my secret place, memories of the time before man came, when this world was ours alone. Memories of flying so high it felt as though we could touch the stars, and of embraces that lasted entire seasons. Of singing, of my terrible poetry, and hunting and the quiet satisfaction of a good fire on a winter's night. Her will devoured them all, fracturing them into a thousand pieces, absorbing them with the same implacable, uncaring efficiency.

'*I promised. I promised to bring you home, and I am here.*'

I felt her hesitate, just for a moment, and hope swelled within me that perhaps some part of her still lived within the creature that squatted within that cavern.

'*The stars are calling us home, my love.*'

'*Stratus?*'

My spirit surged as the weight of her will shifted and I felt the touch of her mind soften.

'*Anakhara.*' I poured my love and remaining strength into her name.

'*Why have you come?*'

'*Because you are mine, as I am yours. Forever.*'

She groaned. '*It is so dark here, so cold. I cannot remember warmth. I am lost, Great Heart. Lost in the dark.*'

I didn't reply. All I could do was share more of my, *our*, memories in the hope that they would give her the strength they had once given me. And if not, that she would at least remember me until we met again.

'Is everything prepared?' Talgoth's voice cracked through the cavern, drowning out even the roar of the maelstrom outside and I felt the connection between us vanish as if it had never been. The weight of her will slammed down again, cutting off any trace of the real Anakhara.

I could just see the mage from the corner of my eye,

a diminutive figure that looked like little more than varnished vellum stretched across a skeleton sat upon a throne carried by four ghouls. A crown of flickering crystals was embedded in his skull like a crown, most likely a conduit to regulate the constant flow of the Songlines' energy required to maintain his mockery of life. The ghouls stepped back as he rose, a glittering staff clutched in his bony hands.

'Yes, my master.'

Seeing him as he was, I finally understood. Even with Anakhara constantly feeding him the energy he required to constantly shield his body from the effect of time, it was not sustainable for much longer, not if his skeletal appearance was any indicator. This is why he sought me, why Navar was tasked to capture me alive. If he wore my flesh, he wouldn't need to rely on her, for I was attuned to the Songlines on a level that no enchantment could ever replicate, and binding his mind and will to him would give him what he wanted more than anything else: immortality.

It seemed I owed Navar and his traitorous ambitions a debt of gratitude. Had he not had other ideas for his own future I might have been delivered to Talgoth in a neat box years ago, unable to do so much as raise as a claw in my defence.

'Then let us begin,' called Talgoth, snapping me from my thoughts.

'Your will be done, my master.'

Anakhara's eyes flared as she drew upon the dark magic around her, the chains embedded in her flesh reddening. The patterns of light intensified and spread from her to Talgoth, then to me and back again, doubling back on themselves over and over again in an increasingly intricate pattern until the air vibrated with them at a pitch that made the crystals vibrate. And then she began to chant, the first of the hundreds of lines that would form the cornerstone of the enchantment that would supplant my true name with Talgoth's, binding him to my flesh and in turn sending my presence, my soul, into the decrepit ruin of his body. By the time she spoke his name out loud it would be too late for me to do anything with it. The healing magics would stop, and the backlash of his long overdue death would snuff me from existence.

This was the end of everything, and even though it was my doom, *our doom*, she was chanting in draconic, and with the voice I remembered from our time together. She had to, for despite the iron monstrosity that she had become, to use her power she still had to be able to merge with the Songlines using her own name, her own unique Song. I watched her, a prisoner in my own body, and listened to the sound of her voice rather than the words she was speaking. It was the last pleasure this life would offer me, and I wondered whether I would feel the moment that my spirit was broken and cast out.

I felt the energies knife into me, the pattern swelling and shifting as it penetrated all of me, preparing to separate spirit from flesh, and I knew that my time had come to an end.

CHAPTER 57

'BY YOUR NAME you are made
By your name you are bound
By your name you are unmade'
I felt the magic scythe into me, loosening the bonds of
my soul. She would intone Talgoth's name next, driving
me from my body and binding his name and soul to it.
I didn't look away from her; I wanted her to be my last
sight. But I was wrong, as wrong as I had ever been in my
life.
'By your name I call you,
By your name I unbind you,
By your name I unshackle your spirit,
Stratus Firesky, the Dead Wind, the Cold Wind of the
North, Destroyer, and Doom of Krandin,
By your name you shall be whole once more, Great Heart,
By your name you are free and whole.'
There was a single moment of pure silence in the cavern
as she sung the last syllable, and then the magic that she
had gathered swirled and poured into me in a jet of *golden*
light. Shaped by her will and my full name in perfect
draconic, the construct was faultless and unstoppable. It
filled every part of me, hurling Talgoth's presence from my
mind. He had been part of the spell from his own free will

from the outset, and could not resist it now, not without risking breaking the spell, which was potent enough to destroy him and his entire castle.

I felt my spirit swelling as the unadulterated power of the Songlines drew me back into my flesh, and the comforting weight of my body settled back around me even as my senses reconnected.

The silence of the cavern was gone, replaced by Anakhara's screams as Talgoth unleashed his anger at her. His staff and the runes etched into the iron that bound her burned star-bright as he made a violent gesture, throwing her from her perch. Iron bent and bones snapped as he slammed her into wall and floor with enough violence to rip at least two of the chains from her flesh. These swung and writhed like headless snakes while raw magic discharged from the ends of them, burning the meat and blood that clung to them. She slid to a halt and lay still, the fires within her eyes dim and flickering. He didn't dare kill her, but he could hurt her. My surprise passed even before she hit the ground, replaced by an elemental fury.

'Talgoth!' The force of my roar set the chains to swinging and shook a thousand crystals loose, sending them raining down around us.

He spun towards me, staff still blazing. I could feel the potential locked within it, far more than I had ever seen within an artefact and certainly more than any living wizard had ever turned against me. I was still trying to recover my wards when he attacked.

White fire lanced towards me, cutting a strip of flesh from my flank as I desperately twisted aside. I smelled my flesh burning some time before the pain hit, but by that time he had already launched another attack and I had no time to worry about it. The beam flattened into what looked like nothing more than a gigantic sword, and he wielded it at me like one too. It sliced through the floor at my feet as I scuttled backwards, leaving behind a deep scar with molten edges.

But Anakhara had not only freed me, she had restored me. My sorcery responded to my mind's call with alacrity, and before he could advance and deliver another blow I loosed a thunderbolt at him. It exploded against his wards, halting his progress for a moment, giving me a chance to close with him before he could trap me against the walls.

He barked a command and his sword fragmented into dozens of glowing arrowheads. I knew what was coming next and threw out an angular wall of force in front of me. It deflected the burning shards, sending them skittering off into the walls where they buried themselves in the rock, leaving the walls pockmarked with molten gashes.

'Fool!' he shouted. 'Your sorcery is mine.'

I felt the dark energies cut the flow of the Songlines off in a single stroke, then swell and dart forward like a thousand vipers, siphoning the energies out of me in great gulps. He launched a barrage of magical bolts at me as I reeled from that onslaught, each one potent enough to do me a serious injury. These shattered against my shield, and while it held steady for now, I now had to renew it from a finite and rapidly dwindling pool of sorcery.

I spooled out a separate strand of sorcery, the effort of maintaining the shield and manipulating this new strand into the construct I needed sent the blood pouring from my nose. The tortures I had suffered stood me in good stead now, for centuries ago the pain would have debilitated me, but now it was just another agony to bear. I released the sorcery, and a glittering ball of flame manifested over my shoulder. It swiftly grew in size and then shot forward, trailing sparks. He was laughing even before it burst on his shields. And kept bursting, filling his field of vision with flares of golden light that blinded his still human eyes. I knew he could disperse it with a thought, but I didn't need it to last long.

By the time he banished it, I was descending on him, the roar of the wind-spells that had propelled me into the air still echoing about the chamber. I could see his staff rising, the tip glowing. It smashed into me, tearing my flesh and breaking at least two of my ribs, but it wasn't enough to turn me aside. He'd have to have killed me outright to have any hope of that, and he needed my body too much to do that.

I smashed my fist down upon him but his physical wards were as unyielding as bedrock. He even had the audacity to lean on his staff and laugh at me.

'You stupid animal.' I felt his magic flex and watched as he let a rivulet of the blood that was flowing from my wounds through the shield to pool at his feet. He dipped the end of his staff into it, then spun and tasted it. 'You don't deserve the power you have. I don't know how you managed that little trick, but it won't matter. There will be no death for you. You will serve me until the end of time.'

I looked at the blood on his lips, then at the stream of blood and where it was soaking into the hem of his robes, and bared my teeth, which only made him laugh again. I swatted at him, knowing that my raking claws would do little except agitate his wards, but I didn't need them to do anything else. I spat a stream of fire bile as my claws rattled across his shield, the viscous fluid pattering to the floor while he laughed again.

I watched the pale stream of bile mingle with the blood he had dipped his staff into. Blood that he had allowed under his shield.

He lifted his staff as the tip lit with a fell light, a spell of terrible potency drawing the dark energies together and

I backed away. His mouth was open, no doubt ready to spout some dire threat, when the bile ignited at his feet.

His spellcasting faltered as flames bloomed at his feet and raced up his dry skin. He staggered back with a screech, and I lunged forward, emptying my bile bladder over him and the floor around him before he could gather enough wit to seal his shield again. The spray ignited as soon as it touched the flames and he staggered backwards as the very air around him caught fire. Realisation dawned quickly, but by then he was standing in a pool of burning liquid. His shield flexed, sealing him away from the heat and flame, but his feet and legs were already aflame and the smoke was thickening by the moment. He summoned a deluge of water, which almost impressed me. In all my years, I had only ever seen a handful of men who were able to function for anything more than a few heartbeats once the fire was upon them.

It was shame for him that, for all his wisdom, he had not learned anything about dragonfire. Fortified by the glow stones and yellow rocks of the great swamps, my fires burned regardless of rain, river or sea, and suffocating them would only win a temporary reprieve for they would burn as long as any fluid remained to burn. His cries became more frantic as the water simply spread the fire that was climbing up his body, and his repeated denials devolved into coughing.

I felt his protective shield wavering and hammered my fists and claws into it, sheathing them in a veneer of sorcery that forced his wards to reset and replenish with every blow. Two of my claws were torn off by the impacts, but I could sense the potency of his spell weakening as fire and fear ate at his control, and I redoubled my efforts. A dozen more blows later the shield gave way with a thunderclap, sending his half smouldering form sliding back across the floor, his staff rattling away across the stones and over the edge of the Vortex.

'Die!' I roared, driving three of my claws through his bony chest, pinning him there as I spat the dregs of my bile across him, coating every part of him in liquid fire. His attempt at spellcasting became a scream as it ignited.

He died as miserably and agonisingly as I had ever dared to dream. While the healing I shared with Tatyana was crude and let her draw as much energy as she needed, the healing energies that Anakhara gave Talgoth were carefully regulated to protect his fragile body and could not be increased to compensate for the damage. All they could do was slow the time it took him to burn to death.

I watched him burn until the pain of my injuries pushed through my anger, at which point I pulverised his skull with my fist, spraying his rancid brain across the floor. I staggered towards Anakhara's still form and was perhaps halfway to her before my legs folded beneath me and I fell.

The impact of my chin on the floor jolted me back into the consciousness I was desperate to cling to. I pulled myself forward with splintered claws until I was close enough to lay a hand upon one of hers. Her iron claws were cool to the touch, the vile runes that marked them dark and silent.

'Anakhara Skydancer.' I spoke her true name, and was rewarded by a faint flicker of light within her sockets. I didn't really know if I was feeling sorrow, grief, joy, or anger. All of them.

'I'm sorry, Stratus.' Her voice was a sigh.

'Sorry? You saved me, my love. You saved *us*.'

A shudder passed through her. 'I dreamt of you sometimes.'

I gritted my teeth as a wave of agony washed over me. 'I

thought you were dead.'

'I am, Great Heart.'

'No.' I meant it to be a shout of defiance, but my treacherous body turned it into a sob. She whispered my *name* and I felt her mind reaching out to mine. I welcomed it, and our memories and thoughts crashed together. Her early memories were fragmented and broken by the torture and enchantments that she had endured at Talgoth's hand. There were glimpses of our life before, isolated moments here and there, but mostly it was a terrible blankness, an indistinct haze filled only with memories of pain, desolation and, through it all, Talgoth's voice. I felt the despair and fear that had overwhelmed her in this time, a corrosive and toxic mixture that had eaten away anything wholesome and good until they were entirely forgotten and that awful state had become all of her existence. It was a crushing, terrible thing, and having felt the strength of his will I could not imagine what it must have been like to be the sole focus of it for every moment of every day for so many years.

'You have to go, my love.' She squeezed my hand with terrible strength. 'The chains are broken and the spells bound to his body will soon unravel. It will be a cataclysm.'

'I'm never leaving you again.'

'You have to.' Sparks sputtered from some of the runes upon her only to turn to blood when they touched the floor. 'My wings are broken. I am broken.'

'I'm taking you home,' I said.

'You will obey!' she snapped, the words and the compulsion within them battering me like a sudden squall. It vanished as suddenly as it had come, and she then shrunk back from me, turning her head away. 'I'm sorry.'

I pulled myself closer, slowly so as to avoid triggering

her defensive wards. They glittered into life as she backed away.

'No, keep away.'

I ignored her protest and instead nudged her snout with my own.

'I'm a monster,' she said in a trembling tone.

'But you're my monster.'

She turned her head and laid it under mine, and we lay quietly, simply together again.

'It's starting,' she said quietly. 'Please Stratus, go.'

I could feel it too, although likely not as keenly as she could. Talgoth's destruction had removed a major component from most, if not all, of the enchantments layered upon Anakhara and throughout the citadel. Like a disturbed or miscast spell, those energies were moving along pathways that now had nowhere to go and were building to a potency that would force its own and no doubt cataclysmic outlet, judging by the amount of power that they had been dealing with.

'I cannot lose you again.' I gathered my will and channelled it into my body, feeding my limbs with new strength and knitting my fractured bones and burned flesh, uncaring of the price I'd pay for it.

'What are you doing?'

'I'm taking you home.'

'Stratus, no! Beyond the mists the wards will strip your power. You'll never make it over the mountains.'

'I'm not leaving you,' I said, a growl at the edge of my words. I slid my arms under her and lifted. I walked to the edge of the floor and unfolded my trembling wings.

'I love you,' I said, and fell into the void.

EPILOGUE

'GOOD MORNING, LADY Henkman.'

I tried to lift my head from my arms and gave up with a groan. It felt like my skull had shrunk overnight and any movement would burst it. I liked Firewater, but I liked it far too much when other people were buying it.

I grunted as I slowly pushed myself to a sitting position and looked at the priest standing in the doorway, then at the four stone walls that surrounded me. There was old, damp straw on the floor and a coarse blanket a mule would reject across my legs. No boots, no sword. Vomit on my tunic and torn trousers. Scraps of the night before flashed before my eyes, and I groaned as I remembered where I'd seen him before.

'How's the cock today, your grace?' I croaked. I knew it was probably stupid to bait him like that, but as usual it was out before I could stop myself.

His already sour expression curdled further at the memory of how my knee had reminded him of his supposed vow of celibacy the night before. Sadly it didn't even raise as much of a smirk from the over-muscled goon standing behind him.

His grimace became a tight lipped smile. 'Laugh all you wish, heretic.'

'Whoa! Since when is being a bit drunk heresy?' I said.

Being a bitch was one thing, but when priests started spouting heresy, even I knew to tread cautiously.

'It is when you consort with devils.'

'Now, hold on, Father. The only devil I tangled with last night came with a cork.'

'Don't take us for fools, woman. You know of what I speak.'

Staying in Falkenburg while Lucien and Jean returned to the capital for the triumphal march had been a mistake. I should have fought harder to go with them and not listened to their bullshit about figureheads for the people. It was nice when everyone was buying me a drink, but it hadn't been a night for good decisions.

'Where is the beast now?' he asked, stepping closer. 'It would go well for you if you co-operate.'

I hugged legs to my chest as I tried to think past the thickness in my head and sourness in my gut. I should have just bought the food and kept walking.

'I don't know,' I said. 'He, it, abandoned me here. Ask Fronsac, he was there.'

'So you wish to name that apostate as your defence?'

'He's a licensed wizard. I want to help you, but I can't tell you what I don't know.'

'It's my experience that people remember more than they think they do. They simply lack the requisite motivation.' He gestured to the goon, who backed out of the cell. 'You have until nightfall to consider your options.'

'What happens at nightfall?'

He smiled then, a proper shit-eating grin that made my stomach twist again. 'That is when we decide how much help you need.'

He slammed the door with unnecessary force, making my skull constrict even more. Despite everything I still managed to pass out again, until sometime later when a tray was slid in the cell. It was just bread and pottage, both of which were remarkable only for their lack of mould or spoil, but there was even a small beer, which I gulped greedily to ease the painful dryness in my throat. It wasn't much, but at least afterwards it no longer felt like my head was going to pop like a tick's backside.

That, however, was a far as the good news went. I was still locked up with a bloody charge of heresy hanging over my head, and quite possibly treason too. I fell back onto the cot with yet another groan. *That bloody dragon.*

I'd been so goddamned angry with him for leaving without me. Hurt too, but mostly just angry, and it didn't help that Fronsac agreed with him, nor that I knew they were right. None of it helped me now in the slightest.

I watched the sky beyond the tiny excuse for a window darken, and soon after heard the tramp of heavy feet outside the cell. I had cleaned myself up as best I could, but still felt quite grubby as four priests and two squires squeezed into the cell. The priests simply stared at me, while the squires hastily set up a small table, book and ink.

'Where is the beast?' asked the fattest of the four without any preamble.

'I don't know. As I said to—'

'How do you control it?'

'Control it? He's a dragon. No one can control him.'

One of the other priests stepped forward now, much younger and almost good looking if you ignored how flat and dead his eyes were.

'What did you offer it in return for it teaching you witchcraft?'

I stared at him as a nasty, creeping sensation crawled through my gut. 'Witchcraft?'

'You deny this?'

'Absolutely. With all due respect, your grace, this is

ridiculous. *A witch?* What is this, the fucking Dawn Age?'

That didn't go down very well, and after a few more pointless questions that I chose not to answer in case my big mouth made things worse, they filed from the room, the squires hastily dismantling the table and running after them as if scared to be left alone with me.

The smug priest I'd kneed in the balls returned the next morning wearing the same greasy smile. 'Would you like the long or short version?'

'Short.'

'The council has deemed you to be a heretic and a witch. You are to be taken for Questioning, after which you will be hung and quartered.'

'What? I saved this city, damn you. I demand to speak to Prince Jean!'

'Heretics make no demands upon the Church, especially not condemned ones.'

He clicked his fingers, and three guards in Church tabards rushed in. I knew what they did with witches, and I fought them with everything I had. It was really a useless gesture, and all it got me was a split lip, swollen eye and bruised tits before they clubbed me across the head.

I knew nothing more until I woke up strapped to a cross shaped table, surrounded by the tools that would be equally at home in either a smithy or a surgery. They left me alone there for half a candle, more than long enough for me to appreciate how badly screwed I was.

I'd forgotten about the enchantment that Stratus had put on me until I licked my lips and found my lip was whole. My eye had gone down too, and even my head had stopped hurting. Which meant he was still alive, which made me smile until I started thinking about how much fun being tortured was going to be if I kept healing. They'd never stop, and would probably take it as proof of my so called witchcraft. As if I wouldn't magic my way out of this shit-hole if I could.

The Questioning began not long after. The cell door swung open and three hooded men marched in. The first two tightened my restraints while the third fired off a barrage of sharp punches to my gut and one to my face that made my eye swell up again almost immediately, which I suppose was a blessing in disguise as it hid my healing. Then he cut my clothes off with a skinning knife, but just my top mind you, since the church deplores vulgarity, even if they don't mind cutting bits of you off or burning you alive. *Those* are pious acts.

'Are you a witch?' said the smallest of them, his northern accent a thick drawl.

'No.'

That earned me a few more punches. Saying yes would only make them stop for a short while before they started with a new and equally damning question, so it was all a pointless charade. I'd seen it before, albeit not from this side of things. *Witchcraft.* Men with gifts were taught to be wizards, but the gods help any woman so afflicted.

'Are you a witch? Admit your guilt and the pain will stop.'

Always deny everything. 'Fuck you.'

They tossed me back into my cell after a good dozen rounds of similarly witty banter. I crawled back onto my cot, and all I could think of was that at least it was just a beating, which meant they wouldn't be able to see that the injuries had faded. There was to be no rest for me though. Whenever I drifted off, some prick would come in and throw a bucket of cold water over me.

They started the burning on the third day, holding a bodkin like poker above my skin until it bubbled like goddamn crackling on a roast pig. I screamed like a banshee, but that pain wasn't anything like what waited for me when they found my skin unblemished and healthy the morning after.

Two priests stood witness to what they did to me over the next few days, taking notes and discussing how they should test how much damage my evil powers could repair. I tried to beat my brains out against the bars of my cell that night but stupidly managed to knock myself out before I could do the job properly. After that they manacled me to the cot.

Time has no meaning in a dungeon. When you're being tortured, it stretches out endlessly, yet when you're not it speeds past so that it feels none has passed. There was no sunlight either, so I had no idea how long I had been down there when the tremors struck. The first of them loosened a few years' worth of dust and soot from the roof, but after that it only grew worse until it felt like the chamber was going to shake itself apart.

'She is using her foul magic!' the first priest shouted, as if I wouldn't have tried that days ago if I'd been able to. This set the torturer's assistant to beating me about the head with a cudgel, but the iron bands they'd used to hold my head to the table while they skinned my arm now acted as a helmet of sorts, which was nice because if he'd managed to hit me I might have missed the moment when five curved claws the length of longswords pierced the roof and ripped it away, flooding their sordid little chamber with dust and sunlight.

Something roared outside, an immense, bestial sound that carried such bottomless rage that my heart skipped and tripped in raw, elemental terror. Unable to obey the need to flee, I felt more helpless and fragile in those moments than at any other time in my life, torture included. I would have shit myself if I hadn't already done so earlier that morning.

Those same black claws reached in through the missing roof and tore the rest of the chamber open, and a moment later a blast of hot air rolled wind in, reeking of burned meat and sulphur. I twisted on the table and looked up to see Stratus hunkered above the hole while stones and smashed timbers rained down around me. I could feel the rage rolling off him like heat from an open oven.

He reached down and ripped my bindings apart with one of those immense and deadly claws. I fell from the cross, but it didn't hurt, not even my skinned arm. I clutched it to me gingerly as I pushed myself to my feet, but rather than the burning pain I expected it felt cool and prickly. I dared a glimpse at it and sobbed when I saw the new, pink skin covering it.

One of the priests lurched towards me, brandishing a bloodied book of prayers, but he'd barely taken two steps before one of those same claws stabbed down through the top of his head and burst out of his arse. Stratus flicked him away as I would a ball of snot, then held his bloody hand out to me. I didn't hesitate and clung to his fingers as he lifted me out and gave me my first look at the devastation he'd brought to Falkenburg.

He'd flattened everything in a two block wide swathe from the town walls to the cathedral of St Tomas, which looked far worse now than it did during the siege. The roof was all but gone and great plumes of black smoke were billowing from the ragged holes where the great windows had been. Fires were raging everywhere, with tongues of orange flame thirty foot high chasing the columns of smoke into the air.

'Are you well?' he asked, tilting his head towards me like the world's biggest songbird while his words reverberated in my chest.

I couldn't help but laugh then. It was good, old-fashioned hysteria but even though I knew that, I couldn't stop. Laughter and tears erupted from me, and I laughed harder than I had ever had before. Or since, for that matter.

'I wanted to come and say goodbye,' he said, his voice vibrating deep within me. 'And then I felt your distress.'

'Goodbye?' I managed to croak.

'The Archmage is dead.'

I stared up at him. 'Dead? You defeated him?'

An arrow careened off the bony ridge on his cheek as he nodded, but he didn't seem to notice. I felt the melancholy emanating from him as I had before he'd left, but it felt different now.

'Oh Stratus,' I said as the pieces fell together. 'Anakhara.'

He bared his teeth in the same lopsided smile he'd had as a man. 'She is free now, and with me forever.'

More arrows were bouncing from his hide now, and I felt his irritation growing.

'Kill the witch!' screamed a voice below us, and we both looked down to where the other priest was exhorting a cohort of archers to loose another volley.

For all of his size, Stratus moved as fast as a striking snake, his head rearing back as he spat a stream of pungent fluid at the group. They staggered back and then burst into flame, their screams becoming something less than human as the flame devoured them.

'Brace yourself,' he said, and launched himself into the air, scattering their burning bodies like leaves. He flew upwards, his huge wings beating with a sure strength, taking us through the clouds and into the serenity that lay above them. I breathed the clear, sweet air and luxuriated in the comforting warmth of his fingers curled around me.

'We are going home,' he said after perhaps an hour of flying. 'To *Draksgard*, but I wanted to thank you for your friendship and to say goodbye properly this time.' He looked down at me. 'Were these hurts because of me?'

'No. These hurts were because men are idiots.' I squeezed

his hand as best I could. 'Thank you, my friend.'

'It is my pleasure.' He looked off into the distance and smiled.

'What's so funny?'

'Nothing. But I want you to meet someone.' He opened his mouth and roared, not the angry, pants-wetting sound of earlier, but something higher and clearer, almost like the cry of a fish eagle.

'I don't understand,' I said, twisting in his hand so I could look out over the wispy surface of the clouds.

His smiled only broadened, and for a moment I felt a terrible fear that whatever horrors he had faced had scarred him in more ways than were obvious to see, but then the clouds in front of us bulged upwards and another dragon rose from them, vapours streaming from its wings and bony ridges as it rose to meet us. It was smaller than Stratus, leaner and more ragged, but here and there I caught the gleam of gold at the edge of its black scales.

It spun in a lazy spiral and slowed so that we were flying just above it. I sagged against his hand, unable to speak as the realisation sank in. I saw him smile once more.

He said something in his own language, a strangely musical sound, and Anakhara spun so she was upside down and looking straight at me, her eyes flashing like amber crystals. She righted herself once more, and with a similar cry she sunk back into the clouds and vanished.

'She likes you,' he said.

'She's beautiful,' I said, forcing the words out around the lump in my throat.

'That she is,' he rumbled. 'The scars of his cruelty will take time to heal, but she will be whole again.'

'I am happy for you, my friend.'

'Thank you. Now tell me, where shall I take you? It seems Falkenburg's welcome has passed.'

I thought about that. With Navar fallen and a dragon in our skies, the kings and princes were meeting to agree an end to the war and argue about who owned what, and from the priests' questioning that conversation clearly included Stratus. I was so tired of all it. I wanted peace, and somewhere warm where I could leave the name Henkman behind, and I said as much.

'I know somewhere,' he said. 'It is a place of spices, endless horizons and storytellers.'

'Is there wine?'

'The finest, and fruit sweeter than any nectar.'

'It sounds perfect.'

'Then it is decided.' A moment later the sun slipped away and he turned west. 'We could all use some time under the sun's healing touch. Rest now, and worry no more.'

He lifted me onto his back and I settled into the same notch where I'd sat when he destroyed the Penullin army, something that already felt like a lifetime ago. I leaned back against a jutting horn and watched as Anakhara's shimmering form rose to skim across the tops of the clouds below us.

ACKNOWLEDGEMENTS

I OWE A debt of thanks to so many people for their support in bringing *Firesky* to life. To my wife Liz for always being there and keeping me grounded; to Dom, Steve, Kyri, and Mark for feeding my imagination; and to the crew at Costa Eldon Street for fueling the rest of me. And to you, for choosing to share in the adventure.

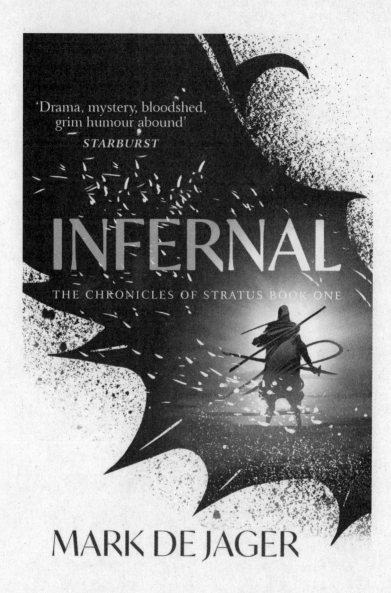

'Drama, mystery, bloodshed, grim humour abound'

STARBURST

INFERNAL

THE CHRONICLES OF STRATUS BOOK ONE

MARK DE JAGER

SHACKLED
FATES

PART TWO OF THE HANGED GOD TRILOGY

THILDE KOLD HOLDT

"Packs a punch worthy of the Thunderer himself. It rocks!"
Joanne Harris, author of *The Gospel of Loki*

⊙ SOLARISBOOKS.COM

FIND US ONLINE!

www.rebellionpublishing.com

/rebellionpub /rebellionpublishing /rebellionpublishing

SIGN UP TO OUR NEWSLETTER!

rebellionpublishing.com/newsletter

YOUR REVIEWS MATTER!

Enjoy this book? Got something to say?

Leave a review on Amazon, GoodReads or with your
favourite bookseller and let the world know!